Praise for

QUICKSAND

"**A remarkable new novel**…Giolito…writes with exceptional skill…[*Quicksand* is] always smart and engrossing…Giolito keeps us guessing a long time, and the outcome, when it arrives, is just as it should be." —*Washington Post*

"[*Quicksand*] provides **a razor-sharp view of modern Sweden and its criminal justice system,** yet is a tonic for readers who have had enough of the brooding, often-bloody 'Scandi-crime' that has been so popular in recent years."
—NPR, Best Books of 2017

"**Astonishing**…a dark exploration of the crumbling European social order and the psyche of rich Swedish teens…the incisive language that's on display here surely involves translation precision that's second to none."
—*Booklist* (starred review)

"[*Quicksand*] is structured as a courtroom procedural, yet it clearly has ambitions beyond that, **addressing Sweden's underlying economic and racial tensions.**"
—*New York Times Book Review*

"**Brilliantly conceived and executed,** this extraordinary legal thriller is not to be missed." —*Library Journal* (starred review)

"**Haunting and immersive.**" —*Publishers Weekly*

"Persson Giolito's craft takes us on **a psychological ride.**"
—*Huffington Post*

"**Expert dialogue and irresistible momentum** make an all-too-realistic story come breathing off the page...Part courtroom thriller, part introspection, *Quicksand* is pulled tight throughout by the suspense, not only of Maja's verdict, but of the elusive 'truth' of what really happened in the classroom that day." —*Shelf Awareness*

"**Sharp social commentary** through the tragic story of a young woman's trial for mass murder...The rhythm, tone, and language are just right...a splendid work of fiction."
—*Kirkus Reviews*

"**A compelling, multilayered study** of a terrible school shooting." —*Boston Herald*

"**A fascinating look** at modern society, class, race, and the definition of justice."
—Sharon K. Nagel, Boswell Book Company, Milwaukee, WI

"**For everyone who wants more** behind the scenes of a courtroom, this is the book. The narrator keeps you so involved in the story. I could not put this book down."
—Shane P. Mullen, Left Bank Books, St. Louis, MO

"**Very well done**...This book provided more insight into why these things happen, and the conditions that lead up to them, than any other book I have read, or any of the mental health talking heads I have watched and listened to on television."
—Diane Scholl, Batavia Public Library, Batavia, IL

QUICK-SAND

MALIN PERSSON GIOLITO

Translated from the Swedish by

RACHEL WILLSON-BROYLES

Other Press
New York

First softcover edition 2018
ISBN 978-1-59051-947-9

Production editor: Yvonne E. Cárdenas
Text designer: Julie Fry
This book was set in Founders Grotesk and Prensa
by Alpha Design & Composition of Pittsfield, NH.

3 5 7 9 10 8 6 4 2

LIBRARY OF CONGRESS CATALOGING-IN-PUBLICATION DATA

Names: Persson Giolito, Malin, 1969- author. | Willson-Broyles, Rachel, translator.
Title: Quicksand / by Malin Persson Giolito ; translated from the Swedish by
Rachel Willson-Broyles.
Other titles: Störst av allt. English
Description: New York : Other Press, 2017.
Identifiers: LCCN 2016032468 (print) | LCCN 2016034069 (ebook) |
ISBN 9781590518571 (hardback) | ISBN 9781590518588 (ebook)
Subjects: LCSH: High school girls—Sweden—Stockholm—Fiction. | High
school students—Sweden—Stockholm—Fiction. | Mass murder—Sweden—
Stockholm—Fiction. | Trials (Murder)—Sweden—Stockholm—Fiction. | BISAC:
FICTION / Psychological. | FICTION / Legal. | FICTION / Coming of Age. | GSAFD:
Bildungsromans. | Legal stories. | Pscyhological fiction.
Classification: LCC PT9877.26.E79 S7613 2017 (print) |
LCC PT9877.26.E79 (ebook) | DDC 839.73/8—dc23
LC record available at https://lccn.loc.gov/2016032468

QUICKSAND

THE CLASSROOM

Lying next to the left-hand row of desks is Dennis; as usual he's wearing a graphic T, ill-fitting jeans, and untied tennis shoes. Dennis is from Uganda. He says he's seventeen, but he looks like a fat twenty-five-year-old. He's a student in the trade school, and he lives in Sollentuna in a home for people like him. Samir has ended up next to him, on his side. Samir and I are in the same class because Samir managed to be accepted to our school's special program in international economics and social sciences.

Up at the lectern is Christer, our homeroom teacher and self-described social reformer. His mug has overturned and coffee is dripping onto the leg of his pants. Amanda, no more than two meters away, is propped against the radiator under the window. Just a few minutes ago, she was all cashmere, white gold, and sandals. The diamond earrings she received when we were confirmed are still sparkling in the early-summer sunshine. Now you might think she was covered in mud. I am sitting on the floor in the middle of the classroom. In my lap is Sebastian, the son of the richest man in Sweden, Claes Fagerman.

The people in this room do not go together. People like us don't usually hang out. Maybe on a Metro platform during a taxi strike, or in the dining car on a train, but not in a classroom.

It smells like rotten eggs. The air is hazy and gray with gunpowder smoke. Everyone has been shot but me. I haven't got even as much as a bruise.

Trial hearing in case B 147/66

The prosecutor et al. v. Maria Norberg

Week 1 of Trial: Monday

1.

The first time I saw the inside of a courtroom, I was disappointed. We visited one for a class trip, and sure, I had already figured out that Swedish judges aren't stooping old men in curly wigs and long robes, and that the defendant wouldn't be a madman in an orange suit, in handcuffs, frothing at the mouth, but still. The place looked like something between a medical clinic and a conference center. We rode there on a rented bus that smelled like bubblegum and sweaty feet. The defendant had dandruff and pleated pants and was allegedly guilty of tax evasion. Aside from our class (and Christer, of course), there were only four other people there to listen, but so few seats that Christer had to get an extra chair from the hallway outside so he had somewhere to sit.

Today it's different. We're in the largest courtroom in Sweden. The judges sit on chairs of dark mahogany with high velvet backs. The middle chair's back is taller than the others'. That's where the head judge sits. He is called the "chairman." On the table in front of him is a gavel with a leather handle. Slim microphones stick up before each seat like bent drinking straws. The paneling on the wall looks like oak, like it's several hundred years old, old in a good way. There is a dark red carpet on the floor between the seats.

Audiences are not my thing. I've never wanted to be St. Lucia or take part in talent shows. But it's packed in here. And everyone is here because of me; I'm the attraction.

Next to me are my attorneys from Sander & Laestadius. I know Sander & Laestadius sounds like an antique shop where two sweaty gay men in silk robes and monocles shuffle around with kerosene lamps dusting off moldy books and taxidermied animals, but it's Sweden's best criminal law firm. Ordinary criminals have a single weary public defender; my public defender is flanked by a whole crew of excited wannabe-suits. They work into the wee hours at a super-fancy office near Skeppsbron, have at least two cell phones each, and all of them except Sander himself think that they're part of an American TV show where you eat Chinese food from take-out cartons in an I'm-so-busy-and-important sort of way. None of all the twenty-two people working at Sander & Laestadius is actually named Laestadius. Laestadius died, I assume of a heart attack, in an I'm-so-busy-and-important sort of way.

Three of my attorneys are here today: Peder Sander, the celebrity, and two of his colleagues. The younger one is a chick with an ugly haircut and a piercing in her nose but no ring in it. Presumably Sander won't allow her to wear a nose ring ("Remove that junk immediately"). I call her Ferdinand. Ferdinand is the type of person who thinks "conservative" is a curse word and nuclear power is lethal. She wears hideous glasses because she thinks it proves that she's got the patriarchy all figured out, and she hates me because, in her opinion, capitalism is all my fault. The first few times we met, she treated me like I was a crazy fashion blogger with a hand grenade on an airplane. "Of course, of course!" she said, not daring to look at me. "Of course, of course! Don't worry, we're here to help you." As if I would threaten to blow everyone to bits unless I received my biodynamic tomato juice with no ice.

The other helper attorney is a guy around forty with a doughy belly, a pancake-shaped face, and a smile that says, "I've got movies at home that I keep in alphabetical order in a locked cabinet." Pancake has a buzz cut. Dad likes to say that you can't trust a person with no hairstyle. But I'm sure Dad didn't come up with that on his own; he probably stole it from a movie. My dad really likes to deliver one-liners.

The first time I met Pancake, he rested his eyes just below my collarbone, forced his thick tongue back in his mouth, and rasped in delight, "Little girl, what are we going to do? You look much older than seventeen." He probably would have started panting if Sander hadn't been there. Or drooling, maybe. Let the saliva drip from his mouth and stain his too-tight suit vest. I couldn't bring myself to point out that I was eighteen.

Today, Pancake is sitting on my left. He brought a brief-case and a wheeled case stuffed full of folders and documents. He has emptied the case and now the folders are on the table in front of him. The only things he left in the case were a book (*Make Your Case — Winning Is the Only Option*) and a toothbrush sticking up from one of the little inside pockets. Sitting behind me, in the first row of the audience, are Mom and Dad.

When I was on that class trip two years and an eternity ago, our class had been given a run-through beforehand, so we would "appreciate the importance" and "be able to follow along." I doubt it helped. But we "behaved," as Christer said when we left. He had been afraid we wouldn't be able to keep from giggling and taking out our cell phones. That we were planning to sit there playing games and sleeping with our chins resting on our collars like bored members of Parliament.

I remember Christer's grave voice as he explained ("Hey now, listen up!") that a trial is nothing to be flippant about; people's lives are at stake. You are innocent until the courts have ruled that you are guilty. That's what he said, several times. Samir leaned back as Christer spoke, balancing on his chair and nodding like he always did, the way that made all the teachers love him. Nods that said *I understand completely, we are on the exact same wavelength* and *I have nothing to add because everything you say is so smart.*

You are innocent until the courts have ruled that you are guilty. What kind of weird statement is that? Either you're innocent all along, or else you did it, right from the start. Shouldn't the court try to figure out which it is, rather than decide what happened? The police and the prosecutor and the judges weren't there and don't know exactly who did what, so how can the court make it up after the fact?

I recall that I pointed this out to Christer. That courts are wrong all the time. Rapists are always going free. There's not even any point in reporting a sexual assault, because even if you were force-fucked by half a refugee camp and you get an entire case's worth of bottles shoved up between your legs, they never believe the girl. And that doesn't mean that it didn't happen, and that the rapist didn't do what he did.

"It's not that simple," said Christer.

What a typical teacher answer: "That's an excellent question..." "I hear what you're saying..." "It's not black and white..." "It's not that simple..." Those kinds of answers all mean the same thing: They have no idea what they're talking about.

But fine. If it's difficult to know what's true and who's lying, if you can't be sure, then what do you do?

I read somewhere that "the truth is whatever we choose to believe." Which sounds even more insane, if that's even possible. Like someone can just decide what's true and what's false? Things can be both true and made up, depending on whom you ask? And if someone we trust says something, well, then we can just decide that it's so, we can "choose that it's true." How can anyone even come up with something so idiotic? If a person were to say to me that he "chooses to believe me," I would know right away that he's actually convinced that I'm lying but he's going to pretend otherwise.

My attorney Sander seems mostly indifferent to all of this. All he says is, "I'm on your side," while his face looks like a thumbnail. Sander is not, like, the excitable type. Everything about him is relaxed and under control. No outbursts. No feelings. No roaring laughter. Probably he didn't even cry at birth.

Sander is the opposite of my dad. Dad is far from the "cool guy" (his words) he wishes he were. He grinds his teeth in his sleep and jumps to his feet when he watches the national team play soccer. My dad gets mad, furious, at pedantic city employees, the neighbor who parked illegally for the fourth time in one week, incomprehensible electric bills, and telemarketers. Computers, immigration officers, Grandpa, the grill, mosquitoes, unshoveled sidewalks, Germans in the ski-lift line, and French waiters. Everything riles him up, makes him yell and shout, slam doors and tell people to go to hell. With Sander, however, the clearest sign that he's pissed off, almost insane with anger, is that he gets a wrinkle on his forehead and makes a clicking sound with his tongue. And then all his colleagues become terrified and start stammering and looking for documents and books and other things they think will put him in a better mood. Kind of like how Mom handles Dad on the rare occasions he's not annoyed but is acting perfectly calm and quiet.

Sander has never gotten mad at me. He's never been upset over something I told him or grumpy about something I didn't say or when I was lying and he knew it.

"I'm on your side, Maja." Sometimes he sounds more tired than usual, but that's it. "The truth" is not something we talk about.

For the most part, I think it's nice that Sander only cares about what the police and the prosecutor have proven. I don't have to worry about whether he is planning to do a good job or is just pretending he's going to. It's like he's taken all the dead and all the guilt and all the agony and turned it into numbers, and if the equations don't add up, then he wins.

Maybe that's how it should be done. One plus one cannot equal three. Next question, please.

But that's of no help to me, of course. Because either something happened or it didn't. It is what it is. All the rest is just beating around the bush, the kind of thing that philosophers do, as well as (apparently) a lawyer here and there. Constructs. "It's not that simple…"

But Christer, I remember how insistent he was before that court visit, he really did everything he could to get us to listen. *You are innocent until the court has ruled that you are guilty.* He wrote it on the board: *a fundamental principle of law.* (Samir nodded again.) Christer asked us to take notes. Copy it down. (Samir copied it down. Even though he hardly needed to.)

Christer loved anything short enough to memorize that could be turned into a test question. The correct answer was worth two points on the exam we took two weeks later. Why not one point? Because Christer thought there were gray areas in memorized responses, that you could be almost right. *No, one plus one cannot equal three, but I'll give you partial credit because you answered in the form of a number.*

That visit to the court with Christer happened more than two years ago. Sebastian wasn't there; he wasn't in our class until our final year, the year he had to repeat. I liked school back then, pretty much, with my classmates and the teachers we'd had in different renditions since our elementary days: the chemistry teacher, Jonas, who spoke too quietly, never remembered anyone's name, and waited for the bus wearing his backpack on his front. The French teacher, Mari-Louise, with her glasses and dandelion hair, who was always sucking so hard on a tiny sliver of a black lozenge that her mouth became as small and puckered as a wild strawberry. Short-haired Gym Friggan, who looked like a freshly polished wooden deck: indistinct gender, a whistle around the neck, and broad, shiny, clean-shaven calves, always surrounded by the odor of gym socks and someone else's sweat. Absent-minded Malin, our bottle-blonde math teacher: dissatisfied and constantly late, off sick on average two days a week, and with a photo of herself twenty years slimmer, wearing a string bikini in her profile picture on Facebook.

And Christer Svensson. Dedicated, in a let's-meet-at-Mariatorget-and-take-a-stand sort of way; ordinary, in a pork-chops-and-mashed-potatoes-and-gravy sort of way.

He thought rock concerts could save the world from war, famine, and disease, and he always spoke in that overenthusiastic teacher voice that no one should ever use for anything but getting a dog to wag its tail.

Every day, Christer brought a thermos of home-brewed coffee to school, with so much sugar and milk in it that it looked like liquid foundation. He would pour his coffee into his mug ("World's Best Dad") and bring the mug to class and refill it during our lessons. Christer loved routines, same thing every day, favorite song on repeat. He had probably eaten the same thing for breakfast ever since he was fourteen: some sort of cross-country skier thing, like oatmeal with lingonberries and whole milk ("Breakfast is the most important meal of the day!"), I'm sure he drank beer and a shot on the side every time he met up with his friends ("buddies"), ate tacos with his family every Friday, and went to the neighborhood pizzeria (one with crayons and paper for the kids) and split a bottle of the house red with "the wife" when he wanted to celebrate something major and important. Christer had no imagination, he went on charter trips, he would never cook with coriander or fry things in anything but butter.

We first had Christer as a teacher in our first year of upper secondary. He complained at least once a week about how the weather had gotten so strange ("There aren't seasons anymore"), and every autumn he complained that Christmas decorations went up earlier and earlier ("Soon there will probably be a Christmas tree on Skeppsbron even before the summer ferries stop running.")

He complained about the evening tabloids ("Why would anyone read that shit?") and *Dancing with the Stars, Eurovision,* and *Paradise Hotel* ("Why would anyone watch that shit?"). Most of all he hated our cell phones ("Are you cows? With those chat apps dinging and jingling constantly, you might as well be wearing bells around your necks...Why do you bother with that shit?"). Every time he complained, he looked pleased, he thought he was youthful and "cool" (not just a Dad word), and that it was proof of how close he was with his students that he could use words like "shit" in front of us.

Christer stuck a pouch of snus under his upper lip after each cup of coffee and collected the used ones in a napkin before throwing them in the trash. Christer liked things neat and tidy, even his garbage.

And afterward, when the tax evader's trial was over and we went back to the school, he was pleased. He thought we had handled ourselves "well." Christer was always "pleased" or "concerned," never overjoyed or totally pissed off. Christer always wanted to give at least partial credit on memorized answers.

Christer was lying down when he died. With his arms around his head and his knees tucked up, more or less how my little sister Lina looks when she's sleeping most deeply. He bled to death before the ambulance arrived, and I wonder if his wife and his kids feel like things aren't so simple in reality and that I am innocent because no court has yet determined that I am guilty.

2.

Mom bought the clothes I'm wearing today. But I might as well be in a black-and-white-striped jumpsuit. I'm wearing a costume.

Then again, girls are always wearing a costume. Dressing up as the pretty, with-it girl, or the serious smart girl. Or as the totally chill I-don't-care-how-I-look girl, with her hair in a purposely messy ponytail, a cotton bra with no underwires, and an almost-see-through T-shirt.

Mom has tried to dress me up as a perfectly normal eighteen-year-old girl who ended up here through no fault of her own. But my blouse strains across my breasts. I've gained weight in jail and there are little round gaps between the buttons. I look like a salesperson who has put on a doctor's coat to dash after people in a shopping mall with my skin-care samples. *Don't think you're fooling anyone.*

"You look so nice, honey," Mom whispered from her spot at the front. She always does that, tosses compliments after me, like trash she expects me to sort. Made-up compliments that have nothing to do with reality. I am not "beautiful" or "good at drawing." I shouldn't *sing more* or *take drama classes* after school. It is terribly insulting for Mom to suggest that I should, because it proves she has no idea what I'm actually good at, or when I actually do look pretty. My mom does not have sufficient interest in me to succeed in giving me a compliment that's actually accurate.

My mom has always been inexplicably clueless. "Run out and play for a while, if you want to," she might urge in those last few months when she didn't have the energy to pretend she wished I would "stick around and talk about your day." *Run out and play for a while?* I was old enough to vote and buy drinks at a bar. It had been legal for me to fuck for three years. What did she think I was going to do? Play hide-and-seek with the neighbors? *One two three four ready or not here I come*, breathless laps around the yard to check behind the same old bush, in the same old wardrobe, behind the same old broken garden umbrella in the garage. "Did you have fun?" she would ask when I came back, my clothes reeking of pot. "Would you hang your jacket in the basement, honey?"

Last night I got to talk to my mom on the phone. Her voice was higher than normal. That's the voice she uses when someone else is listening or when she's multitasking. Mom is almost always multitasking, straightening the house, moving things around, wiping off counters, sorting stuff. She is constantly nervous, fidgety. She always has been; it's not my fault.

"It's going to be fine," she said. Several times. Her words tripped over each other. I didn't say much. Just listened to her too-high voice. "It's going to be fine. Don't worry, everything will be fine."

Sander has tried to explain what will happen during the hearing, what I can expect. In jail I got to watch an informative video in which painfully bad actors performed a trial about two guys who got into a fight at a bar. The defendant was found guilty, but not of all the charges, only like half. When we were done watching the video, Sander asked if I had any questions. "No," I said.

What I remember best about the tax trial we visited on our class trip was that it was so quiet. Everyone spoke in a hushed voice and all other noises became exaggerated — someone clearing their throat, a door closing, a chair scraping the floor. If someone had forgotten to put their phone on silent and got a text in there, it would have roared as loud as when the lights go down at the movies and they demonstrate how they've just installed a new surround-sound system.

And while everything was quiet, the tax evader sat there pushing his greasy hair off his forehead. As the prosecutor read the charges out loud, the man looked at his attorney and hissed out indignant snorts. I remember thinking that he was a moron. Why was he pretending to be surprised? The prosecutor and the moron's attorney talked one at a time, read out loud, said the same thing two or three times, and cleared their throats too much.

The whole show was lame. Not because nothing was "like it is in the movies," but because everyone involved seemed bored to tears; the criminal himself seemed to have a hard time concentrating. Even in reality, everyone was a crappy actor who hadn't bothered to learn his lines.

Samir, though, he didn't think any of it was ridiculous. He leaned forward in his uncomfortable chair, rested his elbows on his knees, and scrunched up his forehead. This was his specialty: showing how earnest he was, that he took serious things seriously. Samir looked like he thought that these polyester-clad losers were the most fascinating speakers he'd ever heard in his life. And Christer was pleased. By the court and by Serious Samir. Samir seldom had to open his mouth in order to French-kiss Christer's ass. We teased him about that afterward, me and Amanda. We liked to tease Samir. But Labbe patted him on the shoulder as if he were his youngest son and had just made the winning goal in a soccer game. "Samir gets it," Labbe said, and Samir grinned. "Samir always gets it."

Things were pretty good at home, too, during my second year. Mom and I still talked about stuff that had nothing to do with what time she thought my curfew should be. Mom was proud of me, or at least of the way she had raised me. She bragged about her effective methods of getting me to do exactly what it took to make her life easier. She told stories like how I slept through the night at just four months old, how I ate "everything" and held my own spoon the very first time I tried solid food. How I wanted to start school a year early, because I thought preschool was boring. How I wanted to walk to school by myself before I even turned eight, and how I "loved" being home alone without a babysitter. She said she let me start riding a balance bike before I used a real bicycle, and thanks to this, she never had to bend over and hold on to the fender to keep me from tipping over. I was able to just *poof!* ride a bike, and she could walk alongside in her flowy clothes and laugh just loud enough. What Mom did for *me*, to make *my* life easier, never came up, but back then, she was thoroughly convinced that I was so easy and trouble-free thanks to everything she had done right.

Today, in here, it is also quiet, I suppose. But not in the same way as during the tax trial. The air feels thick from all the important people waiting for important things to happen. The prosecutor and the lawyers are probably scared shitless that they'll make fools of themselves. Even Sander is nervous, although you'd never notice if you didn't know him.

They want to show what they're made of. When Pancake talked about how he thought it would go, he used phrases like "the odds" and "our chances," just as if he were my basketball coach and I played center on the team. He wants to *win*. Pancake didn't shut up until Sander clicked his tongue.

The day's proceedings begin when the chief judge recites some sort of roll call. He clears his throat into the microphone, and people stop whispering to each other. The judge checks to make sure everyone who is supposed to be here is here. I don't have to raise my hand and say "present," but the judge nods at me and reads my name. Then he nods at my attorneys and reads their names, too. He speaks slowly, but not sleepily; he's bursting with so much solemnity that he might split the seams of his ugly suit.

The judge bids me welcome, he honestly does. I don't say *thanks for having me*, because it's not like I'm supposed to respond, but I think I'm doing all the right stuff. I look more or less as I should. I don't smile, I don't cry, I don't stick my finger in any orifices. My back is straight but not too straight, and I'm trying to keep the buttons of my blouse from zinging right off.

When the chief judge tells the prosecutor that she may begin, she looks so wired that I think she's going to stand up. But she just scoots her chair in, leans toward the little straw-shaped microphone, presses a button, and clears her throat. Like she's taking her mark.

Out in the lawyers' waiting room, where we were sitting before we came in here, Pancake told me that people have been standing in line to get a seat in the courtroom. "Just like a concert," he declared, almost proudly. Sander looked like he wanted to deck him.

There's nothing about this trial that resembles a concert. I'm no rock star. The people who are drawn to me aren't wild groupies, they're just scavengers. When the journalists use me as bait on their front pages, it smells like death, and the hyenas get even more worked up.

But Sander still wanted the hearing to be public. In fact, he demanded the media and the general public be allowed in, even though I'm so young. Not to make Pancake feel like a badass, but because "it is crucial to keep the prosecutor from monopolizing the news reports." This almost certainly means that he is eager to show off his own contributions, but maybe he also imagines that my haters will be swayed if only they get to hear "my version." Sander is wrong. That's not going to matter. They love to hate me. They hate everything about me. *Just like a concert?* It seems highly unlikely that Pancake has ever been in the vicinity of live music that doesn't belong in the dork category. If I had to guess, he listens to the classic rock station and sings along to ads for the perfect family car.

Nine months ago, one week after it all happened, there were riots in Djursholm. A bunch of guys took the metro to Mörby, transferred to bus 606, and rode all eight stops to Djursholm Square. So they could "teach those fuckers a thing or two." Or, as the more articulate ones put it, "those fucking snobs."

Riots usually take place in the thugs' own run-down neighborhoods, among the public housing projects and the youth rec centers and the detoxed motorcycle guys who are "youth leaders" and "neighborhood liaisons" because no normal employer wants to touch them. And when it says in the paper that "the streets are burning," they're usually talking about pimped-out wrecks with tree-shaped air fresheners, not fully insured leased vehicles that are in the company's name and are traded in as soon as one of the side mirrors stops working. But not this time.

For three days and nights, it was all-out war at Djursholm Square and around Sebastian's house down on Strandvägen, the fanciest residential street, by the water. On the second night, there were around fifty people involved. Sander told me, he showed me the articles.

Broken windows in the frumpy shops on the square. What did they loot? A pussy-bow blouse each, plaids, and crystal wine carafes? And where did they go after they were shooed away from the Fagerman estate? Up to our house? Could they find their way? And considering how important my mom thought it was to "say a proper hello to show respect" to the very first beggar who sat outside the Coop grocery store on Vendevägen with a paper cup and a urine-stained blanket, what did she do about the baseball bats and the Molotov cocktails? "Hello there. Have a nice day. Enjoy your weekend." I wonder what Mom said to the National Task Force during the days they helped "keep order" outside our house? "Is everything okay?"

The newspapers Sander showed me speculated on *Why?* Whether it had to do with what Sebastian and I "symbolized," what we were "a manifestation of," and what we had done "had unleashed." Did riots break out because what happened was so incredibly horrible? Were the rioters extra angry because we were rich and they weren't? Or did violence break out solely because a group of small-time gangsters wanted a reason to fight (and because there was no soccer game to vandalize that weekend)? Whatever the reason, those thugs won't be allowed in here.

The gallery is mostly full of journalists. Many of them are typing on laptops. No one is allowed to take pictures; there's a "ban on photography," and presumably they also had to give up their phones before they came in. In any case, some of the journalists are even using plain old pens and notebooks.

There's a poor artist here, too. You'd think I was something out of Dickens, a flea-bitten kid who might get the gallows. Or some Elvira Madigan type from an old broadsheet. *Why, even in this day and age, tragedy may strike.* We sang that song in middle school. Naturally, Amanda cried; she was at her prettiest when she was crying but wasn't sad for real ("adorable!") — it would get her even more attention than usual.

Amanda is described as my best friend. In the newspapers, on TV, in the case report; even my own attorney calls her that. *My best friend.*

Was Amanda the person I spent the most time with, besides Sebastian? Yes. Was Amanda the person I talked to the most, besides Sebastian? Yes. Is she standing next to me in approximately 260 of my Facebook photos? Did I Snapchat with her on average two hours a day during the first four of the six months' worth of phone records they obtained? Did she tag me in over a hundred #bff posts on Instagram? Yes. Yes. Yes.

Did I love Amanda? Was she my very best friend? I don't know.

Week 1 of Trial: Monday

3.

In any case, I loved being with Amanda. We were almost always together. We sat next to each other in class and at lunch; we did homework together and skipped school together. We talked shit about girls who annoyed us ("not to be a bitch, but…"), we climbed and stepped and ran on different machines at the gym, on the road to nowhere. We did our makeup together, shopped together, talked for hours, chatted nonstop, laughed the way girls laugh in movies when one of them is lying on her belly on the other one's bed while the other one stands on the mattress and her nightshirt is way too short and she uses a hairbrush for a microphone and lip-syncs to a good song or imitates one of the dorky girls at school.

We partied together. Amanda got drunk fast. It always followed the same pattern: giggle, laugh, dance, fall over, laugh a little more, lie down on a sofa, cry warm tears that trickled into her ears, throw up, go home. I always took care of her, it was never the other way around.

I liked being with Amanda, being able to tune everything out. With her, it seemed obvious that life was for having as much fun as possible. And her dumb-blonde shtick was also mostly really entertaining. If you asked about the weather, she would say "flip-flops" or "semi-opaque." Or, if it was very cold, she would say "It's frickin' après-ski," and then she would come to school in thermal leggings, moon boots, and a down coat with a rabbit-fur collar.

It would be too easy to say that Amanda was superficial. Sure, she would never be able to moonlight as a columnist for any serious newspaper. She thought "oppression is terrible" and "racism is terrible" and "poverty is super terrible." She stammered all her positives, doubled all her opinions. Really really good, super super cozy, and teeny teeny tiny. (That last one is actually a triple, right?) Her views on politics and equality and really any other issue you could come up with were based on the three and a half episodes' worth of investigative reporting she'd watched (and cried to) on *Mission: Report*. And when she watched YouTube videos about the world's fattest man leaving his house for the first time in thirty years, she would say, "Shh! Not now, I'm watching the news."

What Amanda liked best was talking about her anxieties. She would lean in and whisper about how hard it was to have eating disorders and insomnia ("It's really super super hard"). During a certain period she claimed that she "had to" avoid the color green and the number nine, that she "had to" avoid sidewalk curbs ("I mean, it's not like I choose to avoid them; I have to or else I think I'm going to die, die for real, I mean, like, actually die"). Sometimes she would crank up the volume if she didn't get the reaction she was after. She pretended that a burn scar she got when we tried to make pancakes after school was actually a scar from something else, something she "would rather not talk about." The idea was that people would think it was from a suicide attempt. It didn't even cross her mind that I might tell them the truth.

But it would be too simple to say that she lied, or at least that's not all she did. Sure, she thought life sucked sometimes. And she thought that anxiety was the same thing as worrying that you might miss the bus and that she had bulimia because she felt sick if she ate a bar of chocolate with nuts in under ten minutes.

Amanda was spoiled, of course she was — by her mom, her dad, her therapist, and the person who took care of her horse. But it wasn't just about clothes and stuff. It was something else. She had the same attitude toward her parents, her teacher — all authorities, including God — that she did toward people in the service industry, like they were all concierges at a luxury hotel. She expected to receive help with everything from a pimple on her nose to a lost earring to emergency care and eternal life. Whether God existed or not was uninteresting, but of course he should help her cousin who had cancer because it was "really really sad" and her cousin was "super, super sweet, even though he's bald." She felt sorry for people with problems but was bothered that people didn't feel just as sorry for her in return.

And she was self-absorbed. She devoted so much time to her waist-length hair that you would've thought it was her dying grandmother. People thought she was nice, but she wasn't genuinely nice. She always asked twice if you wanted milk in your coffee ("Are you really sure?") and made you feel fat. She said, "I really wish I could be like you, and just relax and not give a crap what I look like" and "Wow, you're incredibly photogenic," and expected you to say thanks because she didn't get that you got that it was an insult.

And sure, she thought that "politics are super important." But she wasn't politically engaged in the way that makes people want to join youth associations and go to camp and do archery along with other people in shorts. She would never dye her hair black or set fire to a mink farm or even have the energy to read a news article about ozone leaks or shrinking coral reefs, and she was definitely not politically engaged the way all our teachers thought Samir was just because he had a dad who had been imprisoned and tortured for his beliefs.

For Amanda, politics meant that public health care should pay for the gastric bypass operation she was planning to have if she ever weighed "like sixty kilos." It was "only right, considering the taxes we pay." And by "we," she didn't mean her mom, because the only money her mom controlled came from getting cash back every time she went grocery shopping. Her mom would deposit that money into the bank, into what she called her "shoe account," and Amanda rolled her eyes at that account; she despised it. She told me all about it, but only because she thought her mom was an idiot, not because she thought it was strange that her mom could buy a spur-of-the-moment family trip to Dubai, complete with a first-class flight and a luxury hotel, but had to squirrel away petty cash so she could buy herself a new pair of jeans without asking permission.

How Amanda became part of the "we" along with her dad and his money, and how she thought she herself was contributing to the economy, was never clear.

During one political discussion with Christer a few months before it all happened, we got on the topic of Che Guevara.

"I think it's totally horrible to kill children," said Amanda. "Although I'm not too familiar with what's going on in the Middle East."

Samir was sitting diagonally behind her in the classroom, and she had to sort of pause for a moment before Samir caught on that she was addressing him.

"So I totally understand why you hate Americans," she said once he finally made eye contact.

I don't remember what Christer said. Just that Samir looked at me. Straight at me, not Amanda. He thought it was my fault Amanda didn't know who Che Guevara was. That she didn't know the difference between Latin America, Israel, and Palestine. And that she'd somehow gotten the idea that Samir had some fundamental issue with the U.S.

Sure, Amanda was politically engaged in a Disney Channel sort of way, and sometimes it was hard to think that she was super super charming. We seldom discussed politics. It gave me a headache and it made Amanda grumpy because she noticed that it was noticeable that she didn't know what she was talking about.

But there were many times, like when I was lying on her rug and listening to her enthusiastic now-we're-in-a-delightful-teen-movie-where-everyone-jumps-into-their-convertibles-without-opening-the-doors-first voice — as attentively as if it were elevator music — that I thought she and I were so different that we ended up pretty similar. Amanda pretended to be engaged in things and I pretended I didn't care. And we were so good at pretending that we fooled everyone, including ourselves.

The prosecutor hasn't started talking about Amanda yet. She's saving that for the crescendo. Instead she is concentrating on Sebastian.

Sebastian, Sebastian, Sebastian. She will talk about him for days; everyone is going to talk about him. All the time. If there's anyone who seems like a rock star in all of this, it's Sebastian. Sander showed me the photos the media found and published. Sebastian's black-and-white class picture has appeared on at least twenty magazine covers, all over the world, including *Rolling Stone*'s. But there are other pictures. Sebastian lounging with a cigarette in his mouth. Sebastian drunk and with beads of sweat on his forehead. Sebastian standing up in the stern of his boat as we're sailing through the Djurgårdsbrunn Canal on our way to the Fjäderholm islands and I'm sitting at his feet and resting my head against him. There's one from that same trip where Samir is sitting next to me and looking to the side, away from us. He looks like we forced him to come along. As if being near us makes him seasick. Amanda is sitting on the other side, white teeth, tan legs, blue eyes, tons of hair blowing in the right direction. Dennis isn't in those pictures, of course. But there are photos of Dennis in the case report. Sebastian had some in his phone — he liked taking pictures of Dennis when he was drunk, so I don't know why they didn't get their hands on those, too. The fact is, there are pictures of him and Dennis together, equally drunk, high, crazy. Sebastian looks terribly handsome in all of them. Dennis looks like Dennis.

The prosecutor will talk more about what Sebastian did than anything else, because she says that everything he did, we did together. I don't know how I will manage to listen. But it's dangerous to stop concentrating. Because then the sounds will come.

The sound when they came into the classroom and hauled me off, the sound when Sebastian's skull hit the floor, it was hollow. It roars inside me; as soon as I let down my guard it comes back. I dig my fingernails into my palms, trying to get away. But it doesn't help. I can't get rid of it. My brain always drags me back into that fucking classroom.

Sometimes when I sleep, I dream about it. And about how it was just before they arrived. How I try to stop his blood with my hand; he's lying in my lap and I'm pressing as hard as I can. I can't stop the blood from spurting no matter how hard I press. It's like trying to keep water from spraying out when a hose has started to come loose from the spigot. Did you know that, that blood can spurt so hard? That it's impossible to stop with your hands? And Sebastian turns cold, I can still feel it, at night — again and again — how his hands get colder and colder. It happens quickly. And I dream about when Christer drew his last breath. It sounded like when you pour lye down a drain. I didn't know that you could dream about how someone else's skin feels and what noises sound like, but you can, because I do it all the time.

I try to avoid looking at the people in the courtroom who are there to look at me. I didn't even look for Dad when I came in. But Mom touched me as I went by. There was something in her eyes that I didn't recognize. She smiled at me and bobbed her head to the side, and her lips turned up at the corners in an expression that was probably supposed to remind me of what she had said on the phone the day before. A this-is-going-to-be-fine smile. But she shuddered just before I looked away, a microsecond too soon, shaking something off.

Before all of this happened, my mom's greatest challenge was trying to live without carbs. She gained and lost weight so rapidly that you might have thought it was her job, and she was truly proud of herself when she had food under control. And now here she is. Pretty much everything is in that case report. Not just about that day. It talks about our parties, what Sebastian did, what I did. About

Amanda. My mom loved Amanda. She loved Sebastian, too, at least at first, but she probably doesn't want to admit that anymore.

I wonder if Mom believes "my story." If she "chooses" to believe it. But she hasn't said anything about it, and I haven't asked. How could I? I haven't seen Mom and Dad since the detention hearing nine months ago, and our phone calls haven't exactly been confidential, not even in a legal sense.

How weird is that? Nine months have gone by since Mom, Dad, and I were in the same room. Although we weren't really together that time, either. I just saw them through the pane of glass between that classroom-size courtroom at the jail and the row of seats for the public where I'm sure they probably had to sit for fifteen whole minutes before the judge declared that the detention hearing would be held behind closed doors, and everyone, including Mom and Dad, was sent away.

I sobbed during the detention hearing. Nonstop. I was already crying when we stepped in. I felt about as normal as a force-fed foie gras goose, just as nauseated, and Mom and Dad looked terrified.

Mom wore a new blouse to the detention hearing, one I hadn't seen before. I wonder what she was dressed up as that day, when everything was still so unclear. Before she knew. Maybe you're thinking that she was dressed up as a mom who knew, knew without a doubt, that it was all a big mistake and none of it was her daughter's fault. But I

think she was dressed up as a mom who had done everything right, a mom who couldn't be blamed for anything, no
matter what had happened.

The detention hearing took place three days after I arrived
at the jail, and I wish I hadn't cried so much. I would have
liked to shatter that pane of glass so I could ask Mom about
things that really didn't matter.

I wanted to ask if she had made my bed after I went
over to Sebastian's. Tanja didn't work on Fridays. Did it
remain untouched until the police arrived? But what about
after that? What happened then? Had Tanja cleaned, or had
Mom and Dad forbidden her to enter my room, the way
parents do when their child dies and they leave the bedroom untouched for thirty years and it stays just as it was
when their kid was last there?

I wanted that to be what Mom and Dad did, I wanted
them to tell me so, to say everything looked just as it had
when I left, that the police hadn't changed anything, that
life, my life, my life from back then, before, was frozen in
time, preserved, wrapped up in thick layers of mummy
bandages. If I survived this and got to come home again, I
wanted my surroundings to be familiar.

But they couldn't say that, of course. And it probably
wouldn't have mattered whether Mom made the bed or
not. I already knew that the police had searched the house,
because they told me so when they interrogated me. And
they told me that they had my computer and that they had
taken my phone at the hospital (I had to give them all my

passwords, for every forum, every app, every site I had visited), and when I asked what else they had taken, they said "most of it…your iPad and papers and…books, sheets, your clothes from the party." "Which clothes?" I asked, and they responded, as if this were perfectly normal and not weird at all, "your dress, your bra, and your underwear."

They took my dirty underwear. Why did they do that? I wanted to break the pane of glass and demand Mom explain it to me, because I didn't want to ask Sander. "Why did they take my underwear, Mom?" That's what I wanted to ask her. I didn't want to talk to Sander about anything that had my discharge on it.

And what did Mom and Dad do with the stuff they left behind? I wanted to know that, too. I wondered if they had let Tanja wash my scent out of all my other clothes. I've always thought she likes hanging laundry to dry. Smoothing out the wrinkles, stretching out the seams, flattening out the creases. Hanging sweaters upside down, with the arms dangling kind of dejectedly, as if they've given up, like they're crying "uncle." And the socks in pairs, two under each clothespin. So it's easier to sort later on.

I wondered if they had let Tanja clean me away. Or if Mom had looked at the butter knife each morning, the one I always forget and leave out, and thought, *She was just here. Now she's gone.*

Mom? I wanted to scream. Right out loud. *What is going on?*

But there was a pane of glass in the way. And I hardly had time to sit down before the judge sent all the spectators away. I received no answers; I was jailed instead.

One time, long before all of this, I asked Mom why she never asked me about anything important. "What do you want me to ask?" she wondered. She didn't even try to guess.

Today, she and Dad are allowed to stay. They have reserved seats — the "best" seats, I assume, at the very front, closest to me (even though they're still a few meters away). And Mom has gained weight. She's still dressed as a mom who hasn't done anything wrong, but who knows, maybe she's been doing some emotional eating? Gobbling down greasy pasta with butter, cheese, and ketchup. Devouring simple carbs. Considering what I did, she has an excuse to do pretty much anything, even gain weight. Everyone will understand. And they'll despise her anyway, whether she's thin or not.

Mom's neck always turns splotchy when she's nervous, and she always gets nervous when she's trying to explain what she means. It's impossible to concentrate on what she is saying; all you can do is stare at the splotches on her neck. That's probably why Mom seldom says what she's thinking — it's too risky. She sticks to asking what Dad thinks. If he's in a good mood, he'll share. And then a whole evening might go by without Mom saying, "We never taaaalk to each other anymore."

It's beyond me how she can be so concerned that someone doesn't talk to her enough even as she never dares to ask how that someone might be feeling. But I've never hated her for being clueless. I hate her because she doesn't want to know better. And I hate her most of all when she tells me how I'm feeling.

"I know you're worried." "I know how scared you are." "I know how it feels."

My mom is an idiot. "I wish I could switch places with Maja." Did she ever say that? Not to me, anyway.

Week 1 of Trial: Monday

4.

Lead prosecutor Lena Pärsson talks and talks, Jesus Christ, she talks so much. Two of the police officers from the investigation are with her. Beside them are the plaintiffs' lawyers; they're there to call for damages. They, too, have piled tons of folders on the table in front of them, a mini-library. There are two large screens in here, one on the wall behind me and an identical one behind them. Right now, all that's visible on the screens is a number of document icons; the image seems messy, like a slapped-together presentation in social studies.

Amanda's parents are not permitted to sit at the prosecutor's table. Nor are the other families. They're sitting in the audience, I think. Or maybe in the room next door, where people can watch the proceedings on a third big screen. They probably don't want to sit in the same room as me.

Sander has told me that it is the prosecutor's "duty" to "disclose" why we are here. What she thinks I have done and why she demands the maximum punishment.

"Considering your age," Sander has said to me, "you shouldn't get much more than ten years." The law states that a person under twenty-one cannot be sentenced to life in prison. But if I get fourteen years, I will be thirty-two when I go free. And Pancake has told me about the people who call and write, both to him and to Sander. (Pancake is proud that he gets hate mail, too, not just Sander; I can hear it in his voice.) He even told me about the people who trespass in our yard at night and throw feces at the door; Mom and Dad have to power-wash it off before they go to work. He told me this when Sander wasn't there.

So I know. The people who pay the prosecutor's salary, the taxpayers, the general public, everyone besides Peder Sander and maybe Mom and Dad, they don't think that ten or fourteen years are enough, they don't even think that a life sentence would be sufficient. They're not happy just to ruin my life, they want me to die.

Sander said that not much will happen today. But when the prosecutor reads the names of the victims, I hear someone crying.

I'm not prepared for that. Long before lead prosecutor Lena Pärsson is finished, the courtroom fills with the sound. The person is howling. Is it Amanda's mom? It can't be; she would never sound like that. Maybe they found a mom or a grandma for Dennis. Maybe they flew her in so she can sit in this whitewashed room, like Queen Latifah at the Nobel concert.

It sounds like a professional house crier. A crazy person with a black shawl wound around her head, throwing her hands up in the air, staring up at the heavens and standing smack in front of the TV cameras and just screaming after someone got on a school bus and blew himself and fifty kids to bits. Could that type of woman be sitting in here? Would she get through the security check?

One thing is for certain: The journalists will be selling these sobs during the very next newsbreak. They will report it. Live-update and tweet it. Describe how it looks, how it sounds, in 140 characters or less. And all my old "school friends" will retweet it, maybe adding a crying emoji, to show how personal it is to them in particular. I wonder how many of them have made their way here, stood in line for hours, made sure to grab a spot to "work through their memories" of what didn't happen to them.

I don't want to listen to this, but I have to stay here. So I press my palms against the tabletop. The prosecutor talks and talks. I hope she's almost done. She says something about Amanda, something else about Samir, Dennis, Christer...Sebastian and his dad. The chairman looks nervous; he fiddles with the gavel on the table in front of him and glares at one of the guards.

The prosecutor keeps talking, despite the sobs. She clicks, and school pictures appear on the screen, and the howling in the audience transforms into something else — the guard must have told her to be quiet. And my throat burns, I have to press one palm to my lips to make sure I'm not making noise, too. The prosecutor ought to learn to express herself in a shorter, catchier way. She hasn't uttered a single sentence short enough to tweet.

And this is meant to be a "summary" of what she thinks I should be convicted of. This trial is expected to last three weeks, and when Sander told me that, I thought it sounded crazy long, but considering how long this short summary is taking, time might get tight.

I still don't turn around; instead, I stare down at the desk. I assume they'll report on that, too. That I listened to the list of the dead and wounded, that I heard the sobs, this damn crying, without showing any emotion. They like to think that I'm cold as ice. Inhuman.

My whole self is a problem for my lawyers, not just the fact that Pancake thinks I look older than I am. I'm too tall and too strong, my breasts are too big, my hair is too long. Good teeth, expensive jeans. *Not a child.*

I'm not wearing a watch today, or jewelry. But I don't need any of that. The signs of who I am outside of jail are as clear as tan lines around your eyes after a week in the Alps. Isn't the prosecutor almost finished? I want to take a break, I want to change clothes, I have to put on something other than this tight piece-of-shit shirt. Sander says he'll demand a break at least every two hours. It must be time for one. I want to be herded into some room where it's just the four of us and Ferdinand can ask if I want coffee. Always with the coffee. I'm adult enough to sit here, and all adults drink coffee. Except for Pancake, of course — he's the only person over fifteen I know who drinks hot chocolate, even the hot chocolate from the machines in the meeting rooms at the jail. He slurps and sips with those red lips, he digs around in the mug with his index finger to get the sugary globs at the bottom. I have to get out, I have to get out of here.

I pull my shoulders down. It feels like I have a stitch. I think about my last breakfast at home. Anything at all, as long as I don't have to listen. I went down to the kitchen, just like always. Mom and Dad were both there, Dad was reading the paper, Mom was standing up and taking big gulps of that green sludge she lives on. She presses juice from kale, spinach, and green apples and mixes it with avocado in a special raw juicer/blender that cost 9,000 kronor. Before she started juicing, it was a particular kind of tea that she bought from an American health food store online. She drank it every morning alongside her omelet made with four egg whites. Tanja threw out the leftover yolks, once a week, twenty-eight yolks that went stiff in the fridge.

"I can't possibly eat the yolks," Mom would say to her with a laugh, as if it were a joke that Tanja was in on, too. "But maybe you'd like them, Tanja?"

Mom always uses the same tone of voice when she talks to Tanja. The same slow voice, like she's talking to an unruly child. With the exception that she would never talk like that to my little sister, Lina, or any other child, for that matter. One voice for the children, one voice for the help. A little old mass murder would hardly change that. Keep your head up. A roly-poly doll with a lead ball in her bottom, that's my mom.

She likes to pretend that she and Tanja are good friends, sort of like colleagues. That's probably why she's always asking Tanja if she wants something to eat. I have never seen Tanja eat. Or even drink anything other than half a glass of water, which she tosses back as fast as she can, leaning over the sink. Or go to the bathroom; I've never seen Tanja go to the bathroom. Maybe she craps in our flowerbeds and pees in Mom's green juices? Or she holds it until she gets home. I always wondered what Mom thought Tanja was going to do with those leftover egg yolks. Gulp them down like Rocky before a big boxing match, or take them home and make egg toddies for her dreary kids? We've never met Tanja's kids, but Mom learned their names for the same reason she says hello to beggars. *How is Elena these days? Is Sasha doing well in school?*

Waiting on the kitchen table, on that last morning, was fresh-squeezed juice (regular, orange), cheese and but-ter, sliced tomato and cucumber. It smelled like coffee and scrambled eggs, I think; I couldn't see any, but I think it was scrambled eggs. The breakfast looked almost like a ritual, an offering. The radio was unplugged, its cord as limp as an amputated body part next to the cutting board. *We have to talk*, it said. Mom and Dad wanted to get serious. *Had anyone called to tell them? The police? Had anyone called the police?* I didn't want to talk. I refused. Mom looked at me without saying anything, and I looked away without saying anything back. Then my phone rang. It was Sebastian.

I had promised we would ride to school together. He insisted. "You have to." I hadn't wanted to; I still didn't want to. But I didn't want to stay at home either. *Who's going to eat all of this?* I had time to think before I shoved my feet into my shoes and grabbed my keys. They were on the hall table. Will Tanja have to wrap it up and put it in the fridge? But Tanja had Fridays off. She had Fridays off, and they would come search our house before she returned.

"I don't have time!" I shouted at Mom and Dad. "We can talk tonight." But I had no intention of talking to them ever again. How could they possibly understand? It was too late.

Lead prosecutor Lena Pärsson talks and talks and I still don't turn around and look at the audience. I don't want to risk catching sight of Amanda's mom or anyone else who wants me to suffer eternal punishment, preferably in the form of death, but at least by being locked up so they can throw away the key. Why would they be the least bit interested in Sander's arguments about evidence and the sequence of events and causality and intent and all that? *I'm* not even interested.

And the journalists, I don't want to look at them either. I get what they're after, they want to explain me, say that I was like this and like that, my upbringing was this way, my parents that way, I "wasn't well," "drank too much," "smoked weed"; I listened to the "wrong type of music," I spent time with "the wrong people," I was "not the average girl." I convinced myself of some things and didn't understand others.

They're not interested in knowing what happened; they want to box me up into the tiniest compartment they possibly can. That will make it easier to brush me aside. They want to be convinced that we have nothing in common. Only then will they be able to sleep at night. Only then will they believe that what happened to me could never, never, ever happen to them.

The prosecutor, lead prosecutor Lena Pärsson ("call me Lena," she said, the first time she was present for one of my interrogations) with her tacky earrings (authentic versions of those rocks would have been sold with armed security guards thrown in for free), her uneven bangs, and eyebrows that look like they were drawn on with a ballpoint pen, talks. And talks and talks. My head is starting to buzz. I rub my hand over my mouth again. My armpits feel sticky; I wonder if people can see the dark circles there. Pärsson has clicked on one of the documents, obviously nervous. It seems like it's practically a superhuman feat for her to coordinate her movements to bring up those fucking images. But now she's running a little dot back and forth across a photograph to point out what she wants us to look at.

Sander didn't warn me that we would be shown pictures this soon. The prosecutor is already showing us pictures, even though this is only the introduction. How long can an introduction actually take? Isn't this ever going to end? I have to get out of here. I look at Sander, but he doesn't look back. Now she's showing a map of the school. The labyrinth of hallways, the classroom, the nearest emergency exit, the auditorium. You can't tell from the map how low the ceiling is in the school corridors. You can't see how dark it is in there, even on a sunny morning in late May.

She points at the drawing to indicate my locker, where one of Sebastian's bags was found; she points at the doors at the back of the classroom, the ones that lead out to the courtyard. They were locked that day. I assume it's to explain why the police didn't come in that way (they have been criticized for this in the media), even though it's not like it would have mattered. It was all over by the time anyone called the police. She points at the door that leads to the corridor. It was just closed, not locked, but still no one opened it until it was too late. Could anyone but the police have done anything? How? And who? She switches to another image, a drawing of the classroom. I lower my eyes. How long has she been going on? It feels like hours.

Call-me-Lena proceeds thoroughly. I have read the case report, or at least most of it, and in it she dissected me. Call-me-Lena has cut me up, picked me apart, taken out all my innards, sniffed the contents of my intestines. Call-me-Lena has held press conferences about me every week, sometimes multiple times a day, for months. She has analyzed my fucking underwear.

Call-me-Lena-ugly-as-shit-lead-prosecutor-Lena-Pärsson is sure she knows me. It's obvious in her voice. Every word is an unearthed treasure. She holds them up, one at a time, to the light. She is so pleased. She is convinced that she knows everything about me, who I am, and why. What I did. She doesn't point at me, but that's only because she doesn't need to. Look at Maja Norberg, everyone: the killer, the monster, she's sitting right there!

Everyone is already looking.

The indictment itself, the document that states what the prosecutor says I've done and what she wants me to be convicted of, is eleven pages long and contains detailed descriptions. There are exhibits, too, with details about the victims, who they were, what happened to them and what I did, who I shot and who Sebastian shot, and how it was all my fault. There are photographs, legal opinions, interviews with people who claim to know me, that they knew, that they can explain. Lead prosecutor Lena Pärsson has an entire narrative. It is cohesive from start to finish and everyone believes it is true, even if they haven't heard it yet.

I wonder what Mom means when she says everything will be fine.

Week 1 of Trial: Monday

5.

She does in fact wrap things up eventually, lead prosecutor Lena Pärsson. Then the plaintiffs' lawyers speak. They want me to pay damages, but it isn't all that much money. Only one of the attorneys talks for longer than two minutes. And when they're done, Sander finally asks if we can take a break. The head judge almost looks more relieved than I feel. We leave the room. I'm in the middle, with Ferdinand and Pancake on either side. Sander walks ahead of us.

We enter the room they have assigned us and close the door. There is a piece of paper taped to the outside of the door; it reads THE DEFENDANT. As if anyone here believes that I am going to be able to defend myself. It's strange that a court, where the truth is supposed to come out, has such a difficult time saying what they mean in plain language, daring to call things by their true names.

"Do you want anything?" Ferdinand asks. I don't respond, just wait for her to continue. "Coffee?"

I shake my head. *White lilies in my dressing room*, I think. If I said that out loud, Ferdinand would faint, for the simple reason that she has no sense of humor and she thinks I'm the type of person who likes white lilies. But I don't say anything.

Sander stands up for the entire break. He doesn't say anything, either. There is a bathroom attached to our room; I think that's why we are allowed to be here even though it's normally reserved for other uses: We will not have to use the same bathroom as everyone else. Or the others won't have to use the same bathroom as me. We take turns using it. When it's my turn, the seat is warm.

It is dead silent. No one is drinking any coffee. Ferdinand sips from a water bottle. The trial has already been under way for over two hours. The prosecutor's summary took one hour and forty-six minutes.

After exactly twelve minutes, we return. Pancake shuts the door so hard the piece of paper falls off. Ferdinand sticks it back up again. I forgot to ask if I could change clothes.

Once we've taken our seats again, I hear Dad clear his throat just as Sander is about to start talking. I have to force myself not to turn around and look at him. Instead I concentrate on Sander. We're sitting right next to each other, and he has given me a pen and a pad of paper and told me to write down anything I think seems odd or any questions I want to ask him.

"It's important," he has said, more times than I can keep track of, "that you feel everything turns out right."

I like Sander. But I don't always understand what he means. Or, more accurately, I understand the contents of what he says, the meaning itself, but I seldom understand the thinking behind it.

Everything turns out right? That I am satisfied, maybe? I had to ask what he meant. But I might as well not have bothered, because all I got was a long, incomprehensible talk about how he was "pleading my case" and that if he said anything that didn't "correspond with my version of the chain of events," then I had to "point it out."

After a while, I think he realized how idiotic he sounded, because he stopped talking. He looked at me for a moment before saying, "If I say something that makes you angry, scared, annoyed, or anything else like that, you have to tell me. But you can't say so right when I'm saying it, while the prosecutor and the judges can hear. Write it down and we'll deal with it later."

There's more stuff I don't understand the point of. Stuff he says he wants to talk about ("bring up") during the trial. It bothers me that he apparently discusses me when I'm not there, that he "draws up tactics" with Ferdinand and Pancake and all their other colleagues who I can hardly keep straight because they all look the same. He does that without me. They sit at long tables at the law office and discuss "strategies" when I'm not there. I assume that's when they poke around in their boxes of take-out Chinese.

"Maja Norberg admits some parts of the factual allegations but her involvement could not give rise to criminal liability," Sander says, and I wonder if anyone believes that this means I'm innocent, if anyone will be convinced that I haven't done anything wrong, and I wonder what I'll write down on my pad of paper to get Sander to explain it well enough.

Sander says I have to trust him, that he is always "completely open" with me. And what choice do I have? I have no idea how this could ever turn out right.

Sander has a whole collection of *looks*, different ones for different people. He has his focused-but-bored look, for when he's looking straight at whoever's talking, and it is clear that nothing could surprise him, there's nothing anyone could say that he hasn't figured out already. That's the look he gave the police officers while they were questioning me, and I like to imagine he looks at journalists that way when they pose questions he is not allowed to answer ("nondisclosure order"). Right now he is giving the judge and the prosecutor that exact look: politely tired.

The look he aims at Pancake is worse. When Pancake says stuff like, "You have to crack a few eggs if you want to make an omelet" and "Even a stopped clock is right twice a day," Sander's face gets his do-you-think-you're-being-funny? look. And you want nothing more than for Sander to stop glaring. Because best of all is when he is done clicking his tongue and actually *says* something.

The look that means Sander is extremely disappointed, that he was expecting more but he will tolerate this because he has no choice — that's the look most people get, at least now and then. Sometimes Ferdinand gets the opposite: an almost-satisfied look. But that one is almost equally insulting, because it's obvious how surprised he is to find that she is not stupid after all. What Sander doesn't notice is the way Ferdinand looks at him. Or else he doesn't care.

But I like how Peder Sander looks at me. He doesn't want me to laugh at his jokes or ask him what he's up to or inquire about his opinion on something. It would never even occur to Sander to sneak a look at my breasts. He is interested in what I say and he is going to do his job. Period.

I don't have to be afraid that he might have a hard time listening to what I tell him. I don't have to worry that he will be hurt or about how I might make him feel. He looks at me as if I'm an adult, or at least deserve to be treated like one. I assume it's Sander's client look. And that it's one of the reasons he's a celebrity.

I am "pleased" with Sander.

If I asked, Dad would say he chose him because he is "considered to be the best." Is Sander expensive? He is probably more expensive than I can even imagine, but Dad would never discuss that. Because it's "not done," and Dad is a rule follower when it comes to what is and is not done.

It's not as simple as saying that Mom is old money and Dad is new money. Neither of them is the sort of high-class they would like to be. But Mom did at least grow up with money, a lot of money, which Grandpa earned all on his own thanks to a type of instrument that is used in knee surgeries. He patented it back when he was still in medical school and before the pharmaceutical industry had time to figure out that not only was Grandpa's thingamajig brand-new, it was also useful. Within a couple of years it was "indispensable"

(Mom's word). "Everyone" uses it "all over the world" (still Mom's words). Grandpa got "filthy rich" off this thing. (Absolutely under no circumstances Mom's words. Grandpa, though, says this as often as he can.)

Grandpa has the same relationship with money as he has to the weather. It is there, he takes advantage of it, it doesn't seem to run out no matter how he spends it, he got really lucky, might as well make the most of it. Maybe Grandpa's attitude is what made Mom financially constipated. And by constipated, I mean that Mom thinks it is of utmost importance for everyone to think she is richer than she actually is, and she tries to accomplish this by pretending that she doesn't think money is important in the least.

Mom likes to say that the antiques in our house came from "the family." The clock in the kitchen, for example — she doesn't quite know if it's attractive or totally fucking grotesque, so she laughs through her nose when someone mentions it or just happens to glance at it, and she says "family" and rolls her eyes, as if the clock is an inheritance she is obliged to live with so her dead ancestors don't turn over in their graves.

All our furniture comes from various bankrupted estates that Grandpa bid on at Bukowskis and then got tired of and dumped at our house, but Mom would never say so. Not that she's fooling anyone; not a single person has ever believed that Mom is the person she pretends to be. But she keeps pretending anyway. And for the most part, people are polite about it and leave her alone.

Dad's money is hardly even fifteen minutes old. And he doesn't have enough of it to compensate. But he spent his last upper-secondary year at a boarding school outside Uppsala while his proper, super-boring middle-class parents worked on a third-world irrigation project in North Africa. And he thinks boarding school taught him what it takes to fit in, what he has to do for high-class people to think he's one of them. He's wrong, of course.

Dad must be freaking out now. Because people are going to see him for exactly what he is. The newspapers are calling him the Investment Broker. Maybe that impresses people, what do I know? But everyone who counts knows that a "broker" is something you are until you're thirty-five, max, and then you start working with your own money, or else you're just as much an embarrassment as a waitress with saggy boobs and varicose veins. "I work in consulting," I once heard him say. With a crooked smile that said it was far too complicated to explain further. His business card says "asset manager." That doesn't really mean "investment broker," but it's close.

People have always said I take after my dad. Mom says so whenever I get upset, and Dad says so whenever I get my grades. But everything in this courtroom would suggest that Dad will forever after have to be satisfied with being "Murder-Maja's dad — the investment broker." Congrats.

I wonder what Mom is most afraid of. If it's what is going to happen to me, or what has already happened to her. I actually don't give a shit which it is, but I don't want

Lina to be scared. Thinking about how scared Lina must be is almost as awful as thinking about the classroom.

I used to bring Lina into my bed when I had trouble sleeping. It almost always felt a little better when she was beside me, even in those very last weeks. Her hair curled at the nape with sleep-sweat, and she always smelled good, even when her hair was dirty. I would pretend she had come to me after a nightmare. Sometimes I would tell her that: "You had a scary dream, do you remember what it was?" She would look at me, confused at first, and then she would tell me about her nightmare. Most of the time it was full of details, super boring, and incoherent, about Mom and our house and a new toy and bows and maybe a dog or two. Lina wanted a dog more than anything in the whole world. I hope Mom and Dad bought her one and let it sleep in her bed. But most of all I hope that she sleeps in my bed, that she walks in and lies down and it helps her feel a little better than she did before.

I try to imagine that Lina doesn't understand what's going on. That she doesn't have to be here, so she is spared. But it doesn't work very well. Because I can't pretend she would be less frightened just because she doesn't know what's happening. I know what that's like; it is the exact opposite.

"Maja pleads not guilty to the charges against her. Her involvement could not give rise to criminal liability. Maja was not aware of, nor was she made aware of, Sebastian Fagerman's plans, nor was she guilty of incitement or of any act or omission that would result in criminal liability. She did not act with any required level of intent for this crime. Maja concedes that she fired the weapon indicated in the statement, and she did so in the location indicated, but she did so in self-defense. Thus she cannot be found guilty."

"Liable...incitement...reckless indifference..." — the words rattle around in my head and it terrifies me when Sander talks that way, because it sounds like excuses, like we're using legal terminology and strange words for no other reason than to avoid telling what really happened. I want to tell. I don't give a crap what it might lead to. The worst has already happened. And then I wonder if Sander is planning to talk for as long as the prosecutor did. I don't think so. It seems like he's almost finished, and it's only been eleven minutes. I don't know if that's good or bad, but this frightens me, too. Won't people think that he didn't talk as long because he doesn't have anything to say? I run my hand across my pad of paper, press the pen to it. But I don't write anything. Three minutes later, Sander is done talking.

In the real world, it didn't take even three minutes from the time I closed the door of our classroom until the last shot was fired. The police stormed the classroom nineteen minutes after it started.

How many people came in through that door once they opened it? Paramedics, police officers, tons of police officers. With boots, visors, heavy weapons. One of them stepped on my arm; another one kicked me in the hand. Someone yanked me up off the ground, ripped the rifle away. It was chaos. A disturbing number of people showed up. Did they shout? I think so. But I don't remember whether I said anything. Before they touched me, they pulled Sebastian off. They allowed the guns to remain for one second longer than they let him stay with me. I still wonder why.

They lay me on a stretcher. Someone wrapped a blanket around me. I don't know if I was the first one they carried out. I don't think so.

One minute, maybe one and a half — that's how long the shooting went on. It says so in the case report, I don't have to remember it. But still, those calculations confuse me. Sometimes when I think back, it feels like it was over in ten seconds; sometimes I think I was in there for years. Like Narnia, where you ended up if you opened the wrong wardrobe door, and when you returned after several years' worth of war with the White Witch, not even a minute had passed.

Nineteen minutes from when I closed the classroom door to when it opened again. That could certainly be right. More than enough time for everything to end. But that depends, of course, on when you claim it started. Not the shooting itself, I mean, but everything. The police and the prosecutor say we planned it, Sebastian and me, that it grew and grew, our isolation, our hatred, but also that the party the night before, the last fight, was the trigger. The people crowding outside this courtroom throwing cobblestones at each other because they hate me and everything they think I stand for, I'm sure they would say it started with capitalism, or the monarchy, or the conservative government, or when we stopped believing in the Norse gods, or something else absurd that they have no logical explanation for.

I am the only one who knows. I know that it all started and ended with Sebastian.

One of my first memories, not just of Sebastian but of my whole life, is of him sitting in a tree. Mom and I were walking by the Fagermans' house on the way back from preschool. He was only five years old, but everyone was already in love with him. He had longish wavy hair that curled on his forehead. He asked serious, overwhelming questions and wasn't very good at focusing, but he was a thousand percent *on* all the time. He was the kid all the boys wanted to play with and all the girls whispered about. Even our preschool teachers would stare jealously at whoever got to button his jacket, adjust his scarf, dig the right pair of rubber boots out of the drying cupboard when it was time to go outside. And Sebastian would pick out his favorite teacher for the day. *Anneli can help me. Laylah can take off my socks.*

Sebastian called down to me from his spot up in the tree. It was so important, such a crucial moment, that what I remember most is that I couldn't even manage to respond. I'm sure Mom said something, about their yard, the house, whose son he was. (Whispered to me, excited: *Isn't that Sebastian Fagerman? Are you in the same group at preschool?* As if she didn't know already; she was fully aware.) But all

I remember is that my body tingled when I heard his voice speak my name.

"Maja." More a statement than a greeting. I didn't respond. Mom probably did. "Hi, Sebastian," I bet she said. "Don't fall down from there," she might have added, or something along those lines, while I yanked my hand away. I didn't want her to interfere. This had nothing to do with her; I was not about to let her ruin it.

Just one week later, we kissed during playtime in the pillow room. I think about that sometimes, how we never played, not even at preschool; we only made out. With guys he did stuff guys do: kicked balls and each other, and maybe built towers of blocks they could knock down again. But with me it was always physical, he would touch me, stroke me, smell my hair, feel the inside of my arm, pull a blanket over us and lie close and inhale my breath; the warmth and lack of oxygen made me all dizzy. Even at preschool he had a hard time playing regular games with girls. Five-year-old Sebastian touched me. It lasted maybe a week or two, and then I would have to wait thirteen years before he discovered me again. Did I miss it for all those years in between, when he played with others, dated others, was a grade ahead of me and I knew who he was but not the other way around? Yes, I did.

"You can't dictate what they will think of Sebastian," Sander has told me more times than I can count. "You must not concern yourself with how people remember him. We have to focus on you. We have to guarantee that this trial is about what you can be found criminally liable for. That and nothing else."

What I can be found criminally liable for. As if it has nothing to do with what Sebastian did. As if it would be possible to separate, punch out, clip free, cut away, rinse from the rest of it. The prosecutor certainly doesn't think it is. Call-me-Lena thinks it is all connected. Should I make a note on my pad that I think she's right?

6.

Susse from the jail is waiting for me in the garage when we're done for the day. She is wearing some sort of uniform, and she smiles, her grin wider than should be possible, her teeth so white that they look pale blue. Those teeth seem out of place in her spray-tanned face, just waiting for the right moment to escape. Susse asks how it went. I can't muster a response, I just get in the car and squeeze my eyes shut.

I was allowed to bring my pad of paper. I'm still holding it in my hand. I haven't written a word; I doodled instead. Circles, inside each other, on top of each other, next to each other, small, big, around-around-around.

Susse gets into the backseat, next to me. I can feel her watching me from the side, but she doesn't say anything else. She leaves me alone.

How did it go?

I didn't listen very carefully when Sander was talking about the classroom. But I did notice when he started talking about me. "Maja." He was careful to use the first and last names of everyone involved each time he mentioned them, but he called me "Maja." Just Maja, no last name, always Maja, even though it's only a nickname; I'm really Maria. A Maria could be a politician, an author, a doctor. *A murderer*. Maja, though, she's cute and harmless. As sweet as Pelle Svanslös's white kitty-girlfriend Maja. The prosecutor always said "the defendant," once or twice "Maria Norberg." Never Maja, even though she always called me that whenever she attended my interrogations.

"It is important," Sander explained — a lot of things are *important* in Sander's world — "for the court to get to know Maja."

I don't know how Sander's ideas could ever lead to anything other than what we're all expecting, and in "all" I include Sander himself. But his brief summary, which mainly consisted of legal jargon, still managed to mention Mom and Dad, my school, how the adult world failed me, how I'd had a rough time ever since Sebastian came into my life, how I found myself in a situation I couldn't get out of, and how I was only eighteen when it happened — I'd "just come of age."

Sander said that I am "precocious" and "intelligent" but "insecure" and "easily manipulated." Sander has given me IQ tests and made me talk with two different psychologists. He has a bunch of opinions about who I am and why I did what I did and didn't do a ton of other stuff that, according to the prosecutor, I should have done.

Once we're on the highway, Susse takes my hand and I lean against her shoulder. I am a good student. In that way that makes teachers smile when you raise your hand but then never call on you because you no longer need to prove anything. Students like me are surrounded by a special aura. I've had it since I was in first grade. Ever since that first day, when I got one hundred percent on a pop spelling quiz. Ever since the first time I asked for more paper than the teacher handed out when we took a test. I was the only one who needed extra sheets of paper.

I am smart, and all the teachers want to believe that it's thanks to them. I'm what teachers claim they "live for," since it can't be the salary.

Wait, sorry. I *was* that sort of student. I'm not anymore. Now I'm the ultimate proof of the school system's absolute downfall. And Sander can talk till he's blue in the face about how "smart" I am, but he won't be able to change that. I am not going to get an A on this.

And being "smart" is a double-edged sword, at least if you claim that it was an accident that you ended up in a classroom full of dead people and that none of what you did was actually your own fault. When Sander told me about the results of the IQ test, there was something apologetic in his voice. As if I didn't already know it was bad news. As if I haven't already spent years doing everything I could to pretend I am ordinary.

I did what all girls do: complained about everything to do with myself, pretended to be nervous before tests and pretended to be disappointed when exams were over. "Ohmigooood I didn't get to the last questions. I just wrote something down, I bet I did really bad." I played naïve for teachers and friends, guys and other adults, pretended to be dumber than I am, all to avoid seeming too pleased with myself, *she thinks she's so great.* I'm smart enough to realize how pointless it is to be smart, how little it means, and that it's a liability.

During the opening statements today, Sander didn't make a peep about the IQ test. Instead he talked about how I was manipulated, what I was "subjected to," how this "affected" me, that it was "impossible for Maja to predict the consequences," that it is "crucial that the responsibility be placed on those who are truly culpable," and that it is even more important to remember that "we are talking about legal culpability here." Toward the end he let his voice slow down, lowered the volume to get people to really listen.

"Don't be fooled," he said. His voice wobbled a little, because attorney Peder Sander wanted to show the whole courtroom how emotionally engaged he is in this hearing. That what he told the journalists, about how this would be his "last and most important case," was true, not something he made up. I am not just any client for Sander, said that trembling voice. I am Maja. *Falsely accused.* Then Sander raised his voice and sounded almost angry. Disgusted. "Sebastian Fagerman alone," he spat, "bears the legal culpability."

And then he paused and placed his hand on my shoulder, letting it rest there as he waited not only for the chairman but also for each lay judge to look at us. I can still feel, even here in the car next to Susse, how heavy his hand was.

Then he said it: "Of course, we want someone to blame for this tragedy. It is human nature to look for an explanation. But there is no sufficient cause to convict Maja. The responsible party is Sebastian Fagerman. He is dead."

And Dad cleared his throat again. Mom cried. I took a breath.

Mom, Dad, and I had perfect dramatic timing while Sander talked only about what would fit in a paragraph of law.

By the time we turn off at the jail building and the car slows down so that Susse can show her pass, my headache has clawed its way up to my forehead. I swallow and sit up, straighten my back. Open my eyes.

"It went well," I say to Susse as we drive through the gates to the jail. "It went well."

THE AMBULANCE, THE HOSPITAL

7.

The entire area was cordoned off. As they carried my stretcher from the classroom to the ambulance, I saw a big group gathered in the distance and the fluttering blue-and-white police tape all along the street up to the school. I pictured the crowd-control barriers propped up between the cow pastures and the cornfields.

As they hoisted me into the vehicle I heard another ambulance siren, heading for the school. Or leaving?

I don't know which way the ambulance took as they drove me from school to the hospital, because I couldn't see out. I lay there on the cot, under my blanket, and wished I was going home. I pretended that the ambulance was just taking a shortcut, that we would soon arrive in Altorp, the soft, groomed jogging track illuminated all night long by yellow lights, "so practical" (Mom's words), that we would drive past the golf course "just around the corner, so practical" (also Mom's words) and the harbor with all its boats, all with a fresh coat of paint, just returned to the water, ready to go out in the archipelago: "We live right next door to paradise" (yes, still Mom's words).

Sebastian had put his boat in three weeks earlier; we had stayed there on Walpurgis Night. Sebastian slept, I lay beside him looking up at the fogged-over skylight. That happened so recently, and I knew the ambulance wasn't taking me home, but I wanted more than I had ever wanted anything to see places I recognized: Norrängsgården with its tennis courts under curved roofs, the walking path to the Viktor Rydberg School that was too steep to bike up, Vasa School, the rocky trails on Ekudden, the narrow beach at Barracuda, the trees along Slottsbacken, the hammock Dad bought a week ago. If I could just see them, it would mean nothing had happened. But there were no windows in the ambulance and we were driving fast, away, away, away.

Would the schools have to close now? What about graduation? Would it be canceled? Amanda's graduation party? She was going to have her party last of all of us, and she'd said I had to give a speech: "You have to have to have to!" What would happen to her party now? She was dead, wasn't she? I had heard her die, I had heard everyone die, every one of them, they were all dead, weren't they? I saw them die. Everyone but me was dead, and just a few moments ago we were alive.

What time was it? Was it just a few hours after the party had ended and we were walking past Djursholm Square, me and Sebastian? We had finished talking, there was nothing more to say, and he walked ahead of me, refused to walk next to me, and I noticed that the sidewalk sign outside the bakery had tipped over. Did they leave it out overnight? It was warm, it was a warm spring, almost summer. For more than a week the heat had felt wasteful, as if there wouldn't be any left for summer vacation. I had spent the whole walk with Sebastian going barefoot on the asphalt because my feet hurt, carrying my shoes in one hand, holding them by the ankle straps. I had tried to touch him with the other hand, but he slapped me away. And yet I still thought he wasn't angry anymore, that he had calmed down. He seemed calmer than he had been for a long time. That was only a few hours ago, right? Was Sebastian dead now?

That walk. We had gone up to Henrik Palmes Allé. The street was completely deserted, but it was as bright as midday and soon we would go to school and see everyone again. Dennis and Samir and the rest of them. But right there, right then, we were alone. No one was walking behind us, in front of us, or past us. The villas were way up on their hills, the cars were parked in closed-up garages, the doors were locked, alarms set. All of Djursholm had felt deserted; I hadn't heard any birds, or any morning sounds at all, it was just quiet. Deathly quiet, like the minutes following a nuclear bomb, I had thought. What made me think of nuclear bombs? Had I really, or was that something I was thinking only now, afterward? Now it was over. Everything was over.

All the way from the school to the hospital I lay on the ambulance stretcher and listened without seeing. We had been driving for a while when I heard yet another siren in the distance. Didn't a siren mean "urgent"? That it wasn't over? That someone was still alive?

"Isn't everyone dead?" I asked the police officer next to me; I think it was the guy who carried me out. The officer didn't answer. He didn't even look at me. He hated me already.

The hospital staff wore plastic gloves as they undressed me and put my clothes in different bags. I wasn't allowed to wash until many hours later. I saw three different doctors and four nurses before they let me into the shower. I only turned on the hot water, nothing else. I stepped in under the stream while it was still working its way up to scalding, but I hardly felt the temperature change. I still couldn't get rid of the smell of blood. The bathroom door was open, there was no shower curtain, and a female police officer leaned against the doorjamb and stared at me the whole time. They had done tons of tests, scraping under my nails, scraping at me, in me, with instruments made of metal, with freakishly large cotton swabs, and I had to spend the night at the hospital even though there was nothing wrong with me.

Not until much later did I realize that when the police came to talk to me it was an interrogation; not until much later did I understand why I wasn't allowed to talk to anyone but the police, why the nurses and doctors said "We're not allowed to discuss that with you" in voices that didn't even make an effort to sound sympathetic. Not until much later did I understand why several hours passed before I got to see Mom and Dad.

Another woman sat beside my bed, holding the knob of her baton. Once I had been undressed and put to bed, I asked her if Mom and Dad were dead. I don't know why I said it. "Are my mom and dad dead?" But I could tell it made her nervous. She made a call on her phone and then the first policewoman came back; she had boy hips and an eighties perm and a tape recorder. With narrowed eyes, she asked why I had asked if Mom and Dad were dead. Why did I want to know? *Why, why, why?* I didn't get why she asked me that. Not until later.

Two police officers took turns sitting there staring at me in the hospital. Mom and Dad were allowed in to see me for five minutes — it must have been late evening, maybe the middle of the night — along with yet another police officer. There were six of us inside my tiny room, and Mom sat on the very edge of my bed. She didn't say anything, ask anything, no "What happened?" no "What have you done?" not even "How are you feeling?" She didn't say everything would be okay or tell me what to do now, what I had to do so I wouldn't die, even if I said so, that I was going to die, wanted to die, maybe? Mom just cried. I had seen her cry many times before, but never like that. She was a different person. She looked distorted, terrified. I think what she was afraid of was me. I think she was scared to ask me anything, or say anything to me, because she was afraid of what I would say.

It's possible they were instructed by the police (or Sander) not to ask any questions or talk about what was going to happen to me, but my mom has never made a habit of telling me what to do. She tries to wrinkle her rigid forehead and "reason." Out of all the types of moms she chooses to be, she most often goes with Thoughtful Mom. The one who wants to show her daughter that she realizes her daughter is mature enough to take personal responsibility. Not that Mom actually believes this, but it's important to her that other people believe it's true. But I guess that was no time to show what a splendid mother she was. Plus, the chances that she would succeed at that moment, in that place, were pretty slim. Dad stood behind her. He cried, too. I had never seen him cry before, not even at Grandma's funeral.

"I called Peder Sander," he said. No room for argument.

I did actually know who attorney Peder Sander was. I suppose everyone knows who he is; he shows up in newspapers and on the news whenever he defends some child killer or rapist. And in glossy gossip magazines when he's been to a premiere or a party with the king — not just the Nobel Banquet, but the parties where the king himself decides who to hang out with. He's been on tons of other TV shows, too, he comes on as an expert to talk about trials in which no one has been lucky enough to hire him.

It could have been funny. That the only lawyer I'd ever heard of, the only one who exists for real and doesn't just shout, "Objection, Your Honor" on TV or in the movies, hangs out with the king, of all people, a guy straight out of the land of make-believe.

I just nodded.

Mom nodded, too. She blew her nose and nodded. A million hysterical nods. Maybe they'd given her something to help her keep it together, or at least keep her from talking. I was afraid that if I opened my mouth without thinking, I would let out a scream that never ended. I kept my mouth shut. Nodded. Shook my head. Mostly nodded.

Just do it, I thought. *Keep your mouth shut. Don't speak.*

Dad took half a step backward and suddenly I thought he was going to tell me to say "thank you." That he would lower his voice half an octave the way he did when I was little, and ask, "What do you say, Maja?" But he didn't. He left.

I think maybe they could have stayed longer. I'm sure the police would have loved to hear a really good heart-to-heart Mom-Dad-and-daughter talk. But it didn't happen. Mom and Dad left. I don't think they wanted to be there.

Before Mom stood up, she hugged me. She dug her nails into my upper arms. I bent forward to hug her back, but it was a little too late and her breastbone hit my collarbone. If I weren't bigger than she is, maybe she could have kissed my forehead or some other motherly thing. But that was impossible now. When I pulled away from her, I noticed that the rims of her eyes were pink, like a lab rat's. Mom had cried off all her makeup and hadn't fixed it afterward. The magnitude of that. The abyss it hinted at.

After they left, a nurse came in with two pills for me. They were in a plastic cup. I took them. Jammed them into my mouth. Swallowed them with water from a slightly larger plastic cup. Then she left without closing the door.

There was still a uniformed officer next to my bed and another one outside my room.

They believed, of course, that I was planning to kill myself, that I couldn't live with the shame of what I'd done, but this was another fact it took me a couple of days to figure out. I cracked my mouth and called after her. "Thanks," I managed to say. But presumably it would have been more fitting to say I was sorry. *I should have died, but I didn't. Instead I'm alive. Sorry. I'm truly sorry. I didn't mean to. I want to die, I promise.*

I don't know whether I fell asleep that first night. I don't think so. But I did manage to keep my mouth closed. I never started screaming.

The next morning, two police officers came to the hospital. I was thoroughly examined and thoroughly dry-eyed. The woman, the skinny one with the perm, was back, and she had brought along a younger man with eyes that stared; he stayed half a step behind her. Maybe he had been sitting outside my door. In any case, he looked like he'd just woken up. He gaped at us in turn. He ended with me. I thought about staring back until he had to look away, but I didn't have the energy. I was tired, as if I had just been about to fall asleep.

The officers didn't seem rushed, but they still didn't want to sit down. A doctor came in with a piece of paper, and the policewoman signed it. I didn't have to change clothes; they said I could wear the hospital gown. I would only be given new clothes when we arrived anyway. My own clothes, my phone, my computer, my iPad, my house keys and locker key — they had taken it all.

I asked to use the toilet and brush my teeth. They let me, but The Perm followed me into the bathroom. She turned away when I pulled down my underwear, the hospital's underwear, to pee, but I saw her looking at me through the mirror when I wiped.

I didn't ask how long I would be away. Before we walked out of the room, the police officer fastened handcuffs to my wrists, holding one finger between my wrist and the metal to make sure they weren't too tight. Then she put a belt around my waist and chained the handcuffs to it. I hadn't thought I would get to go home, but this might have been the first time I realized exactly where we were going. Although the part I found most shocking was that I was cuffed.

"Are you really allowed to do this?" I asked. "I'm only…" I had been about to say I was only a child, or at least a teenager, but I changed my mind.

Journalists were gathered outside the hospital. Four men with cameras and four women with cell phones gripped in their palms were standing right at the entrance. Two or three more were standing farther off.

They didn't cry out when I stepped through the door, but it was like they all turned around in unison. Grandpa's foxhounds put their noses in the air and start whining as soon as Grandpa pulls on a pair of rubber boots. I was the journalists' rubber boots. The sound of the cameras seemed far away. At a "respectful distance," I thought at first. They were standing where I didn't have to look at them.

While I waited for the policewoman in civilian clothes to open the back door of the gray car we were about to get into, one of the journalists asked how I was feeling. His voice was low; I hadn't noticed he was standing so close. I flinched.

"Fine, thanks," I said. It just came out. I forgot to keep my mouth shut, and out came the only thing that was worse than just starting to scream unchecked. I could feel in my whole body that it was all wrong. "I mean…" I tried to add. And then I saw the journalist's narrow eyes. He didn't feel sorry for me.

The policewoman grabbed hold of me. She absolutely did not want me to start talking.

"Your friends are dead…" the journalist began. But he was not allowed to continue.

The Perm looked like she was about to smack the journalist. "If you don't shut up this minute, if you don't stop asking your questions immediately, you risk sabotaging our investigation. Is that what you want?"

I realized after the fact that The Perm was afraid the journalist would reveal what they hadn't told me yet, and the police wanted to see my reaction to that information. But at that moment I thought The Perm was angry with me, even angrier than she had been before, and I turned red. I'm not some frail little beauty with creamy skin who can blush in a cute way. I have trouble breathing and I start oozing sour, sharp sweat that leaves salty stains. But I tried to pretend nothing was wrong and straightened my back.

As The Perm, with her narrow hips and square nails, dug through her pockets for the car key and the journalist tried to interpret the import of what the officer had just said, the wind took hold of my loose hair and blew it back behind me. The jacket The Perm had placed over my hands and the cuffs fell to the ground. And there I stood, in an oversize hospital gown, no bra, my nipples aimed at the closest photographer. If the handcuffs hadn't been fastened to my waist, I probably would have started waving. A crazy I-just-broke-the-hundred-meter-world-record sort of gesture, a sporty hand on a straight arm, fingers spread, aimed at the speechless crowd that wasn't a crowd, just a dozen surprised (to say the least) journalists with unbrushed teeth and day-old clothes.

My whole body ached when I got in the car. My clothing burned, flames against my skin. Like stinging jellyfish, nettles, third-degree burns with festering blisters, oh my God, it hurt so much. I think I was shaking. I clung to the seat belt that ran right across my arms and hands; I turned away from The Perm. I didn't breathe again until we had turned out of the parking lot and up onto the highway.

Three cars followed us. They kept their distance. I couldn't see them frantically calling home to the editorial offices, fiddling with their phones to send over the photographs, but I knew what they were up to.

The pictures of me. Maja Norberg, spoiled Djursholm bitch, out-of-touch-with-reality nutjob. Killer. Maja Norberg was a crazy killer. Why else would the police react like that? Why else would a teenager be transported in handcuffs? It was only a matter of minutes before I would pop up on newspaper billboards, from fourteen different angles, variations on the same theme.

The Perm quickly settled down. She didn't seem to mind that we were being followed; she stuck a pouch of snus in her lip and poked it backward with her tongue. She lifted her chin and the snus tin to ask if I wanted some. I shook my head.

Oh my God, I thought. *Do we have to bond now, me and her?* I wished I had remembered to ask for a painkiller before we left. Or that I had eaten any of what they gave me for breakfast. I suddenly noticed how hungry I was. When was the last time I ate? It must have been yesterday. But all I could remember was a cigarette I had on a balcony along with a police officer. No one made a fuss when I asked. It took a while for them to decide which balcony I was allowed to be on, and another little while before they dug up a cigarette for me, but beyond that they thought it was fine. So all it took for me to stop sneaking cigarettes was a mass murder.

But had I eaten breakfast today? No. Lunch the day before? Definitely not. Dinner? No, I didn't think so.

I rested my forehead against the glass of the window and closed my eyes. I wished I had waved at the journalists, despite my handcuffs. Then the king's buddy could have pled insanity.

Trial hearing in case B 147/66

The prosecutor et al. v. Maria Norberg

8.

All trials follow the same pattern. There are rules for who is allowed to speak and in which order. Sander has explained all of this. I listened carefully. I don't want to be taken by surprise, I want to be prepared for all of it.

On the second day when we meet in the room that ought to say "killer" on the door, it's not even nine thirty, but someone from Sander & Laestadius has been to the ritzy market at Östermalmshallen for the day's lunch. The food is cold, but it still looks approximately a million times better than anything I have eaten in the past nine months. There's a pile of mint chocolates on the table next to the thermos of coffee and the dishes of sugar cubes and milk in mini containers. It's only been two hours since I had breakfast, but I eat the chocolate and roll the foil wrappers into little round balls, which I pile up into a little stack. I don't ask if anyone else wants a taste, but I do ask if I'm allowed to smoke. Sander asks me to "refrain" (a typical Sander word) because we will never be able to leave this room without the journalists swarming us, and besides, it's "problematic from a security perspective."

Ferdinand asks if I'd like snus instead. Of *course* Ferdinand uses snus. She probably doesn't shave her armpits, either. A couple of my guards at the jail also seem convinced that snus and abundant body hair are steps in the right direction for women's lib. And that a hint of body odor is a sign of natural beauty. Ferdinand reminds me of them, but in a more educated way. I'm not surprised to find that the snus in the tin Ferdinand hands me is loose tobacco, not in pouches.

"No, thanks," I say. I've been offered snus by women more times in the past nine months than most people have to deal with in their whole lives.

"Don't you know smoking is dangerous?" Pancake rasps right into my ear. "You could die young."

I can't figure out if this is a joke or not.

In any case, the prosecutor is going to talk about my death today. About how I ought to be dead.

Her argument goes like this: Sebastian and I decided to take revenge on the people who betrayed us. We rode to school with a bomb in one bag and guns in another, to kill as many people as we could. The killing ended when Sebastian died. I should be dead, too, but I'm not, even though that's what school shootings are supposed to, or at least usually do, look like. One or more nutjobs decide to get revenge on their friends, shoot wildly until they can't keep going or the police arrive, and then they end by shooting each other, committing suicide, or making sure the police kill them. If they don't chicken out, of course. Only cowards survive. And here I sit, very much alive, in Stockholm

District Court, outside Courtroom 1. A yellow-belly, that's the only way to interpret the prosecutor's argument.

I don't respond to Pancake's comments. A security guard opens the door and tells us we can go in. While Sander gathers his things, I rebuild the pyramid of foil balls one last time. Ferdinand asks me, again, if I want any snus. I shake my head. I must really look desperate for a cigarette.

Then, "Nicotine gum!" she exclaims happily: She has just had a brilliant idea. Ferdinand even has time to dig through her floppy purse before Sander clicks his tongue. No way on earth would Sander agree to let me chew gum during trial proceedings. We walk in and take our seats.

Call-me-Lena's shiny cheeks are rosy. Perhaps she started her day by standing on the stairs outside the courthouse and holding a press conference; the weather is nice today, sunny and cold. And I'm willing to bet money that she would love outdoor press conferences on the courthouse stairs. Very Important Person in a Very Exciting Movie. Or maybe she walked here, since it's important to include exercise in one's daily routine? If I had to guess, Lena Pärsson takes the stairs instead of the elevator and thinks that means she can eat two Danishes or individually packaged marzipan punsch rolls on her coffee break every day. Call-me-Lena also looks like she buys bonds and extra retirement insurance and made it through law school without taking out loans (because a person in debt is never free!). It takes almost no effort for me to imagine what it looks like at her home (in a row house): pine paneling in the living room, dream catchers over the children's beds, Sweden's largest collection of ceramic frogs in a glass cabinet, and now it's her turn to talk. Again. I hate lead prosecutor Lena Pärsson.

It's been nine months of newspaper articles and TV programs, in which everyone, absolutely everyone but me, has been allowed to speak, everyone but me has been allowed to cry in prime time, everyone but me has been able to hold a press conference on absolutely any fucking stairs they like while my attorney and my family have been barred from giving public statements. And then — like curdled cream on dioxin-filled salmon — it's the prosecutor's turn to speak. And now she's going to tell the story of the mass murderer who should have shot herself but wasn't brave enough: a fucking coward, who refuses to accept the consequences, who thinks she can get away with it. That's me.

Sander can explain until he's hoarse and I still wouldn't understand why she gets to start. The prosecutor gets to talk crap about me for at least a day, maybe two. Then, after we have been allowed to speak, it will be her turn again. She will call witnesses one by one, and they all have one thing in common: They agree that I'm a monster.

Today, and I don't know how many days more, is lead prosecutor Lena Pärsson's day. Totally and completely hers. Mom is so pale that it looks like she's wearing clown makeup; Dad's forehead is shiny. Sander is perfectly relaxed, he might as well be in his own living room, talking to people he invited over for drinks. But I was not invited to this cocktail party. I am splayed out on the serving table. I am the one they will eat, slice up with the cake server.

We will listen. And then we will look at photographs, drawings, weapons, protocols. We will read my e-mails. My texts. My Facebook updates. We will go through who I called and how long we talked. We will discuss the contents of my computer and my locker at school. We will even read a note I wrote on the inside cover of one of my schoolbooks, a quote from a poem: "When there is nothing left to await, and nothing more to bear." According to the prosecutor, this alludes to a death wish. Next week, Lena Pärsson will bring in other people. They will talk, tell "everything." If it were up to Call-me-Lena, my dirty underwear would be passed around the room so everyone could sniff them.

I am allowed in last of all. I sit down at my spot and stare at the table. It would be impossible to talk to Mom and Dad for even a moment, thank God. Let them hug me, touch me, fix my hair. Pancake would like it if they could do that, because the journalists watch everything I do, and Pancake has nothing against the journalists' staring as long as he can control what they see. He would love it if Mom could brush my bangs out of my face and tuck strands of hair behind my ears.

She has done that for as long as I remember. If someone had taken a picture of each time she has done it — her index finger and thumb, my hair behind my ears — it would be like one of those series of images you can find on YouTube. The same subject for thirty years, films of the glaciers melting or a little girl going from being smoking hot to a toothless old hag in two years because she used crystal meth. Tons of still images, really fast, one after another. Maja's hair brushed out of the way. Short, downy baby hair. Longer, curly little girl hair. The bangs I cut myself on group picture day at day care. The time I gave myself highlights without asking Mom first. The time I asked her to curl my hair for confirmation. Wearing a Midsummer wreath. Lucia glitter. Braids with the hair tie missing. Super-long hair washed with jail shampoo that hasn't been cut in eleven months.

The journalists would take a good look if Mom fussed over me. Pancake would practically shit himself with joy. I remain in my spot and stare at nothing.

When Lena Pärsson turns on her microphone, the loudspeakers crackle.

"Welcome," the head judge states, managing to make it sound apologetic. Then he gives the floor to the prosecutor. Her cheeks are still pink.

"Owing to her actions during the days and hours leading up to the murders, the defendant is guilty of incitement in the murder of..." She is reading from her notes. "...Given that her actions induced Sebastian Fagerman to..."

Why is she reading from her notes? Is it really that hard for this witch to remember what she's charging me with? Is it possible to be a prosecutor even if you're stupid?

"The initial murder was the first step in Norberg and Fagerman's joint plans to carry out the attack at Djursholm Upper Secondary School, in classroom 412, that same morning." Now she puts down her papers. She even takes off her reading glasses. "I will demonstrate that the defendant was actively involved in both the preparation and the execution of these acts," she continues.

"We get to talk last. That's to our advantage," Ferdinand has said. She is wrong, of course. No one will have the energy to listen after the prosecutor is finished here. No one will want to look at me, much less allow me to speak. But what can I do about it? Nothing.

It makes no difference what we say; no one will understand what I mean, no one will buy it when we say we were all playing the same game, just in different roles.

Sander is going to tell "my side of the story." But it will be too late; they will have made up their minds already.

The prosecutor harps on and on about how we were a couple, me and Sebastian. That he was my boyfriend. The prosecutor claims that I loved Sebastian so much that it took over my life. That I would have done anything for him, for our love.

Lena Pärsson continues to lay out how she will prove she is right. "I will call the following witnesses..." "The testimony..." blah-blah-blah... "The evidence..." blah-blah. Ferdinand pretends to be sympathetic, sneaking a sidelong glance at me. *Stop staring.* Pancake switches the positions of two binders. *Sit still.* I wonder why they're even here. They're so pointless. Ferdinand, meant to be my proof that I don't hate brown people, I couldn't help asking her once how she felt about defending me. She got so terribly nervous that I thought she was going to piss herself. It was a "unique opportunity," she stammered. She was "honored to be entrusted" with my case and "hoped her experience could be of help."

What an epic load of bullshit. Ferdinand hates everything about me and this trial. She hates that it's obvious she doesn't have enough experience to be my lawyer but still gets to sit here in the courtroom. She hates that she is "fitting" for my case, because it means she has to do her best — in front of all the journalists and all her jealous colleagues — to look like Sander's token inner-city Muslim even though she was born in Sundsvall and confirmed in the Church of Sweden. It is clear that she thinks, but would never say, that the only thing she likes about this trial is that we are going to lose.

Lena Pärsson keeps talking.

"According to the statement from the medical examiner, see exhibits 19 and 20, Amanda Steen's death was caused by the two initial shots that the defendant, Maja Norberg, fired with weapon 2. A few seconds later, the defendant fired weapon 2 once more. Those three shots, according to the medical examiner's statement, see exhibits 17 and 18, caused the death of Sebastian Fagerman."

We "admit this part of the description of events." That means it's true. I killed them. I killed Amanda. I killed Sebastian. And it wasn't out of love. We can say whatever we want about it — I still did it.

Week 1 of Trial: Tuesday

9.

I never would have bet money on it, but lead prosecutor Lena Pärsson manages to finish her opening remarks before lunchtime after all. After lunch (Ferdinand ran off to warm up the food before we ate it) it's time for her to start presenting the documentary evidence. There are a billion different autopsy reports, documents, police memoranda, and weird maps, and even more reports, lab results, excerpts, and formal opinions, and I can't keep track of it all. It's getting easier and easier not to listen: Lena Pärsson is reading aloud, Lena Pärsson is reading from her notes, Lena Pärsson's voice is whiny, almost a little hoarse toward the end, Lena Pärsson should clear her throat, but she doesn't.

The indictment itself is only eleven pages long, but the prosecutor is harping on like it should have been eleven thousand pages. And the total amount of material is around that size, at least if you count the entire case report.

I'm not allowed to say a single word all day, but I'm not allowed to leave either. I have to be present, endure it. I try not to listen to ugly Lena.

She reads some of our messages aloud. The ones I sent to Amanda, to Sebastian, and to Samir. The ones I received from Sebastian and Amanda. And Samir, of course. At the same time, she projects our conversations on a big screen so everyone can read along. She is ridiculously pleased at how she's put them together. Her *pedagogy*.

I remember when Amanda showed me a letter her grandma had written before she died. The letter contained instructions for how her grandma wanted to be dressed in the coffin and what sort of music they should play at the church. It was some classical piece that was meant to be sung by a particular quartet. Amanda and I had never heard of either the piece or the quartet. But Amanda said the problem was her grandma's best friend had died first, and at her funeral they played the exact same song, so now her grandma had to come up with something different, because she didn't want people to think she was incapable of thinking for herself. But of course her grandma would be dead when the piece was played. The friend was already dead, too. And yet it was important to Amanda's grandma that she didn't seem like a copycat.

It is beyond me why everyone wants to be original, unique, even after they're dead. Oh no, you can't just use "Amazing Grace" like some middle-of-the-road discount shopper, you have to make it special and unforgettable. Which means that some poor sucker has to sing "Tears in Heaven" accompanied by a classic plinky-plonking guitar just so you don't risk embarking on your eternal rest to the tune of banality. Just like at every other "personal" funeral.

People are pathetic to the very end. Not unique.

And now Amanda is dead. Amanda, Sebastian, all the others. I didn't get to attend any of their funerals. The fact that I couldn't get furlough wasn't the biggest hurdle, of course. But I still wanted to know when they took place, and Sander told me. The only one he couldn't say anything about was Sebastian's, because it was organized in secret.

I wonder if Sebastian told anyone what he wanted his funeral to be like. Presumably he didn't. He only talked about death, never about what would happen afterward. Amanda, on the other hand, surely could have had a bunch of ideas about how her "farewell" should have gone. But why would she have planned something like that?

It must have been a challenge to arrange a funeral for Sebastian. They couldn't exactly send out invitations or put an announcement in the paper. *In lieu of flowers, please consider a donation to Doctors Without Borders.*

But surely they must have done something, right? *In private*, at that ceremony with only those closest to him, whoever that might have been, since neither his father nor I could attend. I wonder what sort of music they played. Did they play one of Sebastian's dad's favorite songs? That was what he listened to most. *Preacher takes the school. One boy breaks a rule. Silly boy blue, silly boy blue.* I wonder what they dressed him in. I bet everyone else got to have their "favorite T-shirt." Because *all* dead teenagers are expected to have a favorite T-shirt.

I imagine they put Sebastian in a suit. Majlis, Claes's secretary, probably had to buy it. An expensive one in a conservative color, fit for a mass murderer to be cremated in.

If I had to guess, they probably had a church funeral, with interment right afterward, or else maybe Sebastian's brother scattered him to the wind, out over some secret sea, in order to avoid having a gravestone that might be vandalized and end up in the papers.

I wonder if Sebastian's mom was there, called in from a pill-addiction clinic in Switzerland or charity work in Africa or wherever she was spending her time while her son's condition deteriorated more and more.

I can picture her: gigantic sunglasses, so shaved, waxed, and lasered that her skin has turned shiny and transparent like a jellyfish. With an orange poppy to place on the coffin, perhaps? She would never bring roses; roses at a funeral are so banal, while sunglasses that make old hags look like blowflies, strangely enough, are considered classy.

When lead prosecutor Lena Pärsson shows images from the classroom, I hear my dad shifting in his seat. I don't need to look at him to know that he's the one having trouble sitting still. But when she plays the security camera videos from Sebastian's driveway, the video where you can watch me carry a bag from his house to his car and then sit down next to Sebastian in the passenger seat of the car, the room is so quiet you could hear a pin drop. It looks like I think the bag is heavy (it was). They found it in my locker afterward. But the bomb never went off, it was "substandard," according to the experts Lena Pärsson doesn't quote, because it doesn't fit into her image of the two of us as monsters with unlimited resources.

I never said goodbye to Lina that morning, when I left home for the last time. She was still asleep. I guess she was sleeping in that day? I wish I had gone in anyway, to look at her, I love watching Lina when she sleeps (always on her stomach, hands in fists above her pillow). I've tried to recall the last time I saw her, what we talked about, what she was wearing, what she looked like, but I can't remember.

Dad must have taken three weeks off of work to come to the trial. I wonder if he has to leave his cell phone at the security checkpoint and I wonder what Lina is doing while they're here. Is she with Grandpa? I wonder what Grandpa thinks of all this. Does he talk about it with Lina, where I am? When Grandma was alive, her relationship with Grandpa was based on the fact that Grandpa told her things and she asked tons of follow-up questions so that Grandpa could explain everything to her. Not because she wanted or needed to know more in order to understand, but because Grandpa likes to explain stuff. When Grandma died, Grandpa seemed to lose his grip and become confused. We continued to ask unnecessary questions, but it was never the same. He aged when Grandma died, something had already happened to his posture by the time of her funeral. Nowadays he is an old man (watery eyes and swollen knees), he never takes long walks with the dogs off-leash or uses his whole hand to point at plants you're supposed to be able to recite the species of. I don't know if Grandpa can answer questions about me. I don't know if Lina dares to ask.

More than anything else, I miss Lina. I dream that she places her little hand, light as a birch leaf, on my arm, looks at me, and asks why. *I don't know,* I want to say. But there is no question Lina can ask that I would be able to answer. I never want to see her again.

As Call-me-Lena Lena Pärsson speaks, my neck gets stiff from holding my head upright. When she talks about what we wrote to each other, me and Sebastian, on that night when it felt like a nuclear war had just ended, I want to scream out loud.

Yes! I hear what you're saying, you pedagogical fucking bitch. Shut up.

Now she's reading from her notes again.

"The office of the prosecutor seeks conviction for the following crimes..." And then she starts rattling it all off: "...incitement to murder..." blah-blah..."homicide, or manslaughter, or voluntary manslaughter, or involuntary manslaughter..." blah-blah-blah, blah-blah-blah. It takes her fifteen minutes to spout out everything I should be convicted of, or at least that's what it feels like.

I imagine that Sebastian's funeral ended up being pretty unusual. At Amanda's they played — with one hundred percent certainty — "Tears in Heaven."

JAIL, THE FIRST FEW DAYS

10.

The very first time I met Sander was just an hour or so after my intake at the jail. I had to wait in the visiting room for a few minutes before he stepped in. I sat on one of four adult-size chairs and stared at the play corner. In it was a miniature table, a broken doll stroller, a plastic tea set, and a few books that had been read to pieces, picture books and Astrid Lindgren classics. Lina has never been here to visit me. She has been spared the jail toys.

Each time I meet with Sander we shake hands, and the first time was no exception. On that very first day, it felt like he was my guest, but I didn't know what to offer him. I poured a glass of water and gave it to him with shaking hands, but I didn't spill.

The first time we met, he did most of the talking. He asked about "my view of the charges." But I didn't know what the charges were. I'm sure the police had told me, but in the moment I couldn't remember whether they had actually come out and said it.

"You are under suspicion of complicity in..." He sounded

surprised when he realized how confused I was. I tried to explain, but it was just a mess.

Sander nodded and told me to try to take one thing at a time, that everything would clear up "throughout the day" or "soon enough," that we probably ought to start by listening to what the police said.

"You are under reasonable suspicion of homicide, among other things," he told me then, in a perfectly normal voice, "but the degree of suspicion will likely be raised before the day is out," he explained. As if that would make everything easier to understand.

Just before he left, he handed over a bag full of clothes, my own clothes. He must have received them from my mom. This seemed practical in a way I hadn't expected. I didn't have time to start crying before he had gone on his way.

A tray of cold food was waiting for me when I got back to my cell. I put the bag on the floor of the cell; I didn't eat anything. I said no thanks when someone offered to warm up the food on the plate, and instead I lay on my bed, on my back, staring straight up at the ceiling for an unknown number of half hours (they checked me once every thirty minutes because they still thought I was going to kill myself), and then they came to tell me I was going to be questioned. The Perm from earlier that morning, when I was transferred from the hospital, was back. There was another officer with her. And Sander was there, of course. He had come back, too. And he had brought Ferdinand. She introduced herself with sweaty hands and dry lips. Evin was her name (no last name). The Perm had changed into fresh clothes, and even these new ones seemed to have been washed at the wrong temperature. They were waiting for me in a special interrogation room.

I have been allowed to read transcripts of all the interrogations, even though it was hardly necessary — I remember them in great detail. All those days and months when it felt like all I did was nod or shake my head. I didn't understand a thing back then, but I remember it all now.

The interrogation room at the juvenile detention center was in the same building as "my room"; it was even on the same floor. It had frosted windows. It was impossible to see anything outside, just a haze of no-name colors and shades. Shadows of a Swedish November evening? Or night? But it was almost June. *Where is the sun?* I remember thinking. *Are they really allowed to interrogate people in the middle of the night?* I asked what time it was.

"Are you hungry?" The Perm's colleague asked. They're always going on about food. *Eat, eat, eat.* The criminals of Sweden must be a bunch of bulimics. I shook my head.

It was five o'clock, the officer told me. *Five in the morning?* I wondered, but I didn't ask. Either way, it ought to be light out. It was still summer, right?

There would be dinner waiting for me when we were finished, he went on. So, evening. I wasn't hungry. I couldn't imagine ever managing to eat again.

I got to sit in a kind of easy chair. Sander and Ferdinand sat alongside me, along with The Perm's male colleague, on normal chairs at a normal table. The male officer wasn't wearing a uniform but something kind of pajamalike; it must have been a pair of unironed suit pants. He introduced himself and I immediately forgot his name. Had he been there at the hospital the day before? I couldn't recall. But shouldn't I remember him? That hair evidently hadn't been brushed since he woke up a week ago and, at least in theory, it was unforgettable. His throat clearing would etch itself into the brain of anyone who had to listen to it. Someone in there smelled like yesterday's cigarettes; it had to be him. I asked once more what his name was, and he barked it out again. I still didn't catch it. *It doesn't matter*, I thought, and nodded.

The interrogation would be videotaped, The Perm pointed at a camera above the door and another one directly across from us. She sounded more alert than her colleague, and apparently, despite her gas-station jeans, she was some sort of boss for the investigation. I nodded at her, too, just as I found a dried booger stuck in the crack between the side of the chair and the cushion.

It was impossible to sit normally in my chair. I didn't understand why they wanted me to be half lying down. I didn't want to lean back; it made it hard to breathe, but I couldn't figure out how to explain that so I did it anyway. I could feel it giving me a double chin and I sat back up and had to sit sideways in the chair so I didn't end up leaning downhill.

The Perm used my name. Frequently. *Maja.* Telemarketer style. "Hi, Maja. Have you changed your mind about the question of guilt, Maja?" "No? Maja?" Sometimes she tried to look sympathetic. Then she used a show-me-on-the-doll-where-he-touched-you voice.

"Maja. Can you tell me...can you explain how you ended up involved in this? Maja? Why do you think you're here, Maja? I hope you understand, Maja, that we have to..."

And then the telemarketing voice would return.

"How are you doing, Maja? Do you want something to drink, Maja? Do you think we can start now, Maja? Do you think you could...Maja...Maja?"

I shook my head a few times. When she looked confused, I nodded instead, until she started talking again.

She took out a piece of white paper and a dull pencil. I definitely didn't understand that. Was I supposed to use them? Write down my answers? Did she think I was a deaf-mute?

When I didn't do anything, she started doodling on the paper. A sketch. First a large rectangle — the classroom — then small rectangles inside of it — the lectern and the desks. She marked windows and the door into the corridor. She asked questions as she worked. But after a while she gave up asking about the classroom. She made a few attempts to get me to talk about what I did before. "What did you have for breakfast, Maja? How did you get to school, Maja?"

Did Mom drive me? Head shake. Did I take the bus to school? Head shake. Did I ride with Sebastian? Nod. These questions were a type of warm-up, I assume. Talking about other stuff. Jogging in place. Stretching some muscles.

The Perm gave up on that after a while, too.

"Sebastian was your boyfriend, Maja," she suddenly said, and it didn't sound like a question and I wasn't prepared for it. I don't know why, but I didn't expect her to ask that. It felt too banal. Would she show me photographs of the dead, like they always do on TV? I got the idea that she would start spreading out pictures of corpses on the table like playing cards. Draw them in her sketch, marking the contours of their bodies. Amanda, Samir, Sebastian, Christer, Dennis.

I closed my eyes. And there he was. With eyes that always saw right through me. Hands my skin would never forget. His body, all of him, all the rough and soft parts, hard and sharp, his scent, how he felt when he entered me, and the weight of him on top of me. That, most of all. His body on mine. Up until they came to get me from the classroom. Took him away from me. Carried his body away.

Sebastian, I forced myself to think. She wants me to talk about Sebastian. Nothing more.

No, I thought. *Just nod.* "Mmhmm." *Don't say anything.*

Keep your 'lectric eye on me babe. Put your ray gun to my head. Press your space face close to mine, love.

Don't say anything. There was howling in my head. I pressed my hands to it so it wouldn't go to pieces.

Sebastian was always listening to his dad's favorite music, always, constantly, and when we kissed for the first time (not at preschool — when he kissed me for real for the first time), he called me Sweet Mary Jane. I didn't know it at the time, but that was also from one of his dad's favorite songs. I had climbed onto the Vespa and had just put on my helmet. He said it and handed me the joint he'd had in his mouth. His lower lip glistened with saliva. I shook my head. Mom and Dad were probably spying on us through a window; I didn't understand how he could be so daring. No, thanks. Then he kissed me, leaned forward, parted my lips with his tongue. When he pulled away, he stuck the joint in my half-open mouth. "Maja," he whispered, and I took a drag, didn't cough. He let me take three drags before he kissed me again. Sebastian was kissing me and I was smoking weed a few meters from my parents.

I could have nodded. "Mmhmm." He was my boyfriend. Or I could have shaken my head. "It was over." No one would have understood anyway.

He liked to put his headphones on me, let me listen to his dad's favorite songs while he was kissing me, his hands stroking my skin. Holding me. Refusing to let me go. He refused to let go, refused to give me up, refused.

Was he my boyfriend? That didn't deserve an answer.

"I told him I couldn't handle it anymore," I whispered. I don't know if she heard me. "That it had to end."

I had said that, hadn't I, after we took that last walk? Or did I just think it? *Would you carry a razor, in case, just in case of depression?*

I can't remember whether The Perm looked at me, but I remember that her voice slowed down.

"Listen," she began. "You need to understand that before one can implement the measures we have taken in your case...you just turned eighteen, right?"

I nodded, although I didn't need to. She definitely knew how old I was.

"Well, it's unusual for young people to be detained under isolation and with full restrictions, the way we've done with you. You understand that this means there is something more to go on, it's not just that you are, or were, dating a guy who did something…that you were with Sebastian…There's more to it."

I nodded.

Sander sat up straighter. "What is this about?" he asked.

"We will get into that in a little bit, in detail, once we have finished going through the material we have. But we do have more, and right now I can really only appeal to you to tell us everything at once, and that is for your own good. Because I think you can tell us more about this than what you've told us so far."

I nodded, just out of sheer momentum, then regretted it and shook my head again. Sander was on tenterhooks.

"And we need to inform you of an additional charge."

Suddenly each word seemed more important than it had before, even before she said them.

"It has to do with what happened before you went to school, you and Sebastian. Sebastian's dad." When I didn't say anything, she continued. "Do you think you need to talk with your attorney for a few minutes? We can take a break here."

I shook my head.

"Would you like to talk to your attorney for a moment, Maja?"

"No," I said. No. Why would I need to do that?

And then she told me what Sebastian had done an hour or so before I came over to ride to school with him. She talked, explained, asked. Her mouth was moving. She asked more and more questions.

But I didn't say anything. Instead I opened my mouth. And there it was. The scream. Nothing more. Just the scream. I couldn't stop.

11.

I screamed until my throat started burning and my body stopped working, and thirty-two hours after I came out of that classroom, I fell asleep at last. All I needed was a hysterical breakdown, a doctor in a suit, an injection in my arm. But I didn't sleep for long. And when I woke up, there was chirping in my head. Fragments of music, lyrics that came from someplace I don't remember.

I was no longer in "my room," the place they had brought me at first; I was in a *constant surveillance* cell. Sure, I had never seen one before, but there could be no doubt that that's where I was. There wasn't a single window. Just a rubber mattress on the floor next to a drain the size of a toilet lid. They thought I was going to throw up. A hazy mirror completely covered one wall.

I tried to avoid looking in that direction, at the mirror, because I realized that's where they were guarding me from, back there, as if I were a fish in an aquarium. Instead I stared straight up at the ceiling. I waited for the ceiling to cave in, or turn soft like yogurt, part, crack like a wound, and for a hand to extend down through the hole to pull me out of there, up and away. But it would never occur to Mom and Dad to do such a thing. They were afraid of me now, I had seen it at the hospital, they were terrified. Their daughter was a murderer, she deserved this, she ought to be dead, why didn't she die? *Are Mom and Dad alive?* Now I understood why the police acted so strange when I asked.

As it happens, I am a crier. At the movies. When I see ads with babies in them or when someone sings so fantastically that everyone on *The Voice* jury is totally blown away and they give a standing ovation and say, *Now! Your new life begins now!* I cry when someone is nice even though they don't have to be and I cry when I get angry and can't manage to explain why. Unhappy endings at the movies? I cry. Happy endings? I cry. That's the sort of person I am. But now I wasn't crying. There was nothing to cry for, nothing to do at all. An unhappy ending is only sad if there is an alternative, if it seems unfair. Not if it's unavoidable. In which case there is no point.

I didn't think I would be able to fall back to sleep. I thought I would have to lie there on my mattress waiting for eternity. An aquarium fish washed up on land. But suddenly I felt how sweaty I was. Drenched. In my hair, between my legs. I was freezing. My palms hurt, that's how cold I was. I was shivering so hard I couldn't move. There was no blanket in there and I was shaking harder and harder. My skin itched. My scalp. My palms.

Then I gave up and looked at the mirror wall. There were people everywhere, I just knew it. I could feel them moving around back there, all around me, looking at me even though I couldn't see them. Around my glass bowl where I was swimming, where I was floating belly up. In religion class we had talked about a crazy Danish artist who made an exhibit of goldfish at a museum. Blenders containing ten goldfish each. If the visitors wanted, they could push the On button and start the blender. *Zzzzt!* One second. Goldfish smoothie. Was I under camera surveillance? Yes, of course I was. Did they have to tell me if they were watching me? No. They didn't have to ask before they undressed me, stuck needles in me, gave me medicine I hadn't asked for. I didn't close my eyes. The people were around me without me seeing them, they would open the door, sometimes, often, now and then. I would forget them and remember them and sometimes someone would come in and touch me and their hands would stick to my skin. *Zzzzt.*

How was I supposed to fall back to sleep? How could a little white pill in a plastic cup make me let go? An injection? Never. I couldn't risk it. If I closed my eyes, it would all come back.

The police had asked me to start from the beginning. Then they told me that Claes had been shot. Sebastian had killed him first. When I arrived at Sebastian's house that morning, Claes Fagerman was lying dead in the kitchen.

"What did you think of Claes, Maja?"

"What had he done to you, Maja?"

"What did you think of that, Maja? What did you think when Claes did that, Maja?"

"Can you tell us what you said to Sebastian about his father, Maja?"

"Can we talk about what you wrote to Sebastian when you went home?"

They already knew; that was why they were asking.

They said that Sebastian and I had decided that his dad had to die. That the others had to die.

"Why did they have to die, Maja?"

They said that Sebastian and I had decided to die together, that this was supposed to be the end, but that I couldn't do it. They said it was normal to be afraid of dying.

"Did you get scared when you saw what it meant? When you realized that everything would end, Maja?"

I didn't even know what the beginning was. And now here I lay, in a cell where people could look at me, but I couldn't see out. It still wasn't over.

In one of the many potential beginnings, Sebastian and I liked to hang out in the pool house. It was in the left-hand wing of the house. The guest room attached to the pool house was never occupied, but there were always clean sheets on the double bed and it felt nice and cool. And there were speakers everywhere — on the ceiling, along the floor, in every corner. The acoustics were best in the pool house, the music covered up the low hum of the pool machinery. All the words, the melodies, the most familiar ones. His songs. Mine. Ours. They took over, rested alongside us, enveloped us.

I wondered what they had given me in that injection, because it felt like I was in withdrawal. My head was buzzing, as if I were turning a radio button, listening to five seconds of every channel and then switching to the next one. The static between each frequency, and then five seconds of real sound when a channel tuned in. White noise. Sound. White noise. Sound.

Claes despised drug users; I'd heard him say so. It was just one of the many reasons he hated Sebastian.

And while I stroked the rough wall of the cell with one hand (it did not feel like yogurt), I thought about how that was a long time ago. It must have been an eternity. Or had it just happened? Yes, I had taken something the night before, because when it all happened I was wound up, nervy, high, scared. Claes was despicable, I hated him, he was horrible to me, and he was more horrible to Sebastian. Someone had to tell Sebastian that there was something wrong with his dad. That he was *not right in the head*. That was why I said those things to Sebastian. *That was why he did what he did?*

When I sat up on the edge of the mattress, I realized I was barefoot. The floor was cool against the soles of my feet, almost soft. During my intake they had exchanged my hospital slippers for a pair of sandal-like things without laces. But now those were gone, too. There were usually sneakers dangling from the electrical lines at the

Vendeväg roundabout up by the PLO house. I'd heard somewhere that in New York, if you saw shoes hanging from a lamppost, it meant you could buy heroin there. You definitely didn't have to stand outside and freeze in order to buy drugs in Djursholm. Mom and Dad had rolled joints in a cigar box in the library. They were in a locked cabinet and they were so old and dry that I doubt you could even smoke them, but for Mom and Dad it was titillating enough just to know that they had some at home. *Just in case.* As if Mom and Dad had ever been that type of people, the type with the chance to actualize their "just in cases" and "let's do its" and "why nots." I wonder if the police found their hoard when they searched our house, or if Mom had time to throw it away. Maybe they said it was mine. I would rather smoke rabbit droppings than raid Mom and Dad's pathetic stash.

I lay down on the floor, my head just above the floor drain. It had been a long time since I was this out of it. I had quit all that. Hadn't I? Almost, anyway. That was just one of the many reasons Sebastian was always angry with me, because I said no. I did say no, right? I did say that's enough?

My head was buzzing; I felt sick.

Sebastian had had a guy he could call. To "get a taxi" or "order pizza" or "make an appointment to have the pool cleaned." It sort of depended. The codes were never all that hard to figure out. "Two Italian-crust pizzas with extra cheese. Onion rings. And a bottle of Fanta. There are four of us." But then he discovered Dennis, and the "pizza guy" was no longer needed.

When it came to drugs, Dennis was surprisingly inventive.

Should I tell them that? Do the police want to know how Sebastian got his drugs? Should I say it was the drugs' fault? They're going to think it was the drugs' fault. Is it a good thing if it was the drugs' fault? Does Sander want me to say that? Should I talk about the parties? Sebastian's parties were fantastic. He was legendary. Other people's imaginations stopped at their parents' vintage wines and Bellinis made with Dom Perignon; they thought it was enough to pay a bunch of bikini-clad ninth graders to serve food for the annual guys-only dinner party, but not Sebastian. He rented amplifiers, professional DJs, boats, circus troupes, TV chefs, fireworks, a pizza baker from Naples, and once he flew a YouTuber in from New York to party with us. The YouTuber was too trashed for us to understand what he was saying, but he slept with one of Amanda's friends from the stables, and two weeks after he put up the clip "The Party with Swedes," it had over two million views.

Sebastian had no limits. Everyone loved his parties. Everyone loved him and everything to do with him, at least at first. Everyone wanted to be with him, but no one was closer to him than I was. Sebastian wanted to spend more time with me than with anyone else. *He can't survive without you, Maja.* Sebastian and I left the dinners before everyone else was finished eating, left the dance floor when everyone else was still dancing, went down to the pool house, locked it from the inside, and let the others party without us. When we wanted them to leave, Sebastian cut the power. When the music stopped, they left, at least most of them did. We lay naked on the pool house floor and listened to the hissing of the machinery, which never shut off, it was hooked up to some special generator.

Sebastian chose me. It was inexplicable, I never understood why, he should have had someone prettier, more special. But when he chose me, I became all of that. I became unique. Mom and Dad hardly knew what to do with themselves, they were so happy. Sebastian! Not in their wildest dreams.

At first they were actually happy about Sebastian. Should I say that? Do the police want to know how much everyone loved Sebastian? How much Sebastian loved me? He loved me even when I betrayed him, and he chose me again because he loved me, more than anyone else loved me. I loved Sebastian.

But I hated his dad. I hated hated hated Claes Fagerman. I wanted him to die.

12.

I remained in the constant-surveillance cell overnight. After a while (one hour? two?), with my mouth next to the drain, I got back up on the mattress again. Did I fall asleep? Did I scream? How long did it take for me to wake up again? I don't know, but my head felt different; the walls felt harder. I curled into a ball. Whispered his name. It tasted so sweet at first, but later, like powdered sugar melting on my tongue, it stuck to my palate and filled my mouth with bitter gall and I threw up, far away from the practical drain in the floor. Someone came in and washed it away. Gave me a glass of water, wiped my mouth, left again.

When I was stable enough to move back to "my room," where there was a window and a bed (and where I was still isolated from anyone else), my interrogations with The Perm resumed as well. At first she was always the one who ran my interrogations. Her colleagues were seldom allowed to ask more than a few sporadic questions; they just sat in the corner and picked at their fingernails and were switched out now and then.

I'm sure The Perm was considered the perfect person to talk with me. A "young woman." I thought she was freaking pathetic.

She was always animated at the start of a session. That was the part where she would keep saying my name. She was perky like the host of a children's show. Toward the end of the session she would get increasingly tired and irritated. Then her voice would drop down an octave, and she would start talking like a poorly translated crime drama.

"Really? Then how would you like to explain these messages?"

"I hear you, Maja, I hear you. But I'm having a hard time understanding why you would write that if you didn't mean it. Do you often say things you don't mean?"

In some ways she reminded me of the psychologist Mom had forced me to visit right after Lina was born (she got it into her head that it would be a problem for me, having a new sibling when I was so old). That psychologist had read in his *ABCs of Psychology* that he should wait out the patient, let me speak freely because then I would tell him stuff I actually wanted to keep to myself just to avoid embarrassing silence.

The Perm often tried the same tactics. Just like with the psychologist, this resulted in the two of us sitting in the interrogation room without speaking. At the psychologist's office, ten minutes might go by without anyone saying a word. Here it never lasted long before Sander protested ("My client cannot answer your questions if you don't ask them." "My client cannot be expected to guess what you want to know"), even if he did seem to think that it was absurdly entertaining when I wouldn't say anything and the police officers ended up sitting there staring at their plastic cups of cold coffee that had grown a film at the top. Sometimes Sander remained silent as well, leaning back in his uncomfortable chair, clasping his hands and closing his eyes and seeming to be asleep or meditating, all while his hourly fee ticked on and on.

And when I did actually answer a question, about the party the night before, for example, the fight with Claes, my texts, or what we said when we talked on the phone, when we decided we would ride to school together, or what we talked about when we went on that walk, in the hours before I went home, it wasn't long before The Perm asked the same exact question once more.

"I just answered that," I said.

"Please tell me again," said The Perm.

And Sander sighed.

The Perm would get annoyed, or even angry sometimes, but she never lost control and never started shouting or yelling. She always watched me with the same moist look: not angry, not nice, not empty, just blank. Her colleagues weren't quite as good at that. But if they raised their voices, The Perm would send them away, immediately, no discussion, and without letting on that it was an order. She would ask them to go fetch something, water, documents, some chips, or "maybe something warm to drink." So her colleagues kept their voices under control and stared at me instead, so they would be allowed to stay.

The worst of all was a guy of around twenty-five. He came in toward the end of the first week, and he hated me more than he hated all the girls who had turned him down because you could tell by looking at him how bad he was in bed. But he never let The Perm see the way he looked at me. Because if she had seen it, he probably would have been sent on involuntary vacation, or at least he would have been moved to a different unit, like the one that keeps tabs on whether people are driving too fast or not.

How did I know he hated me? Because he reminded me of the time I took Sebastian along on one of Grandpa's hunts. Grandpa's hunting buddies were seven well-fed, self-satisfied CEOs who dozed out there in the forest, drank already at lunchtime, and told lies: *Oh no, I didn't wound the buck, it was just a wild miss,* all to avoid tracking injured animals with a dog that ran so fast they felt the taste of blood in their mouths after just ten meters. I got to join Sebastian at his standing post instead of going on the drive.

Sebastian hunted with his dad sometimes, so they gave him a pretty good spot, even though he was maybe too young to manage a post on his own. Grandpa had been happy to see us; he greeted Sebastian as if he were a grown man and sized him up with a narrow gaze when he shouldered his rifle. Sebastian was quieter than usual. As long as we were standing in a circle around the leader, receiving our instructions, he was also calmer than usual. As we walked toward the spot where we were supposed to stand, it was like he was walking all alone, almost in a trance. And when we took up our position to wait for the drive to approach our area, he turned into yet another person I had never seen before; it was like his blood was bubbling through his body. I was sitting right next to him, but I could have punched him in the arm and he wouldn't even have noticed I was there. Sebastian's entire being was aimed out at the forest, at the animals he would kill, and when a deer popped up in front of us, almost in slow motion, and turned its head toward us just as Sebastian stood up, leaned forward, and raised his rifle, I had the fleeting thought that Sebastian would rush up and press the barrel of the gun to the deer's neck. Instead he just fired. Two quick shots and the deer fell onto its side, before it even had time to notice us. And when Sebastian walked up and squatted beside the deer, I thought he would take a knife from his pocket and drive it into the hide, just to get blood on his hands, just to feel the deer dying, right up close. But he didn't do that either, he just breathed, short, sharp puffs. His hair curled on his forehead from the sweat. They praised him later on. Grandpa smiled at me, as if I deserved the credit, but I went to bed before dinner, saying that I had a stomachache.

When the policeman looked at me, out of sight of The Perm, it reminded me of how Sebastian acted on that hunt. Because it didn't matter that I was detained, locked up — this police dude would have to kill me because only my blood could calm him down. I wanted to tell him that he reminded me of Sebastian, to see how he would react, but I didn't.

Trial hearing in case B 147/66

The prosecutor et al. v. Maria Norberg

Week 1 of Trial: Friday

13.

I rise from my eighty-centimeter-wide cot and ring the bell. One and a half meters from my bed to the door. I used to wish I would get sick when I was little. Then I would be allowed to lie in bed all day, eating whatever I wanted (marmalade on white toast), reading (Harry Potter), surfing the Web on my phone, watching movies, listening to music.

I don't want to go to court. Maybe I can stay here if they think I'm sick. Stay here in "my room."

I have been living at the women's jail for two months. Before this I spent seven months at the juvenile detention center. "Special circumstances" (legalese for *times we don't have to follow our own rules*) dictated that I had to stay there, even though normally only boys live there. Men behind bars must be kept apart from women no matter what — that may even be why they're locked up in the first place. But they made an exception for me. They rattled off a bunch of special circumstances: The women's jail was overcrowded, I was to be kept in isolation anyway, they did not intend for me to spend time with the other internees there, there were better "resources" at the juvenile detention center "for this type of situation." And so on. But the real reason was just to show "the public" that they weren't handling me with kid gloves. There were special circumstances that meant they had to give me special treatment to reassure the population that they were not giving me any special privileges.

I got to move to a different jail after a fellow inmate in the exercise yard next to mine screamed "CUNT YOU FUCKING CUNT" twenty-four times in a row (I counted). I never saw what he looked like, but his voice was hoarse by the end. Maybe they moved me for his sake.

But it doesn't really make any difference to me. The rooms are almost identical here. Different graffiti scratched into the bathroom wall, but an identical sheet of metal above an identical metal sink. No seat on the toilet (which is also metal) and the same pine furniture. And there are guys here, too, in a different unit, so I never see them either.

I sit on the bed, waiting to be let out. If someone had told me, when I was being driven from the hospital to the jail and I was allowed to take off the handcuffs and my hospital gown and put on stiff, green pants, an equally stiff green shirt, white underwear, and a white bra, that I would be sitting here like this for at least nine months, I'm pretty sure I wouldn't have listened and I definitely would not have understood. But I still would have done exactly what I did at first: started waiting to get out.

Back then, when I still believed I would be allowed to go home a few hours later, I never put on anything but the jail clothes. That stiff fabric against my skin, refusing to conform to my body. I put them on despite the fact that Sander had brought me my own clothes. "My clothes are my identity" was something Amanda liked to say in a voice that revealed she thought it was super smart (it also revealed that someone else had come up with it). When I got here I realized she was right. I didn't even want to look at my own clothes; it was way more logical to put on a bra that was too small and underwear with crumbly elastic that broke when I put it on. The jail clothes meant that I didn't have to be me. It was an incredible relief. *Number one on the list of pros.*

What about "my room"? What is it like? The blanket in my cell smells like dust and unscented detergent, no fabric softener. It's not very comfortable, but at least it will never end up in a report about wasted taxpayer money.

Every other week I am given a toothbrush, a small bar of soap, and a travel-size tube of toothpaste in a paper bag. Every other week they ask if I need pads. Two-centimeters-thick, too-short pads. I nod and say yes please, every time. I keep them in my doorless closet. The room is actually marginally bigger than my old closet. I can see what the guards are thinking every time they lock the door behind me. *Poor little rich girl.* Their schadenfreude when I break down and have to be put under constant surveillance. *Of course jail is worse than Chinese water torture for a chick who's never even been camping without a down pillow and the latest-generation phone, I'm surprised she doesn't crack up more often.*

Up in one corner, just below the ceiling, by my bed, there is an outlet for a TV, but no actual TV. There is another outlet, this one safety-plugged, by the night-stand, but no clock radio. I am on full restrictions so as not to interfere with the investigation. When the investigation was over, they lifted a few of them, but most remain; according to Sander they're going to play games with me until the verdict is handed down and there's nothing we can do about it. *Special circumstances.* Everything about me brings *special circumstances* to the foreground again. It has never been clear to me how my watch, the one they took from me at the hospital, could interfere with the investigation, much less how it could still pose a problem. But there's no point in arguing.

"Pick your battles," Sander says, sounding like a relationship coach on a morning show. I just have to deal with it until I have moved to wherever I'm going to serve out my sentence. *It's your own fault, you cunt fucking cunt. Special rich fucking cunt.* So: If I want to know what time it is, I have to ring the bell and ask one of the guards.

I get up and press the call button once more, holding it down a little longer this time. If they think I'm annoying, they can give me my watch, or hook up the goddamn clock radio. How risky could it be to let me keep track of how slowly time passes?

These days I'm allowed to read the paper, apparently Sander judged that worth going to battle for. He even gave me the ones I missed during the preliminary investigation because he thinks I should know what has been written ("You have been accused of more than you've been charged with, and not even the court would dare to deny it"). But

I've only been given actual physical papers. I don't have the Internet, so I can't follow what's being said about me on Twitter. I can't read about #maja #killer #djursholm-massacre. No Google, no Facebook, no receiving anonymous Snapchat messages, black screenshots in my feed, you-must-die.

Pro number two.

I press the damn call button a third time before I lie down on my bed and wait for them to come open the door. I can reach the edge of the table on the other side of the room when I'm lying there. It feels like I could stretch out my arms and hold on to the walls. This is not home. I don't have to be in our horrible house. *Pro number three.*

We live in a McMansion on a subdivided plot of land, surrounded by authentic early twentieth-century villas; our house pretends to be something it isn't. The first time I saw it I thought it would take 3-D glasses to see what it really looked like. When we moved in, there was a tiny fountain in the front hall. It stood there gurgling for a few weeks before four Polish workers came and took it out and laid new flooring, not just over the hole but throughout the entire hall. Dad says that the person who bought the lot and built the house was "in the DJ industry," he was "the sort of musician who neither plays his own instruments nor writes his own songs."

The "musician" made the driveway wide enough for a Hummer to drive up to the house, but he forgot to make the turnaround big enough to get the car facing back the other way. "That's probably the reason," Dad likes to say "that they sold the house again, without having lived there a single day. Because you don't have to know how to reverse to get an American driver's license."

That's one of Dad's favorite stories; he's told it more times than I can count and he laughs at it every time. It's proof that there are worse upstarts than him, I suppose. Or else he's just jealous that he would never dare to drive a Hummer. My dad really wants to be a chill kind of dude, in suits and T-shirts, no socks, a "type of musician" or an IT millionaire, someone who isn't ashamed of liking '80s TV shows set in Miami.

But at the same time, Dad is far too worried about catching a cold; that might disrupt his marathon training. He wears knee-high Merino wool socks with moisture-wicking silver threads even under his suit pants. Once a week, on Fridays, he takes off his tie after lunch and hangs it on his office chair before he gets back to work. That's it. That's as chill as my dad will ever get.

I am still barred from having visitors. Dad and Mom are not allowed to see me. *Pro number four.*

The fourth time I get up and ring the call bell, I hold the button down for five seconds, counting to myself so I don't wuss out and stop too soon: one Mississippi, two Mississippi, three Mississippi..., the way Grandma counted during a storm between the lightning and the thunder. I can't hear it ringing in my cell, but I know it's ringing out by the guard. Pretty loudly. It must be annoying. But I'm not sick and I can't think of any way to make anyone believe I am, so I might as well get going.

Last night Susse promised that I would get to shower first thing. Before breakfast. "As soon as you wake up," she said. I've gotten pretty good at figuring out when night is over. It should be about five o'clock. I ought to be able to convince the guard it's not too early.

My side of the story. My turn. Not today, but maybe on Monday.

Sander has promised that nothing crucial will happen today. The prosecutor will finish her review of the documentary evidence, which is taking longer than planned, so we are behind schedule. Sander can begin his statements only once that's done. But even if he does get to start today, I won't have to do anything but sit there and listen, and I will get to return to the jail pretty early because even judges (and lawyers, I assume) want to spend cozy Friday evenings with their kids. I will also be left alone all weekend, Sander promised, so I can rest and sleep and I won't have to come to court and listen to Call-me-Lena or Pancake or anyone else.

Today's actually the wrong day to play sick. I should wait until after Sander has given his opening statements. That's when it's time for my "account." Monday or Tuesday, Tuesday or Monday, depending on how far we get today. I will remain in my usual spot, Sander said I don't have to move; there's no witness stand where you sit and look out at the audience. Nor do I have to swear on a Bible; he promised me that, too. But he will ask me the questions we've gone over a million times, and I will answer them right into the live microphone. Everything I say will be recorded, and everyone who is there to stare at me will be able to hear what I say.

It usually takes a while for the guard to come open the door, but it almost never takes this long. I press the button three more times, quick jabs, even though I know they get mad as hell when you ring and ring and ring the bell. What if the guard fell asleep? Maybe it's not even five o'clock, maybe it's only four? If it's not even after three, I won't get to shower. They'll probably be so annoyed that they make me wait until the last second.

If I'm sick today, the whole trial will be postponed for a day. My day will be postponed. Maybe it's a good idea to be sick right now after all, even though no one will give me any marmalade sandwiches. I don't want to be here all weekend knowing that as soon as it's over I have to speak in court. But I don't know how to fake it. There's no way they'll leave me alone with a thermometer, that would mean mortal danger. I might bite it until it cracks and swallow the contents to get out of going. The girl in the cell next to mine swallowed a pen a few weeks ago. They had to take her away in an ambulance. It was chaos in the hallway, impossible to miss, even for those of us in the isolation cells. I made Susse tell me what happened. She was so shocked that she did.

During my first weeks in jail I was constantly on suicide watch. Now and then, while I was in my cell, one of the guards would come by and ask, "How is it going?" After one of them gave me lunch and another picked up my empty tray, they would open the door and just stare at me for a split second before closing it again. They refused to leave me alone. They kept this up around the clock. No knock. A rattle at the lock. Open the door. Stare. Close the door.

At first it made me nervous, because sometimes it felt like they came by every five minutes and sometimes I thought several hours went by between checks. So I started asking them, every time they came, what time it was. Just to know. I was also afraid that night would fall and I wouldn't realize it. I tried to convince myself that I would be able to see it get dark through the window, but since I had such a hard time remembering, at first, when I had last slept (Maybe I had slept for several nights and forgot about it? Maybe I was still at home only yesterday?), I demanded to know what time it was, and I wrote it down on a notepad I received from the guards along with a (really short) pen. (For some reason, I guess they didn't think I would swallow it. Or else it was so small that it wouldn't pose much of a danger if I did.)

On the third — or fourth — day, I was given a stack of year-old magazines, guy stuff, about finances, war, car tires, and naked chicks, preferably all at once. A few days later, they brought a couple of comic books and three dog-eared paperbacks. I paged through them, front to back and back to front, but I didn't manage to read any of them.

It took a few weeks for me to stop acting like a prisoner down for life in a medieval prison (who doesn't brush her hair and uses her bloody stumps of fingernails to scratch the number of days in the cement wall of the cell). But after a month or so I could look at the newspaper ads about pension insurance and light beer and hair products and understand them. I kept the notepad. I took it with me when they moved me to the women's jail, partly to remind myself that I was feeling more normal, partly so I wouldn't forget that everything had a routine. But above all it was because my notes proved that they came once every half hour. So there was plenty of time to kill myself — twenty-nine minutes to be exact. I found this reassuring, even though I didn't know how I would go about dying. There was no breaking the stainless steel plate (the "mirror") on the wall above the sink, so I couldn't use it to slit my wrists. The blanket on the bed (and the extra one on the shelf) was made out of a weirdly fluffy material that was more like compressed vacuum dust than fabric, and my sheets were made of paper. No way could they be used to hang yourself. The bag Sander gave me had come with a shoulder strap, but the guard unhooked it and took it away. I could maybe rip up my T-shirt or my pants and fashion a makeshift rope, but I didn't know where I would attach it. There was no handle on my side of the door, and there were no hooks on the wall or the ceiling. I've never wanted to kill myself, so I've never had to consider how to do it. The jail guards seemed to think I should want to die. They were probably right.

Just as I'm about to push the button again, the guard arrives, just as annoyed as I expected. It's five thirty. I slept longer than I thought. I am allowed to shower. With the soap and the shampoo I bought in the commissary.

Mom tried to send me a whole suitcase full of beauty products, but Sander wasn't allowed to give it to me. I suppose they were afraid Mom would smuggle in drugs or encouraging words in the eyelash-growth serum, what do I know? (No one has commented on the fact that my mom thinks it's important for her alleged murderer daughter to take care of her eyelashes.)

I was allowed to see the list of items they wouldn't let me have. That was a decision I could appeal. Screw it; I chose not to pick that battle either.

Smart little rich girl.

Week 1 of Trial: Friday

14.

When I return from the shower, I get dressed and receive my breakfast tray with the margarine-and-cheese roll that tastes like plastic and the vinegary tea I never drink. Susse steps into my room as I am putting on makeup as best I can in front of the stainless steel plate. She sits on the edge of my bed and watches as I goop on the mascara Mom sent and I was actually allowed to receive. Susse is going to take me to the trial.

Susse seldom works early mornings, late nights, or weekends. And she usually leaves early on Friday afternoons. But not today — she's going to drive me back from the trial, too, and she's wearing her guard uniform. Sometimes she comes to say goodbye after she's changed. In those cases she's usually wearing a tank top and frayed jeans and glittery purple eye shadow and her severely plucked eyebrows are painted jet black. Susse looks like the type who takes out fast-cash loans to buy charter trips to Thailand, and six months later, still just as tan, gets chewed out on that *Luxury Trap* show on TV3 because she spent her entire salary on shoes from Zappos. Susse has a kid and "a guy who pumps iron" (Susse's words). She has her daughter's name (Nevaeh or Angel or something along those lines) colorfully tattooed on one shoulder, but you can't see it when she's got long sleeves on. She always wears long sleeves at work.

Susse often brings me stuff so I'll have something to do. Today she has a bag of candy and a DVD, something insipid (it's always insipid); on the cover is a girl sticking out her lips and her butt as she holds on to fourteen dogs on leashes. I still have no TV in my room, but Susse has talked the evening shift into rolling a portable TV ("the TV cart") into my cell, and she thinks I should watch the movie when I get back from court. "Take your mind off things."

"If you haven't fallen asleep by ten o'clock, Maja," she says, "then take a sleeping pill." When I don't respond, she goes on, "and promise me you'll go outside for break on both Saturday and Sunday."

Susse is my day care teacher. Susse thinks that morning routines and fresh air (there is no bad weather, only bad clothing!) are the most important things in life, with the possible exceptions of free weights and protein drinks in Tetra Paks.

Susse nags me. I should sign up for lessons ("studying," she calls it, even though I don't have any classes to study for). I should go work out in "the gym" (a windowless room with a treadmill, two weight machines, and a gross-smelling yoga mat that is so stiff it stays rolled up all on its own). I should make appointments with the priest, the psychologist, the doctor, anyone who might possibly or impossibly "help me" to "work through it."

Sometimes I say okay, mostly just to shut her up.

"Yes, Mom," I say. That makes Susse laugh; she likes it. She would have to have gotten pregnant at age eight to be my mom, but she likes to be more mature than me, better than me. Susse would never refer to herself as my jailor. I have never even heard her say "correctional officer." She doesn't want to admit that she guards me or that she likes to take too much responsibility for the fact that I feel fucking awful.

I seldom have the energy to protest. So I nod. I don't really know what I'm saying yes to. To the movie or the candy or the sleeping pill or outside break. All of it, maybe. I am very tired today. Tired, but unfortunately not sick.

"Then I'll sign you up for the exercise yard tomorrow morning," Susse decides. Super. I will "get to" wake up early and have the "opportunity" to enjoy the jail's exercise yard in the total darkness of a February morning. I smile at her as best I can. She stands up to leave. She doesn't hug me, but I can tell that she wants to. Maybe she's not the fast-cash loan type despite her clothes, but she is definitely the type to hug murderers and fall in love with the wrong guy (I would bet money that her kid's dad is in prison and that she has worked as his CO/guard/mom, but that it's over now, because her daughter *must always come first*), and she loves to turn around hopeless cases, that that's why she's here, in my cell, on the edge of my bed. She arranges TV carts and Saturday candy for me because she thinks I need to be taken care of and she needs to be my mom.

And suddenly I think of my mom, my real mom. I don't have time to stop myself, and I remember her ridiculous admonitions: When you're walking around with scissors, always hold them by the blade end, always stick knives in the dishwasher sharp side down, look both ways before you cross the street, text me when you get there, don't listen to music when you go for a run in the woods, don't walk through parks when it's starting to get dark, never walk home alone at night, never, never...*fucking goddamn shit.*

I think of Mom because I'm not watching myself carefully enough, and before Susse has time to leave, I'm crying. The tears just pour right out of me and it's awful, because now I have to redo my makeup and Susse starts hugging me, oh my God, of course she does, nothing can stop her from touching me, from standing way too close, from *showing that she cares*, once she gets the tiniest little excuse. And now she's not hugging me anymore; instead she's taking my face in her hands and wiping away my tears, and now we're rushed for time, even though I showered so early and even though I just wanted to put on my clothes and go, not talk, and definitely, definitely, definitely not hug.

Once when we were on a plane, Mom and I, I was maybe six or seven years old, and there was turbulence, a lot of turbulence, and I squeezed Mom's hand as hard as I could and I cried and Mom whispered in my ear, "We're going to be fine," and she comforted me and she was perfectly calm while I thought I was going to die.

I don't want to think about Mom.

When Susse finally leaves to check on our ride, I look at what she brought me *because it's Friday*. It's a jumbo bag of gummy candy.

Sander has explained what will happen as best he can, but it doesn't help. Beyond these walls, neither he nor I have any control. If I let go and think one of the forbidden thoughts, I can no longer move. I become paralyzed with fear; my life is gone forever. If you get cancer, you are declared healthy again after six years without symptoms, but I will never be declared healthy, never. It doesn't matter if I'm sentenced to life in prison or a juvenile detention center, Sander's straight back and half-interested expressions will not help me. It will all go to hell. I wrote to Sebastian that his dad didn't deserve to live. I did it so Sebastian would understand that I cared, to let him know I understood how messed up his dad was. I wrote that I wanted him to die, because I thought if Sebastian could let go of his dad, he would feel better. That he would want to live.

I try to tell myself that at least once the trial is over I won't have to answer any more questions. But I know that's just wishful thinking. I will never get away from all the questions, and they will never, never be interested in the answers because they have already decided that they know who I am.

I hate gummy candy. I throw the bag in my wall-mounted trash bin with a lid and start crying again.

Week 1 of Trial: Friday

15.

By the time we arrive at the courthouse, I have calmed down. Ferdinand wants to give me drops for my red eyes; Pancake freaks out. He thinks it's "excellent" that I've obviously been crying (he doesn't want me to wear makeup at all, because I look younger without it), and Ferdinand tries to give me the bottle anyway, and I think they're about to throw punches when Sander simply takes the drops and gives them to me. I even have time to give myself a few swipes of Ferdinand's jet-black waterproof mascara before it's time. I have to wait in the lawyers' room while Sander and the others walk in. When my turn comes, a man and a woman are standing back-to-back outside the other courtroom, each talking on a cell phone. As I walk by, the woman looks up and our eyes meet for a split second before it dawns on her, the realization (*It's her!*), and I look away. I can hear the voice on the phone behind me, excited; she's speaking Spanish.

Mom and Dad are in their seats, and the judges and attorneys, too. Everyone is there. Mom looks bloated, as if she spent half the night getting drunk and fell asleep without taking off her makeup. But my mom never gets drunk.

She *drinks wine.* And she and Dad go to parties with other forty-five-year-olds, theme parties (like, "James Bond" or "Hollywood"), so the women can dress up as themselves in the '80s, in sequined minidresses they bought on their last trip to New York, and they disco and do the chicken dance. Then they drink cocktails and hold speeches during dinner and laugh at things they did back when they were teenagers and classmates. The men put their arms around the waists of wives who aren't their own and call each other "brother."

I think Mom and Dad have been fighting. Before, they would fight about stuff like how Dad leaves the toilet seat up. Not when other people could hear; when they were at dinners and the women were supposed to be united in the customary our-silly-husbands discussion, at those Mom would just joke about stuff like, "I'm not the one who usually has the headache, hee hee..." And Dad had to respond, "Heh heh, I don't have a headache right now — how are you feeling, dear friends, isn't it time for you to call it a night?"

They preferred to show off "sexy problems," like that Mom wanted to get laid, that she wanted to fuck so bad that Dad had to fend her off. But when their dinners were over, when the artisanal bread and the French cheeses had been eaten, the olive oil with its smoky undertones put away ("We got it from some good friends, they have a house just outside Florence, it's made with their own olives"), and the "flea market" china (which was really from Harrods) was in the dishwasher, the horniness always ended and the banalities took over.

You drink too much, you work too much, why did you let Jossan drape herself all over you all night, put down the goddamn toilet seat, how hard can it possibly be?

I wonder what they were fighting about this morning. I wonder if Lina was there, if they dropped her off at preschool on their way here, and I try to smile at them. They try to smile back.

I assume the toilet seat has fallen on the list of priorities, and they probably haven't been invited to any theme parties recently either. That's just one of the things you get in the bargain when you have a daughter who's been charged with mass murder. You're spared the clichés; you become unique for real.

Soon Sander will talk about the victims. One at a time. Then he'll go through exactly where I was at each precise moment, and he will speak in his low voice, at just the right gradual pace. When he wants the judges to listen, they will listen, and when he wants them to be confused, they will be. And the whole time I will be sitting there beside him, and everyone will be able to look at me.

They all want to look, but no one wants to listen. They're expecting what they think they already know. People like to say that kids believe what they want to believe, but the truth is, it's impossible to fool kids. Adults, on the other hand, want to make up their own minds about which story best matches their beliefs. People aren't interested in what others say or think, what they have gone through, what conclusions they have drawn. People are interested in hearing only what they think they already know.

This had never occurred to me before the interrogations started. But it immediately became obvious. And The Perm was the worst of all. If I happened to say what she was expecting me to say, her eyes opened wide, they literally got bigger, and she wasn't even very subtle about it. And she would bounce around in her chair, like she had to pee. She didn't understand that this only made it even more obvious how worked up she was.

Sander is the exact opposite of The Perm. I never know what he wants me to say. Back in the beginning he would say, "You are not responsible for the investigation." Not responsible for the investigation? What did he mean by that? That I should shut up? Lie? Not help the police?

Sander said I had to tell him everything before I told it to the police. Whether this meant I should tell it like it was, give it to him straight, so that he could then tell me what I absolutely must not tell the police, he never explained. He never asked me to lie or keep quiet or not say one particular thing or another. But at the same time, he said, "Answer only the questions they ask…" It was incomprehensible. What else would I answer?

Was there something else Sander was after? No idea. I didn't even understand whether he was "after" anything.

In that sense, it was easier to talk to the police. I knew they had a plan: They wanted to put me away. The faster I could work out what I would have to say to play into their hands, the faster I could get rid of them. And at first I did want to get rid of them. I didn't want to have to talk to them. I just wanted to stay in my bed, in my room, where it was quiet.

But after two weeks with The Perm leading the interrogations, they sent in a dark-blond guy of around thirty-five to crack me. He had rolled-up sleeves, sat with his legs spread wide, and asked in a velvety voice, "How are you doing, Maja?"

I understood that he had been very popular with the girls at his upper secondary school in Jönköping or Enköping or Linköping or some other fucking -köping. I understood that the plan was for me to fall in love with him and want to tell him everything. But I didn't fall in love. I thought he was ludicrous. The strange thing was, despite that and despite the fact that I knew just how they thought I would react, I still wanted to tell him. When the köping guy said that he knew I hated Claes Fagerman, when he said he knew I was just trying to help Sebastian, that I wanted to "be a good girlfriend." When he said that he would have been "really fucking mad, too" if he had been in my shoes, it was like pressing a button: I started to cry just as automatically as at the end of a bad movie.

It was like it was programmed into me to let him take care of me. I wanted to say, *Yes! I told my boyfriend to kill his dad and we decided to get revenge and end it all*, because I wanted him to feel sorry for me (*Yes! I'm miserable!*) and then I wanted him to say how sorry he felt for me and then he could go away and the police would have gotten what they wanted and would leave me alone.

Sander helped me, I realize that now. At first I thought he was weird, when he suddenly demanded we take a break right in the middle of an interrogation. It wasn't like he interrupted me, or even the police, but he wanted to kind of remind me who I was now and then, make sure I didn't forget.

"Well, then…" The judge spits his words into the microphone. "It is time to resume the proceedings in…" He rattles on.

When the stream of words seems to peter out a bit, Sander asks permission to say a few words about the schedule. The judge nods, annoyed, and Sander explains that in consideration of my "state of health," it is "extraordinarily important" for us to end the day's proceedings at three o'clock at the very latest. There's something Sander "must take care of" and, there we go, he manages to bring up my age again, the "exceptionally long and difficult detention period" I have "had to endure," and the judge nods again, just as annoyed. It's clear that he doesn't enjoy being reminded about this, and when Sander is finished the judge resumes rattling off what the day will "entail."

I thought earlier that it was odd that Sander is always discussing the schedule, that he doesn't want to be done with this trial as quickly as possible, but persisted in submitting petitions about how he couldn't be present this day or that in the second week and this day and that in the third week. The trial has already been postponed once, because the judge insisted on holding it without interruptions. And I have come to understand that it would have been better for me if the trial was divided up into different weeks, four days one week, three days the next, two and a half in the third, and so on, because the more chopped up the trial is, the greater the chance that the judges will forget what we were talking about when we left off. And it's to my advantage if it's hard for them to keep it all straight in their minds. Anything they find muddled and illogical can only be a plus. If the case doesn't seem crystal clear to the judges, then ugly Lena hasn't done her job properly. Even if Sander isn't hoping to "win," he can cross his fingers that the prosecutor will lose.

Sander's plan for a sliced-and-diced trial went to shit. We will convene all day, every day, until it's over. But Sander still insists on talking about the schedule every time he gets the chance.

Then it's the prosecutor's turn. She has only a few records to go through. But the chief judge asks a lot of questions. That's why this is taking longer than planned. Everyone pretends this is not super irritating.

When the prosecutor is finally finished, the plaintiffs' attorneys are given the floor. They start going through the documents that are supposed to show why I must pay damages. I have "caused irreparable harm." And suddenly, at ten minutes to twelve, right in between two attorneys, Sander demands that we break for lunch. Yes, it may be earlier than usual, but Sander seems to think that it's a matter of life and death.

Sander is stalling, I suddenly realize. He doesn't want to start talking today; he wants to postpone it.

The judge suggests that we continue until one o'clock before we take a break, so that we might have time to get through the damages portion. At this, Sander looks even more annoyed. His entire being radiates indignation at their inability to understand that I'm too young to withstand such a strain on my blood sugar.

Once they've gone back and forth on this for what has to be fifteen minutes, the judge finally agrees to break for lunch. We have to be back at one o'clock.

I don't think it will be as rough when Sander's talking. When he speaks, he never seems the least bit nervous, and he doesn't have to think about what to say.

Even back in his opening statements, he talked about what I knew and what I didn't know, and what I did, but above all what I didn't do. Sander prefers talking about what I didn't do.

Before Sebastian and I went to the school, for example. When I got back to Sebastian's house after having slept at home, I entered the house and stayed there for eleven minutes before we came back out again. There was a security camera on the driveway but none in the house. No one can know for certain what happened while I was standing in the hall waiting for Sebastian.

Waiting? Was that what I was doing? How is that possible? The prosecutor said that I did a bunch of other stuff, that I didn't just wait for eleven times sixty seconds. Sander says that I wasn't doing anything. That's a long time. An eternity, you could say. Didn't I think it was a long time? Did I just sit there in the hall with my hands in my lap? Didn't I even look at my phone? Check FB or Instagram? Snapchat? Didn't I even leave a single emoji or like-thumb behind, like the pebbles or breadcrumbs Hansel and Gretel trailed behind them when their dad wanted them to get lost and starve to death in the forest? Isn't there any sort of proof that I didn't do what the prosecutor claims?

No, unfortunately there is not. It was not an Insta-moment.

Week 1 of Trial: Friday

16.

After we've eaten lunch and the plaintiffs' attorneys have made it through all their *thus* and *whether* and *justifiably* and *reasonably* and *intentionally* and *willfully*, there are exactly fifty minutes left before it's time for the promised break for cozy family Friday.

Sander is more worked up than I've ever seen him.

"This is unacceptable," he says in his most acidic voice. "We cannot possibly begin to present our case now."

For a brief moment I think the judge in the middle is going to protest. But he doesn't. He just says "okay" and concludes the proceedings. The prosecutor doesn't protest, either. So we gather up our folders and our pens and our papers and briefcases, and leave, earlier than planned because the trial is delayed. Now begins the wait for Monday.

But my ride back to the jail hasn't arrived yet. We end up sitting in our room, me and Sander, Ferdinand, and Pancake. Everyone wants to go home, but neither Ferdinand nor Pancake dares to ask to be excused. Sander paces back and forth across the room a few times before turning to Ferdinand.

"I want you to check on the status of negotiations between the estate of Dennis Oryema and Fagerman's attorneys."

Ferdinand nods.

In the classroom, Sebastian shot Dennis first. The papers made a big deal out of the fact that the black guy died first. But Sebastian wasn't a racist, Dennis's skin color wasn't the problem. And even if a few journalists wanted to turn this into a tragedy with racist undertones because Djursholm snobs can't handle people who don't look just like them, the fact is, none of the parents have issues with kids from other neighborhoods going to our school. In some ways it's even the other way around. Just-black-enough guys and smart Samir are as welcome on Djursholm Upper Secondary's Instagram as a colorful photograph from a market in Marrakech in my mom's nauseatingly PC feed. Students like that are proof (with or without a filter) of the school's thrilling curriculum, of the tolerant and unprejudiced and multifaceted education on offer.

But Dennis was different. He was no latté-colored hottie from the hip Söder neighborhood, no product of a love affair between a giggly blonde and an exchange student from Africa. He wasn't named after some soul singer and his skin wasn't appropriately light to fit under the rubric of "thrilling." Dennis smacked his food when he ate, asked weird questions in a voice that was too loud, laughed at the wrong things. If Dennis walked up a flight of stairs, he would get so out of breath that for several minutes he could do nothing but rest his palms flat against his thighs, lean forward, scrunch up his shoulders, and wheeze. Maybe he had asthma. But above all he was in crappy shape and lived on trans fats dipped in ketchup. Dennis, surrounded by at least three buddies from the trade program, was always first to enter the cafeteria and always last to leave. And the trade program was not one of the school's bragging points; that department was housed in an annex, set apart from the building where the rest of us had classes. The only reason we knew the name of one of the trade school guys in the first place was that he always had drugs to sell.

Sander has a furrow of concern on his forehead. It's so deep it is visible from the side. He turns to Pancake.

"We will also need to meet for a bit on Sunday afternoon and talk about how to draw the court's attention to the other aspects of Oryema's life."

The prosecutor has made a big deal of how sorry we should all feel for Dennis. How he fled all the way from Africa, all by himself, lived in foster homes, and was threatened with deportation and all that. I think Sander's brow is furrowed because he isn't quite sure how to show the judges that we do feel sorry for Dennis (because we are good people), that we feel sympathy for the fat dead drug dealer, yet still remind them about who he really was (that is, Sebastian's fat drug dealer) without appearing to be prejudiced.

But the fact is, everyone has prejudices about Dennis. Every single politically correct journalist, every single lay judge, all these lawyers, no matter who they represent — their ideas about Dennis are so clear that they might as well have swastikas tattooed on their foreheads. Dennis was not a "friend" and he wasn't "cool" (not even Christer would call him that). Dennis had "difficulty concentrating" (teacherspeak for why his teacher had to pick him up from the bus every morning for him to even make it to class). Dennis's Swedish was a joke, sometimes a pretty funny joke. He never talked to girls without his eyes roving, and his dancing looked like Jazzercise gone wrong. Dennis wasn't even charmingly musical; he probably couldn't have been more tone-deaf if he were actually deaf for real.

Dennis thought that it was fashionable to use pomade, and he would pat his sticky hair as lovingly as he scratched his junk. The girls Dennis hung out with (in the Täby Centrum mall or at Stockholm Central Station) had hair extensions, fake nails, fake eyelashes, and flabby muffin tops that squished over their jeans. They were constantly trying and failing to tug up those jeans to cover their butt cracks. They had incomprehensible tramp stamps and shoulder tattoos, and they wore headache-inducing perfume, chewed gum with their mouths open, and thought french fries were a vegetable. They probably deep-fried hot dogs and Snickers to serve at parties if they hadn't ordered enough kebab-pizzas with béarnaise sauce. Dennis's "sisters" (yes, they called each other "sisters") and "brothers" said "hey man" and "yo man" when they greeted each other. They would make their index fingers and thumbs into pistols and point them at each other for reasons no one could comprehend, and they laughed too loud at pointless jokes. No one imagined Dennis would become a well-spoken, appropriately conservative politician when he grew up.

There is no evidence, technical or otherwise, that links me to Dennis's death. I didn't kill Dennis. Sander will point this out, obviously. He will also do his best to get everyone to understand that I had no reason whatsoever to want to kill Dennis.

Aside from that last night, Dennis never gave me cocaine, hash, or anything to smoke. Sebastian gave me whatever I wanted. I didn't know Dennis and didn't want to; Dennis didn't want to get to know me. If he spoke to Sebastian while I was around, he would stand there tugging at his clothes and trying not to look at my breasts. But he never talked to me. He never talked to "someone else's chick"; he thought "chicks" deserved respect only when they were dating "a dude" you had to show respect to. That last night, when Claes kicked him out, he cried round, waxy tears and dripped clear snot, which he didn't wipe away but just let flow. He was crying because he was going to lose the drugs he'd brought to sell, and, naturally, they didn't belong to him. If Sebastian hadn't killed him several hours later, Dennis's supplier would have been sure to murder him instead.

It would be absurd to claim that I wanted Sebastian to kill Dennis. It would be even more absurd to claim that I needed to convince him to do it.

When the police opened Dennis's locker after the shooting, they found an unloaded handgun. I know Sander wants to make a big fuss about that gun, too. He will never know why Dennis had it, but he will try to use it to make everyone understand that Dennis lived a dangerous life. Almost as dangerous as Sebastian's, or considerably more so, depending on how you look at it.

The journalists claim that we treated Dennis like a pet, but they don't let on that we were hardly the worst. For example, if someone had stuck Dennis in a Ralph Lauren shirt, it would have taken fewer than twenty minutes for the school authorities to demand a search of his locker to find the rest of the stolen goods. And what's more, Dennis earned a ton of money thanks to Sebastian. With every week that passed, Dennis's jeans got more and more expensive, and more and more thick gold chains hid in among the fat rolls on his neck. But no one ever looked at Dennis long enough to notice. Maybe the teachers and the adults at the place where he lived thought his jewelry was fake; maybe they had no idea how expensive his ugly sneakers were. But I think above all they didn't give a shit where he got his money, as long as he wasn't stealing stuff from other students. Because it would only be a few more months before Dennis had to "run away" from the home where he lived to avoid being deported, when his made-up birthday said he was eighteen. And then they would be rid of him and all the problems he caused. Were the teachers upset that Dennis would be deported? Just for pretend. They were actually relieved.

No one believed that Dennis would grow up and get a handle on his behavior. Dennis didn't even know what that meant; he couldn't spell "behavior," and his pay-as-you-go cell phone didn't have autocorrect to help him out.

And the prosecutor and all her journalist buddies can shout themselves hoarse about how no one should have to endure what Dennis did, but not a single one of them pitied him enough to do anything about it while he was alive. Everyone treated him like a doomed man even before he died. At least Sebastian paid him.

I didn't kill Dennis; I didn't even judge him worse than the rest of the world already had. This is what Sander wants to tell the court, I think, but he doesn't know how to go about it.

A day or two ago, prosecutor Lena read aloud some text messages I wrote to Amanda about Dennis. "He's crazy, but he'll probably be dead soon," I said in one of them. A longer one I wrote to Sebastian contained the sentence: "You have to get him out of your life."

"We need a clear way to counter those messages," Sander is saying now. "And I want to do so without touching the other texts. They have nothing to do with each other. That's our main line. Keep them separate."

Sander still hasn't turned to me, only to Ferdinand and Pancake. I assume they usually have a run-through of what happened and what must be done after each day's proceedings, but most of the time they wait until I have gone back to jail. Ferdinand and Pancake seem to think Sander is nagging.

"We shouldn't run into any major problems countering the messages about Dennis. It's perfectly understandable that Maja doesn't want Sebastian to spend time with him," Sander says. Ferdinand nods unenthusiastically. "No one can blame Maja for wanting Dennis out of Sebastian's life."

Pancake shakes his head just as halfheartedly. They've heard this a thousand times. They've had to listen as Sander talks to himself more times than they can count.

I think Sander's right. But no one would admit that if Dennis had been the only one to die, I would never even have been detained. Nor would anyone admit that they would have killed Dennis themselves rather than let him become friends with their children, because they're afraid of seeming racist. But I don't think Dennis felt like our pet. He didn't give a shit how we treated him; he just wanted to earn as much money as he could before he took off.

"I'll need to start with the time line and, in particular, our view of the events that night." Sander is still talking to himself; Ferdinand and Pancake keep pretending to listen. "But when I go through the victims, I'll start with Dennis and Christer. They're the least problematic."

The murder of Christer is part of the general claim that I helped Sebastian do what he did. If people believe that, then I am complicit in Christer's death as well, and if they don't believe that, then I won't be convicted.

Maybe Christer died "by chance." Or maybe any adult who tried to tell Sebastian how to live his life deserved to die. Sander told me that he doesn't want to speculate about what Sebastian did or did not want. The prosecutor doesn't know why Sebastian killed Christer, either. Maybe he was just in the wrong place at the wrong time, or maybe Sebastian didn't care who died — the more the better? The stuff they found in my locker suggests that he wanted to kill a lot more people. Oh wait, sorry. According to the prosecutor, it proves that Sebastian and I wanted to kill half the school.

Earlier in the week, when the prosecutor talked about Samir, I cried. I didn't want to cry, because I knew that was what Pancake wanted me to do, but I couldn't help it. I wanted to say something to make them stop listening to the prosecutor, but because I'm only allowed to speak when it's my turn, I cried instead.

I did not cry when the prosecutor said that even if Sebastian didn't tell me outright, even if I didn't see Claes Fagerman's dead body when I was at his house, I must have had time to figure out that Claes was dead during those eleven minutes, especially considering the texts I sent to Sebastian that night and morning. When she said that Sebastian and I planned that together, and all the rest of it, too, and that we wanted to kill and we wanted to die together, I just looked straight ahead without showing a reaction. I listened as she claimed that even if I didn't realize that Sebastian was serious, even if I was stupid enough not to understand that there were weapons and explosives in the bags he wanted to take to school, I *should* have understood and protested, and since I didn't protest, I am an accessory. And the murders I committed, I did commit them, there is *forensic evidence* that proves it, said the prosecutor, she said *forensic evidence* again and again, she loves those words, her voice got so worked up by them that it almost cracked. But I remained calm.

And when she was talking about Amanda, Ferdinand put her hand on my shoulder. It was light and slender, and it barely brushed me, and I had to bite my own hand so I wouldn't scream.

No one thinks it's a catastrophe that I killed Sebastian. I should have done it sooner, they think. But I killed Amanda, and there's no rationalizing that.

"It was self-defense," Sander will say about the shots I fired.

"Lack of intent." "Self-defense."

He will use a bunch of different words to explain that it was a mistake. I shouldn't be held accountable for it; my actions were meant to ward off a greater danger.

But deep down I know I wasn't trying to defend myself in any conscious, well-reasoned sort of way. I wasn't thinking "help," I wasn't thinking "I have to kill Sebastian or else he'll kill me." It is impossible to explain the terror I felt; it was like something happened to my body while my soul prepared to die.

I have cried several times this week. But not because Pancake wants me to. I don't pretend that crying helps.

When my car from the jail is finally here, Pancake offers to follow me and the security guard down. The journalists are waiting for us when we walk from the elevator to the car in the garage. I'm tired. They take pictures with their giant cameras, that clicking sound: machine guns with silencers. Susse joins us and plants herself in front of me, puts her arm around me. I turn my face toward her neck, she's actually taller than I am, she's almost grotesquely tall, so maybe it looks sweet. Mom-like.

I'm sure Pancake loves that they're taking pictures as I'm being babied. It makes me appear younger and more girlish and sadder. Maybe he even tipped off the press about which way we would exit, where they could stand to take their photos.

"Maja," a journalist calls. "How do you think it went today?"

I don't respond; I let Susse stuff me into the backseat. I sit as far from the cameras as I can. The windows are tinted. But I see Pancake approach the journalists. It's odd that he followed us to the car. Usually the security guard is enough. He and I weren't in the middle of some super-interesting conversation that he didn't want to cut short. And shouldn't he still be in the debriefing with Sander, talking about the situation and, you know, *how it went*? What is Pancake doing here? He must want to reassure himself that I'm behaving. And why would he be concerned with how I'm behaving if he didn't already know that there were journalists in the damp garage?

Pancake won't shut up about how "they" are interested in me. Who I am. It's important that my team "gives me a personality," that I "become a person." My entire defense rests on this, according to Pancake. Who I "am." Sure. As soon as we gained access to the case report, Sander began a million of his own investigations to double-check the conclusions the forensic analysis and the investigation arrived at. But Pancake mostly seems to concentrate on getting "them" to understand me. But it's not entirely clear who "they" are, because I don't think he means the judges. At least not only the judges.

Susse pats my arm. I let her take my hand. Now no one can see me. Yes, the driver's door is cracked, but the photographers don't seem to have noticed. I can hear Pancake talking to the journalists in a low but clear voice.

"We can't talk right now, as I'm sure you understand. It's been a long day." He sounds tired, much more tired than he did in the elevator down to the garage. "Maja is upset. This is difficult for her. She is so young..." There, he said it again. I wonder if the journalists are starting to think it's repetitive. "...It is not common for a girl of her age to be locked up for so long. She has had an exceptionally long and taxing detention period."

I try to fall asleep in the car. I'm tired. That was an accurate perception by the empathetic Pancake. But he is wrong about the other part. Jail isn't excessively difficult. Not that it's a pleasant place to be, because it's not. Not that the food is great, because it isn't, but there's a lot I can avoid while I'm there.

Every day in jail is a cut-and-paste version of the day before, especially since they stopped questioning me all the time. It's such a fucking relief. No surprises. No new people. All the food tastes exactly the same whether it's meatballs, cod, or scrambled eggs. I eat breakfast, lunch, and dinner. One hour in the exercise yard, one hour in the gym (where I only pretend to work out). Class. Ten minutes in the shower. I lie on my bed, I lie on my floor, I use my toilet, I listen to people walking by, I try to read, I listen to music, I sleep more than I ever have in my life. The only visitor I see is Sander. But I'll probably get to spend this weekend on my own. No one will talk to me, surprise me, make me think.

We didn't have time to begin presenting our case today, but when the weekend is over, it will be time for my side of the story, about Sebastian and me, the love and the hate, and how I betrayed him.

SEBASTIAN AND ME

17.

We became a couple the summer before the murders, Sebastian and me. Stockholm was stuck in such an awful heat wave that three weeks in, people weren't even talking about the weather anymore. They complained about broken air conditioners, ice that tasted like old socks, and mealy ice cream at 7-Eleven, but not about the heat — it had become a fact of life. No one could imagine that the weather would ever change.

I was working the last shift of my summer job, night receptionist at a hotel downtown, when Sebastian showed up. I had spent three weeks, from ten at night to seven in the morning, answering the phone, taking reservations, canceling reservations, calling in extra staff for breakfast and cleaning, listening to drunk Finns ("Where are the nice girls?") as they asked whether I could bring some alcohol up to their rooms ("Be a nice girl, will you, hee hee"). There was a panic button under the counter, but I never needed to use it. Sometimes someone would puke all over themselves, usually in their room, but I didn't have to worry about that either. One time some guy sliced up his wrists; he sent the police a tweet about it well before he got going.

On the way to work, I ran into tired tourists. They were on their way to or from cheap restaurants: pop-eyed parents with kids in front-facing strollers or sluggish Germans in sandals, carrying wrinkled maps. It wasn't a stressful job, it wasn't difficult, it paid pretty well, and it gave me "experience" (Dad's word). Dad was "for" my having a summer job; he thought there was a sweet-smelling cloud of Ingvar Kamprad and Young Entrepreneurs around it. Mom wanted me to take a taxi home each morning, but Dad couldn't write it off so she let it go.

Sebastian had been out at one of the clubs nearby, and he came in to use the bathroom. I was working by myself that night; my coworker had gone home early, something about her son's birthday.

We weren't allowed to let anyone but our guests use the bathroom, but I never would have said no to Sebastian. I never found out how he knew that I would be working there that night, I didn't even know he knew who I was. It had been a long time since we went to the same preschool. Sebastian was one year older than me; if he hadn't had to repeat senior year, he would have already graduated. But now we were about to be in the same class. I knew that. Everybody knew that Sebastian had to repeat final year. And then he stepped into the lobby of the very hotel where I worked.

"Maja," he said in his confident voice; he didn't seem at all surprised to see me, and my heart skipped a beat, just like when we were in preschool. He stayed until it was time for me to go home. We took a walk, the city was empty and cooler than the morning before; we walked alongside each other through Humlegården, up Engelbrektsgatan to the Östra Station. From there we took the train to Ösby, in Djursholm. He sat next to me on the train, and when we got to the university he lay down with his head in my lap and fell asleep with no further comment. When the train pulled in at our station, I stroked his forehead to wake him up and he looked at me as he woke. Then he raised his hand and ran his thumb across my lower lip. That was all.

That same afternoon I left for vacation with Mom, Dad, and Lina. Mom had decided that we would do a road trip through Europe, but first we flew to Geneva, where we rented a car to transport us between various boutique hotels that Mom had picked out on a site that promised "secret" and "unique" experiences.

Dad drove. Dad always drove when both he and Mom were in the car (except when they'd been to a party). Mile after mile, we changed the radio station when it began to crackle. We listened to the same music in country after country; the DJs all sounded the same, the same cheerful laughter and friendly *shh* sounds ("shlabablasha Rihanna, shushushu Ariana Grande!"). The DJs spoke different languages, of course, and in Italy they played more Italian songs, and in France there were more French ones, but on the whole it sounded the same all over, and anyway I felt like I was in some sort of shock. Sebastian had exploded inside my head. I was in the wrong place with the wrong people, sitting beside Lina and her barf bag in the backseat, searching. I didn't give a shit that Mom and Dad complained about my roaming fees, I searched everywhere, surfed myself crazy, but I couldn't find anything about where he was, and I didn't dare to ask anyone he knew or add him somewhere he hadn't already added me. So I sat there in the car getting more and more desperate and panicky because the opportunity had slipped out of my hands, Sebastian had lain in my lap, he had looked at me and then I left. How dumb can you get?

We were nine days into our vacation, in Villefranche-sur-Mer outside Nice, when he called. My phone vibrated in my sweaty hand; he had a blocked number and picked me up on a Vespa. Dad looked surprised; Mom seemed almost shocked. Sebastian met all of us in the lobby of our hotel and invited Mom and Dad "and Lina of course" (how did he know her name?) to dinner "on the boat" that evening. His dad's "boat" was anchored outside the harbor in Nice, and I could see Mom tap-dancing in place because she didn't know how she would manage to buy a new dress in time and Dad puffed up to twice his normal size because Sebastian's dad was a great deal more than just "a potential client." Claes Fagerman was potentially a new life.

Sebastian pretended not to notice any of this. He just looked at me.

Amanda had told Sebastian where we were, and Sebastian had decided to come down that same morning. It was all so unbelievable as to be on the verge of surreal. I left with him, on the back of his Vespa. I put my arms around his waist and it was all narrow coastal roads and it was all steep and warm and I slept with him twice in his oval double bed on the boat (under a white sheet) before Mom, Dad, and Lina arrived to eat dinner with us and Sebastian's dad up on deck, right under a million stars.

The boat was almost sixty meters long. The deck was as smooth as silk, the color of syrup, everything was brass fittings and silver details, gold and white marble. The sun had already gone down when the first course was served. We were sitting on the uppermost deck, which was illuminated from below, along the waterline, and around the deck; the velvety black night soaked into our skin and we had more waiters than I could keep track of and Mom and Dad looked at me more often than they usually did. Lina wanted to sit on my lap.

"I had given up hope of seeing Sebastian down here," Sebastian's dad told my parents with a wide grin. "I expect it's thanks to Maja that he decided to honor us with his presence."

I could hardly stop looking at Claes Fagerman that first night. He was a fantastic storyteller, a magical entertainer, and he was even more luminous than he looked in photographs. Mom giggled, as delighted as a little bird. She had bought a new dress and was wearing something in her hair that looked like a laurel wreath made of fake gold leaf. Naturally, it was real, otherwise she never would have dared to wear something that looked so cheap.

Sebastian put his arm around me, and Claes Fagerman told stories about people I'd never heard of. My dad's laughter became more and more manic. Most of the time,

Sebastian's dad was good at getting people to relax; he was never afraid of those gaps that ensue when people who don't know each other have to spend time together; he didn't mind silence or throat clearing or boring conversations. He just smiled and kept talking and his jokes made people laugh in relief. That first evening I didn't see through all of it, I didn't suspect what sort of man he truly was. Mom got so tipsy that she ate her dessert and Lina fell asleep on the sofa; one of the staff covered her with a thin blanket even though the air was gentle and warm.

Once Claes said to me, "I'm rich, you know," and he didn't say it to brag but to explain where he was coming from. He was rich in a way that made it like his nationality. He lived in a country all his own. It had nothing to do with geography. Because the truly wealthy Swedes are more like the truly rich Japanese or Italians or Arabs than they are like any other Swedes. And Dad admired this, because Claes Fagerman had found his way to this nationality all by himself, no inheritance or privilege, at least not in an estate-in-Sörmland-forests-in-Norrland-shipyard-in-Gothenburg-and-member-of-the-king's-hunting-party sort of way.

Dad hated the "trust fund babies" and their "pointless hobby investments." He sometimes came home from work and told us about their projects. "If you want risk capital to develop an app that tells you what a liter of milk costs, there are dozens of twenty-year-olds with a run-down estate, an ancient title, and a new investment firm who think that the average Joe needs an app to figure that out, because Daddy's boys never had to learn that the price is posted right there on the grocery shelf." What's more, the trust fund idiots were not "rich for real," and this particular attribute was the only thing they had managed to do on their own: to not become rich for real.

"It's just pathetic," Mom would respond. (Dad's word; she uses them when she talks to him.) "Pathetic."

And Mom, in turn, might tell us that a colleague or friend had stopped working. "I suppose her husband will buy her a home-décor boutique," she would say, because just as Dad disliked people who inherited money, Mom hated women her own age who did what she dreamed of: giving up.

Mom is a corporate lawyer for a listed company and earns about half as much as Dad does. She cut back on hours when Lina was born so as not to "have a breakdown," but she didn't want to quit. She pretends that everything is fine and that she still has too much to do. No one believes her, least of all Dad.

"They ought to blow all their money on the lottery instead," Dad would continue. "Better odds of turning a profit." (He always keeps talking about his own stuff even if Mom is talking about something else; their best discussions always follow this pattern.)

But faced with Claes Fagerman, both Mom and Dad turned into starry-eyed boy band groupies. For months after Sebastian and I got together, Dad would talk about Claes Fagerman every time he got me alone. He talked about how Claes Fagerman had transformed the crisis-ridden group he'd inherited into "one of Sweden's three greatest fortunes." He succeeded because he "wasn't satisfied with razing forests and panning for gold in some Norrland stream"; instead he began to invest in high-tech branches (like cables and microchips, I never really felt like paying much attention). Dad looked up to Claes Fagerman so much that he couldn't even manage to be jealous.

"The only thing about Claes Fagerman that isn't unique," Dad told me once, "is that he married a former third-place Miss Sweden. Fagerman is one of the greatest men Sweden has ever had. He will go down in history."

And on that first night on the boat, I also liked Claes. He made me feel like he thought I was special. When he made jokes, I felt funny solely because I laughed in the right spot. When he was talking about Sebastian's brother, Lukas, what he did at Harvard, and how smart he was, I thought it was cute that he was so proud. When he said it had "always been obvious that Lukas would go far," I felt like I'd been initiated into some private family secret, stuff Claes only told a couple of people. I thought that a dad who bragged about his older son must also be proud of his younger son. I didn't see that his love for his sons was conditional, that one had to perform to avoid being despised by Claes Fagerman.

Sebastian and I excused ourselves around midnight.

"We were thinking of having a night swim."

"A walk on the beach."

Mom took my face in both hands as if she thought I was a virgin and this was my wedding night, and Dad looked at me with something that actually resembled pride.

"My little girl," Mom probably said.

"Behave yourself," Dad might have said. And then he grinned at Sebastian and said, "Don't do anything I would do," because my dad is always saying stuff like that.

"If only I could understand what you see in him," said Claes Fagerman. "You should know he takes after his mother." And we laughed, all of us, even me because this was before I understood that Claes was never joking when he said cruel things to Sebastian.

Aside from that comment, we didn't talk about the third-place Miss Sweden, Sebastian's mom. Not that night, and hardly any other time after that. She hadn't been replaced by a younger version of herself; she was just gone. Or at least relocated, not present, not important. Had she left Claes, or had he kicked her out? I don't think I ever found out. And compared to Claes Fagerman, she was so unimportant that I never thought about her, not even about the fact that she was absent.

Before Sebastian and I got together, I had had four boyfriends. The first was Nils. We were twelve years old, almost thirteen, and we became an item in the dark at a party his twin sister had invited me to. Christina Aguilera was on the stereo and he kissed me fast and hard and we fell onto a sofa and made out until I had swollen lips and soaked underpants. He touched my breasts, and that was the best feeling I'd ever had, but we never slept together, it never even occurred to us. Three weeks later it was over, and it took me another two months before I figured it out because it was summer vacation, and I spent nine weeks looking at his picture and writing postcards ("I'm at Grandma and Grandpa's out in the country, it's raining and I watched *The Evil Dead*"). I didn't get any postcards from him. When school started up again he wouldn't say hi to me and that was that.

I got my second real boyfriend about six months later. He was a year older than me (more than fourteen and a half!) and he wrote on the timetable at the bus stop next to the school that he thought I was pretty. It took somewhere between six and eight minutes for that piece of gossip to reach me, and I was smart enough to realize that this was the biggest deal of my life so far. Almost-fifteen-year-old Anton had plump lips and curly blond hair. We were together for seven weeks, so long that we were practically considered married. But one Friday evening, at a class party at Friberga School, he got drunk off a mishmash of liquor he'd poured into an old shampoo bottle and declared, "You're too young, Maja. We have to go our separate ways" (yes indeed, his words). I was ashamed, in a backward sort of way, but I wasn't really upset. Nothing about that relationship was particularly interesting: not Anton, not his kisses, which made the bottom half of my face wet, and not this whole let's-be-a-couple thing.

After that came a period in which I only had crushes on much older guys. They had no clue who I was, either because we had never actually met or because the only times we had met were when I saw the backs of their necks six rows ahead of me on the bus. I don't remember a single one of their names. And right after I turned fifteen, I met Markus.

Markus was sixteen. He smoked hash, played bass, and wrote poetry, and his mom had posed for Richard Avedon. He was in high school in the city, at Östra Real, and everyone, absolutely everyone, knew who he was, and when Amanda and I stepped through the door of a maisonette on a fancy street near Karlaplan, Markus and his band were upstairs playing unrecognizable covers of songs. The party had been going strong for several hours, and each of us received a piece of sticky chocolate cake and a creamy drink that tasted like vanilla from a guy with pockmarks and purple nail polish. I danced myself sweaty in a living room that had been emptied of furniture and didn't think even once about how ridiculous it looks when people throw their hands up in the air and shake their heads. Then the power went out and the fire department came and explained that the power was out all over the Östermalm neighborhood; "there's a reason you need a permit to hold a concert." Two uniformed police officers stepped in after the fire department and around then I realized that I was high for the first time in my life. Amanda and I locked ourselves into one of the bathrooms and tried not to laugh ourselves to death. Whether it was the cake or the vanilla drink or both of them that had made us high, we had no idea. We sat there until the police left and Markus knocked on the door. He was naked, carrying a candelabra with five lit candles. He drew a bath, and when he asked, I took off my clothes and bathed with him while Amanda fell asleep on a towel on the tile floor.

Markus had long bangs that kept him from having to look anyone in the eye, and one afternoon later that same week he took my virginity on top of his dad's smocked bedspread. It wasn't bad, it didn't hurt, and I was incredibly relieved that he didn't notice I'd never done it before. When I called him (I called his home phone since he never answered his cell and because I believed him when he said he "opted not to use cell phones"), he pretended he wasn't there. I could tell by his mom's voice how irritated it made her, but I kept calling both his cell and his landline; it didn't matter that I realized he didn't like me, I just couldn't help it. Markus and I slept together four times at various parties (it usually started with taking a bath together; he always took a bath at parties), and I tried to pretend that when he said he loved my breasts it meant he loved me. The last time we slept together was on top of another bedspread (we never had sex under sheets), it was only just before ten o'clock at night, and he turned away as I used my own T-shirt to wipe off my stomach and then he told me that he was with Terese, Tessie for short. And therefore we could not "keep going like this."

Two and a half hours later that same night I met the girl with the dog name as she and Markus came out of the bathroom. Cocker spaniel Tessie was wearing a bathrobe; Markus was naked again. And I hadn't been upset until that point, but now I hid it, I just left.

With the next guy, I was the one who broke it off. His name was Oliver and he said he loved me (not just my breasts) after just four days. When I responded that I liked him, that he was "sweet" but that we weren't "right for each other" (I had become a pro, knew all there was to know about love, knew exactly what to say), he started calling me every day even when he wasn't drunk, and texting me every evening to "say good night."

We slept together for a few months after it was over, but then Sebastian showed up in my hotel lobby and none of what I'd experienced before had anything in common with Sebastian. It was all brand-new. It's not just that I got to start over. Sebastian was my beginning.

I can't remember asking my parents if it was okay if I traveled with Sebastian instead of continuing on through Europe with them, but I must have asked because they brought a new suitcase to dinner, probably the most expensive my mom could find, with all of my stuff in it.

On the first morning, I woke before Sebastian; I always have trouble sleeping in new places. Sebastian was out cold and I didn't want to wake him. When I came up on deck, Claes was sitting there eating breakfast with a folded Swedish newspaper in one hand.

"Come have a seat," he urged. "What would you like for breakfast?" he asked, without looking up from the paper.

Once I had finished my coffee and picked at my croissant (I thought it was a logical breakfast on a boat in the Mediterranean), Claes put down his paper and gave me a friendly look. I don't remember exactly what he asked, whether he even had any questions, but we talked and I felt my anxiety lift. He stayed until Sebastian showed up and sat down next to me in his underwear and a snow-white T-shirt, his hair unbrushed. At that point Claes stood up, took the newspaper, and left. They didn't say good morning to each other.

There were seventeen days left before school would start and Sebastian and I would become classmates. We stayed on Claes's yacht for fifteen days and as many nights. The very next morning we sailed down toward the Italian coast. We were on our way to Capri and it was nothing but azure sea and cool breezes and the same warm nights every night. Sometimes we would stop in the middle of the water and lower a small motorboat from the deck — from there we could dive or snorkel or water-ski. Once we were picked up by a helicopter (it landed on the deck) and taken to a Formula 1, where we got to stand right next to the finish line and smile at each other amid the roaring engines. I never learned the names of everyone on the boat, even though I tried. Sandro (the captain) let me ask a thousand questions about the places we passed, and the chef, Luigi, learned that I liked *citron pressé* and Greek yogurt, melon and croissants for breakfast and chicken or feta salad for lunch, and that I took my coffee black. In the spa, which was on the same deck as the movie theater and right off the gym, they played silvery plink-plonk music and a woman (Zoe) gave me manicures and pedicures and massaged me with an oil that smelled like toothpaste and vanilla pods. She padded around in bare feet, and I never saw her anywhere but in the spa.

I loved that boat, I loved everyone who worked there, they all seemed happy when I saw them and I was fascinated by how quickly I got used to it all, how natural it felt to stay there and just let the days go by. In the evenings we would eat with Claes. It seemed important to him that we were there even though he hardly ever ate more than just the entrée with us. He would ask me questions, four or five of them, and then he would withdraw, but for that hour he sat with us I let his attention warm us. He listened to us when we spoke, nodding; once in a while he was in an extra-good mood and then he would talk to us about topics he considered important.

One time, it must have been the fifth or sixth night, Sebastian's dad took us to a restaurant. He was going to have dinner with a business acquaintance and he wanted us to come along. We didn't ask why, but I assumed we would help make their meeting more relaxed and informal.

The restaurant was on a ledge up in a mountain village, not far from Bonifacio. The plan was to walk the last little bit; all the colors had vanished in the darkness and a truck was parked by the harbor and a tarp was flapping on a container, rising and sinking in the wind. It was still warm out, even though the sun had gone down, and that particular area smelled like garbage. The business acquaintance, an Italian, spoke English through his nose with an accent so thick you could have spread it on bread. He was already drunk.

"Help me," the Italian said to Sebastian, holding a stubby-fingered hand out to him. Sebastian let go of my hand and took the man by the arm. When we entered the little village, I had a hard time walking on the cobblestones in my shoes and didn't mind that we were walking so slowly. The old man swore and sweated, leaning unabashedly against Sebastian and pausing every twenty meters to catch his breath. When we finally found ourselves outside the restaurant, the man planted a wet kiss on Sebastian's cheek, remarkably close to his mouth. Sebastian gave a start and his dad pulled open the restaurant door. Claes Fagerman turned to the Italian and gestured at him to go first.

"I never would have made it up here if not for you, Sebastian," the Italian said, letting go of Sebastian's arm at last.

"It's nice to know he can be of use," said Claes. "That's news to us all."

I didn't understand why he was angry, but he sure was. Furious. Everything I had learned to associate with Claes Fagerman was turned on its head. He hadn't initiated a single conversation since we'd left the boat; if I said anything, he didn't hear me — he looked away, turned aside, walked ahead, hardly responding if spoken to. My stomach was in knots, and Sebastian wouldn't look at anything, least of all me. The Italian, however, seemed completely unfazed.

We were given a window table. The restaurant was so close to the edge of the cliff that it seemed to be floating above the sea. The lights of the boats were visible down in the harbor, and a lighthouse was pulsing at the entrance to the bay, where our yacht was anchored. Sebastian's dad ordered for all of us without asking what we wanted to eat. The Italian laughed so loudly that the guests on the other side of the restaurant turned around, and we listened, appalled, as he changed Claes's order: a different appetizer, and certainly not that entrée, there was something about Corsicans and octopus, everyone knew that, absolutely everyone, and Sebastian's dad didn't say anything, just nodded almost imperceptibly at the waiter, and when the wine list arrived he let the Italian take it and order what he wanted. But Claes didn't drink any of the wine and he didn't even taste his appetizer.

As we waited for the main course, I had to use the bathroom. When I returned, the Italian had moved to my chair. He waved at me to sit in his old spot instead. Sebastian didn't protest. At some point, Sebastian tried to stand, maybe to come over to me.

"Sit down, for Christ's sake," Claes said to Sebastian in Swedish. "Do you think you could manage such a feat? To sit down and shut your mouth?"

Sebastian sat down. He didn't look at me. But he smiled, mechanically and broadly, without saying anything.

When the Italian wasn't trying to get Sebastian to sing "Swedish songs," he was talking business. He had a firm to sell; I understood that much. And while he grew more and more exuberant, the rest of us grew quieter. I was wondering if the Italian was going to drink his way from merely exhilarated to straight up disorderly when Sebastian's dad made a phone call, spoke briefly, and handed the phone to the Italian. When he hung up, Claes raised his glass and allowed the Italian to graze it with his own. The relief I felt was so palpable that it nearly made me feel nauseous.

We ate our way through four courses, cheese, two desserts, and coffee with a silver tray of chocolate pralines, mini-meringues, and marmalade candies before it was time to head home. Somehow Sebastian's dad had managed to get a wheelchair brought up to the restaurant, and the Italian fell asleep in it as one of the men from the Fagermans' boat rolled him back down to the harbor. Just before they got the wheelchair up on deck, he awoke, heaved himself up, and declared that he was going to take a stroll ("I am making a walk!"). Sebastian and I went to bed.

Around four o'clock, voices on the foredeck woke me. When I sat up in bed, Sebastian pulled me back down. "Just stay here," was all he said. "That has nothing to do with us."

We ate breakfast alone.

"Your father took off," one of the white-clad staff, whose name I didn't know yet, informed us. Sebastian just nodded. He didn't look surprised. "He said you can take his room. We will be done cleaning it soon."

We were sunning ourselves when the Italian came up on deck. His face was black and blue and his right arm was in a sling. It seemed like it was in a cast. He stood three meters away and didn't come any closer.

"Oh my God," I managed. I stood up. "What happened?"

The Italian just shook his head.

"Don't go for a walk on the beach late at night," he said with a crooked smile. Then he turned to Sebastian to ask, "Is your father here?"

Sebastian pulled me back down onto the deck chair.

"No," he said, his eyes closed.

"Could you..." the Italian began.

"No," said Sebastian.

The Italian left later that day and we moved into Sebastian's dad's suite. Now we had two bathrooms instead of one. And an even better view, out the front, across the sea; I assumed it was the same view the captain had. You could open the roof above the bathtub in one of the bathrooms, and we ate dinner there, alone, that evening.

"Did your dad beat up that Italian guy?" I asked later that night as we lay in the outdoor pool on deck. "Because he was flirting with you?"

Sebastian wasn't angry. "No," was all he said. "Of course he didn't."

I laughed in relief, trying to pretend it had been a joke. But Sebastian didn't laugh. He put both arms up and leaned against the edge of the pool, his eyes closed to the black sky.

"I asked Dad once. When Mom disappeared. What he had done to her, why she...how he had...to get her to move out..." He stopped talking.

"What did he say?"

"Dad said...'Our family doesn't have to take out the trash. We have people to do that for us.'"

I wanted to ask what he meant. What was he saying? Had Sebastian's mom been kicked out, had the Italian been beaten up, by someone who worked for Claes? But I lost my train of thought. Sebastian was crying. He wasn't sobbing, his nose wasn't running, but he was crying. And I didn't know what to say. I took his face in my hands and kissed him. Harder and harder, I kissed him for a long time, longer than I ever had before, and he kissed me back until I didn't want anything but for him to enter me. And when he did I came almost immediately, I always came faster than he did, more times than he did, more intensely.

Nine days later, we flew home from Naples; we were the only ones on the plane. I had heard Sebastian talking to his dad on the phone the night before. Claes felt there was no reason for us to take the company plane, that we could travel on a commercial flight, and yet the jet was there waiting for us when we arrived at the airport. The car drove us all the way up to the ramp. We didn't have to go through any security.

The boat traveled on without us. It sailed year-round with a full crew. They were counting on leaving the Mediterranean one week later. I don't think it struck me, the surreality of it all, that world of postcard-blue and sparkling sunshine and plink-plonk manicures, until we turned off the highway at the Djursholm exit and everything looked the same as when I had left a month earlier. Exactly the same, even though everything had changed.

We landed at Bromma airport. There was another car waiting there, out on the tarmac. One of the crew carried our suitcases to the car. Sebastian seemed tired, and I don't think I had expected us to still be an item when school started. For some reason, it was hard for me to believe that he wanted me to be part of his everyday life, to the extent that he had an everyday life. It just seemed natural that this was a summer fling — a parenthetical aside for him, the best weeks of my life. The car dropped me off at home and I didn't know how to say goodbye, how to thank him for everything, but Sebastian followed me inside and shook hands with Dad (Dad's face took on that expression that adults get when they're supposed to pretend they're being nonchalant but are about to piss themselves with excitement). He kissed me on the cheek and said, "See you tomorrow," and then he was gone.

The next morning was the first day of school. Sebastian sent a text at seven thirty (but not a single one the evening or night before) and asked me to meet him at the intersection down the street from my house. He picked me up there, and I thought it was so he could break up with me before school started. About halfway there I started crying, maybe because I wanted to get it over with — I would have to cry when he ended it, so I might as well do it right away. When he noticed that I was crying, he pulled onto the shoulder, turned the car off, moved my seat back, and straddled me. He stuck his hands under my shirt and stroked my back and kissed me, then kissed me deeper, touched me, pulled me closer. I could feel how hard he was and I was surprised how relieved I felt, how afraid I had been that he wouldn't want to be with me anymore.

We walked hand in hand from the parking lot to the school, and it felt just like a movie about high school where the most popular guy suddenly shows up with the ugly chick with glasses and weird hair, after she has gotten a makeover and turns out to be a hottie. Not that I had been a dork before, and not that Sebastian was some sort of perma-smiling jock with a side part, but everything about our entrance felt like it had somehow been washed in pastels.

Amanda already knew we were together, of course. She met us by the smoking area, where she gave me a hug and then linked her hands behind Sebastian's neck. She dangled there like a Christmas ornament for a moment before Sebastian wiggled his way out of her noose and we walked into the school.

There was something Sebastian had to take care of before first period, so we went our separate ways by the lockers. When he said goodbye to me, he kissed my cheek again and it felt even more like that movie. Amanda rolled her eyes, just like her character would have done (she didn't have a cheerleader outfit, but otherwise everything was perfect). She was about to go to pieces, she was so pleased that she was suddenly going to have a central role in Sebastian's life. That Sebastian was going to be a part of our lives from now on. The people he had hung out with the year before had moved on, to college, to an internship at their dads' companies, or to study language in the U.S. Now it was our turn. And Amanda was overjoyed. But she didn't say so, of course — she just spouted something about how Sebastian and I should "get a room!" and I tipped my head back and laughed, at the perfect volume, all according to the script.

There are several pictures of me and Sebastian from our Mediterranean trip. I look happy, unproblematically content, a person who screech-laughs when her boyfriend splashes her with water before she's gone all the way in. I'm smiling and my eyes are luminous. I look happy, despite the fact that now, later on, I have trouble remembering that I felt happy. Maybe good fortune is like misfortune in the sense that it takes a while for realization to set in. At first you feel nothing. The feelings come later, perhaps not until the reason for them is long gone.

Only now, much later, do I realize that Sebastian never looked happy. Not even in those very first photos.

18.

But for the rest of us, the first few weeks of school were wonderful. And the first day was the best of all. Amanda wasn't the only one who thought having Fagerman's younger son join our class was the most awesome thing that had ever happened to her; all our classmates had been wondering and talking and hoping since the previous semester, when the rumors that he would have to repeat senior year started. Now it had become a reality and I was in the center of all the action.

When it was time for first period to begin, Sebastian was still off somewhere. Amanda and I went to class on our own and sat in our usual places. Christer didn't ask what we'd done over summer break, of course he didn't. I'm sure it said somewhere in the lesson plans or the school rules that you couldn't ask those sorts of questions, you must absolutely not allow the kids to write essays about "My Summer Vacation," because that might make those who couldn't afford to travel "feel left out." According to the PTO parents, "feeling left out" ("different") is the worst thing that can happen to a person — that, and soda machines in the school cafeteria. And they love senseless platitudes as long as they make the organization appear compassionate. As if it would help if the teachers avoided asking that particular question. We knew exactly where everyone else had been, or at least what they hadn't done.

Christer did his best to find another topic of discussion. He didn't comment on Amanda's '80s tan, or Alice's charter-vacation braids ("Ohmigooood, Mom made me get them, I mean, I'm totally taking them out tonight, I mean, Goooood..."), or Jakob's broken arm (he broke it water-skiing, everyone knew that, probably even Christer). And he definitely didn't comment on the fact that Sofia appeared to have lost twenty kilos since school ended two months earlier (although it did take a few seconds for him to wipe the shock from his face). Instead he talked about absolutely anything else.

Christer wondered if we had read "any good books." Samir was the only one of the guys to respond. He sat with his back extra straight and rattled off three titles; Christer tried to look like he knew exactly what books those were but he didn't ask any follow-up questions so I assume he had no idea.

"You only read three books this summer?" I asked.

And Samir smiled, but only with one corner of his mouth, the way he usually did when I said stuff like that to him, and then he stuck his hand into his thick hair. Sometimes when he was pondering something he would wind a lock around his index finger. Around and around and around, until it looked like he'd cut off circulation. I smiled back. Samir and I had been carrying on like this ever since our first year at Djursholm. We squabbled, discussed, argued. We each pretended we never thought the other was right or had said something funny. It felt nice that this didn't have to change just because of summer vacation.

"Certainly not," he said. "I was only mentioning the three best ones. So that there would be enough time left over for your..." He hesitated.

I helped him out. "I didn't read any horse books, no comics about having your period..."

"But you loved that one about the teenagers who are dying of cancer and fall in love with each other?"

Amanda jumped as though she'd gotten a shock. "Yes!" she said happily. "It's *so* sad, I've never cried that much before in my whole life."

Samir looked at me. We were thinking the same thing: Amanda hadn't read the book; she had only seen the movie. But we didn't say anything. And then Sebastian stepped into the classroom. Did we react to the fact that he was late on the first day of school? Maybe. Just a few weeks later we would react if he showed up on time.

He said a perfunctory "Sorry."

Christer gave a slight nod.

Sebastian sat down beside me; he didn't even have to ask Amanda to move to another desk. And as she took the two steps to the closest empty spot, she rolled her eyes and played an imaginary violin.

I could feel my classmates catching on one by one, as clearly as if a colored gas were filtering among the desks.

From the first row, where I was sitting on one side, Samir on the other, to the last row, where Mela was sitting with her pierced nose and black nail polish. Everyone realized that we were together, and that atmosphere that surrounded Sebastian, the mixture of admiration and curiosity (and feigned I-don't-really-care-about-him expressions) spread, but it was the first time it had been about me, or at least partly about me.

I once read about an actor who moved every year during her childhood. She said that each time she started in a new school she found the same collection of types: the popular kid (pretty mean), the popular kid's best friend (even meaner), the smart kid, the kid who was worst at gym, and the kid without any friends. There was like a given number of roles to be played in each class, and all she had to do when she moved to a new school was figure out which role was open, which one she would play in the year ahead.

I had always played the same role: good student, not the most popular but close, not a victim of bullying, not a bully, in the coolest kid's crowd, and never *dating* the coolest kid. It had never crossed my mind that I could take on a new role, but I'd done it. And it made even Sofia's *Biggest Loser* makeover pale in comparison.

Sebastian took my hand under the desk and I felt my face go hot.

Christer had posed another question, but I'd missed what it was. He looked at me, waiting for a response. I turned to Samir. Maybe he could help me out with a sarcastic comment; those always clued me in to what was going on and what I should say. But he wasn't looking at me. His left arm was crooked on the desk the way he always held it when he was writing, staring down at his notebook. No one but Samir took notes on the first day of school. His hand was gripping the pen, a thick black one, a real fountain pen. His knuckles were white. But he wasn't writing anything.

I had to turn to Christer. "Sorry," I said. "I didn't hear..."

Christer laughed. He was probably relieved that he was finally in the know about the most important news of the summer, relieved he wouldn't have to ask to find out.

"Sebastian," he said instead, "did you read anything good this summer?"

Samir wasn't the only one who laughed, but he's the only one I heard. It didn't sound like he thought it was particularly funny.

19.

No, Samir wasn't happy that Sebastian had joined our class. Sebastian and Samir didn't get along, and this became obvious as soon as Christer asked us to introduce ourselves to Sebastian since he was new to the class. Sebastian looked like he didn't already know Samir's name. Maybe this was revenge for Samir's loud laughter, but it was also possible he actually had no idea. But when Samir pretended he didn't know who Sebastian was it only made him look stupid, because absolutely everyone in our school knew about Sebastian.

Samir was the only one who was upset; the rest of us were thrilled. Even the teachers seemed happy to have Sebastian there. If anyone had asked Christer, during those first few days of school, he would have said something along the lines of "Sebastian deserves a second chance." During the first two weeks, they let Sebastian arrive late, show up whenever he felt like it, leave in the middle of the class period; the teachers made no comment. When he didn't have his stuff with him (which was always), they just said, "You may look on with Maja," or else he would be allowed to borrow the teacher's computer.

Christer never would have admitted that he knew Sebastian would never graduate. *Everyone deserves a second chance.* Samir, though, he never even gave Sebastian a first chance.

It took exactly nine days before Sebastian organized the first party of the semester. Claes was off traveling, and Sebastian's brother, Lukas, had gone back to Boston. Amanda and I were the first ones there. I think I'd said we could help, but even from the driveway it became obvious that this was not that kind of party. Sebastian never needed "help" with his parties.

"Don't take it personally! I mean, people can totally eat whatever they want. But I just can't bear to."

Amanda hadn't started in on her halloumi burger; she was just holding it between her index finger and her thumb, inspecting it from one side to the other, carefully, to try to find the part with the fewest calories. She eyed my meat as if it were a trampled, antibiotic-ridden sow in a cramped cement stall. I wiped some sauce from the corner of my mouth, nodded, and swallowed.

The sun was going down, and most people had already eaten. There were no more than three hamburgers on the grill and the hired grill master was halfheartedly pressing on the lumps of meat, causing grease to drip onto the coals. Tiny, furious flames spit forth and died back down. A waiter in an American flag Speedo was walking barefoot down the soft lawn with a tray of newspaper-print cones full of french fries. Sebastian had vanished into the house along with a half dozen of the guys who always followed him if he let them.

Amanda and I sat on the stone-paved terrace and looked down at the water.

"Where's Sibbe?" she wondered. She was the only one who called Sebastian that.

I shrugged.

"Is Labbe here yet?"

I shrugged again. Just as Sebastian joined our class, Labbe had left. He didn't have to repeat a year, but he ended up having to switch schools. Labbe was the only one of us who knew Sebastian from before, which was probably why Amanda had gotten it into her head that he would be her new boyfriend. But Sebastian didn't have any best friends, he had a swarm of bees. And, since a few days back, that stray dog Dennis chasing at his heels.

Amanda sighed and put down her half-eaten burger. I had already finished mine, and I was working through my fries. I held the cone out to Amanda. She shook her head without even looking at it. The water below us was gleaming a leaden gray. The lanterns at the bathhouse illuminated the dock. I could see a pair of dark silhouettes on the foredeck of one of the two boats Claes Fagerman had moored there. A couple was making out in the basket swing that was hanging from one of the four trees in the yard. A half dozen girls were sitting on one of the patios, at a table with a mosaic top and mismatched cast iron chairs. They were smoking, drinking white wine, and taking turns showing each other their phone screens. Sebastian came up beside me, took my hand, pulled me up, and put his arm around me.

"Shit, what a boring party," he complained.

Then he ran out onto the dock and down into the water, pulling off his clothes as he went. I ran after him, quickly stripping off everything but my underwear, and jumped in, too. We swam fast. The water wasn't very warm anymore, but when he slid up next to me he had an erection. I spread my legs and placed them around his hips and with all of his guests still on land he entered me. I didn't even have to take off my panties, I just let him pull them aside under the water. I don't know if he finished, but when he stopped we went back ashore. Sebastian was so cold his lips had turned blue; his teeth were chattering. Amanda had found bathrobes and handed them to us as we climbed the ladder. Sebastian took me by the hand and we ran up to the sauna.

"This party is dead," he said.

I pulled the bathrobe tighter around myself even though it was too warm and sat down closest to the door. Samir and Dennis were sitting on the top bench. Dennis was startled when Sebastian spoke, as if it were his fault the party wasn't living up to Sebastian's expectations.

When Sebastian saw Samir, he laughed; he was surprised. And he wasn't the only one. I never thought Samir would show up there. And it was weird to see him with Dennis. They didn't know each other, did they?

Sebastian dropped his robe on the floor and stood there naked, pouring water on the unit, letting the steam rise to the ceiling before he sat down, but a few minutes later he left, still naked.

"What a fucking drag. This party sucks." Dennis followed him. These days he always walked half a step behind Sebastian, his eyes on his back; I didn't get him. Dennis wheeled around above, in front of, right next to Sebastian, in mysterious circles, with no explanation. He was more like a bat than a stray dog.

Samir and I were left alone together.

"Did you come here with Labbe?" I asked. Labbe and Samir had become friends when Samir joined our class in the first year. They still hung out, even though Labbe had switched schools.

Samir nodded and looked at me for a moment before he moved to sit right above me. He didn't look like himself; his face was maybe a little swollen and he was definitely annoyed, seriously annoyed. I had never liked to sit in the sauna, but I couldn't exactly leave right then, Samir would think he had embarrassed me.

"I didn't think you and Sebastian — " I began, but he interrupted me.

"Labbe asked if I wanted to come."

Then he stopped talking. But he didn't have to say anything more, I completely understood. Ask anyone if they wanted to come along to Sebastian's house, and they would immediately forget all the crap they'd said about him earlier and accept the invitation. If you got the chance, you took it. So you could say you'd been there if anyone asked what you'd done over the weekend. So you could casually drop into unrelated conversation, *So I was at this party at Sebastian Fagerman's house, yeah, exactly! Claes Fagerman's son…*

I wondered why I had thought Samir was different. But why was he so annoyed?

For everyone but Labbe, this was the first time those of us in our year had been invited to one of Sebastian's parties. Only a couple of people he had hung out with before had come tonight; most of them had already left upper secondary school behind.

Samir leaned down toward me. He had already been sitting too close, and now his leg was pressing against my arm. He smelled like sweat. A strange scent. It didn't seem to belong with Egghead Samir with his ironed jeans and double-knotted gym shoes, head-of-the-class Samir.

"I thought I would come here and see what the big deal is. And your dopehead boyfriend got one thing right, at least. Because this is a fucking drag." Samir shook his head and leaned even closer. "Assuming you don't like snorting shit with the house Negro, that is."

At first, I suppose I just felt shocked. I had never heard Samir talking like that before, not to me, not to anyone else. I stood up to leave. I wanted to have fun, I wasn't about to let him sit there judging me. But Samir was at the door in a flash, blocking my way.

"Does he snort lines right off your naked belly?" The sauna felt claustrophobic. "Is Dennis allowed in on the fun? A bonus for letting Sebastian sample the very latest?"

"Are you done?" Was he trying to be funny? It didn't seem like it.

He lowered his voice. "You know, those of us who live in the real world, we avoid Dennis because he's nuts. He would sell crack on a maternity ward if they let him in."

My heart was pounding too fast. I didn't know whether Samir could tell that I was high, if that was why he was angry, but I wanted to leave.

"Don't you get it?" Samir's voice trembled. "He's a nobody, Maja. He is no one. Take away all of this" — he waved one hand around at the sauna, with his pinky extended as if the condensation-covered wooden walls were the Hall of Mirrors at Versailles — "and he is about as interesting as a tin can."

At last, Samir stepped back. Quickly — the towel he had tied around his waist came loose and he pulled it tight again, hard.

And that was when I figured it out: Samir was drunk. I had never seen him drunk before. But I suppose there's a first time for everything, even for the valedictorian. I was so relieved that I almost cracked up. *He doesn't know what he's saying.* I got the door open, drunk dudes aren't worth the time. There was no point in trying to reason with him. But then I changed my mind and turned toward him.

"I do get it," I said. "You don't like Dennis; no one does. But who bought your booze tonight? If you were pregaming with Labbe, I would bet money that you can thank Dennis for your buzz. You don't like Sebastian. Fine. You don't even know him, but fine. Coming over and sitting in his sauna and drying yourself with his towel, though, that's just fine, too. He's good enough for that."

It was impossible to breathe in there, it was so hot. I wiped my nose on the sleeve of my robe as I left.

The music was roaring from the pool house. Three girls from the other class in our year were running up from the beach; they passed me on their way to the sauna I'd just left. The party seemed to have doubled in size in the short time I'd been gone. Sebastian always invited people he didn't know, usually girls. He met them out on the town, standing in line somewhere, maybe, and took pity on them and their bandaged blisters and let them party with him a few times before he got tired of their tube dresses and H&M glasses and invited some new chicks instead. But he never seemed worried that things might derail. Probably because it was impossible to crash a Fagerman party. Not that the security guards ever bothered us, or stuck their noses into whatever we were doing, but they were always present, at just the right distance.

Amanda called out from the dance floor. She was wearing a bikini and had let her hair down. It didn't look like she had been swimming. Three meters away stood Labbe, in an unbuttoned shirt, staring at her.

"Come on," she mumbled, breathing against my neck.

We had done this before. Amanda loved an audience, and I was a part of her favorite act.

The music pounded. I was still wearing the robe, but Amanda wriggled it off me and placed her palm against my back; she tilted her head back and we danced so close to each other that our waists touched. We were barefoot. She was still wearing her top. My underpants were still a little damp from the swim, but I closed my eyes and tried to get my pulse to slow down. The music — I had to concentrate on the music. What Samir thought wasn't important. He was just drunk; he didn't know what he was saying.

Sebastian was standing by the stereo. He watched us for a while, then came up next to us and put one arm around Amanda and the other around my waist. I loved Sebastian's hands. When he grabbed me, almost too hard, I felt pretty. I pulled his hand farther up my back and he let go of Amanda, shoving her over toward Labbe, who laughed and caught her. Sebastian wanted to touch me, not her.

He was sweaty; his forehead glistened and his eyes were fixed on something in the distance. I looked at Amanda. Labbe was standing in front of her, lifting his hands up and down in some sort of paint-the-wall move. He never danced for real. Only ironically. Something he did to be kind to those of us who liked to dance. To show that he didn't judge us, even though he didn't quite understand the point.

I picked the robe up off the floor and Sebastian placed it over my shoulders; I couldn't find the belt. I left the pool house and went through the living room and the kitchen, past Dennis; Sebastian had told him to remain in the kitchen with his stuff. Dennis gave me a curious look as I walked by, but I shook my head and kept going, up to the second floor, to Sebastian's room. The security team was never allowed to come inside the house unless they were summoned. Nor were there any surveillance cameras in here, a decision made by Sebastian's dad. His reasoning was obvious. Claes didn't want whatever happened in his house to be caught on tape. That sort of thing could be copied, distributed, used for blackmail. When I got to Sebastian's room, I put on a cami and a pair of Sebastian's boxers. Then I went to the bathroom. The evening had just begun and I wanted to dry my hair. My heart was still beating too quickly, but I was no dopehead (what kind of old-timey word was that, anyway?), I had just started off too fast, I wasn't used to it, I should drink something, just drink for the rest of the night, that's it, but first my pulse had to calm down. The hair dryer hummed and I closed my eyes into the warm air. I was in no rush to hurry back downstairs. I kept my eyes shut and breathed, in through my nose, out through my mouth. Once my hair was dry, I heard them. Guys, several of them, maybe a girl. The music stopped.

When I came into the kitchen, two security guards were holding Samir by the arms. Dennis was leaning up against the wall, his nose bleeding. Behind him, an oil painting of a wine bottle had been knocked askew. Dennis looked more surprised than angry.

"Let me go." Samir was standing unnaturally still, the way you do when you're playing sober. He wasn't speaking very loudly, but everyone could hear him.

One of the guards looked at Sebastian. He nodded.

"It's time for you to go home," the security guard said to Samir.

"I wouldn't stay here if you paid me."

Sebastian turned to me. He stood in the doorway. He kept talking, his back to Samir.

"Make sure that other one doesn't bleed all over the kitchen, please. He needs to go home now, too."

Samir looked me straight in the eye from behind Sebastian's back. His lips were moving; he was trying to say something more. To just me. He was mouthing something. It looked like "come." He wanted me to go with him. Or was he mumbling in another language? Arabic? Farsi? I couldn't even remember which language Samir spoke. I didn't care.

Sure, it had occurred to me that Samir liked me, I liked him, too. But now, here at Sebastian's house, he had suddenly transformed into a drunken moralist. He considered it his Duty to Lead Me Away from the Primrose Path. A knight with his lance raised.

Awkward. I thought he was embarrassing. I wanted him to leave, I wanted him to take his holier-than-thou *I*-take-*my*-life-seriously face and run along home. I hadn't asked for his protection, I didn't need it, I wasn't some helpless princess who was dating the wrong prince.

A guy from the mathematics program tugged at Sebastian's arm.

"Wait," the math guy protested. "How am I supposed to..."

"Don't worry," said Sebastian. "We have plenty."

Sebastian took my hand. We walked toward the pool house. The music started again. Nothing serious had happened. Dennis had been kicked out. Samir had gone home. Sebastian brushed my hair off my neck. I inhaled his scent, cold and fresh, I loved the way he smelled. I loved the way he made me feel. I had fun with him. We always had fun. No one should have to feel ashamed of being able to have a good time.

Sebastian whispered, "See? It's not a party unless something gets broken. Now this party is finally happening."

20.

The weekend after Sebastian's party went by pretty quickly. We went into the city on Saturday, Sebastian and me, Labbe and Amanda. On Sunday, Mom and Dad and Lina and I went to a restaurant with Grandpa. Mom was grumpy because I was "tired" and Dad was grumpy because we were at a restaurant with Grandpa. I didn't think any more about Samir, at least not much. On Monday morning, Sebastian dropped me off at school. He had "things to do." I didn't know what that meant, but I didn't care. This was before that sort of thing made me worry. After lunch I had two free periods. Amanda was sick and Sebastian wasn't answering his phone.

The school library usually wasn't very crowded, not since they blocked the Internet on the public computers. But I wasn't alone: Evy from the other class in my year was sitting across the room. She had a narrow nose and wore floral skirts and socks with every kind of shoes, even ballet flats. Evy had won the school creative writing contest (organized by Rotary) the year before, even though she had only been a second-year student at the time. Her story was about her developmentally disabled brother and every-one thought it was true, which is probably why she won. When it came out that she didn't even have a brother, just a perfectly normal sister, people were disappointed, and a lot of them even got angry, because they thought she had "cheated." No one pointed out the obvious: It just made her story that much better.

Two first-year girls were sitting on the sofa set a few meters away from my spot. They were paging through a glossy magazine and they had a bag of candy to share. They were talking just loudly enough so I could hear that they were abbreviating all their words. That was the big thing right then, all the first-years were talking like that. Amanda and I had also made up our own words and expressions when we were younger. But this shit was complete nonsense. It made pig Latin seem more refined than actual Latin.

"Hey bae...listen! He's driving me craaaay, does he want to be with me or not? It's making me so *angs*!"

The other one nodded without looking up from the magazine.

"Totes psychs."

A few days earlier, in English class, we had discussed the Bechdel Test, which you could use to determine whether or not movies were feminist. You had to ask three ques-tions: Were there at least two named women in the movie? Did they talk to each other (without a guy around)? And did they talk about something other than guys?

The teacher pulled up a bunch of movies that almost everyone had seen and we had to decide if they fulfilled the criteria. They didn't (which we kindly pretended we hadn't understood from the start; why else would he have asked?), and sure, I thought it was gross that that's how things are, and I got why people thought it was important for women in movies to produce something other than dialogue about guys, but: In reality, girls talk about guys all the time. Even Mom and her friends complain about their husbands (and how hopeless they are) whenever they get the chance. The chicks in the debate club, with their suits and Young Economist memberships, the theater kids with their plays in French and their Interrail plans, the BFFs right here next to me — they all had one thing in common: They talked about guys. Their guys, other people's guys, guys they wanted, guys they wanted to get rid of. Just guys, all the time. Perhaps, I would have liked to point out, you shouldn't complain about how you are depicted in films when the depictions are a pretty decent reflection of reality.

Samir shoved the door open so hard that it slammed into a rack of brochures about the Royal Institute of Technology, the law program at Uppsala, and adult-education math. Samir's legs were, like, too long for the rest of his body, which made it look like he was always in a hurry. He stopped short at the information desk and yanked his phone earbuds from his ears. His movements were jerky, always full of surplus energy, always one retort, one thought, ahead, before anyone else had even started to think. I suppose it would be easy to assume he was stressed-out. I had never thought so. But this time he looked nervous.

He noticed me before I had time to think about pretending not to see him, and by then it was too late. He almost ran up to me.

"Can I sit for a minute?"

I pretended to look in another direction.

"Hey…bae." One of the girls was whispering to the other, but it was still more than loud enough for me and Samir to hear. "Do you have any tamps?" She laughed in embarrassment. "I forgot to bring any."

I had tampons in my bag. I could go sit next to them, say "you're welcs" and just ignore Samir. He would never jump into a conversation about female bodily fluids. That would definitely stress him out. Incidentally, did period talk fulfill the Bechdel Test? Presumably. But was having your period still feminist if you called it "code red"?

"Maja?" Samir was still standing in front of me, trying to make eye contact.

"I don't work here, you'll have to ask the staff."

He looked surprised. "Huh? What am I supposed to ask them?"

"I'm not in charge of who sits where. But if you sit down here, I'll leave."

He didn't say anything. Then he threw up his hands and cleared his throat.

"It won't take long. I just want to apologize." He lowered his arms. "I wanted to say I'm sorry about Friday.

That was stupid. I don't know why I said all of that, I guess I was drunk."

The besties on the couches had stopped talking. They were pretending to be deeply involved in an article in the magazine that one of them had on her lap.

"What, you were drunk?" I said. Samir caught the sarcasm and lowered his head. The girls were dead quiet, they didn't want to miss a word of this.

"I shouldn't have come to that party and I really shouldn't have attacked you like that. Sebastian's the one I don't like. I shouldn't have..."

"Do you even remember what you said to me?"

He nodded. "Yeah, unfortunately."

His bangs fell down across his forehead. He looked like he expected me to give him a spanking. Did he know how cute he was? Of course he did. There was something about his mannerisms now and then that seemed so practiced; he was well aware of how he looked. This was what he looked like when he wanted forgiveness; I wasn't the first recipient of his look of shame. But at the same time, he really had seemed upset at the party, truly upset, not just drunk mad.

This was a new side of Samir. He always seemed so indifferent, almost uninterested in Amanda and me and our lives outside school. He never asked anyone what they had done over the weekend, and I always figured he thought we were pretty ridiculous. And suddenly I realized that I had found it disappointing, that he had never wanted to talk with me, just with me, about stuff that wasn't school related. But now that he finally did, it was to talk about Sebastian. *Guy talk,* I thought. *Always guy talk. Everyone talks about guys with girls, even guys.* This popped into my head before I could stop it and I smiled, not on purpose, my smile just appeared. *I want him to talk about me. With me. About something other than Sebastian.* Samir smiled back. Not his usual teasing smile — a more relieved smile.

Just then the loudspeakers emitted a signal that made the besties rush off to class with their huge purses and glossy magazines. Samir pulled up a chair and sat down across from me. He made his lips pouty in what I assume was supposed to be a selfie face.

"Sebastian is your bae," he squeaked. "I totes get it." And then he switched personalities again. He put his arm on the backrest, slid down low in the chair, spread his legs, and said, in a thick accent: "Dude is your *shono*. And you're his *guzz*, no problem girl, nuff said, respect."

I laughed. He was horrible at playing gangster. But he was hot, and so what if he knew it? And there it was again, Samir's teasing smile. God, how I had missed it.

21.

A few weeks passed. Six or seven, maybe? In the middle of October, we decided to go out to Labbe's country home for the weekend. "The Farm," Labbe called it, but it was actually an old castle. Labbe's dad's family had owned the place since like the Middle Ages. Labbe's mom's family had a similar place maybe twenty kilometers away, but I'd never been there. Samir had come along, too. I don't remember what I thought about that — it was fine, maybe? I don't think it made me nervous, or that I thought it was stupid. Sure, there was tension between Samir and Sebastian, but it was nothing to worry about.

Amanda and I were lying on deck chairs, each under a blanket, each with our phone. A brimstone butterfly went by, fluttering like a leaf in the wind, across the short grass of the lawn, down to the water. It probably should have been dead already, but it was an unusually warm fall.

"If you had one wish," Amanda said, "and you could have anything in the world, what would you want most of all?"

Behind us, the door to the kitchen was ajar. Labbe's mom, Margareta, was listening to opera and cooking; she didn't want any help, but now and then she would come out and stand not far from us, her hands on her hips, wearing a half smile. She liked having us there. We loved being at her house.

Amanda opened her eyes and squinted at me.

"I don't know," I responded. I wasn't in the mood to answer Amanda's questions. And it's never worth talking about what you wish for when you want for nothing.

"Oh, come on," Amanda protested. "There must be *something* you want."

Amanda loved asking questions that could have been part of conversational games with preprinted cards, "topics" that made the participants "open up." She loved posing follow-up questions about other people's answers almost as much as she loved giving her own responses to the questions she'd made up.

"Come on, Maja." Amanda got up, raised one hand to the sky, and placed the other over her heart. "I'll start." She cleared her throat. "I wish for peace on earth and food for all the children."

Amanda pretended to adjust a beauty-queen tiara on her head, and I laughed.

"But seriously, Maja." She sat down next to me. "Next semester we're graduating. Then it all begins. I'm going to London for my internship, you know? I'll be there for six weeks, and Dad says I'll have to work half the night. I'll definitely have to make copies and get coffee and stuff like that, you have to be prepared for all that, but I still wonder how I'm going to feel. Do you think it's going to feel like a real job? That what I'm doing *means* something? The point is to want to make a difference, right? A real difference. You're supposed to want to do something for the world and for other people and, like, good things, right?"

I didn't answer.

"Because it's, like, of course I want to do that. Doesn't everyone?" She gave a nervous laugh. "But to be honest, most of all I would like to know what I want. Or what it means to do something. Like, have a plan. Do you get what I'm saying?"

I nodded. This was an ordinary Amanda conversation. Amanda always said really obvious stuff and asked if I got what she meant. And then she would get all doubtful and sentimental and her eyes would well up with tears.

"Do you get what I'm saying?"

This could have been a sign that she thought I was pretty dense, that I had a hard time following, but in fact she wanted me to reassure her that she wasn't as stupid as she felt.

"I get it," I said. And smiled.

Labbe's mom came out to the garden again.

"I don't know if I can promise peace on earth, but there will be food for all the children in ten minutes. Can you go get the boys, darling?" Labbe's mom pulled off an oven mitt and ran the back of her hand across Amanda's cheek. Amanda and Labbe had been together for less than a month, yet Labbe's mom and Amanda had already developed a full-blown mother-in-law/daughter-in-law relationship. I had been with Sebastian more than twice that long, and even if I maybe didn't hate his dad yet, that was mostly only because I hardly ever saw him.

Three days earlier, though, Claes had been at home. He had gotten a call from the school, and by five o'clock he had shown up to talk to Sebastian. He had sent me home, but I knew what was up. Sebastian had pretty much stopped going to class. He would ride to school with me almost every day, and sometimes he hung around the schoolyard with Dennis for a few hours, but for the most part he would just go right home again. And even if Claes was never home during the day, he still should have known.

We ate in the so-called summer kitchen, which was right next to the garden. Margareta had set the table with chipped floral-patterned porcelain, different designs on each plate. The Duralex glasses were cloudy from years of being run through the dishwasher. Labbe went to stand beside Amanda. She was standing at her spot, holding on to the back of a bright blue Windsor chair (yes, she already had her own place at the table). When he kissed her cheek, she let out a low laugh; it was obvious how sexy she thought it sounded. Labbe seemed to agree; he bent his back at a weird angle so he could rest his chin on her shoulder. They looked in love and totally goofy.

What's more, Labbe had grown a narrow Freddie Mercury mustache, ironically of course, to show that he was so sure he wasn't gay that it didn't matter if he looked gay. Amanda pinched a few of the hairs on Labbe's upper lip, just at his Cupid's bow, and turned to Labbe's mom and asked, "Do you think he's going to keep this for long, Mags?"

"Well…" Margareta looked at her son. She didn't look particularly impressed. "I think I'll keep my opinion to myself."

I caught Samir's eye. He looked at me and almost imperceptibly stroked his upper lip with his index finger and thumb, and the corners of his mouth turned down and his nostrils flared in an I-am-the-lord-of-this-manor expression. I had to look down at the table to stop myself from laughing.

Labbe and Amanda and Samir were sitting along one side. Samir was next to Labbe's mom, and Sebastian and I were on the other side. Georg, Labbe's dad, would sit across from Margareta, at the head of the table. He entered the room just as we were taking our seats; he was wearing clogs, jeans, a T-shirt with a hole at one shoulder, and reading glasses pushed up onto his forehead. Before he sat down, he held out a folded newspaper to Samir.

"Did you see what Tirole wrote in today's *FT*?" he wondered. Samir began to read. But Labbe's mom gently took the paper from him and placed it on one of the counters.

"No reading at the table."

Sebastian sat down at his place before Labbe's mom had managed to pull out her chair, and he held out his wineglass to Labbe's dad.

"I'm eighteen," he tried.

"Sparkling water," Margareta stated. She and her husband exchanged subtle glances. They had discussed this earlier. "You can drink sparkling water even if you are eighteen."

Could Sebastian's dad have asked them not to serve alcohol to Sebastian? Claes knew Sebastian drank. A couple of times I had had to drive Sebastian's car home, even though I didn't have a license yet. Once Claes was standing in the driveway when I parked there. Sebastian hadn't told me what his dad had said about it, and when I asked, he said, "Ask me about something I actually want to talk about, would you?" and I let it go. Maybe Claes didn't know I wasn't allowed to drive. Or maybe he did know and he had taken it seriously.

Amanda and I helped Margareta place the food on the table. The first course was potato-leek soup. There was crispy wild boar bacon in a separate bowl, and the bread was still warm.

"I thought you were a vegetarian," Sebastian said when Amanda sprinkled a generous helping of bacon onto her plate.

"It's different when it's a wild animal," she said, and her cheeks turned only a little bit pink. Amanda had forgotten all about vegetarianism at the exact second she French-kissed Labbe for the first time. The week before she had gone on a moose hunt with Labbe and Sebastian. I hadn't been able to come — Mom had made me go to Grandpa's birthday dinner — but Amanda had taken part in the drive, heavy petted in hunting stands, fucked in sleeping bags, and gotten her Hunter boots wet for the first time since she bought them.

"I'm going to take the hunter licensing course," she said, passing the bowl to Samir. He handed it to Margareta without helping himself.

"Of course you are," Samir mumbled, just a little too loudly. And I smiled into my napkin. I felt Sebastian look at me.

"What an excellent idea," Labbe's dad said drily. "Nature is in no way a useless place to spend time."

Amanda always played the perfect wife in any relationship. One time (when we had just started our second year) she was dating the bassist of a band from Stockholm who claimed they had a contract with Sony. That time she had even been the perfect rock groupie.

"So what should we talk about?" Labbe's dad wondered when we were halfway through our soup.

"We can talk about the zero-interest policy," Samir said.

"Yeah," Sebastian mumbled. "Pretty please, can we talk about the zero-interest policy?"

"It was a joke," Samir said. His voice was cold as ice. "Have you ever heard of joking?"

"Hilarious," said Labbe. "Really, funny as hell. Zero interest, ha ha ha. But this thing you and Dad have going, all your books and newspapers and Topics and Situations and Currents...are you just trying to make me feel stupid, or do you have some other plan and I just don't get it because I'm too stupid?"

"No worries," Samir spoke again. "I will stop making jokes immediately."

"There, there," Margareta said, patting Samir's hand. "Let's not be like that. Right, Lars Jacob?" Labbe's parents never called Labbe "Labbe." But I had never heard Margareta use his double name before; it sounded like it came from a newsreel. I suppose it was a way to show him she meant business. But Labbe kept eating, unconcerned.

Georg tried to help. "No one thinks you're stupid, Lars. You've been doing great ever since you started at Sigtuna." He stuck a piece of bread in his mouth. "We're grateful, Sammie. You've been such a big help."

"All two exams." Labbe raised two fingers in the air. "Two. And 'great' means I passed. I got a C and a B-minus. Sammie chewed me out. Sammie thinks anything but an A might as well be an F."

"I don't understand why you would be satisfied with anything but an A," Samir said. "I'm with your dad. You are not stupid."

There was something about that response. Maybe he had emphasized the word "you." But everyone heard what Samir meant, what he was insinuating, what he hadn't said: *Unlike Sebastian, you are not stupid.*

"I know what we can talk about instead of the zero-interest policy..." Amanda began, but it was too late.

"How much are they paying you?" Sebastian was looking straight at Samir. "Is the money good?"

Georg and Margareta were masters of pretending nothing was wrong. Labbe wasn't fully trained in that yet, but when Georg showed off the portrait gallery up in the "big house," and pointed out the traitors, the ones who had committed patricide, and the adulteresses, and mentioned how many illegitimate children had been placed out in the village, Labbe would joke that "Keep a stiff upper lip" was on the family crest. And now they were able to show it off:

neutral expressions, thoroughly unmoved faces, not a single raised lip in Sebastian's direction.

But Samir shook his head hesitantly as his eyes ping-ponged between Georg and Margareta, back and forth, back and forth, without making contact. And Sebastian didn't give up. He spoke slower and louder, as if Samir was having trouble understanding.

"How. Much. Do. They. Pay. You? How much do you make tutoring Labbe?"

"Sebastian," said Margareta, quietly but still unconcerned, "eat your soup." Georg offered Labbe the breadbasket. He shook his head.

"Excuse me." Sebastian raised his hands in an I-give-up gesture and let out a laugh. He lowered his voice just enough so that the others could pretend not to hear anything. "It's none of my business who you add to your payroll."

I don't remember what we talked about after that. But I'm sure Margareta thought of some topic of conversation while Georg finished his soup. Changing the subject was another family specialty. And the rest of us did our best to keep up. When Margareta had finished talking and eating, Georg got up and cleared the dishes; everyone but Sebastian tried to do the same, but we were shooed back to our seats by Georg. Not until the main dish was on the table did Margareta place her hand on top of Samir's once more. Then she adjusted her chair to line up with her plate and lifted her silverware.

"Tell us. How are your parents, Samir?"

I had received the same question an hour earlier. Amanda had received it even before we made it from the driveway into the west wing, where we would be sleeping. Margareta always asked how everyone's parents were, whether she knew them or not. Sebastian had to talk about how Lukas was doing in the U.S. Margareta was on top of things. It was extremely unlikely that she'd ever met Samir's parents aside from at a parent-teacher meeting. But she was still interested.

"They're pretty good," Samir said.

"Where is your mom working these days?"

"At Huddinge Hospital."

"Really!" Margareta and Georg looked at each other across the table. "Then it all worked out with her authorization? Oh, I'm so happy to hear that."

"No." Samir wiped his mouth. He swallowed, speaking rapidly, lowering his voice. "She's working as a nurses' aide while she...waits. But she likes working in a hospital."

Georg shook his head. "It's unbelievable that we can't make better use of the resources we have in this country. Unbelievable."

"That's odd. I could have sworn..." Sebastian hadn't touched his food. "I could have sworn you said your mom was a lawyer. Labbe?" He turned to Labbe. "Didn't you say that when Samir started at Djursholm he told everyone who would listen that his mom was a lawyer?" Sebastian dragged out his words, making them longer than they really were. When Labbe didn't respond, he turned to Samir again. "But maybe she has a double degree. Pretty damn impressive, Sammie."

Sebastian wasn't drunk. I didn't think he had taken anything, either. But Samir's nickname seemed to swell in his mouth, the nickname no one but Labbe and his parents used. *Sammie.* Sebastian made it sound like a slave name.

"My dad is a lawyer. Mom's a doctor."

"Aha!" Sebastian nodded, amused. "Sure. That's it, of course. And your dad the lawyer, what does he do here in Sweden?" Samir didn't respond. "Drives a taxi, right?" He turned to Labbe again. "Didn't you say you thought it was Samir's dad who drove us home from the club a month or so ago?" Labbe still wasn't answering, and Samir's face had gone pale. "So tell me, dear Sam, how is it that all the immigrants who come here and start working as Metro drivers and maids…?" He snorted. "Sorry, who drive taxis and work as nurses' aides. How is it that all of them are really doctors and civil engineers and nuclear physicists back in their home countries? Every last one of them. Your mom" — Sebastian's fingers made air quotes — "'the doctor' is in good company. Because there is not a single miserable little maid who actually worked as a maid back home, too. Not if you believe what everyone says. Did *anyone* work as a grocery store cashier in Syria or walk around parks in Iran picking up empty bottles? No way. Only doctors and engineers and lawyers and — "

"That's enough, Sebastian." Georg's voice was low. He had reached the limit of his ability to pretend nothing was wrong. But Sebastian didn't listen. He waved his arm at us and made a face I had never seen before.

"Haven't you ever wondered why that is?" No one answered. He turned back to Samir. "What do you do with people who don't have at least six years' university? Do you shoot them on the spot so they won't take your jobs?"

Claes Fagerman, I thought. *He looks like his dad.*

Margareta grabbed Samir's arm as he stood up. She shook her head at him. Then she turned to Sebastian.

"Sebastian," she began. Margareta was a director at the Ministry for Foreign Affairs, in some department whose name I forget, and it was clear in her voice that she was used to meetings and negotiations, circumstances in which she had to remain polite even though she was furious. Her cozy Mom voice was long gone. The pretend-like-nothing's-wrong stage was obviously over.

"You listen carefully." Margareta spoke slowly. "Some things are hard to understand. For one, it's difficult to believe that many of the refugees who manage to get all the way to Europe, all the way up to Sweden, it's hard to understand that these are people..."

She took a soundless breath. I think she had been planning to say *like you and me* but changed her mind.

"These are, not always, but oftentimes, the people who had their lives in order, were financially stable, and yes, have advanced degrees. Why is that?" She didn't wait for an answer. "Because the people who manage to reach Sweden could afford to pay what it cost to transport their whole family to a better life. It takes money to do that. Not much money in your world, Sebastian, but you should still be able to understand this. You have gotten the impression that everyone who comes here is highly educated. That's inaccurate. And it's just as inaccurate to claim that all the highly educated people who come here would lie about their backgrounds. Because many of the new Swedes are academics. The very poorest and most deprived people in the war-torn countries we're talking about here seldom manage to get as far as Sweden. It is deeply unsettling, but it is not a reason for you to behave like this and blurt out things you obviously know nothing about."

"Sure," said Sebastian. He didn't even sound angry. He didn't seem to notice the contempt in Margareta's voice. "It's really super for Sweden that they come here. And those people who tried to start a tent city in the Humlegården park, they really seem to belong to the absolute elite. The intelligentsia of their homelands."

Margareta cleared her throat. "I have known you your whole life, Sebastian. I refuse to believe that you're really that vulgar."

When she took a breath, Labbe's dad jumped in to take over. He had removed his folded napkin from his lap.

"Sebastian and I are going to take a little walk," he said, in a normal, conversational tone. After wiping his mouth, he stood. "Are you coming?"

Nothing in Georg's voice revealed anything other than that he was perhaps a bit tired, the way he would have sounded if he had to interrupt dinner to take an important phone call for work. But when he went to stand behind Sebastian, waiting for him to follow, I could see the muscles in his jaw working.

"What the fuck is this?" Sebastian laughed. But his unconcerned façade was gone. "You want me to leave? While that freeloader Samir sits here and lies to our faces?"

"Don't make this worse than it already is." Georg took Sebastian by the arm. With a firm grip, he pulled him up out of the chair and prodded him out of the room.

It took a few minutes for Georg to return. I don't know what we did in the meantime. Labbe kept staring down at the table. Amanda had tears in her eyes. Margareta had a mumbled talk with Samir. I didn't listen. If my knees hadn't been shaking, I would have stood up and left.

"Sebastian decided it was best for him to go home," Georg explained before he took his seat again.

He turned to me. "I thought it would be best for you to stay here, Maja."

I nodded.

"Sebastian was not in any shape to spend time with any-one, least of all you," Georg went on as he scraped up the last of the food on his plate. "His dad and I agreed on that."

I nodded again. I was too shocked to do anything else.

"How is he getting home?" Margareta stood and went to clear Georg's plate.

"I asked John to drive him."

Labbe and I had been in the same class from middle school until this year, when he switched schools. I had heard Margareta's bored, even countess voice speak to the headmaster, the school janitor, countless teachers, and other parents. I had fantasized about how she lectured the prime minister with that voice. Throughout all those years, Mom, Dad, and I had watched Margareta simply demand that "this is what we're going to do" (whether the problem was that the city bus timetable didn't match up with the school's hours, or the national school curriculum didn't include something Margareta thought was important, or the weather wasn't good enough for a softball tournament). And each time Margareta made demands, she sounded as if she was only asking for a teeny, tiny little favor. She could call up the king, clear her throat, and say, "Listen, I have a tiny favor to ask of you." And the king would never dream of saying no. No one said no to Margareta; she was awed by no one.

I want Margareta to talk to Claes, I thought. *She could get him to listen.* I wanted to take her by the hand and say it: *Talk to him.* But I didn't say anything. I just sat there, ashamed. That was the first time I was ashamed of being Sebastian's girlfriend.

"So you got hold of his father, that's a good thing," Margareta muttered. "So what did our dear Claes have to say?"

Our dear Claes. Margareta didn't like him.

Georg shrugged. Sort of halfway, a shrug that didn't mean *I don't care* but more like *What do you want me to say?* Or, *You know the answer already and there's nothing we can do about it.* Georg thought Claes was an arrogant bastard, too.

"We'll talk about it later, Mags."

I still didn't say anything. I didn't look at anyone, especially not Samir.

"Would anyone like Italian meringues?" Margareta pushed her dishes away. "With homemade ice cream?"

Everyone wanted ice cream. I forced myself to eat. I stuffed my mouth with dessert, trying to swallow down my worry. *Was Sebastian jealous? Did he feel threatened? Why had he done it?* I swallowed the ice cream so fast that my forehead hurt. I swallowed a little more.

It took a few minutes. I think Amanda said, "Don't listen to him," to Samir, and then the others managed to talk about a trip to Denmark that Labbe's parents had gone on when they were young, to a rock festival, it had rained and they couldn't get their tent up because the mud was too deep. And later they talked about someone who lived in the same dormitory as Labbe. He sleepwalked.

"At least three times a week he walks all the way to the cafeteria and then he climbs up and stretches out on the head table and keeps sleeping there."

They laughed several times, and each time they laughed they sounded a little more natural, a little more relaxed. They took seconds of the ice cream. Then we said thanks for dinner and everyone helped clean up in the kitchen. No one mentioned Sebastian.

My boyfriend.

They pretended nothing was wrong. But what was I supposed to do?

Two hours later, we were watching a movie in the living room when Georg came in to apologize for Sebastian. I forget what movie it was, we didn't even bother to turn off the sound while Georg recounted their conversation.

Sebastian had "made it home." Georg had spoken to him on the phone, and Sebastian wanted Georg to "deliver an apology" (Georg's words). The apology was broad and sweeping, and even though Georg was the one giving it, it sounded forced, the kind of thing you make up when you've forgotten someone unimportant's birthday.

Samir was lying half a meter away from me. He had one arm behind his head. I caught a glimpse of the dark, curly hair under the sleeve of his T-shirt. The inside of his upper arm was so pale it glowed in the light from the TV. He looked at Georg as Georg rattled off the apology, and then mumbled, "It's fine totally fine no problem thanks," and when it was over and Georg left, Samir looked back at the TV, but it didn't seem like he was watching the screen, just staring into space.

When he stood up and mentioned that he was going to take a walk, I waited exactly four minutes before I stood up, too.

"I'm going to bed," I said.

"Good night," said Amanda.

"Sleep tight," said Labbe.

Then I turned off my phone and left it in the room where I was staying.

Samir was sitting down by the water. He was hugging his knees. It was chilly and pitch-black out. I saw him only as a shadow, illuminated by the light from the house. The moon stared at us from across the water.

"I don't need you to comfort me," he said when I sat down next to him.

"I know."

From close up I could see how troubled he was.

He scratched his arm, but it could hardly be a mosquito bite.

"You don't need to tell me that I'm dumb."

"Why would I?"

"Shit, it was the first day of school, when I had just started. I was so fucking nervous. I know you guys weren't, because you know each other, everyone knows each other going back seventeen generations, but for me it was such an insane day, you were all weird as hell, fifteen-year-olds who ask first thing what each other's parents 'do for a living.' How sick is that?"

"Pretty sick," I admitted. *I've never asked you what your parents do.*

We were far from the highway, it took more than twenty minutes on a gravel road to get all the way to the estate, and yet I could hear the faint hum that must have been traffic, because it didn't belong with the other sounds; it didn't fit in with the tree sounds, forest sounds, animal sounds.

"What is your mom?"

"What do you mean?"

"I assume she's neither a lawyer, like you told Labbe, nor a doctor, like you told Georg and Margareta, so what is she?"

Samir pulled a tuft of grass out of the ground where he was sitting. A chunk of dirt followed it and hit my leg.

"I never said Mom was a lawyer. Labbe misremembered. And Mom always says that she would have liked to become a doctor. She was a good student, but she had to quit. And now she's screwed. She can hardly make it through ten minutes of news in Swedish, so there's no way she could be accepted into medical school here. Plus she has to work. And she likes being a nurses' aide."

"Is your dad a lawyer?"

It took a moment before Samir shook his head.

"I get paid, too. Two hundred kronor an hour, they pay me, but..." He didn't continue. "I suppose I should be grateful."

"Grateful for what?"

"That Georg and Margareta didn't kick me out, that they were satisfied with kicking out your racist boyfriend instead."

"Sebastian isn't a racist."

Samir snorted. "Quit defending him. Don't be one of the people who kowtow to him, Maja. Who let him do and say whatever he wants."

Now it was my turn to be angry. "Sebastian knows exactly why people fawn over him. Do you think he doesn't get it? But the teachers don't fawn over him — if they did, he wouldn't have to repeat this year. And was he allowed to say and do whatever he wanted tonight? I thought he got thrown out."

"It's different with Georg and Margareta."

"How so?"

"You know. But if Labbe didn't need me to graduate, they would have thrown me out."

"They would not."

"Do you really believe that?"

"Of course I do. You haven't got a clue, Samir. I think they know your mom isn't a doctor and your dad isn't a lawyer. Because the fact is, they're not stupid. They probably feel sorry for you because you think you need to lie about something so silly. I feel sorry for you because you think you need to lie about it. You are who you are, and it has nothing to do with what your parents do. We don't give a crap where you come from. If your mom never went to school and your dad drives a taxi and you still turned out this great, that's just proof that you fight harder than the rest of us do. People like you even more because you are who you are even though you come from — "

Samir cut me off so quickly that I saw spit fly from his mouth.

"You so don't get it. You're all just naïve as hell. You think you know what you're talking about, but you're dead fucking wrong."

"Don't shout."

He didn't lower his voice.

"I'm not shouting. But you are wrong if you think a good story isn't necessary. All you have to do is watch *Idol* or *X Factor* or fucking *Master Baker*, or whatever it's called, to understand that the backstory is half the point. You all want to be surprised when the fatty sings like a star, you want to feel gratified when he made it 'despite the odds,' and you want to believe that it's just bad luck that my parents don't also live in Djursholm and work as doctors and lawyers, that it's an injustice you are definitely not complicit in, but you can say it's wrong and feel bad that we don't take better care of our immigrants, if they would only be a little more Swedish, learn their new language faster, study a little harder, then the American dream would be just within reach. You love the American dream. You love Zlatan. Shit, you all love him so much. It's like it's just that much better when Zlatan says he's never read a book and that girls can't play soccer, because that's how immigrants are, they're misogynists, they're uneducated, but you like them anyway because you're tolerant and accepting and Zlatan has such a delightful, charming smile. You think it's all about integration and unfortunate circumstances, and that everyone will succeed if only they fight for it, and — "

"Which 'you'?" I started to cry. I couldn't help it. And Samir gave a start, as if I had struck him.

"What?" he asked. "What's wrong?"

"You keep saying 'you.' You said 'you' think this and that and 'you' feel this and that, and so I want to know, who's this 'you'?"

Samir bit his lower lip.

I kept going. "Samir. Everyone gets that it's tougher for you. Only idiots believe that all you have to do is learn Swedish and then all the prejudice will go away. Georg and Margareta aren't idiots. You don't need to be afraid that — "

"You," he said, and he took my hand. "Maja. You know how I feel about you. Labbe is a great guy, and Margareta and Georg are nice." He was sitting so close to me that I could feel how rapidly he was breathing. "You are ... You know exactly what I mean, when I say 'you.' I mean *you*, you and all your..." He waved his other hand, sweeping it around the yard, the forest, the water, up toward the estate house, both wings, the guesthouse, the hunting cabin where John lived, the boathouse. "You know who *you* are, but you don't understand the rest of it. I'm not afraid of you. It's not about being afraid. You just don't get it."

Then explain it to me.

He turned to me. His hand brushed my hipbone. His mouth was close, close to me.

And I thought he was going to kiss me. But he didn't move.

Instead we just sat there. He breathed; I breathed. I didn't dare to look at him. When I stood up, he stayed where he was. I walked back to the house without turning around; I went into my room and closed the door. As I lay down on the bed, I picked up my phone and turned it on. Sebastian had sent one text. Just one:

"If you're planning to fuck him, I hope you use protection."

22.

How did Sebastian and I "get back" to what we had before after that weekend at Labbe's? We didn't. But we kept going. Yes, I think I convinced myself that I needed to think like that, in "before" and "after." No, I don't think Sebastian apologized. Yes, I did say, "I would never...how could you think that of me?" (because I had to say something about the text he sent), and yes, I went straight from Labbe's house to Sebastian's and we had sex while I assured him over and over that *I would never* and *you're the only one I love.*

Make-up sex is supposed to be the best sex, but it's not. It's sex when you're sad and angry but not so sad and angry you can't pretend nothing is wrong after a while. And soon I was angry and sad about something other than the weekend at Labbe's, and that was worse because Sebastian hadn't said or done anything in particular. I just wanted things to be different and sometimes I tried to pretend they were.

The days went by. November went by. It was the first Sunday of Advent. Everything was worth celebrating, in Sebastian's opinion, and I did what I could to agree.

There were lots of people at Montage, maybe even more than usual. We got there earlier than we usually did, too, and we still had to spend a few minutes elbowing our way through before the bouncer saw it was us and pulled us inside. They always let Sebastian in as soon as he showed up. Always, always, always. They usually let the rest of us skip the line, too, even if we came without Sebastian, but it was never quite as fast that way.

Dennis was still outside, his shoulders hunched up. He would never get into Montage without Sebastian, and Sebastian seldom wanted him to come in. Now and then he would take a stroll around the block, his down jacket pulled up to his chin, his hood up, and his hands dangling in front of his body as if they were too heavy for him to manage. But Dennis didn't complain. Thanks to Sebastian he had more customers than ever and they paid considerably more than the sewer rats he could scrape up if he was dealing at Sergels Torg.

The club was decorated for Christmas, with colored lights and thick glittery garlands, silver balls and Swarovski crystals on a tree in the middle of the dance floor. Amanda and Labbe had barely made it through the door before they started making out on a sofa in the VIP section. Labbe was half lying on his back, and Amanda was next to him, one leg thrown over him. Their tongues, two blind, naked rats, were visible side-on each time they kissed.

Thirty minutes after we got in, Sebastian was so high that it was starting to be difficult for the staff to ignore it.

Two of the security guards had joined forces near one of the exits. They were watching him. Presumably they were waiting for him to fall asleep or pass out. Only then would they be able to send him home.

Anytime security tried to interfere before Sebastian was passed out, it all went to hell. The week before, one of them had taken him by the arm when he tried to de-pants a guy who had shoved in front of him at the bar. The guard had been fairly polite; it was a we-think-maybe-it's-time-for-you-to-go-home sort of grip. "Do you want us to call a taxi?" But Sebastian still lost his shit. So he got to stay. The owner came over and managed to get him into one of the private rooms and asked me to sit there with him, and I did, until he fell asleep and Labbe helped me drag him to the car.

Still, they always let him in. Always, always, always. Last in line, first inside. Anything else would be as unthink-able as letting one of the princesses stand outside stamping her feet on the sidewalk to get warm.

I didn't know what Dennis had concocted for him this evening, it was almost always something new, but whatever it was it would hardly make him sleepy. He was working his way around the club like he was looking for someone. Around and around. Again and again. Now and then he would pass by me, demand we go sit on the same sofa as Labbe and Amanda, but before ten seconds had passed he'd had enough and wanted to go to the bar instead. We stood at the bar for a few minutes. He forgot about the drink he had ordered before the bartender had finished mixing it, and he ordered the same drink again from a different bartender. Then he left both drinks on the bar and dragged me by the hand to the dance floor, then left me there because he "had to use the bathroom." A few minutes later, I saw him wandering around again, craning his neck, turning his head. Walking. Around and around. Again and again.

"Should we get out of here? Where should we go? Nothing's going on here. Should we get out of here? I just have to go to the bathroom, then we can get out of here."

I tried to dance. I tried to get drunk. I even tried to talk to Amanda, which was a joke, because she didn't want to talk, she couldn't talk. It's hard to talk when you're getting your tonsils massaged, I get it, it's pretty awkward to talk even if all you have is a tongue in your ear, I'm with her there, too, it's hard to concentrate. But I would have liked to talk to her. To scream-talk over the music, lean close and not even have to say anything, just laugh at someone's ugly pants or weird hair. Instead I tried to keep up with Sebastian. Listen to his questions. They didn't require responses.

"Wanna go now? Did you go to the bathroom?"

"Why? Jesus, you're so lame. We just got here. Want something to drink?"

I was tired of Sebastian. Of Amanda and Labbe, of all of them, of this whole deal. I was tired of being young and having fun, going a little crazy, standing in the cold, screaming drunk outside a party, or inside a VIP room. I was tired of all of it, but I played along as best I could. Night after night after night. Around and around and around. I woke up on

Saturday and Sunday mornings to find a blue ticket in my pocket, crumpled up along with the cellophane from a pack of cigarettes and made-up questions about *Oh my God how did I get home?* I rubbed out the blurry stamps on the back of my hand, cut off the festival armband with nail scissors. And then I said it again, those lines everyone spouts: *God I was so drunk* and *I don't remember a thing* and *Shit, that was totally off the hook.*

But I never had fun anymore. I didn't forget how I'd gotten home. I always got home the same way. I made sure Sebastian got home. I would sleep there while he was half conscious or played video games or just tried to find "something to do."

I didn't want any of it anymore, but I didn't know what I wanted instead. To break up? What would I do if my relationship with Sebastian ended? Would I still hang around with the rest of the squad? I had no plan. I didn't want to have a plan. I just wanted life to be fun again.

Sebastian would lose it if I left him. He had already lost it. I couldn't break up with him now. I would do it soon, once things had calmed down a bit, but I couldn't say anything right now. We watched him, me and the security guards, from our respective directions, but we didn't say anything; we knew that it was always possible to give a little more leeway to the line we knew he would inevitably cross. We said nothing because we pretended it would all be okay, even though we knew that it would all go to hell. The bouncers formed two-man teams, but I was alone. None of us did anything. I was just an extra. We were all extras. That's what happened when you found yourself at Sebastian's side. An extra with no lines. If I said anything, it would be edited out of the action. It was easy to ignore; no one needed to reply to anything I said.

"Why don't we go home?"

"This fucking place, this fucking city. Jesus Christ, it's so boring, it's such a shit hole. Goddammit. Let's go to Barcelona. There's an amazing tapas bar by that church, wait, hold on, that's in Palma, isn't it? I just need to go to the bathroom. Order me something to drink. I'll be right back, I just have to check on something. I need a drink. I just have to go to the bathroom. Fuck it, let's get out of here, Jesus Christ, it's so boring. Can you tell that fucking DJ he has to play something good? Let's go to NYC. I just have to go to the bathroom, check on something, where the hell is Dennis, he has to...go out and get him, tell him I need to talk to him, Jesus Christ, this is so fucking boring."

I said it to Amanda: "I don't know if I love him anymore." We talked about it. She said, "I'm sure it will get better soon." But she and Labbe pulled away. They had been acting strange ever since that weekend out at Labbe's parents'. For them, there was definitely a "before" and an "after." I knew they hung out with Samir without calling us, I knew they thought Sebastian was a problem. But when they wanted to come here, out, to go somewhere, we were still good enough. To avoid standing in line. *We're with him.*

At night, the thoughts would run through my head. When I lay beside Sebastian and the back of his neck was sweaty, he startled in his sleep, turned to me, pulled me close.

There are words that can be felt throughout your whole body. Words can spark a feeling that belongs to a different part of the brain than you expect. Good words feel warm. My mom's whispered "shhh..." when I was little and had trouble sleeping ("My little girl, shhh...sleep now, darling..."). Or Dad's tone of voice when he called "Maja!" and you could hear how he wanted everyone to know that I was his girl, that we belonged together, him and me. And Grandma's voice when she was reading a story ("Once upon a time..."). Sebastian's "I love you," just as he fell asleep, at the tail end of a breath.

I don't know. It wasn't all bad. It wasn't always only bad.

"His dad has to do something," Amanda said to me, but not to anyone else. "Sebastian needs help." Amanda thought it had to do with the drugs, that if Sebastian just eased up a little, we would be just as in love as before. *Amanda's right,* I thought. *Of course Amanda's right. Of course I love Sebastian.*

Don't do anything. Don't say anything. Talk to him. Help him.

But I couldn't say anything. No one said anything. What were any of us supposed to say?

I wanted out. I wanted to leave. I wanted it to be over.

Sebastian would lose it. He had lost it. Sebastian was crazy. He was sick. I had to do something. He needed help.

I loved him. Of course I loved him.

23.

Amanda was asleep in the chair next to mine. Her Lucia tinsel had fallen onto her shoulder and her nylons had a big hole in the knee. On the auditorium stage stood a woman in sky-high heels, tiny earrings, and a gigantic men's watch. Her shiny coal-black hair looked like it would need its own seat on an airplane. She was American, the "editor in chief of the Western world's most-read financial publication" (Christer's introduction).

"You're students of international economics, part of a special program, is that right?"

We buzzed in assent, even though lots of people in there weren't part of the international economics program at all. The other third-year students from the three-year programs were there, too. Plus loads of parents (mostly dads), who were probably skipping their children's St. Lucia performances. The parents had been informed that they were not allowed to ask questions or take up any seats, so they were standing along the walls, and every ten meters stood a broad-shouldered dude in a black suit and an earpiece: the American lady's security team.

"And those of you who aren't studying economics will have to tolerate this anyway."

We laughed cooperatively as the American smiled wider than the entrance gate on a car ferry.

Even Sebastian was there. At five o'clock that morning, Amanda and I had woken him with Lucia songs. Then he offered us and a few other guys "breakfast." But when I refused to ride to school with Sebastian in his car, he got mad. Now he sat on the other side of the auditorium.

An "anonymous benefactor" had sponsored this lecture. I asked Sebastian if it was Claes, and the look on his face told me that was a dumb question. The rumor was that her lecture cost 350,000 kronor, but none of the teachers would discuss it.

The American lady was more than an editor-in-chief; she had a doctorate in economics and had been named one of the world's most influential people by *Time* magazine. She was popular thanks to her YouTube channel, where she explained economic issues using Barbie and Ken, Barbie's house, and Barbie's car. The clip with the most hits was about the American financial crisis. In that video, Black Barbie played an evicted homeowner (a single mom of three). She couldn't pay the mortgage, and good old Ken played the role of the director of Lehman Brothers. The American made the dolls talk: Ken was arrogant and distant, while Black Barbie swore and spoke worse English than your average Swedish preschooler with dreams of becoming a rapper. But no one accused this woman of using racist stereotypes. She herself looked too much like

Black Barbie for anyone to dare. Her critics thought she was too radical, that she used gross generalizations to make her points. I thought someone should at least tell her to be more subtle with her makeup. A shorter pair of false eyelashes would make a world of difference.

Today she was going to talk about the future of the world economy. *Growth or Collapse* was the subtitle, which should have, but didn't, end in a question mark.

"Anyone in here who hates economics? Who actually plans to pursue a career doing something important?" (Gentle laughter.) "Smart decision. You can't trust economists." (Louder laughter.)

She swept her arm across the room. "Name a dangerous economist."

"Karl Marx," someone called from one of the back rows. She nodded.

"Milton Friedman," Samir called. He was sitting in the front.

The American smiled, pleased. "My point exactly."

She picked up a small plastic water bottle and drank from it.

"Economists are dangerous for the simple reason that the global economy affects people. All people. So whether or not you study economics, whether or not you think money is everything or that you are above material objects, listen carefully. I will be talking about you."

As Barbie wagged her index finger toward us audience members, the lights in the auditorium went down. A gigantic screen appeared at the back of the stage, and without further ado she began rattling off a crash course in twentieth-century economics, numbers, historic events, universal suffrage, World War I, financial crisis, World War II, economic boom. In front of her rose hologram charts and spinning 3-D cubes and circles, charts and diagrams of population growth, median incomes, life expectancies. Now I understood why the auditorium had been closed for a week. This felt like it was straight out of a Bond movie. She even had a hologram of FDR that stood beside her on the stage for a few seconds, reciting a few lines from a speech about the New Deal. Not even Amanda was having trouble staying awake.

Barbie spoke faster than a sports announcer. Christer nodded in time with her intonation. Nod-nod-nod-nod, as if he had lost a screw from his neck. Christer was high as a kite on teacher crack, struck by some sort of mental UTI.

"Many people are convinced that economics is a science guided by forces that are like the law of gravity. Expenditures and revenues. If you drop a glass, it falls to the floor and breaks. You go bankrupt if you spend more than you earn."

Barbie looked up at the rows of parents in suits and jackets, then let her eyes move down to us, the students, and continued preaching.

By the Q&A session, Christer started jogging around with a wireless microphone. Sebastian went first. The American smiled at him even before he stood up. *So Claes* had *paid for this.*

I suddenly got the urge to leave. *Black Barbie and Ken Fagerman.* If Sebastian had been sent here to keep tabs on what the most up-to-date fashion darling of the financial world had to say, both Claes and the fashion darling would be disappointed.

Sebastian sounded tired; he stumbled over his words but managed to ask what was written on his card, and as Barbie responded, Christer headed for the next person who had been asked to prepare a question.

When it was my turn, I handed the microphone back to Christer before the American had even begun her answer. I had no intention of trying to ask any forced follow-up questions.

The American nodded thoughtfully at me. She pretended not to think mine was a dumb question (only dumb questions that Christer already knew the answer to had been approved) and she received applause for her response. This was her fifty-third variation on "on the one hand and on the other hand and in my study of this issue I highlight many new factors…they indicate the answer is far from obvious." The 3-D technology had been turned off. Amanda's eyelids looked seriously heavy. She was trying to find a more comfortable position. Barbie was all shell and surface; she would never say anything everyone here didn't agree with. She delivered.

But then it was Samir's turn. He took the microphone from Christer and began.

"We had a mock parliamentary election here in school a few months ago." Samir's voice trembled. He sounded nervous. "All the students got to cast pretend votes, and two made-up racist parties got more than thirty-five per-cent of the vote."

Out of the corner of my eye I saw Christer's gaze darting around. This wasn't the prepared question. He reached for the microphone in confusion, but the Ameri-can pointed at Samir; she wanted him to keep talking. And Samir moved the microphone to his other hand, out of Christer's reach.

"The school decided that the results shouldn't be taken seriously, that it only turned out that way because a group of students got together and decided to sabotage the exercise."

"But?" The American was intrigued.

Someone in the audience called, "Stick to the topic, Samir." One of the dads in the back called, "I think you're at the wrong lecture, kid," but Barbie lifted her hand and the room fell silent again.

"Continue."

"No one took that school election seriously. But it's a good example. Because we are taught that politics is only about...how every problem in every European country is due to immigration, war beyond the borders of Europe, and Islamic terrorism. Things out of our politicians' control. That is all we talk about, the Islamic fundamentalists being the biggest threat. But at the same time, at home there are more and more billionaires, and the poor get poorer. One percent of the people on earth own fifty percent of all the assets on earth. The poorest half of humanity owns less than five percent of the assets on earth. We don't talk about that. I mean…" Samir cleared his throat, losing his momentum for a moment. "Shouldn't we be talking about how these economic issues affect our welfare and democracy; *don't* they affect our democracy, and, I mean, like, our society?"

A guy a few rows behind Samir started humming "The Internationale." Cautious laughter spread through the room. But Barbie raised her Jesus hand again and cut them off.

"Tell me. Samir, was that your name? Tell me, Samir, how do you think these conflicts in our society relate to economics?"

"I think economists ought to use their numbers to come up with concrete solutions to the problems that actually exist. It doesn't mean anything if you say we have to invest one thousand billion in infrastructure if you don't tell us where that money is supposed to come from. Especially not when the debate is only about how we can't afford anything because immigration costs too much."

Something had happened to the American's smile. It looked different, and it took a moment for me to realize that this new smile was genuine.

Samir's voice grew steadier. "Of course public investment is great, but the hard part is determining who should foot the bill. And no one dares to say that these people in here ought to pay."

There was a decent murmur running through the room. The mood had changed; it wasn't rage, but it felt like a room full of adults who want to *explain the way of things*. The row of dads, I could actually *feel* how they wanted to clear their throats and tell Samir (and Barbie), *You don't know what you're talking about*. Because of course *they* didn't have any problem with immigration. *Certainly not!* But right now we're talking about industry in Sweden, they wanted to say. We are supposed to give jobs and welfare and new homes to all these *recent arrivals*. You can't cripple us with taxes. I knew what they wanted to say, because I had heard Dad talking about it. And the dads in the back seemed to have forgotten that they'd promised not to ask any questions, because four or five of them had taken half a step forward with their hands raised. They weren't used to raising their hands, it was clear, but they were squirming. Some of them looked in fourteen different directions simultaneously in an attempt to signal *what a sweet but naïve boy* and *we all want to start a revolution when we're young*, and someone stage-whispered, "My God, we have raised a Communist!" and someone else started giggling uncontrollably.

The American ignored them; instead she pulled up a chair and sat down.

"Bullshit!" shouted the guy who had just hummed "The Internationale."

Barbie looked up.

"Is it?" she said, offering the audience another toothpaste smile. *Don't worry*, that smile said. *I'm on your side.* "It's okay, we're not going to talk immigration politics. I don't know enough about it. But we can talk about how we finance the expenses of the state, how we finance welfare. That's a relevant question, isn't it?" She waited for the murmur of assent. "One percent of the people on earth own fifty percent of all the assets on earth. What's more, the eighty-five richest people in the world own as much as the poorest half of the world's population combined..." She hesitated and made her voice light; maybe she was joking? Maybe she was glancing at Sebastian. "They would fit in a few of the rows in this auditorium. Isn't that a problem?"

One of the dads couldn't handle it anymore. Though he had been given neither the floor nor the microphone, he called, "Excuse meeee," but Barbie didn't even look in his direction. Instead she walked slowly across the stage until she ended up in front of Sebastian. *Now. Sebastian is supposed to prove that he can represent the Fagerman group,* I thought, and my stomach knotted. *She wants Sebastian to help her start a real debate.* I wanted Sebastian to get up and leave. *Get out of here,* I thought. *You hate politics.* And then I had the forbidden thought: *You are too stupid for this debate.*

Barbie went on. Just a few meters from Sebastian. Her tone was more carefree than ever. But she took for granted that he was listening.

"There is a die-hard conviction that from an economic perspective, it pays to be extra generous toward billionaires. That is why we have countries like Sweden, where even the Social Democrats think a zero-percent wealth tax is reasonable." She waved toward the parents. "You have no idea how happy my accountant would be if

I said I was going to move to Sweden. And I'm not even a billionaire."

Then she turned back to Samir.

"But then what happens? When the rest of the population who aren't even millionaires, poor things, what happens when they realize that they finance all public expenses? What will they do?"

She pointed urgently at Samir.

He was still holding the microphone. He answered immediately, as if he had only been waiting for her command. "They will protest."

"You bet they will."

Her natural smile was back. And the dads had gone quiet. Christer executed something that looked like an attempt at a pirouette. He hadn't expected this.

"They will protest," Barbie continued. "How? A bloody revolution? Will your parents be dragged to the city square to be beheaded? We don't want that. Thus it is probably better if we can let immigrants be the scapegoats."

The American squinted and gazed at the back of the auditorium.

"You're laughing," she stated. But no one was laughing. No one said a word. No one but Samir. His voice had lost all its uncertainty and he suddenly seemed ten years older. I had never thought about how good his English was.

"Never in history have the upper classes expected to lose their power; they are always surprised."

"Very true." The American nodded, turning around to aim a challenging look at Sebastian. He had no microphone.

He slouched in his chair when he replied, but we could hear him anyway.

"This is just stupid. Who gives people jobs? Is that you, maybe, Samir? Or your dad, the taxi driver?"

Sebastian laughed as loud as he could. But not even the guys beside him joined in.

The American looked at Sebastian briefly, tilted her head slightly to the side, and then turned back to Samir and waved at him to respond. He nodded.

"The stupid thing is to believe that the more billionaires, the better for Sweden."

Barbie nodded and took over as Samir took a breath.

"And we can talk about dads who drive taxis, too. Because what happens to those dads' sense of taxpayer duty?"

Don't say anything, I thought at Sebastian. *Be quiet.*

And Sebastian made no attempt to say anything either vulgar or stupid. He leaned his head back and crossed his arms over his chest like he was trying to find a comfy sleeping position.

"We're off topic now, I think." The American cleared her throat. "Before my own security guards pluck me out of here so a riot doesn't break out..."

She looked at Samir and the row of parents along the wall, at Christer, who was treading water off to the side. But then she started talking again. Her sentences seemed more thoughtful now that she didn't need the holograms and exploding images.

"Do we need billionaires to create jobs? Prosperity? Successful companies? Wealthy individuals can certainly be good for a country..." She raised her chin at the back rows. "I have no problem with the fact that it is possible to become a millionaire. I don't even completely dislike billionaires." She nodded at Sebastian, who was pretending to sleep. "I do actually believe in capitalism, although some of my fellow citizens think everyone with my...appearance must be a Communist."

Christer cackled but couldn't get anyone to laugh with him.

"But I think you were trying to make a different point, Samir. To say that there is a limit to how unequal a society can become and continue to remain a stable democracy. And you're right. I will explain why."

It was dead silent. Everyone wanted to hear this. We didn't even shift positions.

"We must be cautious about the social contract. Both parties must uphold their side of the agreement. We must have comprehensible equity. It is not fair if the welfare system is bankrolled by low- and middle-income earners. If large corporations pay less in taxes than their small- and medium-size colleagues, that is not what the social contract looks like. And when a nurse pays higher income taxes than a person who has inherited a fortune...You have no wealth tax in Sweden. None at all." She formed her index finger and thumb into a zero. "Nor do you have inheritance tax. Zero percent. In other words, those who don't have to pay income tax if they don't feel like it, they don't pay taxes at all. Is that in accordance with the social contract?

Is that what the Bible means by 'whoever has will be given more, and they will have an abundance'?" She paused and took a sip of water. "Not even in the U.S. are we that generous. And I don't think you have to be a Communist to realize that the opposing sides in the U.S. are starting to reach the boiling point. It would be a mistake to believe that those opposing sides have nothing to do with economics. And I agree with you, Samir. It's no crazy conspiracy to say that there are those who benefit when social ills can be blamed on a minority. To pretend those problems are due to" — she made air quotes — "'the blacks' or, as in the 1930s, 'the Jews' or, as you call them in Europe today, 'the immigrants.'"

She stopped there. The silence lasted for several seconds. No one in the room wanted to acknowledge that there could possibly be a link between their money and anti-immigration sentiments. *We're not racist, we're on the right side, we're not simple, uneducated Sweden Democrats.* But since Barbie hadn't called out anyone in particular, there was no way to protest. Then the American snuck a nearly imperceptible glance at the clock on one side of the room, straightened her back, and pointed at Samir.

"Look at that. Wasn't this unexpectedly fun?"

It was so quiet in the auditorium that the parent who spoke was perfectly audible.

"*Fun?*" he muttered. He sounded like he'd just woken up, but his English was perfect. I recognized him — he was the director of one of the big banks. He scratched his disheveled hair. "It's way more than 'fun.' It's Christmas come early. I can go back to my colleagues and tell them we Swedes live in a tax paradise. Champagne tonight!"

And now the parents were laughing.

The cheery atmosphere was back just as quickly as it had left. *It's just politics. We don't all have to agree.* If the bank guy and his friend didn't feel stung, we didn't have to either. *What does this American lady know about Sweden? Ha ha! Heh heh!*

And then we applauded. The American aimed a few gentle claps at the audience and she smiled at Samir, and he smiled back, as if the two of them shared a secret.

"These are difficult questions you're asking, Samir," she said while we were still applauding. "Keep asking them, and you'll go far."

As Christer went on stage to thank her, I made eye contact with Samir. His cheeks were still a little pink.

Well done, I mouthed. *Thanks*, he mouthed back. I wanted to say more, but by then he had looked away. I looked at Sebastian instead. He had fallen asleep for real.

Christer gave the woman flowers and a book about Djursholm, and we applauded again. We had a free period now, but a whole day of school ahead of us, and I didn't have the energy to listen to whatever Sebastian would say and I definitely didn't have the energy to go to more classes, so I took the bus home. Mom and Lina wouldn't be there for hours; I could be on my own. I didn't have the energy for anything but being by myself.

The doorbell rang after I had changed clothes and was lying on my bed with my laptop on my stomach, watching a movie. Sebastian would just sit outside the door and wait if I tried to ignore him, so I went downstairs to let him in.

But it wasn't Sebastian. Samir had draped his jacket over his arm and seemed out of breath, like he had run to my house.

"May I come in?"

He rested his hand on the doorjamb and leaned in toward me. It made the muscles in his arm contract, and I walked toward him. I stopped right next to him and ran my hand first over his delicate skin and then across the short, thick hair on his arm. When I kissed him, gently, cautiously, it stung my lips. I pressed my tongue to his and my skin burned. He placed his hand around my waist.

"Sure," I said. "Come in."

THE WOMEN'S JAIL

Week 1 of Trial: The weekend

24.

When I have rec time in the morning, I can't take a sleeping pill, so last night I didn't sleep, at least not that I can remember. I tried to watch the movie Susse gave me; I tried three times. Possibly I dozed off for a little while during my last attempt.

When I think back, now that I have time to try to understand what happened, it's easy to start sorting. I would like to divide everything up in carefully demarcated chapters: the first weeks of school, after Sebastian and I returned home from the Mediterranean, when it was "like Sebastian and Maja have always been together" (Amanda's words). Hadn't that been a nice, uncomplicated, easy time? It was at least true that during that period I made new friends, received attention in a new way, other sorts of compliments. Everyone around Sebastian and me (except for Samir) seemed to think nothing was more natural in all the world than Sebastian's and my life and the fact that we were a couple.

The second chapter was more complicated and muddled. And the third chapter, after I kissed Samir, that was when it started to descend into total chaos.

But it doesn't work that way. If I'm being completely honest, not even the first part can be separated from the rest, what happened later. There are no chapters in this mess.

That warmth in the beginning, the heat of high summer, and the colors — maybe that helped? The warmth reminded me of the Mediterranean and blurred out what I should have seen even then, all the strange stuff. Not just the strange things about Claes, how cruel he was, how little he cared. But also the strange things about Sebastian. School was the same old school as ever, but it was like it both shrank and expanded when Sebastian and I started dating. At first he was almost always there, even when he wasn't going to class. He always seemed to know where I was, even if I was somewhere other than I should have been according to my schedule. And I liked that; I was flattered that he was keeping tabs on me, that he wanted to be near me. It wasn't like he was a stalker, he wasn't controlling or weird, nothing like that. When he showed up, suddenly standing in front of me in his white T-shirt, smiling, I would smile back, of course I would, because we were in love — he was happy to see me and I was glad he'd found me.

But that wasn't all. There was always something else in him. It was more than sadness. It wasn't hate; hate is simple, and Sebastian was never easy to understand. I was never afraid of what he might do to me, not even toward the end, but I was always anxious. Even those first weeks were both things, a mixture, difficult, easy and delightful, funny, awful and wonderful.

I hate the first rec-time shift at the jail. I hate it even more because the staff think they're doing me a favor when they assign me to it. They want me to be happy that I'll have time left over for other things, fun activities to fill up all the hours of the day, hours that are freed up when I "wake up and get out of bed in good time." As if I have stuff to do other than wishing I could smoke. Because my least favorite thing about the early shift is that I haven't even had the time to crave a cigarette.

And I crave a smoke even less when they pair me with Doris.

I'm actually supposed to spend my time outside by myself, because I still have restrictions even though the investigation is over. I'm still supposed to be in isolation ("for my own safety"), and I am barred from having visitors. But the jail is full and the number of daylight hours are not sufficient for everyone to receive their constitutionally guaranteed outdoor time if they don't pair a few of us up. Plus they have to consider my age. It's not good to let me go for too long without seeing other people. Locked up in a cell by yourself twenty-three hours per day, that's the kind of thing (imprisoned youth and lack of social contact) that will attract criticism from Amnesty. Ferdinand loves to tell me everything she knows about Amnesty and explain that this is why they try to convince me to meet with the chaplain and the psychologist and the teacher several times a week, and why they don't want me to spend exercise time alone.

Doris is a woman in her sixties whose real name definitely isn't Doris, but it should be. She is considered to be the perfect social-contact companion for me; she's my Amnesty alibi.

It wasn't something I had planned, the way it turned out with Samir. We were ashamed, he was ashamed, I was ashamed; of course I was ashamed.

"I would never sleep with Samir," I said to Sebastian (and myself) after the weekend at Labbe's.

"Never again!" Samir and I said to each other after that December afternoon, when it happened anyway. We could never let it happen again. We shouldn't have needed to say it out loud to know it was true. And yet we said it, over and over, all the time, and yet it did happen again. And again.

Samir called me. He texted. I didn't answer; I deleted the texts, changed my mind, responded, changed my mind again. We saw each other at school. I sat in the library, our secret forest where no one else ever went. It felt real. As soon as I saw Samir, it felt real. Everything else was just a pain. At that point, in December, my life was horrible, all the time, around the clock, until Samir touched me. And then it went on being horrible until he touched me again.

I've always thought it's so freaking weird that people cut up their arms to make their soul hurt less, so that they can *deal*. But in some ways, I guess what happened with Samir was the same thing. It felt so good to be with him that it hurt. Sometimes I thought that it felt so good *because* it hurt, even though I also think that it was all the things he wasn't that made it impossible for me to let go of him.

Samir was *not* always on the verge of a meltdown. He did *not* always want to be doing something other than what he was doing. He did *not* expect to be recognized, consulted, idolized, paid attention to, admitted first of anyone. When Samir touched me, he just wanted to touch me, nothing more, at least that's what it felt like. We had sex everywhere we weren't supposed to. At my house (Mom and Dad were at work; Lina was at day care), when I was skipping class (not Samir, he had a free period). In one of the school bathrooms one evening two days after St. Lucia. The school was open because the choir was practicing in the auditorium, but we didn't know anyone in choir, and at that moment, just as his hands touched me, I thought that it had to be this way. *If it's Samir and me instead, then I won't have to be with Sebastian.* Samir was not Sebastian; he was the opposite, and that was exactly what I wanted. Maybe that was why?

Samir wasn't my knight in shining armor. Quite the opposite — he was the poisoned apple. But back then, during those short days when it was happening, it didn't matter why. The questions about *why Samir?* weren't important enough for me to be able to let him go. I thought about how it was wrong and I shouldn't do it. But I still couldn't let him go. So I didn't bother to think about that either.

Doris spends all her outside time, whether or not we have the early shift, sitting on the cement bench at a cigarette-flicking distance from me, chain-smoking roll-your-owns without ever taking the cigarette from her mouth. The smoke rises around her like she's a pot with a crooked lid. She doesn't say a word to me in any language, even when I say hi. She doesn't look, doesn't nod, doesn't mutter. I did hear her sigh at her lighter when it was raining and she was having trouble getting a flame. But she didn't ask if she could use mine, she just kept trying until it finally lit a few minutes later, and once she had fired up her cigarette she let out a moan. I assume it was of relief. Pleasure, maybe? A very Doris-specific version of pleasure.

I remember asking my mom, when I was like twelve, how old you should be when you have sex for the first time. Mom replied, When you want to have sex so bad that you don't care what I think, when you don't care what anyone else thinks because you'd rather die than not do it, that's when you're old enough. I think she said that to demonstrate how fun she thought sex was, to show how "cool" she was. I thought she was being gross and fake. But she really did turn out to be right. I ought to have listened to her for once. Because I didn't understand what she meant until I met Sebastian. At the very beginning, with him, when he stroked my lower arm and made it feel like it was made of velvet — I understood completely. Sure, I still thought Mom was ridiculous, but I got it. And when it didn't feel like that anymore, I was prepared to do *anything* with *anyone* just to get that feeling back. No, hold on, Samir wasn't just anyone and he definitely wouldn't do just anything. But he made me feel like that, too, like I *couldn't stop.* Even if it wasn't uncomplicated with Samir, even when it was good. He was a version of happiness, but he never made me happy.

Doris's personality is as exciting as wet pant legs and she is fat in the American way — cone shaped — which makes me think of a toy I had when I was little, a bunch of different-colored plastic donuts that you were supposed to stack on top of each other on a pole, in descending order, with the biggest donut on the bottom. Or one of those Slinkys that were popular when Mom was little (it "walks" down stairs); Doris moves like that, but slower, one spare tire at a time, on those few occasions when she isn't just sitting still.

I asked Susse what Doris is in for. Susse is "prohibited from telling me." But whatever it is, it would have been more shocking to find Doris out in the world than behind lock and key. If you looked up "female inmate" in an old dictionary from the 1800s, you would find a sepia photograph of someone who could be mistaken for Doris, with the possible exception of her clothing. Because Doris doesn't wear a jail uniform (oh, no!), she wears Crocs, tube socks, sweatpants, and a fleece sweatshirt. Over that she wears a gigantic raincoat, with pockets the size of garbage cans. That's where she keeps her tobacco. And possibly also a freshly drowned litter of kittens.

Every time I go outside with Doris, I make up new stories about what she might have done; it's become a challenge to always think up a new crime. Doris is too old to be in jail for having just killed her newborn baby. She seems too fat to have killed her husband (unless she straight up sat on him), and I can't imagine who would want to get it on with Doris, or that there could be anyone in the world who Doris cared about enough so that she'd want to sit on him or her. Doris is the ugliest woman I've ever seen in my life.

The first thing I thought of when Samir joined our class was how beautiful he was. Not good-looking, beautiful. Ask anyone, and they'd say that wasn't what was important about him, because everyone always has to pretend that beautiful people are a certain way inside, that they're smart and nice and funny and all sorts of stuff, but of course that was Samir's most important quality. It was crucial, even. His smart comments and good grades and political engagement and everything he knew that other people his age had no clue about would have been unbearable without that toffee skin and those dark brown eyes, which were almost as black as his ridiculously long doll eyelashes. My eyes felt as colorless as rainwater when he looked at me. Samir smelled like tar and salt. He was the most beautiful guy I had seen in my life. How could that be unimportant?

Doris is the pale gray of an earthworm and smells like wet dog. Last weekend I pretended that she ran a brothel full of enslaved whores who had been kidnapped from their families in poor Eastern European countries. I made believe that she would sit there smoking her gray-brown cigarettes next to an old-fashioned Bakelite phone with a corkscrew cord. There she would take orders for degrading sex acts, which she would make her stable of twelve-year-old junkies perform. She had a half dozen slaves with bad breath and dirty beards to help her out. It was one of the slaves, I thought, who called the police and turned her in when she didn't pay him.

Today I'm more into the idea that she ran the books for some drug lord (she refuses to testify against him because he would kill her), or maybe she concocted explosives for her youngest son, a pimply underling who works for the Russian mob. Maybe she speaks fluent Swedish and she just pretends to be doing this silent-movie routine, she was actually born here, maybe she wanted to be an actress when she was young but couldn't get into acting school because she's too ugly so she started drinking and wrecked herself and after a few years she started taking in foster children because it paid well. Maybe one of her malnourished foster children ate so much coleslaw and lingonberries in the school cafeteria that the kid had to go to the hospital. And a doctor's examination revealed Doris's neglect and now she's sitting in my exercise yard, refusing to say a word.

I have nothing else to do all day but think up these sorts of situations. Doris is the most effective antismoking campaign I have ever been exposed to.

"Imagine a place where you feel safe," Mom used to say when I was little and had trouble falling asleep. I would close my eyes and pretend to do as she said, but I never really did it. Now I do it all the time. Weekends at the jail turn time into clockworks in my head. Rusty cogs chew up my brain, one micromillimeter at a time. Only once in a while do I think about what is real. Often I imagine my way to other places, where no one else exists.

I think up places where I should feel safe: beaches, oceans, wide-open spaces, emptiness, sunsets, and winds. Sometimes I picture the forest. I imagine walking barefoot in the moss, even though it's fall and spruce needles poke me and mud gets stuck between my toes. I don't hate jail; it is perfect solitude. You cannot be a different person, but sometimes you can avoid being anyone at all. Even if that nice feeling never lasts very long, maybe only for a few seconds (like a belt that feels nice a split second before it is pulled too tight), I feel a tiny bit better.

I pretend that I'm walking on a beach, for example. Not that I've ever been on a beach all alone, but it's easy to imagine, a long beach with gray shells and white sand, seaweed and driftwood. I fantasize about walking on it, the tide is going out, the sand is heavy and hard as asphalt when the water retreats. Far off on the horizon, the waves are crashing, the cliffs around the bay are black, white foam swirling around them, exploding several meters up toward the sky. There are sounds and smells; even when the sea is calm, it is moving, everywhere. I know it sounds a little like a movie where Ryan Gosling is walking hand in hand down the beach with some chick whose hair gets in her face, and

I hate that sort of movie, but I still like thinking about that place. But without people.

All the places I imagine are deserted. As soon as I think about a person, Samir or Sebastian or Amanda comes back, my brain forces me to think of them. And I can't handle it. Mom's method doesn't work anymore.

Aside from my shifts in the yard with Doris, I am kept in isolation. "For my own safety." But I know that's just what they say. I'm not in a single cell so I can feel safe, I'm there so everyone outside the jail can feel safe knowing I'm properly locked away. But all the same. Despite the water damage above my steel sink (it bows out like the belly of a fish). Despite the fact that they give me sleeping aids (which make my tongue feel like a hamster in my mouth when I wake up). Despite the smell. I never get used to the smell, it's like a layer of primer, it never changes and reminds me a little of the food smell in the school cafeteria (a mixture of industrial kitchen and sweaty gym shoes).

Despite all of that, I am glad to be alone in jail. I can think. About the sea and the beach and the forest, all those super-pathetic clichés. All the opposites of this place. I don't think I would feel safe in the forest, or on the beach, or at home, but I feel a little safer by being locked up and thinking about places like that.

There are forbidden thoughts, too, other than those of Amanda, Samir, and Sebastian. Forbidden: home, the path down to the water, biking to Ekudden with Lina on the back, swimming by the diving tower in Barracuda Park, walking barefoot on Aludden, brushing ants off Lina's feet, grilling out on Cykelnyckel Island, reading aloud on the couch with Lina on my lap, sitting on the kitchen stairs with Mom's cashmere blanket over my legs and drinking tea, Lina's sweaty hand when it's a scary chapter, the lamp on my nightstand that buzzes after it's been on for a while, scary movies with Lina, my fingers sticky from hot buttered popcorn, Lina eating filled apple donuts and trying not to lick the powdered sugar from her lips, Lina squeezing her eyes and mouth shut and scrunching the tip of her nose when I put sunscreen on her cheeks.

The most forbidden thought, more forbidden than any other: Lina.

Close your eyes, imagine a place, anyplace at all, as long as Lina isn't there.

When the trial is over and I've been convicted, I will have to move away from the jail. I didn't ask Sander, but he told me anyway, that he will ("if the situation arises") demand that I be sentenced to some kind of juvenile hall. But it might be "tricky" because I'm already eighteen.

I asked Sander if I could stay at the jail. But he didn't seem to believe I was serious. I was.

If I'm sick for a few days, it will be even longer before I have to be moved away from here. And wherever they move me, I will no longer be in isolation. Sander and the others think that the worst thing about jail is the isolation, but I don't know how I will manage without it. There will be tons of people all around me. They will talk to me, touch me, ask questions, sit next to me at the dinner table, demand answers from me.

Will I have to see Lina? Presumably. I refuse to fantasize about that.

Trial hearing in case B 147/66

The prosecutor et al. v. Maria Norberg

Week 2 of Trial: Monday

25.

It's raining on the way to the courthouse. The window I'm gazing through is covered in diagonal stripes of water. Sander is sitting in the backseat with me; he met me at the jail so we could "go through a few things" on our way to the hearing.

"Did you sleep well?" he wonders. I nod.

When I was little, I thought that if you had a nightmare, you were supposed to tell someone about it so it wouldn't come true. And as soon as you spoke the terrible dream out loud, it wasn't real. It was like it fell out of the framework of things that could happen in real life.

Fairy tales say that trolls will turn to stone if sunlight touches them. I think that's supposed to mean that if you just expose terrible things, make them visible, they stop being terrible. But in reality, with truly awful things, the opposite is true. Too much sunshine and "truth" and "speaking out" and "putting your feelings into words" and "daring to talk about your problems" helps people see what a monster you are. Your ugly emotions become as glaring as hairy warts.

Sometimes the sun blinds those who look at the troll. And then all that light, all that glitter, can make the monster turn into the most beautiful object in the world. That's what it was like with Sebastian. His spotlights were so bright that it was hard to see anything but that he was Claes Fagerman's son, the party thrower, a cool guy. It was almost impossible to see who he really was.

I no longer believe that I can stave off catastrophes by putting them into words. Evidently things happen no matter what I say. The most horrible things can't be swayed by superstition and myth, statistics and likelihoods.

"Thanks," I say to Sander. What can he do about the fact that I can't sleep? "Just fine."

Then I go back to looking out the window. The heat whooshes through the car's ventilation system. It's too warm, but I don't say anything.

I used to talk about what I imagined, about my dreams, everything I pretended and made myself believe. I talked about them and everyone listened. Dad would pull me up on his lap and say he loved my "vivid imagination." When I was too old to sit in laps, it changed. He started to hate it when I talked about my outlandish ideas. He only liked it when I was commenting on what someone else had already said, if I was kind of snarky and distant. That he would listen to. Sometimes he almost laughed. If I involved myself too much, he thought I was lame, and then he would try to look like he wasn't even listening. He did his best to show that he wasn't interested in the least. If I spoke in anything but a whispered monotone, he would tell me to chill ("Calm down, Maja").

But it wasn't just Dad. Sebastian was the same way. So was Samir. Samir even more so than Sebastian after we slept together. ("Calm down, Maja. What are you getting worked up for?") All guys are like that once you've slept with them. All girls know it.

Girls are never supposed to laugh at their own jokes. They are never supposed to talk too fast or, worse, too loudly. A girl who talks too loudly about something she's worked out on her own might as well start practicing public urination and exposing her tits outside Parliament. *PMS-y, teenage female hormones.*

Dad only liked my imagination in theory. In reality, he was afraid of it. And he's hardly alone in that nowadays. My imagination is a part of the person they think I am, proof that I am dangerous and out of control. So I don't talk about my nightmares, or about what I'm afraid of. I no longer believe that it will make the evil go away. Superstition is no cure for reality. Hypochondriacs contract fatal diseases at the same rate as everyone else.

We arrive at the courthouse. Park. Get out of the car. Take the elevator up.

"What did you want to discuss?" I ask. Only then do I realize that we were silent during the entire ride. Sander shrugs. For a split second I think he's going to pat me on the cheek, like Grandpa might have done.

"You're doing well, Maja," he says instead. "Very well."

Sander always listens to me. Even when I'm not saying anything.

The courtroom seems darker than usual. Not that the windows usually let in tons of daylight, but today we are wrapped in a damp, gray darkness, even indoors. The air is dry; it feels stifling even before we begin. There are two weeks left of the trial, and I already feel like we've been at it for an eternity. I know the drill.

Start at ten, end at four, a little earlier on Fridays if possible. When Sander told me about the schedule, it didn't seem like the days would be all that long, but I had no idea how exhausting it is to be bored. I had no idea that my own trial would be boring. The prosecutor's documents, reading of records and forms, reports and statements (we will "revisit" them once it's time for the witnesses to read out loud from those same documents), even more records, even more statements.

We spent more than half of last week listening to the prosecutor go through what we will *revisit*; it will never end. This trial is a nightmare where you can't stop looking for something but you've forgotten what it is. Or when you try to scream but your voice doesn't work and no matter how hard you try you can't utter a single croak. It's not a scary dream in the sense that you're frightened, you don't get all sweaty, but you still know that everything has gone to hell and there's nothing you can do to stop it.

Today Sander is going to present my case (and he will submit our own goddamn documents, which he will *revisit later on*). In some ways, presenting my case means telling my story, but he also told me that he's "laying the groundwork to explain why you must be acquitted."

Sander has never said "It's going to be fine." He doesn't lie to me. Ferdinand has said "Don't worry" a few times, but she barely even tries to look like she means it. And since the way I'm feeling can't be defined as "worrying," I don't bother to respond.

I don't care about what Pancake says.

It's two minutes to ten when the chief judge turns on his microphone. He starts by blowing his nose. One of the lay judges yawns without covering his mouth. Not a single one of the judges is sitting all upright the way they did for the first two days. We are just about to begin and they're already more bored than the guard at the door. Sander's teeth are the only bright spot in here. He is full of energy; he thinks I'm *doing well*.

As soon as the chief judge has made it through the prefatory words ("The court is now in session. We continue with the hearing in case B 147/66..."), which he rattles off indifferently, like "in the name of the Father, the Son, and the Holy Ghost" or "on earth as it is in heaven," it's Sander's turn to talk.

"According to the prosecutor, Maja Norberg is guilty of murder, incitement to murder, and is an accessory to murder and attempted murder."

I'm not sure this crowd needs to be reminded of that, but Sander seems to think it's a bold opening.

"Maja Norberg denies responsibility," he continues, and now it's Sander's turn to rattle off words, rattle off the exact stuff he said back in the opening remarks about my view of the main charges and alternative charges, and it is so immediately boring that I want to leave. But then he lowers the volume of his monotonous rhythm another notch. And you have to make a serious effort to listen.

"The prosecutor claims that Maja Norberg incited the murder of Claes Fagerman and that she planned and carried out the crimes in question at Djursholm Upper Secondary School..."

Sander's voice is icy through and through. It says: *This is* absurd *what the prosecutor claims, it is totally preposterous and unreasonable.* The voice says that each of ugly Lena's claims is so ridiculous that Sander cannot bring himself to repeat it with even a shred of engagement.

He concludes with a hint of a sigh. "Maja Norberg denies all of this."

Sander looks from one side of the panel of judges to the other. The tired lay judge yawns again; this time he turns aside.

Sander continues. "The prosecutor's account of the crimes includes..." I wonder if it's Sander's turn to yawn. "A description of — how should I put it? A peculiar murderer, to say the least."

The prosecutor shifts in her seat. She doesn't look sleepy. She is obviously annoyed, staring at the chief judge and trying to get his attention.

Sander relishes his words; he looks pleased and lifts his head as if he thought of something else just this very moment.

"The prosecutor's portrait of Maja as the perpetrator is in certain ways exceptional. Unique."

I try to look like the opposite of unique. Unobtrusive. Average. I want to show everyone how ordinary I am. *Exceptional?* Why did he say that? Isn't that a good thing? Is the prosecutor's portrait of me a good thing? Sander makes it sound like the bubonic plague (or, well, mass murder). But no one is looking at me. Everyone is staring at Sander; they're afraid of missing a single syllable.

"Is that who Maja is?" I give a start. The sentence is a lash of the whip. "Is Maja really who the prosecutor says she is?"

Now the prosecutor's chair is scraping at the floor. She can hardly sit still, she's so worked up.

Sander allows the question to hang in the air. He doesn't bring up my privileged status, the fact that I'm from Djursholm, that I am "uniquely well-off," out of touch with reality, isolated, all the things the prosecutor has talked about. Sander's rhetorical question is about whether I am uniquely evil.

Most of the statistics are on my side. For starters, my gender makes it unlikely that I would walk into a school and start mowing people down. Sure, there have been a few female school shooters, but not many. Sebastian, on the other hand, who has been one of a kind all his life, is a typical school shooter in all ways but one. Aside from the richest-guy-in-Sweden bit, it all matches: a white guy with mental health issues, a drug user, trouble at school, separated parents, familiar with firearms. Sander included a statement from a psychiatrist in his submissions. The psychiatrist will be called as a witness.

"Maja did not make Sebastian crazy," the psychiatrist will say. "He went crazy all by himself." Me, on the other hand, I'm not as simple to fit into a template. "Maja isn't the school shooter type," our expert will point out.

Statistically, and this is Sander's point, I ought to be innocent. The only problem is that not all murderers are typical. And in the few cases where a school shooter was female, she always did it with her boyfriend. But Sander won't mention that. The prosecutor, however, is sure to have a bunch of expert witnesses to remind everyone of that particular fact.

And now the prosecutor has had enough. She has turned on her microphone, her mouth is scrunched up into a prune.

"Shouldn't Mr. Sander, for reasons of time if nothing else, concentrate on presenting his case and save this for his closing statements?"

The judge shakes his head. He looks annoyed, too. But with ugly Lena more than Sander. The judge doesn't appreciate being told how to run his trial.

"Mr. Sander is well aware of our schedule and how much time he has at his disposal." He looks at Sander. "Isn't that so?"

Sander nods and continues, noticeably energized.

"The prosecutor's version of events is an exceptional story. The whole world is fascinated by Sebastian and Maja: Sweden's most unlikely partners in crime. And the prosecutor has received assistance in weaving her tale, not least by the journalists who have spent the last nine months explaining how Maja Norberg supposedly convinced...I'm sorry, *manipulated* her weak, powerless boyfriend into taking bloody revenge on those closest to them."

The prosecutor sighs, loud enough for everyone to hear. She never said that, her sigh tells us. But she did — maybe not straight out, and yet everyone knows what she meant. The judge reluctantly raises his hand toward Sander and moves it in circles. *Get on with it*, his hand says. *This bitch is a nag, but she has a point*, it says. *You can come back to this later.* I look down at the table. I know what Sander is doing. But it's still Sebastian and me he's talking about.

"By this point, we know the story. Maja and Sebastian were a young couple with lots of problems: with drugs and alcohol, with school and each other, with their parental relationships and their friends. The prosecutor is trying to show that Maja's search for affirmation knew no bounds, that she felt unreasonable hatred for the people around her and Sebastian, that she wanted revenge, that Sebastian was weak, that he felt threatened and challenged and that Maja was the only steady point in his existence, that he sought affirmation from her."

The prosecutor clears her throat again. Even louder this time.

Sander is unmoved and keeps talking. "We have heard the prosecutor describe the events that preceded the murder of Claes Fagerman and the tragedy at Djursholm Upper Secondary School. Maja concurs with large portions of that description."

Once again, Sander gives a nearly inaudible sigh. "With certain crucial differences."

Sander looks down at his papers and pages through them in silence for a moment. He doesn't need those papers; they just give us time to think. He wants to give us time to grow eager for the next part of the story.

When the chief judge realizes that Sander is finished with his introduction, he reaches for his pad of paper. I actually appreciate this about him, that he takes notes and listens. Sometimes, such as when he thinks Lena Pärsson is talking too fast, he raises his hand in a "stop" gesture to get her to slow down. One time, when Lena Pärsson was presenting the text message I sent to Sebastian the night before, he asked her to stop talking while he wrote down the time stamps. He even said "shh," although that was probably by accident. He also said "just a second" right afterward. And Lena Pärsson did stop talking. The judge wanted to write down all the times on his own piece of paper, even though he already had all the documents and even though Lena Pärsson was doing her pedagogical read-out-loud-from-the-display-on-the-big-screen thing. I like that about him, that he takes everything seriously and doesn't trust that everything Pärsson says is correct.

Sander continues.

"This case has received an exceptional amount of attention. We have all heard the prosecutor's story. She has heedlessly fed it to the media for a very long time. Now it's time for us to take a step back. This is the first time Maja has been able to tell her side of the story. Please listen to her. With an open mind. Try, as well, to remember that only after we have reviewed all the evidence and heard from all the witnesses will we be able to summarize what we actually know. What is fact and what is speculation? Only after the proceedings are over can we compare the facts of the case with what Maja has to say."

Somehow the prosecutor manages to produce a noise that is the sonic equivalent of a person rolling their eyes. *Don't talk to us like we're stupid*, says the noise.

Sander nods at Ferdinand. She rises and approaches a utility table with a computer on it. In her hand is a small gadget; it looks like a pen. It's connected to the room's two screens and with it she can aim a red laser dot at the images displayed there.

Like the Laser Man, I think, and I feel a sudden laugh rise in my throat like a sour burp. Just in the nick of time, I succeed in transforming the laugh into a cough, and Ferdinand brings up a surveillance video from Sebastian's driveway. There's a time stamp in one corner. There is no sound.

"So...what do we know?" Sander asks. "Let's start with a time line. Maja states that she left the Fagermans' house just after three a.m. on the day in question. Material gathered from the Fagermans' surveillance cameras indicate that this is accurate. Maja left the house at three twenty.

She states that she returned just before eight a.m. the same morning, and this is also confirmed by the video."

He clears his throat and nods at Ferdinand; she brings up the transcript of an interview with one of Claes's security guards.

"According to an interview with the Fagermans' security guard, his last contact with Claes Fagerman occurred via the camera-equipped entry phone, after Maja left the house at three twenty. What conclusion can we draw from this? Claes Fagerman was alive when Maja left."

Ferdinand clicks back to the surveillance video and lets the red dot dance around the screen.

"One more time. The surveillance cameras from the driveway show Maja Norberg leaving the Fagermans' address at twenty minutes past three in the morning, and she does not return until seven forty-four."

Sander clears his throat and allows the video to finish playing. They have edited the security footage into one film. First we watch me walking out of Sebastian's front door and down his driveway, and then we see me return. Ferdinand uses the laser pen to draw circles around the time stamps.

After this, Ferdinand displays an autopsy report on the screen.

"According to the forensic report, Claes Fagerman died a few hours before Maja returned to the house just before eight a.m. The evidence indicates that Claes Fagerman was shot and killed at approximately five o'clock Friday morning. This time of death is supported by the medical examiner's observations on the scene and by the subsequent forensic examination. Thus the investigation shows that Maja Norberg was not present when Claes Fagerman was killed. Maja has stated that at this point in time, from approximately three thirty to just before eight a.m., she was at her home, just over a kilometer from the Fagerman home. This statement is corroborated not only by the security guard who was working at the entrance to the Fagermans' property during the night in question but also by Maja's parents' statements."

Out of the corner of my eye I can see the prosecutor shaking her head. She thinks this is unnecessary, too; she wants to demonstrate that she still thinks Sander should get to the point. But her version of these events was not this clear. It was more difficult to understand what she meant to say.

"Thus we can unequivocally state that Claes Fagerman died during a period of time in which Maja was not in the house. Additionally, this is consistent with the prosecutor's version of events. Thus far my client has no objection."

For a moment I think Sander won't bother to say anything about the texts, that he's going to pretend they don't exist. But of course he can't.

"So what happens while Maja is in her parents' home or is on her way to or from the Fagerman villa? This is the point at which the prosecutor's version of events moves from being an account of what we know to sheer speculation."

Ferdinand brings up the overview of Sebastian's and my text history from the night before it happened, the same one the prosecutor presented during her statements. I immediately feel like I'm freezing. My scalp contracts. It did the same when Call-me-Lena read them aloud last week. I don't want to look at them again, ever again. Sander lets the image shine down as he continues.

"The prosecutor's account of the sequence of events contains a number of statements that Maja disputes. But first let me quickly remind you of what Maja concedes. During questioning, she stated that Claes Fagerman initiated a violent argument with his son. The argument continued after the teenagers who were at the house for a party left the property. Maja and Sebastian left to take a walk together, but after they returned to the house, the argument between Sebastian and his father resumed. Sebastian and Claes were still arguing when Maja left the house to go home to sleep. Thus far there is nothing to dispute."

The party. I feel sick when I think about it. Once Claes had kicked out Dennis, Labbe, Amanda, and everyone else, the villa was quiet. At first it was a relief. Then Claes started screaming. Not just at Sebastian; he screamed at me, too. We had to leave. We went outside and stayed there for a pretty long time. I was scared. Sebastian's dad frightened me. When he was sitting in his office, when he was talking to the people he paid to make his life easier, you could barely look straight at him without being blinded by all his excellent qualities. But as Sebastian's dad, he was a completely different person.

When we came back after our walk, Claes was wearing his robe; he was waiting for us in the kitchen and he didn't even have a newspaper to cling to. He was hardly recognizable. He looked somehow like his face was missing makeup, even if he'd never looked made up before, ever, not even when he was on TV.

Just an hour or so earlier, when Claes kicked everyone out, he had appeared gigantic, even larger than he usually seemed, but now that everyone had gone home and he had finished screaming, had destroyed everything, he had become shorter and uglier. All his businesslike glitz had been scraped away. All that was left at this kitchen table was a pale old man in a robe, a shark circling in black water, a blind, white fish at the bottom of a deep sea. Sebastian's dad lived on darkness and unicellular water creatures. It was obvious to look at him.

I don't think I ever hated Claes Fagerman more than I did at that moment.

"However." Sander has raised one long well-manicured index finger. We await his point. We wait for him to explain why it is I disagree with the prosecutor. Meanwhile I watch the red dot seem to crawl up the screen and get stuck on my first text. Ferdinand has put down the laser pointer; the dot has landed there by accident. My first text:

We can manage without him. You don't need him. Your dad is a terrible person.

I don't read the rest.

I wrote many more texts that night. Everyone can read them. I look down at the table.

The last one reads: *He deserves to die.*

26.

"By the time Maja returns to the Fagerman home the next morning, she has sent Sebastian nine text messages. Sebastian has sent three replies, and he has called Maja twice. So what did these teenagers say to each other? The prosecutor claims that the plan was formed during their conversations. The first call lasts for two minutes and forty-five seconds, and it takes place just after Maja has left Sebastian's home and before she has reached her own house. The second takes place just before she leaves her own home to go back to Sebastian's. It lasts for less than a minute."

Sander looks at Ferdinand. She aims the laser pointer at the phone records, where the two calls are highlighted. The red dot trembles slightly. How could anyone ever understand why I wrote what I did? How horrible Claes was. That the worst part wasn't that Claes Fagerman shirked his responsibilities, what he should have said to Sebastian — the worst part was the stuff he actually said and did.

Sebastian had never before wanted to see this side of him. He idolized his dad. Claes was the only person Sebastian looked up to. But on that very last night, Sebastian was forced to acknowledge what I already knew. And yet he seemed more tired than angry when I left. The fight and our walk and everything we'd said had left him exhausted. I assumed he would go to bed. Was I angry? I don't know. My emotions hadn't mattered for a long time; Sebastian was the important one. When he sent the first message, *What should I do?* I wanted to show him I was on his side, tell him that I, too, had realized who his dad truly was, and that he would be okay without him, that it would all work out. His dad didn't deserve him; he didn't have the right to demean Sebastian.

We can manage without him. You don't need him.

I refuse to read those last few words. But when I wrote to Sebastian that I thought Claes deserved to die, I meant it.

Sander doesn't mention anything about that, about what I was feeling. Even though I've explained it to him. Instead he raises his finger again, even higher this time, urgently; he demands that we listen.

"What do these phone records tell us? For one thing: Sebastian and Maja talked to each other and they texted each other. We don't know what they talked about. We do know what the texts say, but do we know what they mean?"

He raises another finger.

"Maja has conceded that she did not like Claes Fagerman. That she thought he neglected his duties as a parent. Maja based this view on the treatment to which Claes Fagerman subjected his son. However, at no point has Maja acted in such a way that it can be considered proven that she caused Sebastian to kill his father, or that what she said can be considered to fulfill the criteria for incitement in the eyes of the law."

But I wanted him to die. How will Sander get around that?

"We will discuss whether there was intention, whether the message 'he deserves to die' means that Maja wanted Sebastian to kill his father, or that she was at least indifferent to the possibility that Sebastian might interpret it as a suggestion to commit murder. We argue that Maja did not have any such intent. But there is an even more important reason that the prosecutor cannot be considered to have fulfilled the criteria for incitement. The fact is, Sebastian himself wanted to kill his father. He did not need Maja to convince him. And we will revisit this."

The journalists are loving this. I can't see them, but I can feel them collectively leaning forward in their chairs so as not to miss a single word. They listen so intently to each word about empire builder Claes Fagerman, how the evil billionaire treated his son like a disobedient slave. They adore that Sander is turning Claes Fagerman into a monster, that they will be allowed to hear all the details about how he ignored his son, shamed him, insulted him, ousted him from the family, kicked him out of his house. A functioning father would have made sure that Sebastian received care and attention, but instead Claes Fagerman spat upon him again and again. I can't see the journalists, but their excitement has raised the temperature in the courtroom by several degrees, thanks to this new story. They are eager to tell it, and they have already forgotten that they were telling a completely different story just moments ago. Now they will allow their readers and viewers to get to know Sweden's richest man for real. Claes Fagerman — the billionaire who drove his son to mass murder. The fact that this story might also affect the stock market is a bonus these journalists can hardly handle, they think it's so terrific.

"Let's get back to the time line. One of the facts we know with absolute certainty is that after Maja spends eleven minutes inside the Fagermans' house, Sebastian Fagerman and Maja Norberg get into one of Claes Fagerman's cars in order to drive to Djursholm Upper Secondary School. In the car with them they have two bags. The prosecutor claims that Maja was aware of the contents of those bags before she helped Sebastian put them in the car. The prosecutor is of the opinion that the very latest point at which Maja would have been made aware of the contents was during the eleven minutes she spent in the Fagermans' house around eight a.m. on the day in question."

He lowers his hand.

"Maja denies this. It is pure speculation on the prosecutor's part that Sebastian would have told her what he had done and what else he planned to do. As Sebastian and Maja drive to the school, Maja does not know that Sebastian has killed his father. She has not learned what Sebastian is planning to do inside the school. Maja believed that Sebastian was not planning to sleep at home for the next few nights and thus needed to bring luggage.

She assumed that he planned to sleep on one of the family's boats and would take his bags there after school. Should she have asked what the bags contained? Should she have figured out that Sebastian had killed his dad? In hindsight, she has said during questioning, she wishes she had. But we can't blame her for not knowing. It is also impossible to speculate about what might have happened if she had figured it out. Would Sebastian have killed her and the security guards and gone to the school alone? Perhaps. It's impossible to know. And what's more, when it comes to the criminal charges, it is irrelevant. Because the crucial point is this: The prosecutor cannot demonstrate that Maja planned any of the murders in cooperation with Sebastian Fagerman; the prosecutor cannot demonstrate that Maja was even aware that Sebastian had made any such plans."

"Get out of my house," Claes shouted while the others were still there. I wasn't the only one who heard it; he said it to the security guards, too. "I'll give him twenty-four hours. Then change the locks. After that he may not under any circumstances come onto this property. Do you hear me? Do you hear what I'm saying? I don't want anything to do with him. He is of age; I am no longer responsible for him. He is out of here. I've had enough. The police will have to evict him if that's what it takes."

Sander doesn't mention any of that now. But the security guards will be questioned later. He will ask them to talk about it.

Sander raises his first finger again.

"Maja was not aware of Sebastian's plans. She did not help him with preparation or planning. Nor did she help Sebastian commit the crime, either directly or indirectly. During the coming week we will have the opportunity to examine the deficiency of the criminal charges in these areas, but even now I want to remind you about the prosecutor's forensic evidence. Is there anything in the case report to indicate that Maja knew the bags did not contain Sebastian's clothes, that she was aware they held weapons and explosives? The answer is no." Ferdinand brings up a report the prosecutor has already discussed, but now it's our turn to examine the same document. "All firearms involved in the investigation are owned by Claes Fagerman and were — prior to the crime — kept in a weapons safe locked with a security code. Maja was not in possession of that code. The bags are Sebastian Fagerman's bags. She did not help pack those bags, nor did she assist with preparations in any other fashion. We will revisit the technical investigation and demonstrate that it, too, supports Maja's story."

To be perfectly honest, I think Sander's account seems a little disjointed, but the chief judge seems to be listening and the lay judges don't look like they're about to fall asleep. Sander talks about how we drove to school. How long it took. Where we parked. Ferdinand clicks at her computer and points with her laser pen. Pancake skims through his binders. Now and then he hands a page over to Sander.

Sander says that when we arrived at my locker, Sebastian placed one of the bags inside it. That was the one with the bomb.

I have been asked at least sixty-three times why I let him put it there, why I said, "Sure, go ahead," like, "By all means, put your bomb in my locker." The prosecutor wonders, just as the police did when they were questioning me, why I didn't tell Sebastian to leave his stuff in the car. Why would he bring his luggage into the school if it was headed for the boat?

I've tried to explain, to answer honestly. Because the truth is, Sebastian probably didn't even ask me if he could leave his bag in my locker, he just did it. I didn't have to give him permission because I never would have said no.

So if you didn't think it was strange for him to leave one bag there, why wouldn't you think it was best to put both of them there? Why didn't you think it was odd that he would drag a bag full of his clothes to the classroom?

The other bag didn't fit. He couldn't put both of them in one locker. Why my locker and not his? Sebastian didn't have his locker key. He never did. I don't even think he knew where it was anymore; at least, I'd never seen him use his own locker. If he needed a locker, he used mine. He also used my books, my pens, and my paper on those rare occasions that he bothered with that stuff. It wasn't odd in the least for Sebastian to bring the other bag to the classroom instead of leaving it behind.

When Sander is done talking about my locker and the bags, he looks at Ferdinand and waits for her to click to the next picture. It's a drawing of the classroom. I can feel the vomit rising in my throat. I think about covering my ears with my hands, but I know I can't. I have to listen. I have to look like I will make it through this.

"The exact series of events in the classroom is not known. But according to what Maja has been able to reproduce, it looks more or less as follows. Once inside the classroom, Sebastian Fagerman places the bag he has brought on one of the desks near the back of the room."

Ferdinand points with the red dot.

"More or less immediately after Fagerman has entered the classroom, he opens the bag and removes weapon number one, a hunting rifle registered to Claes Fagerman. The rifle is a .308 Winchester semiautomatic Remington. Maja is standing just behind Fagerman as he opens fire. Weapon number one is fitted with a standard magazine containing four rounds. Fagerman fires two shots and strikes..." Ferdinand points at Dennis's spot, which is marked with the number 1. "Fagerman subsequently empties the magazine, removes it, and then attaches another standard magazine and fires another shot." Ferdinand points out Christer's and Samir's positions. "He does not put the weapon down and it takes him a few seconds to reload. Immediately following these shots, Maja Norberg picks up weapon number two. This, too, is registered to Claes Fagerman. It lies fully visible in the bag. This gun is of the same model as weapon number one and is also fitted with a standard magazine containing four rounds. In addition, there is one round in the chamber."

Ferdinand sweeps the laser to the point on the diagram that marks Amanda's position when she was hit, and then she lets the dot land on Sebastian's number. She clicks on her computer and the image shows how Sebastian's and Amanda's numbers and my filled-in circle (I have a circle rather than a number) moved around the room.

"It is highly likely that the safety on this weapon is already off when Maja picks it up, and as she tries to figure out how to turn off the safety, she fires — by mistake — first one shot and then another. A few seconds later she empties the magazine."

Ferdinand brings up new positions on the diagram using the gadget in her hand. *Clickety-click-click* and the numbers that symbolize my friends move around until, one by one, they go perfectly still and it makes me think of the flip-books Grandpa used to make me when I was little, with a stick figure in the corner of the pages who would run when you flipped them really fast. Once Grandpa drew a man hanging himself. On the last page, he was dead. That made Grandma angry.

"When the shooting is over, Maja waits for the police and paramedics. When they arrive, Maja allows herself to be disarmed; she does not resist."

There are tons of photographs of the inside of the classroom after the bodies were removed. But Sander doesn't show them. Just sketches and drawings with dots and numbers and dashed lines. No blood. My version of events, or rather my attorney's version of events, is bloodless.

"Now we reach the heart of the prosecutor's argument." Sander looks at me from the side. "The prosecutor claims that Maja and Sebastian jointly planned to shoot everyone present, let the explosive device detonate in Maja's locker, and finish by shooting themselves. The prosecutor claims that when Maja fires the first shots with weapon number two, she does so with the intent of killing Amanda. The prosecutor claims that Maja willfully killed Amanda and that she did not kill Sebastian out of self-defense."

Sander pauses again. No one is yawning now. The straight backs have returned. The judges look at me when Sander stops speaking. I wipe my eyes with the back of my hand and return their gazes. Pancake gives me a tissue. I accept it and ball it up.

Sander speaks again, in a low voice. "Maja denies responsibility. Maja did not plan this with Fagerman. When she arrives at the Fagerman house to ride to school, she is not aware that Claes Fagerman is dead. Nor is she informed of this. She does not know what the bags contain. We can only speculate upon what happened between the Fagerman father and son while Maja was in her parents' home. Perhaps the argument escalated to the point that Sebastian decided to shoot his father. Perhaps he had already planned what he was going to do. But during this trial we must not speculate about Sebastian Fagerman's motives and actions. The sole task of this court is to establish Maja's role.

"When the shooting first begins, Maja is shocked. When she picks up one of the weapons Fagerman has brought into the classroom, it is to protect her own life and those of the others, to stop Fagerman. He shoots his first three victims quickly. Very quickly. Maja is not used to handling firearms, and in addition she is terrified. When she first fires the weapon, Amanda Steen is hit, but this is not Maja's objective. Maja is unfamiliar with how the weapon she found in the bag works; during the investigation she explained that the first shot was fired as she was trying to find the safety. When the gun went off, she was alarmed and she fired, again by accident, another shot. Only then does she manage to gain a certain amount of control of the weapon, and when she shoots again, she hits Fagerman. During this entire period of time, Maja is obviously defending herself. The only way for her to save her own life is to take one of the weapons Fagerman brought into the classroom and use it to protect herself."

Now Sander stands up; he can no longer sit still. He approaches Ferdinand and takes the laser pen from her and lets the red beam whirl across the drawing without pointing at anything in particular.

"Does the investigation show that Maja planned this with Sebastian? No. Does it show that Maja was aware of Sebastian's plans? No. Will the prosecutor be able to show that Maja killed Amanda with intent? No. The answer to all of these questions is clearly and without a doubt no. The charges are not supported on any of these points. Did Maja kill Sebastian in self-defense? Of course."

For the second time, the prosecutor has turned on her microphone. She sounds mad as hell.

"I must protest. Is it really too much to ask for the attorney to keep to the presentation of the facts? Could the attorney perhaps return to this line of argument in his closing statements?"

The chief judge nods reluctantly. "Mr. Sander?"

Sander turns to me instead. He raises his hand suddenly and the red dot lands on my shoulder. I give a start. Sander seems angry. And he doesn't care the least little bit that the judge and the prosecutor think he should change topics. They will have to throw him out of here to get him to stop. It doesn't even seem like he's addressing the judges any longer.

"Please tell me what Maja…a teenager, in shock, fearing for her life…what else could she do?" Sander lowers his hand, turning to the panel of judges, and I can exhale. "Please explain to me what you would have done in her place. Explain to me how you can blame her for this."

The prosecutor clears her throat, too loudly and for too long, into her live microphone.

The judge nods again, a bit more decisively this time.

"We need to move on, Mr. Sander. I assume there is some documentary evidence you intend to go through?"

Sander turns to Ferdinand and shrugs, then hands back the laser pen and returns to his chair. By the time he is seated, his voice has recovered its usual dry tone.

"We do have a certain amount of documentary evidence to present in the case. Yes."

A certain amount. Typical Sander humor. He has kilos' worth of documentary evidence.

Ferdinand has gathered up a pile of thick binders. The judges each receive one. The chief judge gets his binder first. Ferdinand ends by placing four binders on the prosecutor's table. Beyond Sebastian's psychiatrist's report, the one from right after what happened two days after Christmas, there are supplements to my personal case study and copies of all the supplementary investigatory measures Sander had his colleagues arrange and carry out. He did not trust a single one of the prosecutor's analyses; he ordered his own inquiries into the weapons and crime scenes. He even conducted a reconstruction of the school shooting. Sander did a nearly exhaustive parallel investigation.

He will go through every last document. Document after document after document. We will "revisit" most of them. Lunchtime arrives, afternoon arrives, and pretty soon it is right back to boring as hell.

It is three twenty-five by the time Sander drinks the last of his water and puts aside the last of his papers. The judge holds up his hand and writes frantically on his pad of paper.

Sander lets him finish. Then he places his hands before him, his palms flat, his eyes straight ahead.

"We sometimes like to say about particularly difficult cases that word is against word. This is simpler than that. The technical investigation shows that Sebastian packed the bags and was the sole person to handle the weapons and explosives, and that he planned the deed alone. Maja was not present when Claes Fagerman died. Maja shot the perpetrator. And what do we know about his background? We know that Sebastian had serious problems. So serious that Maja was not the only one who feared that his life was in danger. After the incident around Christmas, she was constantly worried. During the spring, Sebastian became more and more violent and difficult to handle. A number of people close to him have testified to this. Sebastian's irrational behavior escalated and eventually resulted in the catastrophe in which Maja became one of the victims. Maja, on the other hand, never demonstrated any tendency toward violence, not until her life was threatened."

Sander gives me a sidelong glance. I suddenly feel like he's going to take my hand. I place it in my lap and look at the chief judge instead. He looks me straight in the eye as Sander concludes.

"Maja Norberg fired a weapon in her classroom. She did it to save her own life. And now it's our turn. Now we must save Maja."

27.

And then the room is silent. Dead silent. Almost like in church when someone has just sung a fantastically beautiful solo and you can't applaud. Sander is famous for being Sweden's best criminal defense lawyer. This might be the first time that I've realized that the rumor is actually true.

He tells a good story. But I hadn't realized how gifted he is at persuasion. Pancake is always just being cocky, and that's probably why he's never allowed to speak in this case, even though lots of people think that's the way it's done: If you just appear to be *one hundred percent certain,* you'll get everyone on your side. In reality, no one believes that kind of presumption. Politicians really should catch on to this, that we're waiting for sentences that end in a question mark. That we long for someone who doesn't understand everything but might have a suggestion. *I'm not sure it will work but I'd really like to give it a shot.*

Sander lets everyone tag along in his own doubt, every step of the way. When he says, "We asked ourselves the question: Could this really be true?" everyone is curious. When he says, "We decided to investigate the matter ourselves," everyone, even those who said earlier that it was a waste of both time and money to repeat what the police had already done, thinks this is a perfectly marvelous idea. And every single person is listening when he says, "The results were a surprise" and "We have arrived at the conclusion that..." Although they used to be totally confident that he was wrong, they can't help but let down their guard and think, *Maybe...just maybe he has a point after all?*

Right now, the atmosphere in the courtroom is different from the way it was this morning. The journalists behind me are writing so energetically about this fresh new angle of The Narrative that you might think they'd forgotten the old version — even though they were the ones who made it up. The chief judge is looking at me; he has looked at me a number of times today even though he doesn't need to. He's never done that before.

It doesn't really matter as much anymore, I think, that I sent those texts to Sebastian. It's the first time I've let myself think that maybe it isn't proof enough for them that I carried the bag, that they found the bomb in my locker. Maybe it's not enough to say, *It's obvious that you wanted to blow the whole school sky-high.* I have time to think all of this. I have time to think that this new atmosphere implies that the people in this room have also adopted a new view of me, that maybe they've changed their minds about who I am.

I'd rather die. He must go. He deserves to die. Is it possible to have those thoughts without wanting to murder someone? Are those things you're allowed to say? Sander thinks so. It is not a crime to tell your boyfriend you hate some-one, according to Sander. He claims it doesn't matter what I said to Sebastian; he still would have killed his father, he still would have done what he did. It would have happened anyway, even if I hadn't done what I did. *Maybe he's right*, I have time to think. Maybe?

"The court thanks the defense," the chief judge says, start-ing to gather up the few documents he has before him. I look at the other judges on the panel. The ones who never ask any questions, the ones who look at me, but only when they think I don't notice.

"We will hear the statement from the defendant tomorrow?"

Sander nods. I unwillingly gasp for breath. *My turn. It's time.*

The judge looks at his watch. "Then that's all for today." He reaches for his briefcase and puts his notes inside. "Unless there's something more. I understand there is a problem with the injured party's schedule, is that correct?"

Lena Pärsson clears her throat.

The chief judge looks at her. She straightens her back and gives a firm nod. She is still annoyed, but this has reminded her that the trial is far from over. Unfortunately, it has reminded me of the same thing.

Sander has done his job and tomorrow it's my turn to tell the story. But if the people in this room have any doubt that I'm the killer the prosecutor claims I am, it's extremely temporary. It's not going to last very long.

Lena Pärsson leans toward her little microphone and turns it on. Because as soon as I'm done talking, it will be time for the prosecutor to turn the tables again. For the fact is, there is someone who doesn't agree with Sander, who is planning to remind everyone that I killed my best friend. This person says I picked up the gun much earlier than I say I did, and that I wasn't aiming at Sebastian at all when I shot Amanda, that it wasn't a mistake in the least.

Lena Pärsson starts to speak.

"As I have already notified the court, I will open with the testimonies of witnesses one through four since the injured party is unable to appear this week. The witnesses in question have been notified of and approve this schedule change. Accordingly, I have asked the injured party to present himself at ten o'clock on Monday, as instructed by the court. I expect we will need the whole day."

I can see Pancake out of the corner of my eye. He doesn't look happy; he doesn't look like we're in the process of *winning this thing* at all. And I happen to think of what one of the jailors said to me once back in the beginning, as we were walking alone from the interrogation room to my cell: "You know he never wins any cases, that Sander, don't you? They never do, those star attorneys. They take on the most despicable clients, the ones everyone knows are guilty, because they like hopeless cases. Then they lose. And no one has lost as often as Sander."

Naturally, Pancake knows this. He knows that when a star attorney takes on a case like mine, it's not to win, it's because he wants to show he's prepared to lose for the principle of the thing: *Everyone has the right to a trial, even the most despicable criminals.*

The people in this room like hearing Sander talk, seeing *the pro in action.* But it won't stop the inevitable from happening. I did what I did, and there is someone who was there when I did it. I have the right to the best lawyer in Sweden. But I don't have the right to win.

The judge nods and strikes his gavel on the table. It feels like he's hammering it right into my forehead. *You deserve to die.*

"Then that's that. Samir Said will testify at ten o'clock on Monday. We'll resume tomorrow."

SAMIR AND ME

28.

"Diplomas in the bathroom?" Samir returned to my room, laughing, lay on his back on my bed, and tucked his hands behind his head. "Do people really do that? Hang up their diplomas in the guest bathroom so you can see, oh *my*, they went to the Stockholm School of Economics *and* INSEAD?"

I tried to respond to his grin with an unconcerned laugh and got up to crack the window. It was Saturday morning, the week before Christmas, and it was stuffy in my room. It was five days after Samir kissed me for the first time, and now he had slept over, and what was I supposed to say? My dad was a fucking tool, no news there. Sebastian was off hunting in South Africa all weekend. Mom and Dad were in London. They had taken Lina with them. It would be more than a day before any of them returned home.

"It's supposed to be ironic somehow; Dad thinks that kind of thing is funny. But really he just doesn't want to admit that stuff is important to him."

"The guest bathroom." Samir was still laughing. "Where did your mom hang up her report cards? In the guest room?"

But Mom would never show off like that, even though her grades were better than Dad's. Once I found their old report cards in a box in the attic. When I told Mom, she wasn't happy like I expected; she just seemed annoyed. "I got better grades in college, too," she snapped. "I was first in my class in my Master of Laws program." As if I had said something mean, insulted her. Both of my parents are weird, but in different ways. I went back to the bed and straddled Samir.

"It's important for my dad to show that he's worked hard to get to where he is. But nothing is more important to him than pretending he isn't pretentious."

Samir pulled me toward him by the hair and kissed me, pushed his tongue hard into my mouth, just a little too far in. Last night had been the first chance we got to go slower than as fast as we can before anyone notices. We had slept together five times in six days. Plus three more times in the past day. It felt strange to fall asleep and wake up with him; his fingers felt different, I hadn't gotten used to seeing his entire naked body at once.

"Worked hard, you say." Samir shook his head in amusement. "Your dad wants to prove that he worked hard to get to where he is today? Didn't he live in the same dorm Labbe lives in now?"

"Yes, but..." I knew what Samir was getting at, I got his point, but you can still be proud of what you've accomplished even if you didn't grow up on the streets, right? "Dad didn't go there because Grandpa and Grandma were rich; they lived abroad, he *had* to go to boarding school."

"I get it," Samir mumbled against my neck, pressing his crotch up against me. "It must have been really tough. Your poor, poor dad." He laughed again, then he finally stopped talking. As Samir pulled up my T-shirt I looked at our fuzzy mirror image in my window. He pressed his hand to my stomach, his mouth to my breast, and I leaned back, lay down, let my head and my hair fall over the edge of the bed so I could look right at our reflection. I loved the way we looked, how Samir felt, how his hard edges and big hands looked when he touched me. He wasn't gentle and experienced, but I wanted him to keep going, touch me harder, breathe closer. We looked incredibly hot together.

I was the one who decided how we had sex. In fact, I had to. Samir was happy to make the first move, but he left everything else to me, let me show him, guide him. If I lay down on my back, then that's how we did it; if I got on top of him or knelt on all fours, we did that instead. If I didn't do anything, he got annoyed. "Come on," he would say if I didn't pull off my tights or take off my underwear or spread my legs or whatever it was that had to happen before he could enter me. Only if I told him, *Take off my panties, spread my legs, enter me*, only then would he do it.

Afterward, we lay head to foot. He was half sitting across from me, leaning against my pillow and twisting a lock of his dark hair around his finger. When he looked at me, for a little too long, my stomach jumped. *We could get really good at this, him and me*, I thought. *Once I break up with Sebastian.*

"What are you doing over Christmas break?"

He didn't answer at first. Instead he closed his eyes, pulled me up from my side of the bed and made me lie down next to him, and kissed me again. I stuck my hand into his thick hair. The bed wasn't wide enough for us to fit like that, so it felt like I was about to fall off the edge.

Then my phone blinked. The sound was off, but it was impossible to miss the screen glow. I leaned into Samir, didn't look at my phone, ignored it completely, raised my hand, and laid it on Samir's shoulder.

"Scooch in, I don't have room."

He wiggled over a few centimeters but rose when I shifted even closer, then climbed over me and off the bed, grabbed his underwear, and pulled it on.

"I have to study."

I looked at him in surprise. Was he angry at me for getting a text?

"You have to study right now?"

I hadn't called Sebastian even once since Samir got here. I had responded to his texts, but I locked myself in the bathroom while I did. It wasn't like I could ignore them. Samir couldn't be mad at me if Sebastian texted; I had explained the situation to him and he had said he understood.

"Over break. You asked what I'm doing over Christmas — I'll be home, studying."

Once Samir got his underwear on, he put on his T-shirt. It was best to let him be.

"I'm going to shower," I said. I left the phone on the nightstand. Samir could read my texts if he wanted, I didn't care. I was going to break up with Sebastian, of course I was, but not right now. I couldn't exactly break up with him over the phone, even Samir had to realize that.

When I came into the kitchen, he was sitting there drinking black coffee from our espresso machine, the machine he had dissed the night before.

Samir had made a number of comments about the décor. The ceiling light: "A memento from the abandoned factory, I see." The knife rack: "Why buy knives that can't be sharpened?" The coffeemaker: "They could never sell that machine in a country where people know what real coffee tastes like." The stove: "Your mom *cooks*?" The wine cooler: "I need to get one of those! Everyone knows what happens to the champagne if you let it mingle with the proletarian milk."

He had hardly touched his dusty cornflakes, which he'd found in the pantry and poured into a bowl. I had made an egg and toast and now I had a headache; I couldn't think of anything to talk about. Outside, the sun was shining for the first time in ten days, but we could hardly take a walk and hold hands or go somewhere, sit down at a café and lace our fingers together or go to the movies and make out in the dark. I always ran into someone I knew when I went out.

"What are you thinking about?"

"I have to go home soon."

"Where did you tell your parents you are?"

He shrugged.

I got up and put my dishes in the dishwasher. Samir remained seated, lifting his hands so I could clear away his mug.

"I'll talk to Sebastian. But..."

Samir snorted. "I didn't ask you to do anything."

"I know. But Sebastian isn't well. He — "

"Stop it, Maja. You can keep up that shit together, about poor little Sebastian...but don't drag me into it. There's nothing to feel sorry for him about. If life is so rough at home in his mansion, why doesn't he move out? If he can't deal with going to school, why doesn't he drop out? Your boyfriend is an asshole whether he's high or sober. If I were his dad, I would have kicked him out a long time ago. And why you've got it into your head that you have to take care of him, I have no idea."

I swallowed. "He needs..."

"He doesn't need you, Maja. Sorry to disappoint you, but he doesn't need anyone. Everyone is interchangeable to Sebastian Fagerman. He doesn't care about anyone, not even you."

I had no time to react, to think of what I should say to make Samir understand. My phone started buzzing. It rang soundlessly; the vibrations made the phone creep across the counter. We looked at it until the voice mail picked up and the screen went dark.

"There's a bus in twelve minutes." Samir rose. "I'm going to try to catch it."

He left the soggy cornflakes on the kitchen table and went to the hall. I followed him. I leaned over to kiss his cheek, and as he tied his shoes I unlocked the door; the keys were in the inside lock. When I opened it, Amanda was out front, locking up her bike.

"Hi," she said, her hands dangling at her sides.

Samir walked past both me and her.

"Hey," he said to Amanda. His voice was indifferent. Amanda didn't respond. Once he got to the street, Samir broke into a jog.

"See you," he called. Neither of us replied.

When I looked at Amanda again, she was staring at me. When she was sure I had realized that she knew what was going on, she unlocked her bike, rolled it into the street, and rode off. I couldn't follow her. It was too cold to have a fight in a T-shirt and underwear. I was no fucking Bridget Jones.

When Amanda had vanished from view, I went back into the house, locked the door, turned off the phone, dragged my down comforter into the living room, lay down on the sofa, watched three episodes of *The Walking Dead*, and ate macaroni and cheese straight from the pan. I waited for four hours. Not because I didn't know where Amanda was or because I wasn't going to do anything about the situation before everything blew up, but because I needed to be alone.

The sun had almost gone down by the time I went out the front door again. It was snowing. As I walked, I called Samir. He didn't answer. It wasn't real snow, just the kind that reminds you that winter isn't all that great. I walked through the slush and December darkness; my shoes got soaked through and all the windows in the stables were fogged up on the inside from the heating system and the horses' body heat and warm breath. I walked straight to Amanda's stall. The door was wide open.

"Can we talk?"

Amanda didn't respond, so I walked in and sat down near Devlin's head. Amanda was running the brush across the horse's hindquarters, scraping it off after each pass. His coat was already smooth, but Amanda couldn't stop now — she would have to look at me.

What was I doing there? Why did I immediately feel like I had to explain myself, that it was my duty to reassure Amanda? I hadn't done anything to her. And yet I was there to explain that nothing serious had happened, that nothing in her life would change, that everything was just like always. And to apologize. That's the way our relationship worked. I said I was sorry, whether or not I had actually done anything. It was never the other way around.

Devlin lowered his head and blew warm breath into my hair. I stroked his muzzle. It must have been six months since I'd visited the stables. I used to practically live there. Dad always said as soon as I started "liking boys" I would stop riding, and I hated that he was right. Every time I stepped inside I told myself I would start again. But I never made the effort.

"Amanda," I tried. Might as well get it over with.

"You can't..." Amanda turned to me, raised her hand, and shook the brush at me. She was so upset that her voice was trembling. "I don't know what you're thinking, Maja. I don't know what you want me to say. Don't you see how sick this is? Don't you get what you've done?"

I nodded. It was best to play along. Maybe it would speed up the process.

"I mean, it's not like I don't know things are hard with Sibbe..." She started crying. Amanda was convinced that this was about her. "But Maja, he doesn't deserve this. He feels like crap, Maja. You can't do this to him."

If you say "Maja" one more time I'm going to smack you, I thought. I had to force myself not to say anything for a moment. Count to one hundred. Let her get it off her chest, I didn't have to listen, I just had to let her talk. But she couldn't do anything about what I was thinking. She couldn't make me stop wanting to scream at her that she just didn't get it. She was clueless. She didn't even notice that the nickname she'd made up for Sebastian made our boyfriends sound like a couple of cartoon characters. Labbe and Sibbe. Tudde and Ludde. Huey, Dewey, and Louie. I swallowed. I couldn't deal with Amanda. I couldn't deal with anyone who thought she knew what it was like to be Sebastian's girlfriend. *I* was his girlfriend. Just me. I didn't want to be, but I was. And no one had any clue how fucking awful I felt. Amanda was too much. I couldn't cope with this. But I still couldn't bring myself to argue.

"I'm not...it's not..."

"What about Samir? It's not very nice to him either. Are you in love with him?" She snorted so scornfully that you would have thought we were talking about a chubby small-time politician in gabardine pants with grown politician kids.

Why not? Why couldn't I be in love with Samir? Was it really that implausible? Ever since she started dating Labbe,

Amanda had talked about Samir as if he were her own personal charity project. *Samir is so smart. Samir is so funny. And smart. And really funny. Did I mention smart?*

"No." I shook my head as I spoke. "No, no." I didn't have the energy to double-check my feelings — maybe it was a lie, but I didn't have the strength to care. "I don't know. But things have been really hard, Amanda. I like Samir, he's not so difficult all the time. I've been...Sebastian and I haven't..."

I didn't have to finish any of my sentences. It was better to let Amanda fill them in with whatever she wanted to hear. I really should have cried, too. We couldn't cry at the same time; Amanda hated sharing attention. But I should start crying as soon as she stopped. To really get her on my side, I also ought to let her console me. I doubted I could handle that, though.

"It just happened. Things with Sebastian are so rocky and Samir is..." Amanda glared at me in fury. "I'll talk to Samir," I assured her. "I'll talk to Sebastian, too, but you have to promise not to say anything. You can't say anything to Labbe or Sebastian. Because Sebastian can't find out. He would flip out if he knew."

Amanda nodded. "Of course I won't say anything."

I wondered if she'd already told Labbe.

"Great," I said.

"I always keep my secrets." She sniffled, annoyed.

Learn to talk, I thought. You keep your *promises*. And you don't *reveal* your secrets. But I could hardly point this out.

"Thanks, Amanda," I said instead.

29.

It was pitch-black outside, nighttime at four o'clock in the afternoon. *Welcome to December in Sweden.* Once I was done consoling Amanda about all the things I hadn't done to her, I left the stables and called Samir again. He still wasn't answering. I called four times in a row. I sent a message. He was "online," but once my message was marked "delivered," he went offline. No response. As I approached Vendevägen I could see the bus coming from the square. I got on and called one more time. His voice mail picked up.

We needed to talk. I didn't want to wait for Sebastian to get home. I wanted to do what I must before anyone could stop me, before I had time to change my mind. And Samir had seemed angry when he left, even before Amanda showed up. I didn't want him to be mad at me, didn't want him to think I was ashamed of him. I wanted him to know I was serious.

There were two open windows in the Metro car. Icy air streamed in. Yet the car still smelled like booze and intensive Christmas shopping. Between Mörby Centrum and Östermalmstorg, all the seats and aisles were full of people and shopping bags, and it took a long time to reach Gamla Stan. I could hardly see out the windows, it was so full, but it got better after I transferred.

Christer had told us about a research study that had examined the link between longevity and which Metro station people lived near. There were like fifteen years' difference in average life expectancy between the Bagarmossen and Danderyds Sjukhus stops. And there were no old people on the train with me for the last three stops before I arrived in Tensta. There also wasn't a single girl my age, just guys and two moms with strollers, veils, and floor-length dresses. Maybe all the girls my age were locked up in their apartments so they wouldn't accidentally trip over an erect penis or fall off the balcony.

In my pocket was the Mace my mom gave me; she had brought it from France. One time I happened to press the spray button while it was still in my pocket. I didn't notice until I took my hand out of my pocket and ran it through my hair, and my eyes exploded. They stung and teared up for more than two hours afterward. Mom wanted to drive me to the emergency room, but Dad stuck me in the shower and washed my face with lukewarm water until it felt a little better. Then he phoned a doctor friend, who called in a prescription for an ointment and a rinse that helped the swelling go down. Dad demanded that I get rid of the Mace after that, but Mom refused. I could be cited for possession of an illegal weapon, but Mom "didn't care" because "my safety was more important." More important than what? one might wonder, since if the police caught me I would be the one who landed in the shit, not her. But I was glad to have it now. When a guy sat down across from me on the train, I fingered the can and looked at the floor.

I was careful not to make eye contact with anyone. I thought about moving closer to the moms with their strollers, but they had parked them in the middle of the aisle so no one could reach the empty seats.

Tensta Centrum was the next-to-last station on the Blue Line. All but two of the people in my car got off when I did. I walked slowly, so I would be last onto the escalator. I had looked at the GPS on my phone earlier and programmed in Samir's address, figured out which way to go when I got up to street level, but I didn't want to take my phone out; I didn't want to make it obvious that I didn't know my way around and I didn't want to show off my phone either.

There were more people up on the street than there had been on the train; the women from my car were picked up by a boy of about eleven, and I saw the backsides of three other baggy women coming out of an ICA store a little farther off, but otherwise it was just men. Guys, guys, guys.

Samir had never told me that he lived in Tensta. Was I surprised when I looked up his address? Maybe. Maybe because it was Tensta, one of the ghettos with the worst reputations, it seemed too extreme somehow, like it was made up. But I don't know what I expected from the neighborhood itself; I had never been there before. Fruit and vegetable stands? Unrolled carpets with sales on fake watches and plastic handbags with Gucci logos glued onto them? Roasted almonds and chestnuts, families with nineteen children playing soccer, old men hunched over chessboards and Rocky types with taped-up hands being applauded by everyone they ran past with their sweat-suit hoods pulled up? Pit bulls and Red Bull? Saffron and garlic? Bocce and raucous laughter? Maybe. Or else I thought it would look like the neighborhood Dennis lived in. Sebastian and I went there once, and even though we picked him up a ways from his actual house, you could see what a boring and insignificant row-house neighborhood it was. The kind you forget as soon as you leave, a place as meaningless as a disposable plastic cup. But this? This was just incomprehensible. An idea without a purpose. Broken Tupperware with no lid.

Maybe it was better in the summertime, when it wasn't as dark and the trees had leaves, but right now it was just one of the ugliest places I'd ever seen in my life. All those politicians and journalists who made a big deal about how *they* "still lived in Tensta," they must have been really stupid. Or else they also had overnight apartments in the city.

I counted four broken streetlights just in the square next to the Metro entrance, and Christer's voice popped into my head. His serious, solemn teacher voice. If he knew I had come here, he would be so pleased, nodding slowly and saying earnestly: *This is the real Sweden, Maja. This is what it looks like.* But this was not the real Sweden, any more than ritzy Östermalmstorg or the Stockholm archipelago or the million-dollar homes on Strandvägen were. Things aren't more real just because they're ugly.

I sat down at a bus station on the other side of the square and took out my phone with one hand. I had to. I kept the other hand in my pocket with the Mace and did my best to convince myself that it was not at all racist to be scared. Mom's voice in my head: *Being careful doesn't mean you're frightened.* Then I got my bearings. Samir didn't live far from the station: The map said it would take five minutes to walk there. When the guy who'd gotten off the Metro with me got on a bus that was in such a rush to leave the stop that it started rolling before the doors were completely closed, I started walking along a paved pedestrian path. It was deserted, too. No one was out walking his dog or making sure her baby got some fresh air. No one was jogging; no one was on their way somewhere. I hurried past the graffiti, the parts of bikes chained to an overturned rack, through a tunnel that smelled like urine, and past two empty playgrounds.

Samir lived on the first floor of an apartment building. It looked like apartment buildings always do in teen films about *the projects,* but without the Ingemar Stenmark woolen caps, the vampires, the grandpa bikes, and the snow. The stairwell echoed, the door was propped open — guess I wouldn't need the security code. The front door of Samir's apartment was right next to the elevator, and there was a *ding* when I rang the doorbell. A younger version of Samir answered the door. But Samir himself appeared before I could explain who I was.

Both his mom and dad were at home. I didn't know that he had two little brothers, but they all looked so much alike that they had to be siblings. I introduced myself to all of them and I thought maybe we would sit down in the kitchen, which was visible from the hallway — a narrow strip with a door out to a balcony. It appeared to be crammed full of empty boxes. Had I expected his parents would want to talk to me, ask how Samir and I knew each other, insist I sit down for a bit, have a cup of tea and eat some sticky cake, or at least look at me with curiosity? Maybe. None of that happened. They didn't seem interested, and his mom was obviously super annoyed. She said something in a language I didn't understand and that was the last I saw of her. His dad took my outstretched hand but dropped it again without saying his name, then turned around and sat down in front of the TV; there was a soccer match between two teams I'd never heard of. The TV was gigantic, at least twice as big as ours. At first I thought it was on mute, until I saw his dad had put on bulky bright green headphones.

I didn't understand why Samir looked so angry. Was it because I hadn't warned him I was coming? He had shown up at my house without notice, too. That's how this had all begun.

I wasn't asking him to introduce me as his girlfriend, but he could have said, "This is Maja, she's in my class."

We could have gone to his room, I would have liked to see it, it didn't matter to me if he shared a room with his brothers. I didn't care that he lived like this.

I wanted to tell him that: *You don't have to be ashamed, I don't care.* But it felt weird. I didn't say anything. *Can we talk?* I managed to produce something along those lines. But that was it.

And Samir nodded and stomped his feet into a pair of sneakers I had never seen him wear to school. He had changed clothes, too, into shiny track pants. *The ghetto uniform,* I thought.

"We're leaving," he said. I turned around to go back to the living room and say goodbye to his dad, but Samir took me by the arm and pulled me out the door, back into the stairwell with its half-open door.

It was obvious he was irritated I had come. He was extremely annoyed. I just wanted us to be alone and talk, *about how Amanda knew.* I wanted to ask him, *What do we do now?* I didn't want to have to make any decisions on my own. I wanted him to say, *Break up with Sebastian,* because then I could have said, *I'll do it tonight,* and I wouldn't have felt so alone. Why couldn't he see that it was considerate of me to come to his place instead of asking him, *Can you come over here?* I hadn't ordered him to come to see me. I wanted to show him that I was happy to come to him. That it didn't matter to me, that I didn't care where he lived.

It was so moronic. All this *I don't care, Samir.* I wondered why I thought it was so urgent for him to understand that *I didn't care.* Did Samir think Tensta was an awesome neighborhood, a thousand times better than everywhere else? Hardly. If he did, he wouldn't have put up with a daily commute that took an hour in each direction, just to get to Djursholm Upper Secondary. *I got it.*

Maybe I should have said I understood why he hated this intolerable place where he was forced to live, that I truly understood why he was doing everything he could to get out of there. Because he deserved better than Tensta. He was better than the place he'd ended up in. Maybe that's what I should have said. His apartment, the stairwell, the path to get there, the path to get away, his polyester track pants — I didn't think he should be ashamed, because it wasn't his fault. But I couldn't say that either. Because even that would make him feel ashamed.

Without a word, he started walking away from the building ahead of me. I didn't know where we were going. It didn't matter. I didn't know where people went to talk in Tensta, I was ready to go anywhere, the laundry room, a storage area, next to a graffiti wall or a youth center or a neighborhood coffee shop or a skateboard park. As long as we could talk in peace and quiet.

It took a while for me to realize that we were on our way to the Metro station. Then I grabbed him, forced him to stop.

Even before I told him why I thought we needed to talk, Samir was giving me a strange look. It only got worse as I kept talking. To be honest, I don't remember exactly what he said, but he didn't think I needed to break up with Sebastian, not for his sake, definitely not. "We're not a couple, Maja. We slept together a few times, that's not the same thing."

It wasn't like he called me a whore, or cheap, nothing like that. But intellectual, super politically aware, future foreign correspondent, world's best Samir was looking at me with new eyes. His don't-be-an-idiot expression.

He didn't want to stand still. Apparently we would be walking as he talked. He wanted to get me out of there as quickly as possible, and what I had to say was of no interest. He took me by the arm again, I was a stubborn little kid who refused to come home from the playground. By the time he had finished speaking, we had arrived at the subway, but he didn't leave me alone there either; he stood there stomping his ugly white sneakers on the platform until my train arrived, and then he got on with me and rode all the way to T-Centralen.

What did he think I was going to do? Secretly stay in Tensta and get a bunch of awesome friends and my own dingy apartment with a six-foot ceiling clearance and a linoleum floor? That I would be his new neighbor, get a big pregnant belly, a matching tracksuit, and wrap a patterned shawl around my head *just because it's so so stylish*?

I took a seat; he remained standing even though there were tons of empty spots in the car. By the time we reached the central station, he seemed to have calmed down a little, he placed a hand just below my shoulder before he left me. "Bye, Maja. See you at school." I wish I could have thrown up on him.

I walked all the way home from the Danderyds Hospital stop. The pedestrian tunnel from the Metro entrance to the parking lot outside Mörby School, it all looked nice as hell, almost cozy, compared to Tensta. But I was freezing long before I had come to the soccer fields by Stocksunds IP. The wool mittens Amanda had given me ("I found them in a super-cute shop in SoHo") were wet, from sweat on the inside and slush on the outside. They were heavy as shag rugs. I tossed them into a garbage can next to the oak at the border where Djursholm started and clenched my fists in my pockets. It didn't help.

When I finally got home I was so cold I was shaking, so I went straight to the bathroom and didn't undress until the bathtub was full. The water was too hot, but I got in anyway.

I had thought Samir had a crush on me. Maybe I had even taken it for granted: that he was super into me, he always had been (right?), and I had gone all the way to his house to tell him I liked him back, and I had assumed he would understand. That he would think I was worth the trouble. He didn't.

Once I was warm and wrinkly and the bathwater was getting cold, I put on Dad's robe, went to the living room, where my down comforter was still on the sofa, and crawled under it to call Sebastian. Sure, he was supposed to come home from South Africa the next night, but I had to get it over with right away, before I changed my mind. We talked for almost twenty minutes. When he answered I could hardly hear him, but he moved to a quieter room, or maybe he went outdoors, and I said what I had to say and he responded, his response was calm and collected, he didn't lose it, and I said we could talk more once he got home, and he said, "What do you want me to say?" and he didn't sound upset, but he seemed to have understood it all so we said goodbye and hung up. Ten minutes later, I wasn't sure he would remember what I'd said, so I sent a text as well.

When he didn't answer, I sent another. The same words. I wanted to be sure it was the first thing he would see when he looked at his phone, in case he forgot everything, even though he hadn't sounded high.

I waited until it was long past midnight to call Samir. Maybe he hadn't thought I was serious when I said I would do it. Maybe that was why he'd acted the way he did. He answered right away. I think I woke him up. I hung up without saying anything. He could see my name on the screen, so I expected him to call back. When eight minutes had gone by, I called again. Samir's voice mail message told me he would call back. "As soon as I can," said the message. I fell asleep an hour or so later, still holding the phone in my hand, its ringtone volume all the way up. Samir never called. Neither did Sebastian.

30.

When things ended with Sebastian (and Samir), I didn't do any of the stuff you're supposed to after a relationship falls apart. I didn't watch movies I thought were sad when I was little, I didn't eat ice cream straight from the carton or listen to songs about what dicks guys are. But I did get a cold. For two days I dragged myself to school anyway, but when the last day was over and it was finally Christmas break, I got a really high fever.

On the first day of vacation, Mom gave me a double dose of ibuprofen, a blanket, and a pillow to use in the car. I slept for most of the trip, waking now and then because my back, neck, throat, or legs hurt. I was sweaty and Lina looked at me from the other side of the backseat with a tiny wrinkle of concern between her dark blue eyes. Dad woke me up when we stopped to eat and I had to come along into the roadside pub. They served hot dogs with packets of ketchup and dark crinkle-cut fries, but I would rather have stayed in the car.

"It's too cold," said Dad.

"You have to eat something," said Mom.

We arrived at Grandpa's house just after seven in the evening and found that the road up to the house was plowed. In the summer I liked to take long walks with Grandpa's dogs on that same road. Grandpa lived three kilometers from the newsstand and the ICA store, and when I was little Grandma thought I should play with the neighbor kids, which I refused to do because I didn't know them. Instead I walked back and forth from the newsstand to buy an evening paper for Grandpa, then back to buy an ice cream for myself. I kept it up. The road back and forth. Sometimes I would walk so many circuits that not even the dogs had the energy to come with me. In the summer, the gravel road had a line of grass down the middle; when it rained, deep puddles would form and mosquitoes would land on the shiny film of gasoline. Now the road was framed by two meters of snow on either side and it was the second Christmas we would be celebrating without Grandma. On what was now only Grandpa's porch stood an undecorated Christmas tree and two lighted lanterns.

The tile oven was burning in my room; Grandpa had put a heating pad in the bed. I didn't change clothes; I fell asleep in the clothes I'd arrived in. Mom came in twice. The first time she removed my clothes and wrangled me into a cool, freshly ironed nightgown. It had been Grandma's. The second time she gave me a fizzy drink that tasted like oranges and bitter almond — flu medicine she'd bought in the U.S. — and I slept, I slept and slept and slept while everyone else made a gingerbread house (I could tell by the smell) and decorated the tree (I heard Dad carrying it into the house and Mom chewing him out for tracking so much snow into the hall), making meatballs and roasting ham (the smell again) and making gravlax (Mom brought some up on *knäckebröd* when it was finished, but I couldn't eat it).

I lay there under my down comforter as Grandpa came up and put more wood in the tiled stove, and he let in one of the dogs, who fell asleep under my blanket with her nose pressed to the backs of my knees. I lay there as Mom carried up a tray of tea and cheese sandwiches; I couldn't eat those either. I pulled the blanket up to my chin and half sat up as I licked at a vanilla ice cream bar and Lina showed me the drawings she had made as Christmas gifts. When the ice cream was gone, I curled into a ball and fell asleep again as Lina kept talking.

Not until Christmas Eve did I get out of bed, take a half-hour shower, wash my hair twice, and put on clean clothes. Mom changed my sheets, and I ate three helpings of rice pudding with strawberry sauce. Lina poked around in her pudding until she found the almond; I hadn't gotten the almond in years because Lina still got so excited.

"Where does Santa live, Maja?" she asked with her mouth full.

I hesitated. Because we had already been through this. It shouldn't come as a surprise. "There is no Santa."

"I know," Lina sighed, biting her lip. "But what about those flying reindeer, where do they live?"

We were the only ones celebrating Christmas with Grandpa this year. Mom's siblings had decided to spend it with their in-laws; it was no longer *the first Christmas without Grandma*. But that was fine with me. Christmas was quieter without all the rowdy cousins who would take turns crying and forcing the adults to get involved in unintelligible arguments about nothing.

Christmas Eve brought a record-breaking amount of snow (the most since local record keeping began) and the satellite TV and Internet were out. We listened to music on Grandpa's stereo and ate lunch in the kitchen because it was warmer there, and when we were done eating we sat in the living room, all watching the same DVD, which Dad had picked out. I fell asleep and woke up with my head in Mom's lap. She was stroking my forehead, and I kept my eyes closed longer than necessary. Lina taught me a card game she had made up, and Dad stood in the kitchen, peeling potatoes. The rest of us took a walk ("We have to enjoy the sun while it's still up"); the cold air tore at my throat. When we came back, I built a fire in the kitchen fireplace and I received so much praise you would have thought starting a fire was a greater feat than discovering penicillin.

While we were out on our walk, Grandpa stuck an envelope in my pocket. He stroked my cheek and smiled. It was for my grades; I got paid based on how well I did. The envelope was thick, it was always quite full, and this time was no exception. I was still making it through well.

I had made it through.

"Thanks," I mouthed. Grandpa looked happy, and I was happiest about his smile; I loved the fact that Grandpa could smile even though it was the second Christmas without Grandma.

In our philosophy class at school, we had talked about emotions, how there are six negative elemental feelings and only one positive one — joy. I raised my hand. "We all get scared in about the same way, everyone knows that," I said. "We can always understand what a person means when he says he is ashamed. And the purest feelings, the ones that make us cling to life, those are always negative."

It makes my skin crawl to recall it now, how I sat in that classroom trying to show that I was deeper and more sensitive than everyone else. I thought I knew how it felt to be angry. I thought that I knew how to lose control. But, newsflash! Eating two loaves of bread with cheese and butter while you're coming down from a high does not count. Pretending to hallucinate from some pill, fucking on coke and saying, *That was so good I thought I was gonna die.* That's all just pretend. I knew nothing, absolutely, positively nothing about wanting to die. I had only been to one funeral in my life (Grandma's), and I had never been truly afraid or truly alone; I had never wanted to die. I had never shattered into a thousand pieces. Clever Maja at the head of the class with her hand in the air. *I know the answer!* No, you don't. *You know nothing.*

These days, after the classroom, I know: Elemental feelings are tasteless and uninteresting; only a madman goes around roaring with laughter all day.

I laugh sometimes; it's a hysterical reaction. Shame. Fear. Sadness. Hate.

The compound feelings have vanished, the mixture of colors in an art shop, sixteen shades of eggshell. Yellow and blue make green. Friendship? Jealousy? Tenderness? Consideration, sympathy. Happiness. I miss happiness the most, the mixture of everything, of all the negative emotions, a drop of surprise and a lot of joy. Happiness is the perfect blend, but no one knows the recipe.

Those Christmas days at Grandpa's were the last time I was happy. I laughed and said things to Mom without thinking that I was only saying them because she wanted me to. Lina got a walkie-talkie set for a present, and she made me come out in the snow to see how far apart it would work. And once we'd done that, we built a snow fort and a snow lantern, which we lit with a candle, and we made snow angels and threw snowballs into the lake to see how far they would go. I ate marzipan dipped in chocolate and almost thought it tasted good, and I ate mustard-grilled ham on *knäckebröd* because there is nothing more delicious, and Grandpa shushed me so I would listen extra carefully when Jussi Björling sang about tears and ill-fated love.

For three days I was only sad for tiny breaths of time and not afraid even once: That Christmas was the perfect mixture for happiness. Christmas Eve, Christmas Day, and the day after Christmas.

But then. If you mix all the primary colors, all you get is brown sludge. And eventually it all turns black. Because two days after Christmas, Mom woke me up just before seven a.m. Claes Fagerman had called. They had spoken for ten minutes. He was sorry to call so early, and Mom was sad to have to tell me this, but I had to go to the psychiatric ward at Danderyd Hospital because Sebastian had tried to take his own life.

31.

Two hours later, a helicopter landed on Grandpa's lawn, the lawn that sloped down from the house to the lake. Snow whirled up as I jogged to the open helicopter with my suitcase. Grandpa kept up with me as best he could; his legs were a little stiff. For a moment he talked to the pilot, whom I got to sit next to; he was going to "drive" me "to the city," and then a car would pick me up and drive me the last little bit to the hospital. Claes wasn't there, unfortunately, but he "sent his best," he "truly appreciated this," he "had no choice" but to be somewhere else. I wasn't listening.

Sebastian had tried to kill himself.

Grandpa made a strange gesture with his head, kissed me on the cheek, and let me go.

Not until I was already in the helicopter did it occur to me that no one had asked whether I wanted to go to Sebastian. But what would I have said? No, he'll have to manage on his own?

I have to go. Of course I have to.

Sebastian had an IV in his arm, a white bandage, and a pale blue nightshirt. As I stepped through the door, he started to cry. I sat down beside him, stood up again, walked around to the other side, the side without the IV, lay down next to him on the bed, pressed my nose into his neck, and started crying myself.

It had started with "a probable overdose." Mom's cheeks had turned pink when she told me. "He needs you, Maja," she said. She was scared and sad, but there was something more, I could tell. Dad had also looked at me with that weird expression he got sometimes. *Our daughter is so mature*, they were thinking. *She is responsible. She and Sebastian have problems, but he loves her and she knows she has to support him, help him through this.*

They knew it was over between us. But "in this situation" they seemed to forget. No matter what our teenage quarrel was about, it was clearly more important that I "help out." And they were proud of me, Mom and Dad. For what I did, despite everything.

But I wasn't brave and mature. I had been unfaithful to Sebastian and then I left him because I "couldn't deal with it anymore," and I cried against his neck because I didn't know if I wanted to be there. It scared the shit out of me. For the first time I realized how easily he could have died, that death is just a single heartbeat away from life, and I reached for his wrist and pressed my fingers to the bandage harder than I dared to because I had to feel the veins underneath. I was more frightened than I'd ever been in my life. Sebastian could have died.

And it was my fault. I had betrayed him.

"I'm sorry," I whispered, my mouth right next to his jugular. I couldn't help him, I couldn't, how could I? *Sorry.* How do you tell a person not to want to die? *I will love you when no one else has the strength to. I promise. I will never leave you alone again.*

I stayed in the bed as Sebastian told me the story. He had been out the night before Christmas Eve, Dennis tagging along, he was always game and what else did he have to do? But when the ambulance picked up Sebastian, Dennis was gone. Sebastian was lying on the sidewalk outside Urban Outfitters on Biblioteksgatan, and the doctor said whoever called it in had done so from an unregistered pay-as-you-go phone. But Sebastian didn't blame Dennis. He had been granted permission to stay in Sweden until he finished this year at school; after that he would be deported. It would be considerably harder to run away from jail than from the home where he lived. He couldn't risk being picked up by the police now, especially not now.

Sebastian was taken to the emergency room with a suspected overdose. His dad came to see him during visiting hours but left after just twenty minutes. About twenty-four hours later, on the night between Christmas Eve and Christmas Day, the hospital staff found Sebastian in his bathroom.

The mirror was broken and blood had flowed out under the closed bathroom door. He had lost a great deal of blood. Since then he had been on the psychiatric ward; they had waited to call me because they didn't want to bother me during the Christmas holiday.

Claes had spoken to the emergency room doctor. The nurses had told Sebastian so when he came to.

"Could the doctor have told my dad not to come here?" Sebastian asked me. "That I'm not allowed to have visitors? Could the doctor have said that?"

Sebastian wanted me to answer, but I didn't. Because he didn't want those answers. Yet even though I didn't say anything, he became extremely upset and said, "You don't know what you're talking about," and "My dad has to take care of the firm, you know," and "My dad can't just sit around at a hospital staring at the walls." Sebastian said so several times, that his dad *couldn't,* and I had to *accept that.* I just kept quiet because we both knew it wasn't true.

Claes would be here if it was your brother, I thought, but I didn't say that either. Because Sebastian's brother would never try to kill himself; Lukas never did anything wrong.

But in the end I did say it — that Claes *should have,* that *any normal dad would have,* that *a dad isn't allowed to act like this.* And first Sebastian grew even angrier, but then he didn't have the energy to shout anymore. He cried instead. "He isn't a normal dad," he whispered, in a voice that begged me to agree and then he stopped talking and I didn't want to make him any sadder. So we talked about his mom.

"They haven't been able to get hold of her. I wasn't the one who asked them to try. I don't think Dad would call her, even for this."

"Why not?" I dared to ask. "Why won't he call her? Why don't you ever see her? Why did she leave you?"

This time Sebastian wasn't angry.

"I don't know if she did leave us," was all he said. "Dad says he kicked her out. But sometimes I think she left him, and I don't know if she wanted to take us along or if she just wanted to be by herself, but Lukas didn't want to move so then I didn't either and Dad would never let her..."

He started over when his voice steadied.

"Lukas called yesterday, he's called twice. He called me. He called. And I think if Mom was the one who left him, she wouldn't be allowed to see us. Dad wouldn't let her. Never. He can't handle being slighted. And Mom is..." I wiped his mouth and nose with toilet paper and whispered, "Keep going," and he cried even harder, and when he was done he blew his nose and said, "I'm not like Mom at all. Dad always says I am, but I hate her, I'm not like her, she's an idiot. I don't give a shit if she was the one who took off, I'm sure she was, because she can't deal with anything. Lukas says so, too. She's totally fucking hopeless."

And I didn't say anything more.

His mom and dad weren't there with him. Nor was his clever big brother Lukas, who was also afraid to stand up to Claes — he would sneak a phone call only while Claes wasn't around. But I came to the hospital. I had hurt him, too, but we left it at that; what I had done was unimportant, it was a minor detail, and when I whispered, "Forgive me," he said, "It's okay, you're here now, it doesn't matter," and I kissed him and he kissed me and he stuck his good hand under my shirt, into my hair, he held on to my neck and kissed me again and kissed me again, because he couldn't live without me, it was a question of life and death.

Did I really believe that? That he needed me to live? Yes. Because it was true. By the time he was moved to the psychiatric ward, his dad and brother were on a ski holiday in Zermatt. From there, his dad flew to another city to work and Lukas took off for the U.S. again. It sounds like a joke, but the only person who visited Sebastian on the psych ward before I got there was Claes's secretary, Majlis. Maybe you think I'm making that up, but I'm not, and the worst part is not that Claes Fagerman sent his assistant; the worst part is that Claes Fagerman knew exactly how sick this was but he did it anyway.

Sebastian lay in his hospital bed and cried for a long time. I lay beside him, and I could tell by looking at him how close he had been to death; I could tell by looking at him that he wanted to die, and I thought that if I just stayed with him I could make him better. I would get him to look at me that way, like he'd never seen anything like me. Make him feel gone, like he had lost his footing and all he could remember was one thing: that he wanted me. And then I would figure out, then I would *know* how to save a person. And everything would be fine. Sebastian would be okay again.

Was I thinking of Samir? Maybe. But he didn't want me; I didn't fit into his life, and he didn't want to adapt himself to mine. Samir didn't need me.

As I lay there in Sebastian's hospital bed and the two of us cried, I wanted to light up the world for him, show him what he meant, come with him, to him, for him.

Oh, shit, you're thinking, but that's only because you know what happened later. But right then, no one knew anything. And no one asked me, *Do you want to? Can you? Or* said, *We will help you, you can't do this all by yourself.* Because everyone knew this was the only option. There was only me.

No one asked if I wanted to save Sebastian, but you all blame me for failing.

I don't know what the doctor said when Claes Fagerman explained that he couldn't come visit his son on the psych ward because he was busy skiing and celebrating Christmas, but I know that no one ever made demands of Claes Fagerman. Not even doctors. Maybe in the break room, when Claes couldn't hear, they said to each other, *Someone ought to set him right,* but they themselves were never that someone, *no one was that someone,* and if and when they encountered Claes Fagerman and could in theory say anything at all, they forgot whatever had been so important before. *What the hell is wrong with you, you're his dad? His brother? Where is his mom?* Not a chance that they would ask. They were so blown away by Claes Fagerman that they never dared to say anything they weren't certain would please him. And they were terrified that Claes Fagerman might turn his hatred and contempt away from his son and aim it at them instead.

I lay in Sebastian's bed and hugged him until he was done crying, until he had fallen asleep, and I lay there until he woke up again.

Not a single person in the whole world stood up and shouted until someone listened: *Can someone please go get*

Sebastian's fucking piece-of-shit parents and force them to love him the way he deserves to be loved?

When he cried so hard he couldn't talk, I kissed him. He kissed me back. It was uncomfortable and his snot got in my mouth and his bandage was in the way, but right then, at the hospital, Sebastian was love. He was all I needed, he was there with me and not headed somewhere else, and I truly believed that I would be able to change something. Not the world, I wasn't that naïve, but I thought about what it would be like after he was discharged and we would lie on his double bed, naked and alone, and he would trace paths on my stomach and I would inhale the air he exhaled, and no, we did not need anyone else. We sure as hell didn't need his despicable father. "He should die, not you," I whispered into Sebastian's ear. Did I mean it? Of course I did. I hated Claes Fagerman. I wanted to sacrifice it all for Sebastian. The only problem was that I had no clue what "all" meant. Because greatest of all is love up until something else becomes even greater.

I got to the hospital by helicopter and car; it was obvious that I had to go. I went back to Sebastian and I stayed. Because Sebastian needed me. He didn't have anyone else. He loved me. *We're so lucky to have each other.*

What I miss now, after everything, is what it was like when I could feel those lukewarm mixture feelings that resembled happiness. What it was like over Christmas at Grandpa's, when there was snow all over and my head felt like after a good rain and my emotions were diluted into a just-right blend.

Love? No, I don't miss love. Love is not greatest or purest, it's never a perfect blend, just an impure liquid, the kind you should really sniff before you taste. But the risk is you still might not notice it's poisonous.

THE WOMEN'S JAIL, NIGHTTIME

Week 2 of Trial: Early morning, Tuesday

32.

Even in the middle of the night, in the darkest hour, a faint mist of almost-light finds its way into my cell. It comes from the city outside, where it is never completely dark, never completely quiet. When I wake up, I lie on my back for a while to let my eyes adjust, and then I can see the contours around me. The thin yellow blanket over the sheet rises and falls as I breathe; I rest my hand on the headboard and feel the indentations my fingernails have left in the soft pine. That is when I am most alone.

I had a pine bed when I was little. I wanted a bunk bed and Mom bought one from IKEA, but I was never brave enough to sleep on the top bunk, so I would crawl under the bed and lie flat on my back and draw on the bedposts, leave secret messages for posterity. Sometimes I made Amanda creep under there with me. Perhaps our friendship was at its best in those days, when life was made up of Popsicles, glitter tattoos from packs of gum, and investigations into who could draw the best horse head. But it was crowded under the bed; we never stayed there very long.

When I got a new bed, a Gustavian style one with a lacy canopy, that was the end of my graffiti. I kept the canopy bed until it was time for Lina to sleep in a real bed. Then it went to her and I got a new bedroom and a double bed and Amanda got a real tattoo, a lily on her wrist. It was hardly visible when she wore a watch.

Sebastian never slept over at my house. Not that Mom and Dad would have had a problem with it, but Sebastian kind of did best in his own surroundings and we were never completely alone at my house. He preferred us to be on our own. And this became even more important once he was allowed to leave the hospital. *I want quiet. Can you just shut up?*

In my cell I don't have to turn on the light to use the bathroom; the steel ring of the seat is shiny even in the dark. I sit down on it and it doesn't bother me anymore that it's hard and narrow and uncomfortable. When I'm done, I find the flush button without fumbling around because I know exactly where it is. I have lived in this room for so long now that it's stuck in me, branded into me with a red-hot iron, a forever-and-always-etched-into-my-skin-with-burning-ink tattoo. I never wake up anymore and wonder for one sweet second where I am, and I never wonder a refreshing *Why?*

But I still have my dreams. And sometimes I get to be with her, Amanda, as she laughs with her mouth wide open, takes me by the arm, and pinches because it's her and me forever.

Her and me. And Sebastian and me.

Just the thought of him, what it was like when it was Sebastian, causes a reaction in my body. It doesn't matter if my brain protests; my body remembers, even my skin remembers him.

Before Sebastian, I was a girl who said yes or no. Never anything else. But with Sebastian, I became like one of the guys. It never made a difference that I knew I would hate myself afterward. I would say "oh, come on," I would plead "please," "more," "one more time," "just one last time." There is only one thing my body remembers more clearly than how much I wanted him and that is how it felt when he was gone.

It's my turn to talk. In just a few hours. First Sander will guide me through my account, and then the prosecutor will ask her questions.

I can hear in my head what the prosecutor will say. How could you? What did you do? What did you know? Why didn't you stop him? *Answer me.*

"It's not up to you to explain why Sebastian did what he did," Sander says. "The faster you realize that and let it go, the better. You have to concentrate on your own role in this story."

Sander doesn't think I should talk about how I loved Sebastian; that "has nothing to do with this." He doesn't want to listen when I explain how I betrayed Sebastian. How it was my fault that he wasn't mentally stable. Or how Sebastian needed me. When I talk to Sander about that, he always starts flipping through some papers or turns away from me or searches his pockets for his glasses. Sander doesn't want to hear about what Sebastian and I had. The story of our love is "inconvenient." He thinks that our love in and of itself makes me appear guilty. Or stupid, which is more or less the same thing.

It has nothing to do with this. You don't need to talk about it. You can keep it to yourself. It is not judicially relevant.

But there are some things Sander doesn't understand. When he was young, the king didn't have to kiss Silvia on the palace stairs when they were newlyweds. The king didn't have to hold an after-dinner speech on live television: "Silvia, Silvia, I love you...blah-blah-blah..." in front of the entire country. It didn't take speechwriters to satisfy the plebes' need for claims of, "We have been through hell and high water together, we did not choose the easy route, but greatest of all is love." In Sander's day, you got to keep this kind of thing private. In Sander's day, you were supposed to keep your life to yourself, anything else was embarrassing. But those days are gone. And I know what it will take. I know what I personally would have wanted to know: I would have wanted to know everything, I would have demanded every last detail about Sebastian's and my dirty, sick, poisonous love. In order to understand why I said his dad deserved to die and why I shot my boyfriend and my best friend.

Maybe it's not up to me to explain why Sebastian did what he did. I'm sure *it's not judicially relevant.* But I was there, he was my boyfriend, I knew him better than anyone else in that classroom — I definitely knew him better than his own parents did. And I killed him and Amanda. If I don't explain, who will?

Why? I want to know, too. And "why" is an infinite concept, it takes complete openness, and complete openness demands that I am more cautious with my words than I've ever been before. Because as soon as I say something, it will become true.

On the day it's my turn to talk, finally, after all the delays, I wake up long before I should.

It's the worst, waking up at the darkest time. That's what happens today, and even before I open my eyes I know I won't be able to go back to sleep. I feel sick; I get up and stand with my head tilted above the sink, let the water run, the tap water in jail never gets truly cold or truly hot, but I rinse my face, the neck of my nightgown gets wet and I pull it off. Then I stand there naked in my room and breathe, in and out, in and out. I'm freezing and sweating.

Sander has prepared me for what will happen today; we have practiced, we have practiced and practiced and practiced, and no, it's not that Sander has made up a story full of lies for me to memorize, but he knows that if I start stammering and blushing and sweating, it won't matter what I say, how honest I am — no one in that courtroom will listen to me.

The defendant. That's me. I will be allowed to speak; it is time for me to *present my account*.

Sander told me that I have the "right to remain silent." That means I have the option to completely keep my mouth shut during the trial. No one can force me to speak; no one can force me to answer questions. If I want to remain silent, I can remain silent.

Sebastian talked at the hospital, but once he left he stopped speaking. I let him be; I didn't ask him a thousand questions and I didn't demand any answers. I understood that he needed to be quiet. His friends did their best to pretend nothing was wrong. None of them had insisted on coming to the psych ward, but once he was back home it got harder to pretend that their playacting was for Sebastian's sake. Dennis was best at it; Labbe was worst. The first time Sebastian saw Labbe after Christmas, Labbe started crying and hugging him, which made Amanda try to do the same, and it was awful. Sebastian hated it.

I'm freezing when I get back in bed. There's an extra blanket in my cupboard but I'm shaking too hard to get it. When I close my eyes, they burn. I turn onto my side and try to put my arms around my knees, try to breathe under the blanket. My shivering fits come and go; I almost have time to get used to their rhythm, like having the hiccups, and then they stop just as suddenly as they started.

Once I have told my story, there will be no going back. But here, at night, there are versions of this story, lives parallel to my own. I can't stop thinking about them. In one version I never kiss Samir, I never let him take my hand, I never go out to his neighborhood, he never starts hating me or feeling ashamed of the way I make him feel, he doesn't feel responsible for me and he finds stuff besides Sebastian to get worked up about, and I never get a crush on Samir and I don't have to break up with Sebastian and Sebastian doesn't try to kill himself, he doesn't get worse the way he did after Christmas and the very last party never happens and his dad doesn't freak out and Sebastian never loses hope that his dad will love him and he never fires the first shot or the other shots and I never kill Amanda and I never kill Sebastian and we just keep living our lives and that is a better ending, a better beginning, a better life.

Because it's when I break up with Sebastian and he realizes how easy it is to die that he becomes a murderer. I didn't figure that out until it was too late.

In another parallel universe, I shoot Sebastian sooner — the night before, right after the party. I don't know why I would have done that, or how, but it still would have been better because everyone else would still be alive. In a third version, I never go home after the party and Mom and Dad call the police early in the morning and they find me dead near Barracuda. I drowned myself, and the police go straight to Sebastian and force their way into the house to talk to him and he can't do what he did in the house and he can't go to school to do what he did there.

In a fourth version, I never leave Sebastian's after the party. I refuse to go even though his dad orders me to, and I stay with Sebastian, I force him to stay with me, and if I had been there he wouldn't have killed his dad. Then everyone else gets to live. Amanda gets to live. And all these versions have one thing in common. I can't stop thinking about them. Not yet, anyway.

"It's important that you tell us." The Perm, the officer in charge of my interrogations, said that more times than I could keep track of. "Do it for Amanda."

People always think they know what the dead would have wanted. *Amanda would have wanted you to be brave. Amanda would have wanted you to tell the truth. Amanda would have understood.*

This is such an incredible load of shit. Amanda would have liked me not to shoot her. Amanda didn't want to die. That's the only thing I think we can be certain of.

The truth is, everything after I went back to Sebastian happened because I couldn't manage to stop it.

Should I talk about all the other stuff that Sebastian was, too? The evil? Sure, why not? It's not my responsibility to defend him. He is alone now, as alone as I am. But I'm not sure it will help me, or even that it's particularly important. Because today I'm going to talk.

And after that it will be Samir's turn.

Trial hearing in case B 147/66

The prosecutor et al. v. Maria Norberg

33.

Yes, Samir survived. Sebastian shot him three times: The shots to his stomach and shoulder didn't exit, and one went straight through his arm. He needed six operations, and they removed his pancreas. I'm not sure what that means, but it says in the indictment that he'll have to take medicine for the rest of his life, that he has limited use of his left arm, and that he has recurring back pain.

But he is well enough to be in school, at Stanford of all places, and according to Pancake that's thanks to the settlement he received from the Fagerman Group.

Samir isn't just one of the victims, one of the injured parties. He is also the prosecutor's star witness, Ugly-Lena's only witness from inside the classroom. She has built her whole case upon Samir's testimony. And naturally, I know what he has said. The transcripts of his interrogations are included in the case report, and I have read them. I have read them so many times that I practically know them by heart. Samir said that I shot Amanda on purpose. That I picked up my weapon calmly and quietly, that Sebastian didn't seem to be worried in the least when I did so, that Sebastian begged me to "do it now, come on. I want you to do it" before I shot. First Amanda. Then Sebastian.

The courtroom is silent when I come in to take my seat. The air is trembling with anticipation, as Grandma would have said. Even the judges look different. Puffed up with importance again, just like on the very first day. Samir won't give his testimony until Monday next week; there was something he had to do at Stanford and the court decided that was fine, but I have to go today. That is why everyone is on tenterhooks, because I'm going to talk. But considering we all know what Samir's going to say, I don't get why everyone is so worked up. There's nothing I can say to make his story go away.

Sander says that Samir's testimony "must be judged in light of the situation in which he found himself," and he says he can "point out inconsistencies in what Samir observed." But I know that once they hear what Samir has to say, they will trust him. Samir is the kind of person you trust.

Sander starts by asking questions about me. He asks how old I am, even though anyone who still doesn't know can't possibly have a pulse. He asks where I live, and I don't reply "Djursholm"; I say "with my mom and dad and little sister...she's five and her name is Lina." Then he wants me to talk about how I'm doing in school, and I say "pretty well." "Very well," corrects Sander. When the warm-up is over, it's time to start talking about "what happened."

Sander told me that he does not intend to "focus" on Samir's "interpretation of events," but that I will have to talk about the classroom. But we begin with Sebastian's suicide attempt. I have to talk about how sick he was before, his partying, how I wasn't a fan of it, how I started seeing Samir, what Sebastian said when I broke up with him, what we talked about at the hospital.

"Tell me what it was like after Sebastian came home from the hospital. Can you do that?"

Sebastian was allowed to come home one week after New Year's, the same day school started. But he was allowed to take another two weeks off sick, and he spent them at home. At first I thought he was getting better. It didn't get better, but I thought it did. Sebastian stopped going out, he stopped inviting two hundred people to parties at his house and booking weekend trips to Barcelona, London, and New York. He wanted to be with me. Preferably all the time, even when I was supposed to be in school. He also stopped talking about what we would do, where we would travel, how we would party. Instead he wanted us to spend time alone. Just the two of us. At his house, where his dad hardly stuck around long enough to switch suitcases. I thought that was a good sign. He wasn't getting as drunk, he wasn't high as often, and never the way he used to be. When his friends phoned while I was there, he would screen their calls. If we were supposed to spend time with anyone else, he wanted to do it at his home, and if anyone showed up there, it wasn't unusual for him to disappear to some other part of the house. Sometimes not even I could find him. He was just gone.

Of course it was obvious that he was depressed, but at the same time Sebastian had never been as in love with me as during those few weeks after he came home from the hospital and walked around in his pajamas. And that's probably when I loved him the most, too. Why was that?

At the end of Harry Potter, in the middle of the biggest battle with Voldemort, Ron and Hermione kiss each other. They do it because they believe they're about to die. Right after that, Harry and Ginny kiss each other for the same reason. I think Sebastian loved me more than ever because he knew he could have died. And I felt the same way, because I also believed he could have died. It's only now, now that I know what happened, that I think maybe he knew even then that not only *could* he have died, he *would* die, or at least he knew it was easy to die, if that was what he decided he wanted.

It passed. That intense feeling of love.

We talk about Claes. Sander asks me to talk about what Claes said, what he did and didn't do.

"Was it difficult for Sebastian?"

"Was Sebastian disappointed in his father?"

"Did you talk about it?"

And I tell him. I talk about the others, too. About Lukas and his mom and Labbe and all the parties and Dennis and the drugs and Samir. I tell him everything.

"Can you tell me how Sebastian's health changed?"

I tell him that, too.

It took almost until Easter break for me to admit to myself that nothing had gotten better, that in fact it was worse. Everyone else had figured this out much earlier, even Amanda. Because even back in late February, Sebastian didn't have to demand to be alone, he didn't have to dodge calls or pretend to be sick to avoid going out to things. We were alone because no one wanted to be with us.

Living happily ever after with the person you love only works in books; "ever after" is only long enough if you're fictional. And love can't rescue anyone into eternal life.

Two things are important for Sander. One is that he wants to show that Sebastian had a conflict with his dad and I was in no way responsible for it. That I didn't convince him to kill Claes, that Sebastian would have done it no matter what I did or said. The other is that he wants to show that Sebastian and I had not made a joint plan for revenge, that we didn't lie around in Claes's villa devising plans for our murder pact. Sander wants to make the court understand that I *missed* my friends, I didn't *hate* them, that Sebastian just kept getting sicker and sicker as well as angrier and stranger. Sebastian, not me.

So I tell the judges about this, too, and the journalists and everyone else. I talk about his growing cruelty. The first time Sebastian shouted "Shut up!" at me even though I hadn't said anything. "If you don't shut up, I'll smack you." And when I became convinced that he would hit me. And do the other thing.

"Were you afraid of Sebastian?" Sander wonders, and the chief judge leans forward a smidge, looking at me, waiting for my response.

But I wasn't afraid of him, not then, not that first time. Not the second time, either. It's hard to explain. I don't have a formula to help people understand exactly how I felt.

"Is that really true?" Sander asks. "You weren't afraid?"

Instead of responding, I feel the tears rising up; I can't stop them. I shake my head, and now I can't say anything at all because I'm crying too hard.

"Yes," I manage to say at last. "It's true. I wasn't afraid for my own sake. I might have been scared, but not that he would hurt me."

"What do you mean by that?"

"I couldn't leave him."

"Did you think he would try to kill himself again if you left him?"

I nod. The panic fills my throat. "Mmhmm."

"Why did you think that?"

"Because he said so. And it was true. I knew it was true."

"And you didn't want that to happen."

"Of course I didn't."

"Did you talk to anyone about this, Maja? Did you explain how serious the situation was?"

I nod again.

"Yes," I say. "I did."

SEBASTIAN AND ME

34.

We didn't know Claes would be home. But he was. He was having dinner in the kitchen with four other old guys. One of the men was standing by the stove. I recognized him; he usually wore his shoulder-length hair in a dorky bun (I guess he wanted to look like a soccer star) on one of the three million cooking shows on TV. That day his hair was greasy and loose and he was standing in Sebastian's kitchen and grasping a fish by the neck in one hand and a knife in the other. The TV chef was wasted.

Claes was in the middle of one of his showpieces, a story about the time he was hunting in South Africa and was ordered by one of the lead hunters to fetch more ammunition. Everyone must have heard this story at least twenty times, but they all laughed out loud at just the right moment.

"Sit down," Claes said in the middle of a sentence, before resuming his story. We sat. Why? Because Sebastian always did as Claes said and I always did whatever Sebastian did. "Can you grab a couple plates?"

He turned to the man closest to me, a guy of around sixty. I recognized him, too — he wasn't the minister of finance, but he was some other sort of minister, maybe the minister of industry and trade; I had met him before. Looking confused, he stood up and turned to the row of cabinets. The minister had no idea where the plates were and plus he, too, was super drunk. He had to put a hand over one eye in order to see properly. He pointed a stubby index finger at the refrigerator and wondered, "Where do you keep the plates?"

I stood up. "I'll get them," I said. I wanted to get out of there, speed up whatever Claes wanted us for.

"And what's the matter with you today, Sebastian?" Claes had finished his story. "You look sober. Are you sick?"

Sebastian gave a faint smile and poured us each a glass of wine. He drained his, filled it again, and raised it toward his dad in a toast before gulping it down.

"He takes after his father, I see," said the TV chef, coming to stand beside me. He leaned over to place a platter of dill potatoes and a bowl of snow peas on the table. "And he has good taste, too," he added, pinching my arm before he went back to get the fish.

"Well, unfortunately you're wrong about that," Claes said as he took a ladleful of potatoes and passed the platter. "He sure as shit doesn't take after me. I checked a few years ago, and remarkably enough he is mine, but he is a hundred and twenty percent Miss Jönköping. He even knocks the original out of the water. Makes his mother seem both stable and smart in comparison."

Claes's drunk friends laughed. A little hesitantly, perhaps, but they did laugh. No one could believe he was being serious.

The TV chef returned, pulled up a chair, and squeezed in between me and Sebastian. He sat so close that I could smell him, a mixture of fish guts, sweat, and heavy cologne.

"But please, tell us," Claes went on. "Sebastian, the family's filthy black sheep. How are you?"

"Do you care?" I mumbled, trying to scoot my chair in the other direction. I didn't think it had been loud enough, but Claes looked up from his plate. Was he going to start laughing?

"Do I care?"

The TV chef put his arm around me.

"He's just joking, girly. Relax. Try the food." He took my fork, speared a piece of fish, and brought it toward my mouth. "Here comes the airplane...open up, take a bite for Daddy."

Claes cracked up, burst into peals of laughter, and a split second later everyone else was laughing again. I opened my mouth. I don't know why I did it, but the TV cook prepared another bite. He *zoom-zoom-zoomed* it into my mouth. As I swallowed, he wiped my lips with his napkin. I couldn't see Sebastian anymore, but I could hear him laughing, too, that laugh he always managed to produce when his dad started in on him. It nauseated me. Sebastian was stuck with this, he couldn't get away from the bullying, and he never would. Couldn't he see how sick it was? Of course he could. Didn't he see how sick his dad was? Yes, he did. How disgusting his behavior was? Naturally. Why didn't he do something? Why couldn't he grasp that you can't treat other people like that? Why did the rules of decorum apply to everyone but Claes? Claes Fagerman could do anything he liked. The rest of us just opened wide and swallowed.

Maybe it was the TV chef preparing a third bite that gave me the strength to act. I placed both hands on the edge of the table and shoved myself away from him and his fucking fork.

"Little girly..." the chef tried to protest once I'd gotten away. "You need to eat to grow big and strong."

"Open wide," someone cackled. I couldn't hear who. The minister maybe, and I heard Sebastian laugh again. *Like his dad.* I scrunched my eyes closed, fast and hard, white dots danced on the inside of my eyelids.

I turned to Sebastian. "I'm going home now."

He didn't respond. I don't think he even looked back. I was always the loser when he had to choose between me and his dad.

"That's probably a good idea," Claes said, reaching for the bowl of potatoes to take seconds. "This is fucking delicious," he continued, turning toward the chef.

I took four steps and planted myself directly in front of Claes.

"Do you really think..." I managed to say. My throat ached. My voice barely held. I would start crying in a few seconds and I had to get out of there before it happened. But I had to say this. "Do you think this is okay? Aren't you going to do something about it?" I swallowed. I was screwed; I was already crying. "You don't give a shit that Sebastian is sick, that he can't handle... you're not going to do something about it?"

Claes looked up at me. He smiled.

"Do something?" His voice was cold as ice. "Tell me, Maja...what is it you want me to do? What do you think I should do that I haven't already done? Please explain to me exactly what that might be?"

I tried to look back. I tried to keep my gaze steady, but I couldn't. Would he say that we need to talk about this in private? That this wasn't a fitting topic for a dinner among gentlemen? No. Claes wasn't ashamed, why would he be? He was never ashamed; nothing could threaten him, there was nothing he couldn't say or do in front of the entire world. Claes Fagerman leaned back. He had put down his silverware. Everyone else had stopped eating, too. They looked at me.

"We're listening, Maja. Tell us what's on your mind. Tell us what you think I should do." He swirled his wine-glass. The yellow liquid swished around inside it. His other hand remained still next to his plate, his fingers slightly spread. He had a signet ring on his little finger; he tapped it against the table.

"Nothing," I forced out. It was just a whisper. My throat was burning with exertion. "You don't have to do anything." Then I turned around and left. Sebastian didn't follow.

Mom and Dad were watching TV in the living room when I got home. I went straight to my room. I didn't want them to see that I had been crying. But I slammed the door as hard as I could behind me. I suppose I just wanted to make sure they knew I had come home, so they would know I wasn't sleeping at Sebastian's even though I always stayed there on Saturdays. Three minutes later, Dad knocked at the door. I had taken off my jeans and gotten under the covers. I was done crying.

"Is everything okay, honey?"

I turned over to face the wall.

"Sure."

"Do you want to talk?"

"I want to sleep."

He walked over to my bed, bent down, and stroked the hair from my cheek.

"Good night, darling."

The next morning, Mom sat down across from me as I was eating breakfast.

"What's going on, Maja?"

I shrugged.

"Did you have a fight?"

I shrugged again. No one said anything for a moment.

"How is he doing?"

"Not good."

"We figured that much out. Do you want us to do anything?"

Yes, I do.

"No."

"Are you sure? Promise you'll tell us if there's anything we can do. We know it's not easy, that Sebastian has issues. We've spoken with your teachers, and they understand as well. They realize that you need to miss school sometimes. And you're still doing very well, they're not worried about you."

I swallowed.

They should be worried about me. I'm really fucking worried about me.

"You're making a big difference, Maja. He needs you, and you're there for him. Not many people could handle that at your age. Promise you'll say something if you need help?"

"Nothing. There's nothing you can do."

Mom smiled. A bit too quickly, a bit too broadly. She was relieved, it was almost comical to see how incredibly happy she was not to have to deal with this. At the same time, she was pleased, proud of herself. This was a super morning for her; this was the Mom role she loved playing best. *Listen to your child.* Check. *Ask if there's anything you can do.* Check. *Show that you care.* Check.

Do something? What might that be? Tell me, explain to me, you have to say how I can contribute. It's not my responsibility. *My God! Sebastian does have parents of his own, after all.*

I had promised to take Lina to gymnastics. She pushed her own stroller, which we had brought so she could ride in it on the way home; she was usually tired by then. Samir got on the bus near our school. He hesitated when he saw us. He was about to walk past us and sit farther back, but when Lina said hi, he took the seat in front of us, turned to the side, and looked at us.

"How are you?"

"Do you go to school on the weekends, too?"

He shook his head. "I left my math book in my locker."

"And what a catastrophe it would be," I said, "to have to make it through a whole Sunday without your math book."

A little dimple appeared in Samir's cheek. And suddenly I was crying again. I was tired of crying. It didn't make anything better. But it was easier not to cry when Samir wasn't smiling. Everything was easier when he was grumpy and acting super weird and treating me like crap. I tried to smile back, to dry my tears without him noticing, but it didn't work. I looked out the window, leaning as far back in my seat as I could. I didn't want Lina to see.

"Hey..." he attempted.

Go to hell. I hate you. Don't look at me like that if you don't want me.

I wiped the tears with the back of my hand.

You're a coward, Samir. If you weren't too scared, it could have been you and me.

"What's your name?" Lina asked. She had clambered up in her seat, kneeling so she could reach, and I felt so relieved that I gave a nervous giggle and ran my hand over her hair.

I don't want to cry anymore.

Samir laughed, too. He leaned toward Lina, his face just a few centimeters from hers.

"Samir," he whispered, and Lina giggled in delight.

Lina could be our alibi. We could let her babble on about the stuff that meant the world to her; we wouldn't have to deal with our own crap as long as she was talking.

I'm too tired to be angry, Samir. Not at you, too.

Lina asked her usual twenty questions about nothing. Samir responded. Now and then he looked at me, and I had plenty of time to force my tears back down. But then Lina stopped talking, sank back down in her seat, and took out the book she had brought to page through on the way. She pretended to read, and a small wrinkle appeared in Samir's forehead.

I shook my head. Shrugged. Cast down my eyes. Went through all the motions you make when you want the person you're talking to to realize that it's just shit, everything has gone to shit, but you can't say so because that's not the kind of thing people say.

I don't want to talk about it. Make me.

He nodded.

"You aren't responsible for him," he started.

"Yeah," I said. "I am, actually."

"He's crazy, Maja," Samir whispered. "And the stuff he does isn't less illegal just because he's doing it at home instead of on Stureplan. You don't have to take care of him. It's not your responsibility."

It's not the drugs, Samir, they're not the worst part. Not anymore. He's turned into a different person. Something is growing inside him. At night, he hurts. It's in his head and he screams out loud, just screams, whatever's inside him is poison, sometimes he can't even deal with light, not even the tiniest little beam of light. I don't know what to do. Help me.

I swallowed, fiddled with Lina's ponytail, then leaned over and sniffed her hair. She had used Mom's shampoo.

Samir nodded. And I thought he understood. Understood how fucked up everything was and that was why he wasn't asking if there was anything he could do. That the reason he didn't ask if he could help me was because he knew how bad it really was.

But I didn't say anything. Anything at all.

Lina and I got off two stops before Mörby. We walked the last little bit to the gym, and as I helped her change clothes, I received a text.

"It will all work out," Samir wrote.

I should have responded, but I didn't. Instead I deleted his text. He didn't get it. Nothing was going to work itself out.

I didn't want to be in contact with Samir because Samir wanted nothing to do with me. He was afraid to, because he was a fucking coward.

I should have responded: *No, it's not going to work out.* Or at least: *You're a fucking idiot, Samir Said.* But I didn't.

Maybe that's why it all went to shit. Because of course Samir would try to help. And maybe he wanted to help me because he had a guilty conscience. Samir was the kind of guy who thought he could help. I should have realized that.

Trial hearing in case B 147/66

The prosecutor et al. v. Maria Norberg

Week 2 of Trial: Wednesday through Friday

35.

After I was done talking, it was Lena Pärsson's turn again. Since Samir couldn't appear in court when he was supposed to, the lead prosecutor started by bringing in the person who had made the first call to the police. The call was played in the courtroom.

We listened to the panicked voice before the round, enraptured eyes of the judges. The voice screamed about a shooting, and a calm voice responded: "Where are you calling from? Where are you right now? Have you informed the school authorities? Have you begun evacuating the school?" We could hear the sounds of the evacuation in the background: students running, crying. We could also hear the calm voice growing more and more tense: "We are on our way. Emergency vehicles are on their way. Can you hear them? Can you hear the sirens? Can you get out of the building?"

It was obvious from looking at the judges that the emergency call made them feel like *they were there*. The sounds, the real sounds, the panic, the real panic. The screams. But the emergency call made me feel the exact opposite:

What we were talking about, listening to, had nothing to do with what had happened to me. I couldn't remember any of those sounds from inside the classroom. The emergency call could have been about anything, anyone. It could have been made up.

Call-me-Lena posed eight questions (I counted) to the woman who had made the call, a janitor I had never seen before. She didn't start crying until the fourth question. But she didn't give any new information, nothing I hadn't heard before. Sander didn't ask any questions.

Then Call-me-Lena brought in the three police officers who had been first on the scene. One at a time, they talked about what they had seen, what they had felt when they made the decision to enter the classroom, what they had seen there, what they had and had not done. Two of them cried — or, one of them cried and the other had to clear his throat and swallow a few times to keep from crying. The one who had taken the gun away from me and talked to me, I didn't recognize him, but he looked at me, and when he did so, he seemed tired. More tired than upset or angry. He didn't cry. But the lay judge to the left of the chief judge sure did. She even had to blow her nose.

Sander showed them a sketch of the classroom and asked if they could confirm that Samir and Amanda had been found in the marked locations. They could.

The prosecutor also questioned two students who had been out in the hallway when the shooting began. I didn't know them, but one of them started shaking when she looked at me, shaking for real, as if I were a zombie or, like, Charles Manson — so terrifying that even just being near me would give you epilepsy. But when she started to blather about what she'd heard about me and Sebastian, that "everyone knew what we were up to," the chief judge interrupted.

"I think we'll stick to the subject at hand," he said, and the girl, who was pretending she knew me but really had no idea what Sebastian and I were like, blushed.

Sander asked three questions of each of the students: "Did you know Sebastian personally? Do you know Maja personally? Was the door to the classroom closed?" They responded: "No. No. Yes."

Labbe testified by videoconference. He refused to be questioned if I was in the room, and the chief judge had decided that this was acceptable. Labbe said that "everyone had been worried" about Sebastian, that "everyone knew he had issues," and that Sebastian and I had "stopped going out like before." He didn't mention that they had been avoiding us except for when they wanted to party, and he didn't start crying until he talked about the last party, when he explained that he had come down from his boarding school outside of town "because it seemed important" and that he had slept over at Amanda's house after the party. When he had to explain that he had stayed in bed when she left for school the next morning, he wailed even more. You could hardly hear what he was saying. I was glad he wasn't in the courtroom. I didn't have to look at him; I never want to see him again. Sander didn't ask him any questions. "Thank you," said the chief judge when Labbe was finished. "Thanks," prosecutor Lena mumbled into her mike, but by then Labbe was already offline.

Then Call-me-Lena examined the crime-scene technicians. They got to explain which weapon had my fingerprints on the trigger and which one had my prints only on the barrel. They got to talk about which weapon had, according to the investigation, killed first Amanda and then Sebastian, and on what grounds it was considered proven that I had fired it. Sander's questions to the technicians revolved around shot angles and margins of error and my position when I fired the gun, and he presented the report from the investigation he had ordered and allowed them to share their thoughts on how reliable it was. I don't know if I would have understood why he was asking all those questions if I didn't already know that he was trying to show that it wasn't unusual for someone (me) who wasn't used to firearms to be so off target (and hit Amanda instead of Sebastian).

When he was done talking about where the techs thought I had been standing when I fired the gun, he started talking about the bag in my locker. The prosecutor had asked, "Is it possible to rule out that Maja handled the bag?" The technician had said it wasn't.

Now it was Sander's turn. He wondered: "How likely is it that Maja could have handled the bag without leaving any fingerprints on or in it?"

"Not particularly likely."

After this it was time for him to discuss the "bomb." In the case report, it was called the "explosive material."

In the prosecutor's accusatory part, the "explosive material" was mentioned as a factor that indicated Sebastian and I had planned "still more extensive destruction" and that "an even greater attack on the school could not be ruled out as its purpose." The investigators had managed to trace the "bomb" to a couple of construction workers who had done some work on Claes Fagerman's house. It was really only half a bomb, you might say, because it didn't have the actual fuse part. Presumably, it said in the case report, Sebastian had snitched the stuff when they were there to blast away a boulder that was in the way of what would become Fagerman's boathouse. Or maybe it had been left behind and Sebastian came across it and kept it for his own purposes. In any case, the construction workers had never reported it stolen, or wanted to admit that they had done a poor job of keeping track of their materials.

The prosecutor argued that the "bomb" indicated that Sebastian and I had been planning the attack for some time, but Sander was of a different opinion. The fact that Sebastian and I were not even a couple when Claes's boathouse was built was only one of his objections. Sander also wanted the technicians to admit that the object in my locker never posed a threat. It couldn't be detonated, at least not in the state it was in at the school. Thus it was inconsequential, in Sander's eyes, to discuss the "bomb" and its purpose, since it couldn't even be defined as a bomb.

The prosecutor claimed that Sebastian hadn't known it was worthless. She claimed that whether or not the bomb was functional was "immaterial to the motive." She and Sander argued about that for a while until the chief judge interrupted them and said that "speculation about Sebastian's insight into the functionality of the object in question can be left at that." He thought it was uninteresting whether Sebastian was stupid enough to think the "bomb" was functional.

Sander asked the technician a whole bunch of questions. The tech gave lengthy answers. I didn't understand the half of it. But when the chief judge asked what Sander was trying to get at, "considering that the charges only encompass the fully executed crimes," Sander became impatient.

"Given that this entire criminal investigation has been based on the wholly unjustified assumption that my client planned to level her school to the ground, I am of the opinion that it is extremely important to show that (a) my client cannot be linked to either the bag or its contents and (b) the contents of the bag never posed any danger."

After that, the judge allowed him to continue with his line of questioning. But I still think it was dumb of Sander, because the judge looked annoyed the whole time. He gave deep, audible sighs, and once he even looked at his watch, which he'd never done before.

When they were done with the bomb talk, Sander moved on to "the lack of evidence to link the bag, the gun safe, and the other firearms found at the scene of the crime to my client."

"How likely is it that Maja packed the bag? Opened the gun safe, handled the other firearms?"

"It can't be ruled out."

A wrinkle appeared on Sander's forehead.

"Did you find her fingerprints anywhere but the handle of the bag? On the zipper? Inside? Did you find her prints on the gun safe? The other firearms?"

"No. No. No, no, no."

Sander stopped asking questions after that, but the wrinkle didn't go away. And the chief judge still looked angry.

I don't think that this particular part of the trial was going too well for us.

The medical examiners got to talk about the autopsies. How old the victims were (Dennis was estimated to be between fifteen and twenty years old), when they died (Dennis, Amanda, and Christer were declared dead in the classroom; Sebastian died in the ambulance on the way to the hospital), and how they died (it wasn't enough to say that they were shot; they had to talk about exactly what sort of damage the bullets had done and how they could tell which wounds were fatal and which weren't).

As the expert witnesses spoke, I scrutinized them; I observed their faces intently. I wanted to see if their manners of speaking, scratching their noses, biting their lower lips, brushing hair out of their faces, could give me any clues about the answer to an unsolvable riddle.

It didn't work. It just made me want to throw up.

I had asked Sander to let me leave the courtroom while Amanda's mother was testifying, but he refused. Amanda's mom had requested that I sit in the next room over and watch her testimony over video, but the chief judge refused. And Sander had protested as well, even though I told him I thought it would be less unpleasant that way.

Amanda's mom had to sit in a spot not far from me, sort of diagonally next to me. She was in profile to me. She had lost all her color and half her hair; she'd gone from thin to emaciated. I hardly recognized her. The prosecutor let her talk about Amanda for a long time: who she was, what she liked to do, what she was planning on doing after graduation. The judge didn't tell her to stick to the subject.

Amanda's mom didn't have to talk about when Amanda died, because of course she hadn't been there, but she did mention that she'd thought it was odd that Amanda and I had spent less and less time together during that spring, that Amanda had told her Sebastian and I preferred to be on our own, that she, Amanda's mom, had been worried — worried about me and Sebastian, but never about Amanda.

When it was time for Sander to ask his questions, I thought it was all over. If there was one thing I understood about his tactics, it was that he never asked a question unless he was certain of the answer. I thought it was obvious that he would want Amanda's mom to be done talking as quickly as possible.

But when I heard what he said, I wanted to tug at his arm. Get him to take the question back. *Don't you see how she's looking at me?* I wanted to say. *Don't you see how she hates me? She wishes I were dead instead of her Amanda.* I had never seen someone hate me that much. *Can't you see?*

"Do you think Maja would hurt Amanda on purpose?" Sander asked. His voice was completely flat.

And Amanda's mom cried for a moment before she responded. Then she turned her head and looked right at me.

"No," she said. "Maja would never do that. Maja loved Amanda."

THE WOMEN'S JAIL

36.

I refuse. I stay in my cell all weekend. Not a chance they'll get me to go out for "break" or convince me that I should put on my workout clothes and crank my feet around and around on that broken stationary bike or that I should agree to "talk to someone." I want to throw up at the very thought of letting a clammy weekend sub in her last year of studying psych sit there and check her notes without posing a single question because the checklist doesn't include any questions, just stuff to "be vigilant" about.

Is she sleeping poorly? Does she show signs of being nervous? Of anxiety? Sudden mood swings? Is she frothing at the mouth?

I stay in my bed. *I show signs of mood swings.* They'll have to put me in a straitjacket if they want to get me out of here before it's time to go back to court. I refuse.

Amanda's funeral took place on a Saturday at three o'clock in the afternoon, five weeks after I killed her. The service was held in the Djursholm Chapel.

Amanda and I were confirmed in the Djursholm Chapel during the summer between eighth and ninth grades;

we wore identical white gowns and we wore them over our equally white dresses, hers was Chloë, mine was Stella McCartney. Hers was new; Mom had found my dress at a secondhand shop on Karlaplan. But they looked nearly identical. Bell skirts, just low cut enough, glossy cotton; we each wore a white gold cross necklace on a thin, extra-long chain. We had already received presents from our parents that morning: We each got a watch, the same brand, different models, and we laughed at that, that our parents were so alike, that they did the same dorky things at the same time, without even having to discuss it ahead of time. But mostly we laughed at how alike we were, Amanda and me, we could have been sisters. Dad even said so when we went to pick up Amanda so he could drop us off at the church an hour beforehand.

You two could be sisters.

There were no examination questions, of course. We weren't nervous. A rumor had gone around confirmation camp that we would have to study, that we might get asked a question in church and we would flunk if we didn't give the right answer. But everyone from camp was confirmed in the end. We had prepared little skits from the Bible, and we started each skit by saying who we would play and we squeaked with suppressed laughter when everyone else presented themselves. "Hi, my name is Jacob, I'll be playing a regular person." "Hi, my name is Alice, I'll be playing Jesus."

A few kids had chosen to read a Bible verse. Amanda was asked to give a "spontaneous" talk about "something important she had learned," and she read what she had written about "why lying is bad." The priest had read it beforehand and made a few corrections without admitting that he wanted to be in charge of exactly what she was going to say.

There's a jail priest here, too, with acne scars and shoes with two-inch-thick rubber soles. I have no intention of talking to him either. I plan to stay in my bed all weekend, waiting for breakfast, then lunch, and finally dinner. Sleeping. And then I'll do the same thing for another twenty-four hours. Next week is the last week.

"Then it will be over," Susse says when she comes to "wish me a good weekend."

Sure it will.

It's impossible to wash out blood. I saw that mind-numbingly boring *Macbeth* with Mom at the theater. Blood leaves a stain, no matter how hard you scrub. And if you scrub hard enough you'll make a hole in your skin and then more blood comes out. It will never be over. Amanda's mom will never forgive me. I will never forgive myself.

And what about all of you? What do you think? I know what you've done, what you're still doing: You spend your time trying to get me to fit the image of what you think I am. You refuse to acknowledge that I don't conform to any mold, positive or negative. I'm no student council go-getter, no courageous rape victim, no typical mass murderer, no decently smart, decently pretty fashionista. I never hail taxis in high heels. I don't have any tattoos or a photographic memory. I'm no one's girlfriend, no one's best friend, no one's daughter. I'm just Maja.

You will never forgive me.

I bet you're the type to walk by beggars on the street and think, *That could have been me,* and get a little teary-eyed because you're such empathetic and good people. And you think, *Anyone can get sick* and *It takes so little to end up in a financial crisis and maybe get fired or evicted* and *Oh, that could have been me.* With soiled pants, head hanging, waiting for some change, buying a coffee at McDonald's. You want to show empathy. *Because it's what good people do.* You all want to be good people. But in fact, you're just pretending. No way you actually believe that it could be you. And besides, it is the height of egotism to think that you must feel personally affected in order to experience empathy. Empathy is the exact opposite. It's all about feeling that this gross lowlife who smells like shit and has absolutely nothing in common with me shouldn't have to live like this. Because no matter what he's done, he doesn't deserve to live on a urine-soaked mattress. If you were empathetic for real, you would know that this goes for me, too.

Samir says that I wanted Amanda to die, that I shot her on purpose. From his very first interrogation, he has said he saw it clearly, how I aimed and fired, and he says he thinks I allowed myself to be swayed by Sebastian, that no one in my world was more important than Sebastian, that I did everything he told me to, that I sacrificed my life for him, that I killed Amanda and Sebastian because Sebastian told me I had to.

"Who's this 'you'?" I had asked Samir before it all happened. "You don't get it," he replied.

I think you're all on Samir's side because you like him better than you like me. And you think that makes you better people. Samir's fate has made an impression on you; he's the one you identify with. I'm just a rich bitch.

I take a sleeping pill at eleven in the morning and I'm sleeping when lunch arrives. But they let me be. So far they've left me alone. Sure, they check on me now and then, but not often enough for it to be clear that I'm under heightened monitoring.

They know that listening to Amanda's mom made me "upset." They know they "need" to leave me alone but must still "keep me under watch" because I might be a danger. A danger to myself, since I'm under "great pressure."

But my most recent lunch tray included a full set of plastic utensils. Both a knife and a fork to try to shimmy down my throat, if I had the energy.

One of the guards came by with the evening papers, placed them on my desk, and left again.

He didn't say anything in particular about the papers, which probably means there's nothing about me in them; usually they say so right away.

"Want to read?" they ask, pointing at the headline (always on the front page), and for the most part, I do want to. If I don't, they take the newspaper when they go. But today they don't say anything. I just leave them there. Because even if he didn't say anything, that guard, there's the risk that there might be something about Amanda's mom or Sebastian's mom or some other goddamn mom. And if there's anything I can't deal with right now, it's shit like that.

In conjunction with her questioning of the medical examiners, lead prosecutor Lena Pärsson displayed Amanda's autopsy report on the screen. She read it out loud. She read out loud about where my bullets struck Amanda and what those bullets did to her body. She used a drawing of the classroom to show us where Amanda's body lay and where I was sitting when the police stormed in. She even brought the weapon into the courtroom. It was in a taped-shut plastic bag. The bullets, five of them, were in two separate, tiny plastic bags. One bag for Amanda, one for Sebastian. She had brought those, too. I have counted silently to myself, up to five, one, two, three...It takes an awfully long time...four, five...How could I fire so many shots?

She had not brought Amanda's body. That was cremated and buried.

I was lying in my room on the day Amanda was buried. No one interrogated me; they left me alone that whole weekend as well. I don't think it was because they were showing me any particular consideration; I don't think they knew that I knew that Amanda was being buried and that it would be "difficult" for me. It was probably just pure coincidence. And it was only in the beginning that they interrogated me every day; after that it calmed down. They knew where I was and they knew that I wouldn't go anywhere, so there was no reason for them to work weekends if they could help it.

I thought they were giving me extra-odd looks, the guards who came and went. Maybe they knew it was Amanda's day, maybe it was in all the papers, maybe it was front-page news item, maybe it was the lead story on both major news shows. But I wasn't allowed to read the papers back then, and they didn't say anything to me, they just stared.

But I knew which day it was. Sander had told me, and I hadn't forgotten.

I spent the entire day of Amanda's funeral sitting on the floor in my cell. After lunch I rang for a guard four times, to find out what time it was, and when they said it was two thirty, I started counting silently to myself. Thirty times: one Mississippi, two Mississippi all the way to sixty...And when I was almost certain that it was three o'clock, I put on the music I had prepared. Mom had sent my old iPod. It took almost two weeks for me to actually receive it, because the police had to make sure it couldn't access the Internet and they had to listen through all the songs to make sure — well, I don't really know what they had to make sure of, but I assume they were checking for hidden messages inserted between Mom's boring-ass hoarse-lady-singer-with-a-gap-between-her-teeth music and Dad's middle-aged I-listen-to-this-because-I-wish-I-had-an-electric-guitar-and-a-mild-drug-problem music. Or that there was nothing on there to finally make me up and decide to kill myself. When they were finished inspecting it, they gave it to me, and I listened to it in my cell during Amanda's funeral at the chapel where we were confirmed, dressed as sisters.

Besides the music I had loaded, Mom had managed to download my three most-listened-to Spotify lists. From those, the police had removed three innocent songs but left two that proved that if someone actually *had* listened through all the songs to make sure I wouldn't hear anything that made me suicidal, he or she was pretty dim. But I didn't complain. The only songs I could tolerate in the first place were the ones that really hurt.

When I thought it was three o'clock, I lay down on the floor of my cell; there wasn't much room, so I had to lie crosswise with my feet under the bed. And then I pictured what the chapel looked like. How it was full of people. How the whole school, all, all, all of them, were there. They were dressed in white, just like Amanda and I had been at our confirmation, and they had brought flowers. Amanda's two siblings and her parents greeted people at the entrance. They had cried until no tears were left. Now they just looked tired and confused. Especially Eleonora, Amanda's little sister. Amanda's brother was angry. There wasn't enough room for everyone in the chapel, so those who hadn't been specially invited had to remain outside; they stood along the drive with their flowers. Those who didn't know Amanda well enough to be inside the church, they still had tears left. They cried and hugged as the TV crews filmed and the church doors closed and those who cried the most and hugged the longest hoped to end up in the picture so they could see on the news how sad they had been.

Mom and Dad and Lina couldn't have been at Amanda's funeral. They could hardly have sent flowers or a card. They would have been thrown out, burned — such gestures would have been seen as taunting.

But I could still feel, with my whole body, how Lina tugged at Mom's hand and asked, *Mom, can I go? I want to give Amanda a flower,* and Mom replied, *No, honey, you can't go.* Even if it was just in my imagination, I could feel it in my body. I could hear the words Mom would never say out loud to Lina: *They don't want you there.*

It's strange how my body remembers. I can remember what it felt like to hug Dad when I was little and my nose pressed against the hard bone of his hip, how I wrapped my arms around his legs. I can remember what it felt like when he bent down and picked me up so he could hold me. I can remember the feeling of his hands reaching around my waist. But I can't remember exactly when he did it. I can't remember the first time or the last time, not a single specific time. I can't remember it clearly enough for it to stop hurting.

Does Lina know that Amanda is dead? Has she begged, *Please, please, can I go say goodbye to Amanda?* My body aches when I think about it. Can my body remember things that have never happened, or does it mean she really did ask?

At Amanda's and my confirmation, I read a Bible verse. I had chosen it myself. Amanda and I had spent an entire night lying on the uncomfortable camp mattresses trying to find a good one. Luke, John, Psalms, or Ecclesiastes — those were the priest's suggestions. There was a bit in Psalms about God striking "all my enemies on the cheek," knocking out their teeth, something along those lines. We laughed at that, Amanda and me. We laughed hysterically at most of the verses; there was something about the language and the priest's expression and Amanda's gestures. It was impossible to take it seriously. And it only got worse when the priest wanted to discuss the way Jesus washed the feet of the disciples ("He's demonstrating his love; this is about you!"). I couldn't even look at Amanda's expression of disgust without collapsing into spasms of giggles.

I have a Bible in my cell. During my second or third week, someone (probably Susse) asked if I wanted to see the jail chaplain. I said yes. It was always easier to say yes than no. Let time pass, be guided through corridors, walk through doors the guard pointed at, sit down on offered chairs, drink from glasses within reach.

That chaplain at the jail gave me a Bible. I brought it back to my cell with me. And as I lie on the floor and think about Amanda's funeral, I take it down from the shelf and page through it. Amanda and I had found a bit about someone "conceiving evil." He was "pregnant with mischief." It swelled and grew until he birthed all this devilry. We had laughed at that, too. Then we read a bunch of hallelujah and sing praise and glorify the Lord, and Amanda stood up on her bed with her Bible in one hand and the other over her heart and I almost peed myself laughing, and the Bible is a bunch of crap, I thought that back then and I know it now, because the guy with evil inside *fell into his own hole*, he but no one else suffered because of the wickedness inside him. Our confirmation priest thought God was just and good, and he read verses where the bad guy died and went to hell, and I wonder what the hell the priest said about "the fair and just God who loves the little children" at Amanda's funeral.

Evil doesn't strike justly. In reality, no one falls into his own fucking hole.

And on Monday, in less than two days, it will be Samir's turn to talk.

I never managed to picture Amanda for very long. I hadn't been able to bring myself to think about our confirmation since I lay on my floor, trying to imagine her funeral. I hadn't been able to think about Amanda's funeral either, not since that day.

The weather outside my window was lovely. Maybe I should ask to go out for exercise time after all. I could lie down full length on the slice of cement and smoke. It had snowed the weekend before. When I went out for exercise time, the snow lay there taunting me, hopeful and white. By the next day it had turned into cement-gray slush, slippery as snot, and the wind stung — shards of glass right in the face. But at that moment it had been easier to breathe outside. A little easier than in my cell, at least.

I still have the playlist I had made for Amanda's funeral. The songs we danced to. The songs we sang together, so loudly that we lost our voices. The songs we knew all the words to. If someone played them, we raced to the dance floor, just me and her, and went nuts. *Party girls don't get hurt, can't feel anything, when will I learn, I push it down, push it down.* Songs that would never ever be played in any church.

At our confirmation, I read out loud about when Jesus ran off to church to "be with his father" and his mom and dad were worried because they didn't know where he was.

When I had finished reading, I had to say something (in "my own" words, which the priest had "helped me" with) about how it was important to spend time alone on occasion when you're a teenager. And that the church can be a place for that.

If they asked me to choose now, I would have read the part about emptiness. That's the only part that's true. *Everything is empty and futile.* Chasing after the wind. We never get what we want. The priest said I should read something that made me feel like it was talking about me and my life. I should have read that. And skipped the part about how you should rejoice in your youth. Because that's bullshit.

I ring the bell after all. I will demand to go out for exercise time. I will bring my iPod and I will listen to our songs and smoke until I feel sick.

The very last night before it happened, when Sebastian's dad sent everyone home, everyone but me, in those few short hours before the murders, Amanda kissed her fingertips and waved her hand in my direction as she walked through the door and out to the stairs.

I pretended to catch her kiss in my palm and press it to my chest. Dramatic, dorky, silly, theatrical, just like Amanda.

That was the next-to-last time we looked each other in the eye, and everything around us was chaos. Sebastian was crazy, Claes and Samir and Dennis and everyone else were crazy, and Amanda sent a kiss sailing through the air to me to say, *It'll be okay, Maja, it'll all work out,* and I played along because I didn't want to reveal that both of us knew she was wrong, that she was so hellishly wrong, and nothing would ever be okay again.

Amanda tried to console me. I lied to her. To be nice, I think. Amanda was always nice to me. She was nice to everyone, even Sebastian, long after everyone else had stopped bothering.

Always.

But wait, you're thinking right now. *Hold on a second.*

You've gone on about how much you disliked Amanda. You despised Dennis; you have confessed to hating Claes Fagerman.

Plus, you are whispering to each other, *you aren't just anyone. There is a reason that you are sitting in that cell.* Because you don't want to think, *It could have been me.* You want something to be wrong inside my head. You want to be sure that you have nothing in common with me. You're not going around thinking my thoughts, you would never do what I did, say what I said, dear God, it's so important for you to think that what happened to me would never ever happen to you, because I deserve it, I fell into my own hole. I was obsessed with Sebastian, I was incapable of empathy, spoiled, out of touch with reality, and maybe I was even an addict, can't we pretend that's the case?

You're not obsessed, you don't use drugs, you would have called the police, you are not me.

Why did Sebastian choose me? There has to be a reason! Why did he come to me at the hotel that night? Why did he track me down in Nice? Why did he stay? Why did he try to kill himself when I broke up with him?

Someone once said coincidence is God's way of remaining anonymous. Anything meaningful is the result of chance. That's true whether you're born rich or poor, as a woman or a trans person, whether you make it as an artist or win twenty-five million in the lottery. Just a coincidence. You've got to play to win. And if that's true, if good can only come to us through peculiar back doors, then that must be true of evil as well.

Coincidence is the proof that God doesn't exist, is what I would say. Because truly evil events can arise due to planning or heredity. But they can also be due to coincidence. They can verge on the ordinary.

Evil has no meaning. That is the very definition of evil. But just because something hurts doesn't mean that the reason for the pain is evil.

I have done things that have caused many people pain, the very deepest sort, in the worst of ways. I don't understand what the meaning was of Claes's and Christer's and Dennis's and Amanda's and Sebastian's deaths. Or the meaning of my survival. Or that I tried to save Sebastian but instead helped him to kill and die. I don't understand it. There is nothing to understand. But I'm not evil. I might not be good either, but you refuse to acknowledge that because you are incapable of empathy.

When the guard comes, I pick up the evening papers from my desk and ask him to take them away. I don't want to read them. I want him to take away all the articles about better mental health care for teenagers, gun control in school, surveillance cameras, and drug checks. I say that I want to have exercise time. "I'll check the schedule," he says as he leaves. He's annoyed, but he can't say no, he's not allowed to, or Ferdinand will get Amnesty after him.

And then I crawl onto my cell bed, gather the gross yellow blanket, curl up against the wall, and cry. For the thousandth time I cry. *I couldn't live without you now, Oh, I know I'd go insane, I wouldn't last one night alone, baby, I couldn't stand the pain!*

I know I fired the shot that killed Amanda, but I just wanted to live, I wanted to stop Sebastian, I wanted to make him stop what he was doing, that's why I shot him. I killed Sebastian, it's true that I killed him, and I meant to do it, but what else could I do? I just wish I had killed him with the first shot, I wish I hadn't shot Amanda. I wish that more than anything I've ever wished in my life, but I had never used a rifle like that before. I've shot clay pigeons a few times, but those guns have a sluggish trigger and they're heavy. This was so easy, I hardly had to do anything. I just picked up the gun and when my finger touched that thing, I thought I had to take off the safety, or I don't know what I was thinking, I just pressed it, I pressed it five times, because that's what it says in the case report, and I didn't kill Sebastian the first time or the second time, but then I killed him and before that I killed Amanda, and what does it matter what kind of person I am and what kind of impression I make and what happened and why and why not? What I did matters, that's the only part that means anything. And I killed Amanda.

Amanda will never dance again. She'll never sing. Or listen to music she doesn't really like but knows that you are "supposed to" like.

I loved that Amanda blew kisses through the air and made me catch them. She was superficial and silly and out of touch with reality and selfish, and I loved her. Of course I did. She was my very best friend. I never could have hurt her. *Never, never, never.* But I did it anyway.

SEBASTIAN

37.

I don't know what to say about the last few weeks. The days passed. Sebastian got worse. And worse. I went to school more often, because he no longer demanded my company all the time. But I just sat there in class, at the back of the room, and when school was over I went back to Sebastian's house even if he hadn't asked me to come. Occasionally he gave me a ride to school. Once or twice he even came to class. Sometimes he sat outside waiting for me to be done. Now and then a teacher came by and asked how he was doing. He would say "okay" and the teacher would tell him he "had to start coming to school." He nodded, and then they said goodbye. Christer tried to get him to "shape up."

Then Christer got this idea that a few of us from our class should perform together at the last-day-of-school assembly. It happened at the last minute, we had no idea if we could scrape together a decent number, but according to Christer this would help to solve the "identified conflicts" that existed "in our group." He organized performances like this every year. They were always "appreciated." Amanda loved the idea, Dennis probably got it into his head that it might be good for his residency application, Samir would do anything a teacher asked him to, but Sebastian thought it was a bad joke. Christer was insistent. "At least come to our first meeting and we'll talk about what we could do. I'm open to suggestions." In the end, there was only one meeting.

A couple of the other teachers called Claes to talk about Sebastian's "problem." At least they said they had later, when the police asked. According to the case report, the headmaster even sought him out "at a few junctures." He couldn't get hold of him, he was "hard to reach," but he left messages and a letter was sent to Sebastian's home. Because Sebastian wasn't going to pass his third-year classes this time either, and the school was obliged to inform his parents even though Sebastian was of legal age.

It says in the case report that the headmaster's letter was found in Claes's office when the house was searched. It was unopened.

What about Sebastian's mom?

Sander found her. The evening papers found her, too; there are paparazzi photos of her outside the building where she lives, and there is an interrogation with her in the case report. I know Sander considered issuing a subpoena, having her speak in court, because I know he had this idea that she might be able to shed light on what happened between Sebastian and Claes, that she could explain that their relationship was doomed from the start (not Sander's words), that he might be able to get her to talk about "what was wrong with Claes," explain why he was such a monster of a father (also not Sander's words), why he did what he did, and what it did to Sebastian. Ferdinand thought it was a terrible idea; the fact is that if Ferdinand hates anyone more than she hates me, I think it would be Sebastian's mom. She said that it was just "too much." And I think she meant that whatever explanations there could possibly be, there was no getting around this: Sebastian's mom was an egotistical idiot and Sebastian's dad was emotionally disturbed. It couldn't be a good idea to have Sebastian's mom testify "for me," because no matter what she said, no one wanted to be linked with that shrew. It would be like having Hitler's mom as a character witness.

I think Sander figured at first that Sebastian's mom could attest to his theory that Sebastian didn't need me to convince him to kill his dad. But then he dropped it; I guess he realized that it might stick to me, the distaste a person would automatically feel when that bitch tried to explain why she had chosen to desert her children. So Sebastian's mom was allowed to vanish once more, far, far away.

But I've read her deposition. She mostly talked about herself. About how she hadn't been able to live with Claes (I'm with her up to that point), that at first she thought she could "heal him" (that sounds like a phrase she learned from a therapist), get him to love her even though he wasn't "very good at emotions" (more therapist words, presumably), but she was later "forced" to leave him, at which point he "refused" to let her have the children to "get revenge." "What could I do?" she asked, a rhetorical question she had to answer herself in order to get the response she wanted. "There was nothing I could do. Claes refused, and I had no way to fight him."

Lukas has refused to cooperate with either the investigators or Sander. He won't speak to anyone. He has taken over the Fagerman Group and settled with all the victims and survivors. But he won't talk. Not a word.

After Sander presented the story of Evil Claes Fagerman, the evening papers wrote about his upbringing at boarding schools, au pairs instead of parents, employees rather than family members. Psychologists who never met Claes or Sebastian or Lukas have expressed their opinions that Claes was probably never able to bond with his children because he was never allowed to bond with his own parents. The same psychologists have also said that Sebastian likely inherited this same behavior from his father; one even spouted the good old neglected-children-suffer-even-if-they-have-their-own-room-in-a-luxury-home-in-Djursholm rationale, but Sander would never resort to such cliché, he's smarter than that. *We have to concentrate on what you have done and what you can be held accountable for. Sebastian's problems are not judicially relevant except to the extent that they emphasize your innocence.*

But to the press, his problems are relevant. Very much so.

I've been curious about Sebastian's mom and why she left her kids. Whether she was sick or a drug addict, whether there was some other reason. Maybe that's why she hasn't given any Exclusive Interview About the Truth

Behind It All to the Most Important Reporter in the World. Because she hasn't. Not a single interview. Maybe she has stuff to hide, stuff she's ashamed of, stuff Claes knew and held over her head. Or maybe she's lying. Maybe she didn't want her kids, maybe she forced Claes to take them, I don't know. Or maybe she was actually terrified of him, as oppressed and hated as Sebastian. No one knows. *It's not judicially relevant.*

But it's still important to me. Part of me wants to believe that she loved her kids, that it was something she couldn't help. I want it all to be Claes's fault, so that he really did deserve to die. I want to believe that Lukas is a victim, too, that he's as scared of Claes as everyone else is. But all I know for sure is that neither Sebastian's mom nor Lukas was there, not when Sebastian needed them, not those last few weeks. I was the only one. And it was too much for me to handle.

Sometimes I tried to do something other than be with Sebastian. I wanted to get away from him on occasion. Because the calm, numb Sebastian who came home from the hospital had long since been exchanged for a different person. Sometimes he was wild with rage, sometimes he was detached. One day he might scream at me that I was an idiot if I came to his house without calling first, and the next day he might turn off his phone and later chew me out for blowing him off, not paying attention to how he was doing, what he was doing, ignoring him, ignoring everything. So once in a while I thought I should go downtown with Amanda, read a story to Lina, eat dinner with my family. But I had forgotten how. They were my everyday people, and spending time with them should have been a no-brainer, as automatic as breathing or falling asleep when you're tired, but they felt like strangers. So I avoided them. I stopped picking up if Amanda called, I went to bed if I was at home while someone else was there, I sat by myself at school when I bothered to go.

Mom and Dad went out of town with Lina over Easter. I said I was going to Antibes with Claes and Sebastian, but Sebastian and I stayed home. We didn't venture outside; we mostly stayed in the pool house, having food delivered; we smoked and listened to music chosen by Sebastian. Dennis came by sometimes. He didn't usually stay very long. When I saw Mom and Dad after they came back, they wondered how our vacation had been.

"Fine," I said.

"How are you doing?" Mom wondered.

"So-so," I said as I headed for my room. "I think I'm getting sick."

They didn't ask any more questions; they didn't think it was weird at all that I was paler than when I left.

What was going on?

The truth is that during those last few weeks, there wasn't really a turning point, no one said anything that made a crucial difference. The days went by and life wasn't great. It was fucking awful, but one day after another began and ended and sometimes Sebastian wasn't high, wasn't acting crazy, and sometimes he didn't get mad and sometimes I thought it felt a little better, but apparently, as I realize in hindsight, I only thought things were better because they weren't noticeably worse.

Many, many of those days were horrible. Especially on the weekends. Weekends when the only people I saw for forty-eight hours were Dennis and Sebastian. But worst of all was when Claes was home.

I tried to get Sebastian to understand this, but he didn't want to, didn't do anything about it. The worse he was, the nastier his dad became. Claes Fagerman belched up one insult after the next in a remarkably blasé manner, which just made them that much worse. He didn't care, Sebastian fell apart, he cared even less. Sometimes I thought he wanted Sebastian to kill himself, because that would have solved the problem, the problem he brought up as often as he could: *What the hell am I supposed to do with you?*

After the dinner with the TV chef when I tried to tell Claes off, I, too, ended up on the list in his Book of Idiots. Presumably because I could neither get Sebastian to stop doing what he was doing nor get him to start doing what he refused to do. Claes stopped greeting me when we ran into each other, he talked about me in the third person, he never looked me in the eye. He despised me because I was with his son.

Yes, I think it was Claes Fagerman's fault. If he'd been a different person, if he hadn't done what he did and said what he said, then what happened never would have happened. I have told Sander so: I wanted him to die. I meant it, I meant each and every word I said and said again and wrote in my texts. I thought Claes Fagerman deserved to die because he was Sebastian's dad and he should have loved him.

Sander says that still doesn't make me guilty of the murder. He says the prosecutor must be able to demonstrate that I "persuaded" Sebastian to kill him. That she must show that there was a "causal relationship" between my words and actions and what Sebastian did, that they are linked, that one wouldn't have happened without the other. It's not even enough that I *wanted* Sebastian to kill him, if Sebastian would have killed him anyway, no matter what I thought.

To Sander, it's obvious that Sebastian decided to kill his dad *because of* the way Claes treated him.

The last party, that fits into Sander's template. That party makes what happened easier to understand. Sander is of the opinion that Claes's actions — he kicked Sebastian to the curb, ordered him to move out, disappear, go away — they were the last straw for Sebastian. He had nowhere to go, he was failing in school, all the factors that made up his identity had been taken away. And I let him say this in court. But the reality, which Sander can only guess at, cannot be explained so pedagogically.

"Tell us about the first time Sebastian hit you," Sander requested when I gave my statement. He wanted everyone to hear about it because it sounds so horrible and Sander wants the court to feel sorry for me. I told the story, but I didn't mention that it was no big deal, or at least not a big enough deal. I let them think it was horrible.

We were at Sebastian's house; it was right after Easter. Claes and Sebastian had been sitting in the kitchen, "planning" Sebastian's "graduation party" ("I'm not sure I'll be in Sweden that weekend; you'll have to ask Majlis to work out the practical details") when I arrived. I hadn't said a word while Claes was around, but once he left I couldn't keep it in any longer.

We fought, not because it was clear that Sebastian wouldn't be graduating — we didn't fight about that sort of thing — but because I was mad that he allowed Claes to keep pretending nothing was wrong as long as he didn't have to give a speech in Sebastian's honor at the dinner. Claes didn't care what the graduation party cost, he would pay anything. But there was no way he would attend it.

"I don't understand why you let him treat you like shit. He hates you, Sebastian, he always has. You don't deserve to be treated like that."

I said this even though I knew Sebastian was upset. I could see how much pain it caused him, what Claes had said, that he would never manage to make his dad proud or even pleased, that his dad hated him. But I said it anyway. Would it help? No. Sebastian was always being punished and never, ever taken care of. Maybe I said it because I wanted to make him even more upset. I was being terribly cruel and I knew it, but I did it anyway.

I was inciting him. I was inciting him against his own dad.

And then Sebastian struck me right in the face. He didn't say anything, it didn't hurt all that much, but I ran off and closed myself in the bathroom but the door didn't lock. There was no way to lock any bathroom in the Fagermans' house, not since Sebastian had returned from the psych ward.

I sat there for a while before he came in. As I heard him approach the door, I pulled as hard as I could on the handle. The door opened outward, but Sebastian didn't tug at it, he didn't try to prize it open from the outside, even though it would have worked because he was stronger than me. It took a while for me to figure out what he was doing instead, it was maybe a few minutes before the heat made its way from his side of the metal handle to my side. Sebastian was heating it up. With the help of a butane torch from the kitchen he was making the handle white-hot. He didn't say anything in the meantime, he didn't even touch the door, and when I was forced to let go the door just opened.

He walked up to me and pushed up my dress — it got caught around my neck — and then he unclasped my bra and looked at me in the mirror.

"Can't we close the door?" I whispered. I could hear Claes downstairs. The cleaning lady was there, too, and someone was riding a lawn mower, and I'm sure the security guards were in their usual spots on the driveway. Sebastian didn't respond. He didn't even look angry. His face was swollen and he had black rings under his eyes and he looked tired, but not furious. He unbuttoned his pants, unzipped his fly, pulled down his pants, and struck me with the back of his hand, an apathetic smack, right on my temple, his watch caught my cheekbone, almost up by my ear. I lay down on the floor, the tile was cold, I let him pull off my underwear, my dress was still bunched around my neck. He sucked on one of my nipples and grabbed my other breast in his hand. He squeezed it, then pulled on it. And I didn't want to be raped, I wasn't raped, because I took his hand and moved it toward my vagina, he pressed two fingers into me, I felt him against my thigh, and I raised my foot, I didn't want him to force me, and I braced my feet against the edge of the bathtub and then he entered me. It didn't take long for him to finish. Then he left.

When Sander asked me to talk about when Sebastian hit me, I complied. But I didn't mention that what filled me when it happened was a sense of relief. That my blood bubbled, my head thundered, that I actually believed I was in control. That he would no longer be able to do anything to me once he hit me. If he finally beat me up, everyone would see it, everyone would realize what kind of person he was, and that would set me free from something, possibly even from him. I would have a reason to leave and never return. No one would ask me to take care of him, to comfort him, to follow him. Even I would realize that I had to let go. You're supposed to leave the first time someone hits you; you never stay with someone who is physically violent, no matter how many times he begs for forgiveness. Everyone knows that.

But Sebastian never apologized. My cheek swelled up a bit, but it was hardly visible; if I didn't touch it, it didn't even hurt. No one noticed what had happened. And where was I supposed to go?

38.

The last night arrived; it was the last week in May. There was no graduation party; it never came up again after what happened in the bathroom. He hadn't gone to Labbe's party, even though he was invited (neither did I), and I didn't think he would go to Amanda's.

On a regular old Thursday, with school the next day, Sebastian said he was going to throw a party. The air had a special scent that afternoon; the sky was bluer than usual and that made me happy. I suddenly remembered what summer could be like, and for a brief moment I thought about nights out and grilling, skinny-dipping and bare feet.

"Are a lot of people coming?" I wondered.

"Not too many," said Sebastian.

It was warm, more than twenty-five degrees Celsius. I thought we might hang out by the pool, or maybe by the water if the temperature held, drinking but not getting drunk, talking, listening to music. It almost felt like the previous summer. *Almost?* When "there's nothing better to do" was all it took for Sebastian. When "let's have a party" was something fun.

Sander told me that he believes Sebastian had already made up his mind, that this was literally his "last night." That maybe what his dad did made him switch from just suicide to what actually happened, but that Sebastian had already planned at least his own death. The investigators have not found any evidence to indicate what Sebastian had planned, if anything. And Sander can only speculate. No one knows. But I think Sander's right.

Dennis was first to arrive. He brought two friends. Sebastian hadn't told me that Dennis was coming, but I wasn't surprised, maybe not even disappointed. But I couldn't quite figure out why Dennis had been allowed to bring his buddies. We had never hung out with his friends before. At first they kept to themselves on the terrace and by the pool. They didn't seem timid; they mostly just laughed. Like they couldn't believe their eyes, but not in a good way.

Then came the chicks I'd never seen before. They hadn't been invited. They'd been hired; it was obvious. They cost money, but not a lot (that was obvious, too), and they awaited further instructions with drinks in hand.

I thought Dennis had brought them. But Sebastian was the one who greeted them, although Dennis got to go first.

"You go first," Sebastian said.

Dennis was wearing shorts, and he bent down to tug at the cuff of the tube sock on his left foot. The elastic was loose. He tried to pull it into place anyway, and he took off his cap and placed it upside down on the dining room table. I wasn't standing that close, but I could still see the dark ring left by sweat and flakes of skin. Dennis and his friends went into Claes's bedroom. *But not Sebastian*, I thought, *never Sebastian*. He didn't do stuff like that.

You guys go first. And I sank. Right down into the quicksand, and I looked at one of the girls, the one closest to me had a snag in her black nylons, it was too warm for tights and it was about to turn into a run. She put down her drink, her thumbnail was bitten down to the quick, and I wanted her to look at me but she wouldn't. If only she would look at me, if I could just see her eyes, she would become real, an actual person, someone who counted, and I could get mad, sad, crazy with jealousy, *rush out of there*, but she avoided my gaze and she went into the room along with the other two, and I sank deeper and deeper. I could smell her cheap perfume and sweat, but I didn't do anything. I didn't scream. Didn't cry. I couldn't do anything, because I would drown.

Sebastian went in after Dennis and his friends came out, which I think was around twenty minutes later. I didn't ask why. I didn't say, *Don't do it*. I didn't cry. Labbe and Amanda had just arrived. Before Sebastian closed the door, he turned around and looked at me. His eyes were black, already dead.

"Are you coming?"

He didn't wait for an answer. He closed the door behind him.

And I didn't hit anyone, didn't spray spittle every which way. I didn't walk into the bedroom after them and yank my life back; I couldn't move. Sebastian didn't want me anymore. He had made up his mind.

He wanted to die in peace. This was how he left you, Maja.

And Dennis laughed at me when he saw my face, he laughed out loud, his mouth open and his head tipped back. From his ugly shorts he took a small plastic bag. He removed what was inside; it was no larger than a stamp. It took so little, all I had to do was let go. I could forget all of this. Sebastian didn't want me. *Are you coming?* he asked. *Get out of here,* he meant. *There's nothing more you can do, Maja.* I couldn't move. If I let go now, my chin would sink into the quicksand, I could let the darkness come. A black sinkhole.

"Open wide," said Dennis. I looked at him. *He gets it,* I thought. *He knows what to do to keep yourself from drowning.*

Later, the house was full of people. Music roared in the pool house, I sat on the edge of the pool with my feet in the water. There were flashes from the disco lights someone had set up, lights flying around the room, up and down the walls, into my head, where they exploded. I lay down on the edge of the pool, my dress wet on one side, and I watched it sparkle; someone had tossed a champagne bottle into the water, and it bobbed out of time with the music. Glitter on the surface, tiny sparks in my head, giant, tall, turquoise flames. I would need to take something else soon because what Dennis had given me was about to wear off.

I don't know how long I stayed there. The music blurred together, I felt it in my chest, it was trying to blast its way out. It didn't matter what Sebastian was doing, I didn't care, but I could see her, blurry at first.

"Amanda," I called, or at least I tried. She didn't hear me. I whispered to myself. "Amanda." She could help me, drag me up out of here. Help me take something else, help me get Sebastian, help me go home.

She was holding Labbe's hand. They looked around, searching for someone. Only when Labbe grabbed his shoulder, causing him to turn around, did I see.

Samir. With his phone in hand. And then I realized what he was filming.

Sebastian had his back to Samir. He was cutting lines on the floor, and two of the three naked hookers got down on their knees to snort them up. Sebastian grabbed one of the girls by the hips, pulled her ass up, and thrust his crotch against her. Dennis laughed.

Samir was still filming.

I don't know how I got up, but Labbe grabbed me before I got hold of the phone. I don't think I screamed, but Amanda was holding on to me too and they dragged me off, into another room, the music was so loud, and the last thing I saw was that it was Sebastian's turn to snort two lines. He picked up the leftovers with his tongue, then turned toward the other girl and let her lick it up.

I think I was crying. Samir must have followed us. He was still holding the phone and looking at me.

"We have to put a stop to this." Did Amanda say that? Maybe. Or else it was Samir.

"We have to turn him in."

It was definitely Samir. Fucking Samir. He wanted to do something, *the right thing.* Oh my God. He wasn't supposed to be there. If Sebastian hadn't been *busy,* Samir never would have gotten in. He couldn't do this, it wouldn't solve Sebastian's problems. And then I suddenly became frightened. Absolutely terrified. And for the first time, it was for my own sake.

If the police showed up, the shit would hit the fan.

"You can't do this." Now I was screaming. "You can't call the police, you can't rat him out. I won't let you. If you call the police..." I started over. My heart was racing, beating too fast. "If you call the police, Sebastian won't be the only one who's screwed."

"We have to do something. He can't go on like this."

I took out my phone. It happened so fast. It was totally automatic. Like I wanted it to happen. As if I had planned it. I pulled up his phone number and handed the phone to Samir.

"Call him. Call him instead!"

Did I think he would dare to do it? I was prepared to force him to. Anyone but the police. Samir dialed the number on his phone.

"What are you doing?" I asked. Maybe that's when it really hit me — what I had done, what it would mean. Samir looked proud, disdainful. His eyes were brimming with *You never thought I would*, and I wanted to smack him. "What the hell are you doing?"

The music roared. It was so loud we had to shout to hear each other. And yet I heard the swish, the sound of the text message going from Samir's phone to Claes's private cell. Samir hadn't written anything; he'd just attached the file, the video he had just taken.

You fucking idiot, I think now. *Call the police. Call the police,* I want to scream from my jail cell on the other side. *Ask him to call the police. Demand that he call the police. If only you had called the police instead.*

It took only ten minutes for all hell to break loose.

Trial hearing in case B 147/66

The prosecutor et al. v. Maria Norberg

Week 3 of Trial: Monday

39.

When Samir enters the courtroom, he looks like his regular old self. Almost, anyway — maybe thinner, a little older somehow. He doesn't look at me as he takes his seat. But I look at him. I look and look and look, and for the first time since the trial began I feel something that does not resemble panic. His hair is longer than it used to be and he runs his hand across his beige jeans, as if it's sweaty. He clears his throat too much so no one will notice that he's very nervous.

Samir is alive. He really is, they weren't just saying that. He survived, because he's sitting here, so close I could stand up and touch him. It doesn't matter, I think, that he's here to say I killed Amanda on purpose. The important thing is that he's alive.

The prosecutor begins. She allows Samir to speak uninterrupted.

"Tell us in your own words..."

Samir talks about why he attended Djursholm Upper Secondary, how he knew Sebastian, Amanda, and Labbe, how he knew me, exactly how well he knew me, how he, Amanda, and Labbe were worried about Sebastian and me, how they had decided to "do something"; he talks about what happened at the party.

The security guards arrived first. When Claes Fagerman got there, he had even more with him. Samir said that one of the security guards who arrived with Claes took his phone. He was given a new one, a nicer one, its packaging unopened, in exchange.

Samir's old phone (and Claes's) are part of the evidence. We have already watched the movie (and a second one that Samir had taken just prior but had never sent to Claes) and now the prosecutor plays them again. You can tell how high I was, you can hear how frantic I get when I realize Samir is filming. I scream, "What the fuck are you doing? Are you crazy?" The clip ends with my sweaty face in the frame; the prosecutor lets me stare out at the audience for a long moment before she clicks me away.

Samir talks about the chaos. How Claes lost control and went from being his usual distant, icy self to dragging Sebastian out of the bedroom, where he had retreated with the hookers. Sebastian was naked. Claes punched him in the face in front of everyone, and when he fell to the floor Claes kicked him in the stomach.

"Three times, I think," Samir says. "Maybe only two. I'm not sure."

One of the security guards pulled Claes off Sebastian and another came out of Claes's bedroom with Dennis and the hookers. Dennis was totally out of it, his pants in his hand and his swollen-earthworm dick tucked between his fat, almost dark blue thighs.

Samir says that he was driven home by one of Claes's guards. He had asked to be dropped off before they arrived at his building so his mom and dad wouldn't see the car. But the guard insisted. Samir's parents hadn't noticed anything.

It takes Samir nearly fifty minutes to give his account of what happened in the classroom the next day. The prosecutor asks all her questions in a slightly quieter voice than usual. Each time Samir starts to cry (three times), the judge asks in the same low voice whether he needs a break. He just shakes his head, he fights to keep his voice under control, he wants to get out of here, he wants to get this over with, he rattles off everything he said in his deposition almost verbatim, the exact same words. He is "certain" he "knows what he saw," what I did.

By the time it's Sander's turn, Samir's forehead is shiny. He has pink dots on each cheek, just above the spot where he usually has dimples. He seems annoyed even before Sander has asked his first question.

Sander's voice is kind, too, but he speaks at his usual volume.

"When you were first questioned, you said it took several hours for the police to arrive."

"Um."

"Do you recall that?"

"It felt like several hours."

"In reality, it wasn't even half an hour, was it? I have the report here, and it says that the classroom was opened fifteen to seventeen minutes after the last shot was fired. That is nineteen minutes after the first shots were fired."

"Does it matter?"

"You also said that the first person to be shot was Christer."

"Yes, but..."

Sander lowers his voice. "You retracted that statement as well the next time you were questioned."

"I was still pretty out of it. I had just undergone an operation. They questioned me while I was still in the hospital... I was..."

"I understand that, Samir. I understand it wasn't easy for you. But there were a lot of things you said the first few times you were questioned that you took back later on."

"That's not true at all."

"How many days went by before you were questioned?"

"Four."

"Was your family with you during those four days?"

"Yes."

"You talked about what happened, didn't you?"

"I didn't talk very much."

"Because you were in bad shape, I know. You were given a lot of pain medication, it says in your record. I know you weren't feeling well. But your mom and dad... did they talk to you about it?"

"Of course we talked about it. I don't understand why that would be a problem."

"You need to answer the question, Samir."

"Mom mostly cried, she just kept crying."

"What language do you speak with your parents?"

He hesitates. "Arabic."

Pancake hands Sander a few documents. He takes them, flips to the last page, and goes on.

"We've spoken with the hospital staff. One of the nurses said that you asked what had happened to Maja." Sander turns to the chief judge while Ferdinand hands out copies of the nurse's transcript. "She speaks Arabic, too."

"Mmhmm."

"And she told us how your dad responded."

"What's wrong with that? Why shouldn't my dad answer me if I ask him a simple question?"

"Do you remember what he said?"

"That she was in jail, I think."

"She said your dad told you that the police had taken Maja into custody and that Maja deserved to rot in jail for what she did."

"Is it so strange that my dad thinks Maja should be punished for what she did? That he was angry?"

"Your dad said that the police had found a bag in Maja's locker. Your dad also told you what was in that bag, didn't he?"

"Why wouldn't he? The police did, too, they found the bag in Maja's locker, was my dad supposed to lie to me?"

"Your dad told you that Maja and Sebastian acted jointly, that she and Sebastian had carried out the shooting together."

"They did do it together."

"Your dad told you this two days before the police conducted their first interview with you, correct?"

"I don't know. Maybe he did. But he was just telling me the facts, it's not like he made it up, it was — "

"I don't think your dad made it up. I think he read it in the newspapers and I think he believed it. Maja was in jail, and your dad is not the only one who thinks that a teenager would hardly be locked up if she weren't guilty. I think you've fallen into the same trap, too, and that all your memories from inside the classroom, everything you didn't understand while it was happening, have been colored by what you heard later on."

"So you think I'm making it up? Bullshit. Maja was put in jail because she shot her — "

Sander looks sad as he interrupts Samir.

"Your dad, indeed, your whole family, everyone who visited you at the hospital, had been told that information about the case was subject to a nondisclosure order. Do you know what that means?"

"Yes."

"It means they were not allowed to discuss anything relating to the case with you."

"Dad didn't discuss anything with me."

"And the reason your dad was not allowed to talk about the case...about Maja, or what he had read in the papers or what he thought he knew, the reason was that the police wanted to make sure that you would not be swayed by anything you heard about the crime or about Maja. They wanted to question you before you could form an interpretation of what had happened."

"I formed an interpretation of what had happened because I was there when it happened. Why would I make up — "

"I don't believe you have consciously made anything up, Samir. But I believe you want to…that more than anything, you want to understand your traumatic experience, and this fabrication seems the most logical."

"Dad never said that Maja and Sebastian were working together."

Sander looks up skeptically. "But he told you she was in jail."

"Yes."

"Did he tell you why she was there?"

"He didn't need to…"

"No, maybe he didn't need to. I'm sure it was enough to say that Maja was in custody for you to figure out what the police suspected Maja of doing. But he did talk, Samir. Your dad did tell you what he had read in the newspapers and what he was convinced was true. The nurse who overheard your conversation, I have her statement here with me. We can call her in, if you like. She heard how upset your dad was, and what he wanted to do to Maja, because she 'had tried to kill you.'"

"It's not that simple…Dad just wanted me to know that — "

"I understand, Samir. That's actually exactly what I want us to talk about. How it's not that simple to explain what happened."

Sander lets this statement hang in the air while he takes a sip of water.

"How did you know you had been shot?"

"He...Sebastian shot Dennis and then Christer and then..." Samir clears his throat. "He said..." Samir starts crying, clears his throat again. "'You're going to die,' he said. Then he shot me. I thought I was dead." He cries for a moment.

Sander lets him finish and then continues.

"Where was Maja standing when Sebastian shot you? Do you remember?"

"By the door."

"Was she holding a weapon at that point?"

"I don't know."

"But Maja didn't shoot you?"

Samir gives a snort. "I never claimed that Maja shot me. But she —"

"When did you realize you were still alive?"

"When I heard them talking to each other."

"Who?"

"Maja and...Maja and Sebastian."

"You said during questioning that —" Sander reads aloud from his document. " — 'they thought I was dead, and that saved me.'"

Samir raises his voice. "If they had realized I wasn't dead..."

Sander lowers his voice. "You played dead so you wouldn't be shot again."

"Yes."

"Did you close your eyes?"

"Not all the way."

"So you were looking?"

"I watched without opening my eyes completely. Yes. Yes, I could see enough."

"Weren't you afraid they would notice you watching them?"

"I was terrified. I've never been more scared in my life."

"Were you in pain?"

"I've never been in so much pain in my life."

"It must have been difficult to lie still and play dead."

"I had no choice."

"You said during questioning that — " Sander picks up a sheet of paper and reads from it. " — 'they did it together.' What was it, exactly, that they did together?"

"They..."

"When Sebastian shot Christer, Dennis, and you...was Maja shooting, too?"

"No. She — "

"Was she holding a weapon at that point?"

"No, I don't think so. I don't know."

"But she did have a weapon when Sebastian told her to...What did he say?"

"He said, 'You know you have to do it.'"

"And do you know what he meant by that?"

"Kill Amanda."

"Maja claims that when Sebastian said 'do it,' he wanted her to kill him, that she had to kill him so he wouldn't kill her."

"Then why did she kill Amanda? Why would she have shot Amanda unless Sebastian had told her to?"

Sander doesn't say anything for a moment. But it's not because he thinks Samir has a point. It's because he wants everyone's undivided attention.

"You were there when the police did a reconstruction of the shooting."

"Yes. And when —"

"But you weren't at the reconstruction we did."

"No. I wasn't invited. And what does it matter? I was there when it —"

"The person who played you, or whatever I should call it, do you know what he said about what he could see from where you were lying?"

"How am I supposed to know that?"

"He said he couldn't see Maja."

"I could see Maja."

"He couldn't see Maja. In order to see Maja, he had to turn his head. But if he turned his head, he could no longer see Sebastian. So he couldn't see both Maja and Sebastian at the same time. Nor could he see both Maja and Amanda at the same time. Did you turn your head to see Maja?"

"I don't know. Maybe."

"You were pretending to be dead, right?"

"Yes."

"Were you lying as still as you could?"

"Yes."

"Do you know what else our reconstruction man said?"

"How the hell am I supposed to know that?"

"He also said, the man who played you in our reconstruction, that from your position it didn't look like Amanda and Sebastian were standing in the same line of fire, it looked like they were standing next to each other. But from Maja's point of view, that is, from a different perspective, Sebastian was standing in front of Amanda and to the side. Do you think it might have looked different to you than it looked to Maja?"

"Maja shot Amanda."

"We know that Maja shot Amanda, Samir. But we don't know why Maja shot her."

"Because she wanted her to die, I guess."

"Are you certain of that?"

"They hadn't...they weren't...Sebastian and Maja had gotten totally..." Samir is crying again. "Amanda said that Maja had stopped calling her, that they didn't hang out anymore, that she was acting strange. Amanda was worried about her, but Maja didn't want anything to do with Amanda. She only spent time with Sebastian. She was obsessed with him. She didn't care about anything but Sebastian."

"Have you ever heard Maja say she wanted Amanda to die?"

"No."

"Did Amanda tell you that she was afraid of Maja?"

"No. But I didn't understand that Maja wanted to...I didn't understand it until the classroom."

"When the paramedics arrived at the scene...the first one who examined you, while you were still in the classroom, she stated that you were unconscious."

Samir shrugged.

"Were you?"

"I think so."

"Do you remember being taken out of the classroom?"

"No."

"Because you were unconscious?"

"Yes. I have never claimed to remember what happened once the paramedics arrived."

"How long were you unconscious?"

"Not long."

"We have spoken with your doctor, and he says it's not out of the question that you lost consciousness right after you were shot."

"I didn't."

"Are you sure of that?"

"I know what I saw."

"And what was that?"

"I saw Maja aim at — "

"But you couldn't see both Maja and Sebastian from where you lay. Or Maja and Amanda. Unless you turned your head, of course, but you said you didn't do that because you didn't want to risk them noticing you were still alive. Nor could you have seen whether Maja was aiming at Sebastian or Amanda, because you were at the wrong angle."

"Sebastian said — "

"He said, 'You know you have to do it,' even Maja has reported that. But do you know *why* he said it?"

"I…"

"You have to be careful with what you say, Samir. You must be certain. Do you know why Sebastian said that?"

"No."

"Do you know — with absolute certainty — why Maja did what she did?"

"How could I — "

"I just want you to answer honestly, Samir. Do you know why Maja shot Amanda?"

"No."

"Can you be sure that she did it on purpose? That she wanted to kill Amanda?"

"No."

"Thank you. I have no further questions."

SEBASTIAN

40.

I stood in Sebastian's hall for eleven minutes. I didn't wander; I just waited for him. I heard him call down to the guard, "Dad's going to work from home today. He doesn't want to be disturbed."

The guard didn't ask questions; I'm sure he didn't think it was particularly odd, so there was no reason to react. Considering the evening and night before, it would be natural for Claes to want to sleep in, to be by himself.

I didn't want to risk seeing him, so I stayed in the hall.

Why would I refuse when Sebastian asked me to help him carry the bags? I thought he had packed his belongings because he was going to go stay on the boat for a while. Maybe he would go abroad somewhere. Maybe he would just disappear. Stay at a hotel. I don't know what I was thinking, aside from that I didn't want to see Claes but didn't want to leave Sebastian there on his own, that I didn't want to be there but I didn't dare to leave.

Who would guess that two heavy bags might contain guns (wrapped in a sheet) and explosives (wrapped in another sheet)? I would have been less surprised to find that the bags contained ten million dollars in cash or the crown jewels.

No, I didn't ask Sebastian what he was planning to do. No, I didn't ask about the bags. I didn't want to ask because I didn't have the energy to care.

But, you protest. If that had been his luggage for the sailboat, why would he want to bring it into the classroom? Why did he want to leave one of the bags in my locker? *Didn't that strike you as odd?* I don't know. I didn't want to know. Why didn't I ask what it was? Why didn't I ask any questions? I didn't want to ask Sebastian anything. I was tired. I just wanted the day, the semester, the school year to end.

If I had stopped to think about it, I might have found it unusual that Sebastian wanted to go to school. Why did he suddenly want to attend Christer's dorky planning meeting? But I guess I had stopped questioning what Sebastian did and didn't want long before. Anytime I thought I knew why he did what he did, I turned out to be wrong after all. I understood nothing. If he wanted to go to school, even though he would never entertain the thought of getting up on stage and singing with Samir and Dennis, it was far from the most incomprehensible part of my life.

Maybe I suspected that he wanted to confront Samir and Amanda. Chew them out? Punch Samir? Or maybe I just thought he wanted to get hold of Dennis for a refill; Claes's army of security guards had rid the house of drugs. Sebastian needed to see Dennis, and if I'd thought about it I would have assumed they had arranged to meet at school.

Christer's plan for us to perform together on the last day of school was typical. He thought there was no teen problem so severe that it couldn't be worked out by forcing the teens in question onto a stage and giving them three microphones to share. And just think what a pretty picture it would make for the school Web site! Diversity, togetherness, integration, and solidarity. "It's too bad none of us is in a wheelchair," Sebastian had commented when Christer told us of his plan in the hallway one afternoon, two weeks before it happened. Sebastian had come to school that day, and when Christer caught sight of us he jogged to catch up, calling to Amanda and to Samir, who was standing nearby, making them listen, too. "I talked to Dennis," Christer had said. "Come to one meeting, at least. I'm sure we can come up with something everyone will think is fun." And Amanda was genuinely happy; she loved to sing, she sang at every year-end performance. And Samir put on a good face; he probably thought, like I did, that a performance would never actually happen.

But we came to the meeting. Sebastian walked into the classroom ahead of me. He tossed his bag on one of the desks near the door, sort of heaved it up — I know I reacted to the sound. It sounded strange, like there was something hard in the bag.

"Go ahead and close the door," Christer said to me, and by the time I had done so Sebastian was already holding his gun and standing in the middle of the classroom, and as I let go of the door handle he started shooting.

The gun was deafening. Dennis was shot in the face and chest; I saw it happen as I turned around. I gaped as Sebastian shot Christer and Samir, and then he stopped. Afterward I heard Dennis asthma-wheeze three times, and then he was quiet. I think Christer said something, half shouting, before he was shot, but I don't know for sure.

I had never heard a gun fired indoors, and it was so loud I almost didn't react. It was too surreal. I don't know what I was thinking when I realized that Sebastian had taken the gun from his bag, and I don't know how many times he fired. They've asked me about fifteen hundred times, but I don't know.

When I turned away from Dennis, Amanda was sitting down; I don't know where she was standing when Sebastian started shooting or when she moved, but she was by the wall alongside the window when Sebastian stopped shooting and he screamed... No, hold on, he didn't scream, no one was screaming right then I don't think. He spoke to me in a normal tone of voice and behind him I could see Amanda shuffling away a millimeter at a time, she was crying and her lips were moving, but I couldn't hear what she was saying because my ears were ringing, and Sebastian was talking to me so I stopped looking at Amanda and looked at him instead.

The bag, the one he had carried into the classroom, was right in front of me. It was open, the zipper was as far as it would go. The smell was stronger now than it had been right afterward and I don't think Sebastian was looking at Amanda, just at me, and there was another gun in the bag, I could see, I saw it clearly, and when Sebastian started talking again, Amanda was farther away but still not that far away because Christer was lying there and she didn't want to go in that direction and she turned toward the wall, I think, and when Sebastian started screaming, because he did start screaming, she stopped moving and I couldn't see her eyes anymore, or her mouth. I don't know if she was saying anything, I don't think so, I could only hear Sebastian screaming at me. He had screamed a few hours ago, too.

"Shut your fat mouth, you fucking asshole," Sebastian had screamed at Samir as the security guard dragged his dad off him, and Samir screamed back, too, I don't know who at, but he screamed like he had gone crazy. He *had* gone crazy. Everyone had lost their minds. When Claes Fagerman came in, dragging Sebastian behind him, Samir looked insane, almost as insane as Sebastian, but Claes was worst of all. If the security guards hadn't pulled him off, he never would have stopped hitting Sebastian, never stopped kicking him.

After everyone had left and Claes was screaming at Sebastian to get out, and he took off, I followed him, we walked out of the house, walked away, and I thought he seemed calm. We didn't talk about the night. We didn't talk about what Sebastian had done. About the girls and his dead eyes. I didn't tell him I had given Samir his dad's number, but who else could it have been? Sebastian must have figured that out. It couldn't have been anyone but me. And yet he seemed calm on our walk, even though it was my fault, even though I was the reason his dad showed up, it was all my fault. Sebastian didn't want to touch me, hold my hand, but he didn't seem upset. He had left me. He had left everything.

The bag was open and I picked up the gun. Sebastian didn't scream at first. But then he screamed louder than he'd ever screamed before. I had no idea how many shots he'd fired but I did know why he was screaming, of course I knew. At first he spoke in his normal voice, and then he screamed. He aimed his weapon at me, and I understood why. And then I fired the gun and fired it again and again and again. What other choice did I have?

I don't believe in coincidence. I don't believe in God either. What I do believe is that everything that happens is connected to whatever happened before, like links in a chain. Is it predetermined? No. How could it be? But that's not the same as saying that something just happened. The law of gravity isn't random. Water heats up and becomes condensation. That's not random, nor is it proof of divine justice. It just is.

We once had this teacher who said that everything can be traced back to the propensity of gases to explode. He was an idiot, I still think that, because what does the big bang have to do with me taking the gun out of the bag? And Amanda? Sebastian? A few minutes later, or maybe just seconds, when everything had shattered from the inside, had been shot to pieces, and the only thing that was still moving was the second hand of my watch, ticking forward above the numbers, unperturbed, what did that have to do with the origins of the universe? Why didn't Sebastian shoot me so that Amanda could have lived? That shitty, incompetent teacher could hardly have explained that.

Everything, absolutely everything, was quiet and still and unreal. Sebastian had fallen away from me, he was dead, I had killed him, but I pulled him to me once more, as close as I possibly could. Amanda died and I didn't hold her as it happened.

I didn't see Sebastian take the gun from the bag. But I looked at him as he was holding it, as he started shooting. It sounded too loud to be real, there was no room for the noise, it exploded in my head; I saw what happened, but I couldn't comprehend it.

I picked up the second gun because there was nothing else I could do. I realized he wanted to die, that I had to kill him or else he would kill me. I didn't see it when I hit Amanda, but when I realized she was dead I knew that I was the one who had shot her. *The greatest of these is love,* they say. People use that quote all the time, and some even seem to think it's true. The prosecutor said I did what I did because I loved Sebastian. That my love for him was the greatest thing in my life. That nothing else was more important. But it's not true. Because the greatest of all is fear, the terror of dying. Love means nothing when you believe you're going to die.

I know that I ought to have an explanation for why it happened. That I should be able to do what Sander does, fashion it into something that either does or does not fit into the word of law. That I should say that first *x* happened, then *y*, and it turned out like *z*. *It wasn't my fault. I am innocent.* Or *It was my fault. I am guilty.* But I can't. You all hate me for what happened, but I hate myself even more because I can't explain it. There is no explanation. It's absolutely meaningless.

Trial hearing in case B 147/66

The prosecutor et al. v. Maria Norberg

Week 3 of Trial: The last day

41.

I try not to fall asleep on the night before the last day of the trial. Because at night there are no lies. I think the silence is to blame. When even the birds are quiet and the night sky is black, that's when the dreams come, and dreams don't follow any rules, no one can rule over their contents, they are ruthless. My memories fly straight into me, dead silent, a murder of black crows, my spine turns to gravel, sand, dust. I try not to fall asleep, but I can't move; exhaustion overpowers me. I can't sleep away the pain, sleep is no savior, my dreams leave me exposed for truth.

No, I never planned to kill anyone. No, I didn't want Dennis and Christer to die. Yes, I wanted Sebastian's dad to die; no, I did not want Sebastian to kill him. Yes, I killed Sebastian, yes, I did it on purpose, I wish I hadn't. And yes, I killed Amanda, yes, I would do anything to have it undone.

We rode to school together, but I didn't know what Sebastian was planning to do because he didn't tell me anything. When Samir told me that Sebastian didn't need me, I thought he was wrong. I thought Sebastian needed me in order to stay alive. I was convinced I was the most important person in his life, but the truth was, he didn't need me for anything, not even to die, even though I was the one who killed him.

All I had left was the idea that Sebastian needed me, but I meant nothing.

People say that all humans are of equal worth. That's what you say because you are polite, well-bred, and maybe have an advanced degree, but that doesn't make it true. In reality, everyone knows that people have different value. That's why, if a plane crashes near Indonesia and four hundred people die, the news reports double if there was a Swede on the plane. One pathetic, sweaty little sex-tourist Swede is worth twice as much as four hundred Indonesians. That's why it makes the front page (with pictures) when a healthy, young, pretty woman with a successful career dies in an avalanche, but there's only one paragraph alongside ads for movies and breast enhancement when an incontinent, divorced, childless retiree is robbed and murdered on the way home from the Metro. That's why all the articles about the "Djursholm Massacre" contain at least one photo of Amanda, while a picture of Dennis is included much less frequently.

Only idiots pretend that who you are and what you do don't matter. They talk about the value of a human life as if it's not something we have completely made up.

The value of a human life is absolute, blah-blah-blah... eternal, constant, fixed, we are all the same, blah-blah-blah. Hitler's life is worth the same as Mother Teresa's.

But not Sebastian. He knew. Sebastian grew up in a house with its own white-sand beach brought in by plane and boat from a former French colony. How could he have pretended to be anything but a god, equal to no one, superior to everything? Every single day of Sebastian's life witnessed to the truth: He was worth more than everyone else. Money is easier to understand than all the philosophical drivel about the absolute value of a human life.

Sebastian's problem was that he also knew his worth depended on his dad. Without his dad he was no one. All the teachers who let him show up late, all the parents who didn't bother to forbid their kids from hanging out with him, all the lines he jumped, all the friends he had, all the people who took pictures of him, gossiped about him, talked about him — they only did it because of his dad. *Claes Fagerman's son.* And when his dad said he no longer wanted anything to do with him, that he was worth nothing, when he spit on him and kicked him, Sebastian knew Claes was right. Without Claes, his life was over.

He was good at one thing. He could kill. He was a good hunter. He could use guns to accomplish things on his own; he even received praise for it.

I was the one who gave Samir Claes's phone number. I was the one who begged Samir not to call the police. I was the one. Maybe I wanted to get revenge on Sebastian, maybe I wanted Claes to see what he had done to those girls because I knew Claes would punish him worse than anyone else would be capable of. Or maybe I was just afraid of getting caught because I was high as a kite. But as

I walked home from Sebastian's house that very last night, in the morning light, my high-heeled shoes in one hand and my sweaty phone, which would soon be filled with desperate messages, in the other, Sebastian and I both knew I had betrayed him again. Of course he didn't say anything to me. Of course he could have killed me, too.

At night I am like the air on a day with no breeze, when everything is still and nothing can take flight. I remember too much. And the truth, to the extent you are interested in it, the truth is that I am guilty.

Week 3 of Trial: The last day

42.

When lead prosecutor Lena Pärsson clicks on her microphone, clears her throat, and begins her closing argument, the summary of everything she wants to have said, she almost sounds sad, like she doesn't want to be here.

"It is every parent's worst nightmare...sending their children off in the morning only to find that they don't come home that evening."

But the sadness passes. After just a few sentences, she sounds grim and furious. Her voice says that we are not going to get off that easy.

"It's difficult to understand, nearly impossible to comprehend, how young people can be filled with enough hatred to kill. But we mustn't let that keep us from recognizing what happened. And what the court must determine today is the guilt of the defendant. The court must have the courage to do the right thing and find that the defendant is guilty of incitement, complicity, and murder. The defendant's criminal liability has been proven beyond a reasonable doubt."

Her voice grows stronger and stronger as she works through her argument; after just a few minutes she sounds almost triumphant.

Two things are clear: She has not allowed herself to be swayed by Sander's questions to Samir, and she stands firm in her conviction that I should be punished to the fullest extent of the law.

"Interpretations," she says with a sniff, "are not so simple if you want them to correspond with the truth. And what…" She hesitates, unsure which word to choose. "What the defense's experts have arrived at is just one of several possible interpretations. Which is not to say that their results are in any way conclusive."

The defense's experts. Everyone knows what she wants us to take away from this. *I paid them. The defendant is trying to buy her way to freedom.*

Rich fucking bitch.

"The police investigators are no amateurs. They know what they're doing; this isn't their first investigation. Nor their second, nor their third. No one tells them what to look for, which results are desired. They perform their inquiries without presuppositions, not on orders from the accused. And remember," she says, "remember what Samir said from the start, what he has said throughout the entire investigation, what he has maintained even though time has passed. Samir was there. He saw clearly what happened in the classroom during those nightmarish minutes; he was able to explain the actions of the defendant. Was it necessary for him to turn his head in order to see? Perhaps.

What does it matter? He saw what he saw. And Samir has hardly been vague about the role of the accused. The value of a first interrogation must never be minimized, particularly not when the information obtained is confirmed by the technical investigation, and on the police's side, the technical investigation was performed by the NFC, our National Forensic Center."

She emphasizes "National," as if that word on its own would be enough for anyone to understand what was right and what was wrong. *State experts. Not Sander's amateurs, not the defendant's mercenaries.*

So the lead prosecutor is sticking with what she's claimed all along. But one thing has changed. And it takes a moment for me to figure it out, but once it occurs to me, I can't let it go. Because as she lays out her story, when she talks about how Sebastian and I, isolated from the world around us, planned our murderous revenge, she is no longer addressing the chief judge. She's looking at the lay judges, the ones who have no formal education in law.

"There is no doubt in my mind that this has been a difficult time for the defendant. Maria Norberg surely regrets her actions. It is possible that she even felt regret in the classroom, once she found out what death really looks like. She was probably frightened. Once Sebastian Fagerman was dead, she no longer wanted to die. But that doesn't absolve her of her guilt."

If Lena Pärsson had been playing the infuriated prosecutor on an American TV show, she would have been leaning over the jury box at this point. Staring the jurors in the eye, one by one, to see whether they were about to start crying. She's using the full scale of emotions right now, because she knows that if she can get the lay judges on her side, I'm screwed. Each lay judge is just as important as the chief judge when it comes time to make the decision. They have one vote each, no more, no less. The chief judge and his statutes can be steamrolled, easy as pie.

I look at the lay judges, try to read in their expressions what they're thinking, what their opinion might be. But I see nothing, nothing I understand, nothing I can interpret, just faces.

When Lena Pärsson is finished, the chief judge thanks her. No questions, nothing. And then it's Sander's turn. *Go ahead.* Sander doesn't start speaking right away. He lets Ferdinand start up the computer monitor. She brings up a newspaper billboard:

MASSACRE AT DJURSHOLM UPPER SECONDARY
SCHOOL — GIRL IN CUSTODY

Then a different image. Another billboard looms over us:

CLAES FAGERMAN MURDERED — SON'S
GIRLFRIEND'S DEMAND: "HE MUST DIE!"

And another:

SOURCES CONFIRM: SHE KILLED HER BEST FRIEND

And another. And another.

When the sixth billboard flickers up, Sander clears his throat. He reads the first part of it aloud:

EVERYONE HAD TO DIE,
THERE WAS NO OTHER WAY OUT

But we must read the subheading on our own:

HOW SHE LIVES NOW — SEVEN PAGES
ON THE DJURSHOLM GIRL'S LIFE IN JAIL

Then he continues. "I wanted to tell you how many articles had been written about Maja by the time this trial began. But I can't. The fact is, it's impossible to determine. In the first fourteen days after the murders, my client appeared on every front page of the three largest national newspapers. Every single one. She, or the crimes she is alleged to have taken part in, was the lead story on *Rapport*, *Aktuellt*, and the TV4 news for three days after the incidents, and they were among the lead stories for eight days after that. When the police released the information about Claes Fagerman's death less than twenty-four hours after the events at Djursholm Upper Secondary School, the attention was as explosive in the international media as it was here. And they had hardly been uninterested before. My colleagues have informed me that when they Googled 'Maja Norberg' the night before this trial was to begin, they received over seven hundred and fifty thousand hits, even though most of the Swedish media had not yet made her name public. The term 'Djursholm massacre' resulted in over three hundred thousand hits, and the combination of Sebastian Fagerman and Maja Norberg gave nearly the same amount."

He sighs. A deep sigh. He regrets that he must discuss this. He looks at the chief judge. Unlike Ugly Lena, Sander is addressing him. *We lawyers, we don't allow ourselves to be swayed by trivialities like evening papers and the Internet, professional pundits and debate shows, foreign news, and so on for all eternity.* Sander's entire being radiates *I'm depending on you,* but it's also saying that it is up to the chief judge to explain this to the lay judges, should it become necessary.

"Incitement. My client is charged with inciting the murder of Claes Fagerman. This portion of the charge is also fundamental to the claim that my client, along with the late Sebastian Fagerman, planned and jointly executed the murders at Djursholm Upper Secondary School that same day."

My client. Sander has seldom called me his client during the trial. But now he is using his dry-as-a-desert voice. His lawyer voice.

"In order for the conditions for incitement to be fulfilled, the prosecutor must demonstrate both that my client had intent to incite the murder of Claes Fagerman and that there was a direct connection between my client's words or actions and the murder itself. In order to prove this claim, the prosecutor has referred to a number of text messages my client sent to Sebastian Fagerman during the night and morning in question, messages in which my client expressed what the prosecutor interprets as exhortations to commit murder."

I don't get why Sander is harping on this. He knows I hate having to listen to what I wrote, and yet he persists in bringing it up. Ferdinand is up by the projector again. She brings up an image on the big screen. It's from Sweden's most-followed Instagram account, which belongs to a sixteen-year-old girl from some small town somewhere, and it's a photo of ice cream with sprinkles. "I'd rather KILL MYSELF than eat paleo," is the caption. I hear a few brief laughs behind me. The chief judge isn't laughing, but two of the lay judges smile.

She clicks onward. A photo of a chicken peeking over the edge of a pot. Next to that is another photo from inside a chicken factory. The text reads: "Carnivores = MURDERERS!"

Sander lets his arms drop in a gesture of resignation as Ferdinand clicks through the images.

"We sometimes choose our words poorly. Even adults express themselves in dubious ways. I often say to my wife that I'd rather die than watch yet another schmaltzy pre-Eurovision quarterfinal, and yet I watch all of them without committing suicide during the sketches between songs. Sometimes I text in my vote for the most terrible entries just because my grandchildren say I have to. I like to accuse them of trying to kill me. But I don't think that's their true intention, at least not primarily."

They have found tons of examples of teenagers online wanting to "waste" other teens who listen to music they don't like, demanding a famous actor who was unfaithful be "publicly whipped." Ferdinand also shows us the comments on one of the Swedish *Idol* contestants' blog, and three or even four soccer banners that look like they came from Snapchat.

Then Sander waves his hand in irritation. *Shut it off,* says his hand. *I don't want to see this crap. It's nonsense.* His voice is dead serious once again.

"I don't mean this to be a joke. The situation we must judge is no laughing matter. Maja had no reason to kid around, and her texts to Sebastian during those last few hours were anything but comical. I'm only trying to point out the obvious: We use words and expressions that refer to death without truly meaning it. Teenagers often express themselves not only carelessly, but inappropriately. Is that criminal? Does that mean the legal qualifications for incitement have been fulfilled? No."

The screen goes black and Ferdinand sits down.

"But let's play with the thought," Sander says. "Let's assume that Maja meant every word. That she found herself in such a desperate situation that she saw Claes Fagerman's death as the only thing that could save Sebastian. Let us assume that she truly wanted Sebastian to kill his father. In that case, is she guilty of incitement? No. For the prosecutor must still be able to prove that Maja's actions were decisive and that Sebastian otherwise would not have killed his father despite what Maja thought. Has the prosecutor succeeded in proving this causal relationship? No."

Sander points out that Samir was not the only one who gave testimony about the party on that last night. They questioned Labbe, they questioned the hookers, they questioned the security guards, they questioned everyone who didn't die the next day. And sure, their stories were inconsistent, all had their own versions, but everyone mentioned Claes Fagerman's rage. How he hit Sebastian and kicked him until the guards dragged him off. They had the chance to talk about what it looked like, that Sebastian was bleeding, that he seemed to be in shock, angry maybe, but no one was able to say how Sebastian felt. I did mention what I suspect, but it's hard to trust me.

"Instead, the image that has emerged is of a wounded relationship, a relationship between a damaged boy and his father. We don't know the details of what happened during those early-morning hours when Claes Fagerman died, but we know that father and son were alone when Sebastian shot him, and we know that they had violently come to blows immediately beforehand. We also know that Sebastian Fagerman was under the influence of heavy drugs. That he had been abusing drugs for a long time and that he was mentally ill. Does it seem likely that Maja's sporadic messages were a crucial factor in Sebastian's actions? Or is it more likely that the explanation can be found in the relationship between Claes and Sebastian Fagerman and in Sebastian Fagerman's state of mental health? I am convinced that the court will come to the same conclusion as I have in this matter."

Then he talks for a while about the consequences this has for the rest of the charges, that the court "must" come to the conclusion that I did not cause Sebastian to kill his dad. And then his dry voice is back again. He walks us through the "concrete" evidence the prosecutor has against me.

"Are there any factors, witness statements, or other evidence to indicate that my client was involved in planning the crimes at Djursholm Upper Secondary School along with the late Sebastian Fagerman? No. Are there any factors, witness statements, or other evidence to indicate that my client was made aware of Sebastian's plans? No."

Sander repeats what he already said during the trial. No fingerprints on the inside of the bag, on the zipper, on the gun safe, that whole spiel. He also points out (again) that Sebastian obtained the explosives (which couldn't even be detonated) far ahead of time, before he and I knew each other.

"Is there anything in the rather intense cell-phone exchanges between Sebastian and Maja to indicate that Maja is aware that Sebastian intends to kill his father before he actually does so? No. When Maja returns to Sebastian's house, Claes Fagerman has been dead for nearly two hours. Is there anything in the investigation to suggest that Sebastian informed Maja of this before she arrives? No. Is there anything to indicate that Maja became aware that Claes Fagerman was dead while she was in the house? That she learned Sebastian killed his father? No. There is nothing of that nature in the prosecutor's material. Instead I will have to use my time to remind you of what the prosecutor has *not* been able to prove. The prosecutor has not been able to show that Maja might have known the security code to the gun safe where the weapons in question were kept, nor have her fingerprints been found on or inside that safe. The crime-scene technicians were, however, able to secure fingerprints from Claes and Sebastian Fagerman both inside and outside the gun safe. Thus there is no technical evidence to suggest that Maja helped handle the gun safe. Nor were Maja's fingerprints found in either of the bags or on their zippers, only on the handles and on the underside of one bag. Nor is there any evidence to link Maja to the explosive substance that was retrieved from her locker. Maja's fingerprints are on the weapon she used later, but not on the trigger mechanism of the one Sebastian was using."

Sander pauses briefly, pages through some documents, takes a little sip of water. He takes his time. Then he starts anew.

"Are there any factors, witness statements, or other evidence to show that my client assisted Sebastian Fagerman in executing his plan? To show that she had intent to kill? Yes! There is, actually." He sounds exaggeratedly surprised. Sarcastically surprised. "The prosecutor presents the testimony of a witness. A testimony that was gathered under dubious circumstances and from a gravely wounded boy who — just to be on the safe side — had been made aware long before his first interrogation that my client had been jailed under suspicion of guilt in the very crime the boy is being questioned about. During the questioning, this boy states that he observed Maja's actions in a way that is at odds with what she herself claims happened. In addition, he says that he heard my client consulting with the late Sebastian Fagerman and that he later watched my client intentionally shoot one of the victims."

And then he goes through the details of the investigation he ordered into Samir's testimony. Details we've already heard.

"And what does the prosecutor have to say about this investigation's unambiguous results, which are in favor of my client? Why, the prosecutor is of the opinion that it wasn't performed by sufficiently competent personnel on sufficiently free and unbiased grounds." Sander looks up from his documents and shakes his head slowly. Then he picks up one sheet of paper from the pile and starts to read from it.

It is a description of the people who participated in the analysis, their educational backgrounds, the control methods they used; it's peppered with technical terms and it's ridiculously boring.

He continues along those lines for a while longer. His voice drones on and on and I have trouble breathing. I unfold the crumpled napkin in my fist and crumple it up again. I want to stand up, I want to run up to the judges. *Listen*, I want to scream. *Do you hear what he's saying?* Because the truth is, I realize — it socks me right in the gut, totally out of the blue — that I want to believe Sander. I want to believe he is right when he says I shouldn't be found guilty, that I have the right to a future.

I want him to be right.

You all probably won't even remember how this trial ends, whether I'm found guilty, or what I'm found guilty of. You'll be talking about me at some party in a few years and say,

That's what happened or *She wasn't even charged with that* or *That's weird. Are you sure? I think she…* My truth will soon exist nowhere but in the binders full of material from my trial, archived in a cold basement.

You'll have to Google it to be sure, see what happened, how it turned out. Or else you'll say that it was a well-written verdict, or that the police did a botched job, or *Well, good thing she was nailed,* to show that you are in the loop, that you know.

No matter which version you choose, you'll remember me as a murderer. But I don't give a shit about you and your fucking opinions. I still want to get out of here. I want the court to believe Sander.

The exhaustion that overcomes me when I let myself think the thought is so debilitating that at first I think I'm going to fall off my chair. But I hold on tight. I have to get through this, I don't want to be here. I want to get out of here.

My grandma had a rocking chair. She would rock in it, back and forth, reading or sewing, and it's still there at my grandpa's house and I want to rock in it again. I want Grandpa to whisper in my ear, "You have your whole life ahead of you," and I will nod to make him happy. *Anything can happen.* I want to make someone happy. *Anything is possible.*

And I don't want to have to think about how it's when anything can happen, when all the doors are open, that you get a cross breeze and everything slams shut and locks itself. I am eighteen years old and I want to be a Disney princess and cry in a shrill whine: "I will follow my heart and be happy!" And no one will believe that I am Snow White's stepmother, who follows her evil, black heart and decides to kill. I will get an education, sit in an office, twenty-eight stories above the ground but the floor won't give in, the building won't collapse, and I won't fall. I want to find a place where I don't have to imagine the masses settling over me and burying my body.

Listen to Sander. Chief judge and lay judges and journalists. Agree with him. Let me be.

With his reading glasses low on the bridge of his nose, Sander stares at the chief judge. *Now,* I think. *Now he'll say the words that make everyone understand. That force them to let me go.* But he doesn't.

"The prosecutor has not met the burden of proof," is all he says.

After that he says nothing.

The chief judge speaks instead.

And then it's over. It's all over.

43.

We have a new room to wait in. The chair I'm sitting in is bowl shaped and plastic. One side of my butt is asleep, even though I haven't been sitting here for very long. The coffee I'm holding is muddy. Apparently I said *yes, please* to both cream and sugar, but I can't remember being asked.

I thought I would be driven back to the jail. We all thought so, that was the plan, my ride was waiting. But the judge had other plans. In his concluding statements he said, "Blah-blah the hearing in this case is hereby concluded" and "The court will take a brief deliberation period after which a verdict will be delivered." And then he turned to Sander and nodded at the lead prosecutor and said, "You can wait here, we'll call the case when we're finished."

A buzz of *What does this mean?* went through the courtroom, and all around people turned to each other and stared, waiting for an explanation. I turned to Sander. *What does this mean?* Mom turned to Dad. *What does this mean?* But no one responded, no one had a clue, and I thought it must be because everyone knew that only an open-and-shut case, the kind where the only solution is to send the horrible criminal straight to death row as quickly as possible, only the guilty receive their verdicts so quickly.

It's happening too fast. I don't want to.

And we stood up, we all stood up and left.

It was over. It was all over.

And I thought I was going to throw up, right then and there, or suffocate, but I didn't do anything. I just sat down and apparently said *yes, please* to a cup of coffee.

Sander isn't sitting down. Pancake is out there dodging questions from the media; Ferdinand is typing frantically on her phone, I don't know about what, I don't know to whom.

Sander doesn't respond when spoken to. He looks nervous; I've never seen him so nervous before, he's trying to pour himself a cup of coffee but the plastic mug slides away and the coffee ends up on the table and Sander swears out loud. *What the hell!*

I think this is the first time I've heard him swear.

We wait for an hour. Nothing. Five minutes later, Sander sits down. He reads something on his phone. Ferdinand looks at me, offers me her snus tin. I shake my head and she gives me a blister-pack of nicotine gum and I press four pieces into my palm, shove them into my mouth, and start chewing.

We wait for another twenty minutes.

"How long do we have to wait?" I ask. No one answers. I ask again. "How much longer?" My voice sounds like a whiny little kid. *Are we there yet?*

"There's no way to know," Sander says at last, but he doesn't look up from his phone, reading, reading. How can he read? What is he reading?

Two hours of waiting. And eleven minutes.

Then the loudspeakers crackle. And our case is called.

Sander stands just behind me and places his hand at the small of my back as if he's going to guide me to the table. Or to my execution? With a bag over my head. Where are we going? Are we there yet?

We walk to our places, the judges are already seated, Lena Pärsson has pushed her chair back and is pressing her legs together tight, her feet primly placed side by side. Her hands are folded in her lap. When the chief judge begins to speak, my ears ring. I can hardly hear what is going on, I don't know what it means, I watch Sander as the judge talks.

"The written verdict will be delivered later; it will comprise a more detailed account of the findings of the court."

What does that mean? What is he saying?

And I hear Dad gasp for breath, it sounds like he's in pain, as if someone has socked him in the gut. For an instant I think he is angry, that he's about to shout the way he does when he loses his temper, but then I see that he's crying. He cries and cries and Mom tries to soothe him; her voice cracks as well and that's when I notice my own tears. The journalists' murmurs grow louder and louder, and soon they're straight up talking, interrupting each other, there is no longer order in the court. There is a piece of paper in front of the chief judge. But he doesn't need to look at it to know what to say.

"The court dismisses the charges against Maria Norberg. The prosecutor has not proven that the defendant had intent to murder or that the necessary conditions for incitement were fulfilled. The defendant is free to go."

44.

Mom and Dad are sitting on either side of me in the back-seat of Sander's car. Dad has his arm around me, his back is straight as a rod, he is taking short breaths through his mouth, and he has been holding on to me without letting go ever since the judge said I was free to go home. Dad even held on to me as he hugged Sander, two fingers on my shirtsleeve, he squeezed my shoulder as he shook hands with Pancake and he had his hand around the back of my neck as he pulled Ferdinand close. It would have been a group hug if only Ferdinand had realized that she was sup-posed to be embraced.

Mom's entire body is warm, she's trembling a little and she is clasping both my hands, she strokes my fingers, my nails, my knuckles, as if she needs to count them, make sure everything is where it should be, that I'm truly here, that this isn't her imagination. Now and then she leans toward me, sticks a hand in under my seat belt and smooths out some wrinkle in my clothing. She pats my cheeks, breathes into my hair. We haven't spoken much. We haven't said that we're "glad." We haven't said "I love you," we haven't said "thank God." Dad has mumbled a thousand times *thank you thank you thank you.* To everyone he encounters he says *thank you thank you*, and Mom whispers *I'm sorry* as she hugs me, she whispers the same thing each time. *I'm sorry I'm sorry I'm sorry.* Only I can hear her, her voice is so low that it's almost a breath, and I hug her back. *I'm sorry.*

I don't say anything. It's impossible. I can't.

My mom.

Sander says that we can stay at his country home for a few days to get away from the media. It's by the water, we take a boat the last little bit, a passenger ferry, but we're the only people on board, so it must be chartered, rented just for us. *How did he have time?* There are no journalists here, no one asks how I'm feeling, whether I'm happy, whether there will be an appeal. When they asked the prosecutor, "Are you going to appeal?" Lena Pärsson sounded sulky: "I must have a chance to read the verdict before I can comment." Sander sounded much more certain: "We are satisfied with the result. The court had no trouble finding my client not guilty, and it would surprise me if the verdict leaves the prosecutor room for an appeal."

Did Sander sound confident only because it was a journalist asking? I don't think so. He doesn't sound confident without cause. He leaves that sort of thing to Pancake with his time-to-loosen-my-tie and goddamn-we're-good smile.

I walk out on the deck, stand with my stomach to the rail and my face to the wind, closing my eyes against the ice-cold air; my eyes tear up. The wind, I didn't know I missed the wind, the smell of oxygen, the cold feels like it's been set free out here on the sea, it doesn't cling to concrete and bars and barbed wire. I stand there for a moment, my cheeks stinging, and then I realize that Sander is beside me. He is wearing a thick coat I've never seen before, and lined leather gloves, a fur cap with earflaps that flutter in the breeze.

He reminds me of Grandpa.

"Grandpa is waiting for you," Mom said in the car. "He's so happy, he's missed you."

Sander hands me a well-worn handkerchief made of fine cotton. I carefully dab my nose and eyes. The handkerchief smells faintly of pipe, and I fold it up in my hand.

Do you smoke, Attorney Peder Sander?

There's so much I don't know about you. May I call you Peder?

"Is it over now?" I ask instead. He doesn't respond. He looks at me; a smile flickers across his face, but it doesn't take hold; he keeps a stiff upper lip and claps me on the shoulder.

"Yes," he says. He claps my shoulder three times and lets his hand rest there when he's done. He may be the best lawyer in Sweden. And yet it's clear that he's lying. "It's over now."

I take his hand and take half a step toward him and embrace him, a long hug in the ice-cold wind, harder than I really dare to. It's over for him, at least. He has saved my life and sent the invoice to the court. I put the handkerchief in my pocket.

We dock at a private pier, and the engines stay on as we get off. It's colder out here than it was in the city, there's snow in the air, the sea is steel gray, and dusk is starting to fall over the islet, to sneak up along the cliffs. My belongings are still at the jail, I have no bag to carry. I start to walk up toward the house and I see her on the stairs.

She's sitting on the porch; she's taller than I remember. Her hair appears unbrushed, her curly bangs fighting in a thin tuft at her forehead. I break into a jog. When I crouch down right next to her, I see that she has lost two of her top teeth. But she doesn't look me in the eye. Her gaze wanders, impossible to catch, like a dancing sunbeam.

"Are you coming home now?" she wonders.

I nod, I don't trust my voice, and then she slides close to me, winds her skinny arms around me, hooks her legs around my waist, clinging to me and crying into my neck. And that piece inside of me that has been hard for so long, gripping me with sharp claws, finally melts and flows out through my body.

"Yes. I'm coming home."

CREDITS

The song lyric on p. 22 ("Why, even in this day and age…") is from the ballad "Visan om den sköna konstberiderskan Elvira Madigan" by Johan Lindström Saxon, 1889: "Sorgeliga saker hända, än i våra dar minsann." Translation by Rachel Willson-Broyles.

The quote on p. 83 ("When there is nothing left…") is from the poem "Stjärnorna" by Karin Boye: "När inget finns att vänta mer, och inget finns att bära på." First published in Gömda land (Stockholm: Albert Bonniers förlag, 1924). Translation by Rachel Willson-Broyles.

The song lyric on p. 89 ("Preacher takes the school…") is from "Silly Boy Blue" by David Bowie, from the album David Bowie, Decca, 1967.

The song lyric on p. 100 ("Keep your 'lectric eye…") is from "Moonage Daydream" by David Bowie, from the album The Rise and Fall of Ziggy Stardust and the Spiders from Mars, RCA, 1972.

The song lyric on p. 101 ("Would you carry a razor…") is from "Young Americans" by David Bowie, from the album Young Americans, RCA, 1975.

The quote on p. 388 ("All my enemies on the cheek") is from Psalm 3:7, New Revised Standard Version, 1989.

The quotes on p. 388 ("conceiving evil," "pregnant with mischief") are from Psalm 7:14, English Standard Version, 2001.

The song lyric on p. 390 ("Party girls don't get hurt…") is from "Chandelier" by Sia, from the album 1000 Forms of Fear, 2014.

The quote on p. 390 ("Everything is empty and futile") is from Ecclesiastes 1:2, Wycliffe Bible.

The song lyric on p. 393 ("I couldn't live without you now…") is from "Addicted to You" by Avicii, from the album True, 2013.

The quote on p. 439 ("The greatest of these is love") is from 1 Corinthians 13:13, New Revised Standard Version, 1989.

Malin Persson Giolito was born in Stockholm in 1969 and grew up in Djursholm, Sweden. She holds a degree in law from Uppsala University and has worked as a lawyer for the largest law firm in the Nordic region and as an official for the European Commission in Brussels. Now a full-time writer, she has written four novels including *Quicksand*, her English-language debut. She lives with her husband and three daughters in Brussels.

Rachel Willson-Broyles became interested in Sweden and the Swedish language at an early age. She majored in Scandinavian Studies at Gustavus Adolphus College in St. Peter, Minnesota, graduating in 2002. She started translating while a graduate student at the University of Wisconsin-Madison, where she received a PhD in Scandinavian Studies in 2013. Willson-Broyles lives in St. Paul, Minnesota.

▉ OTHER PRESS

You might also enjoy these titles from our list:

THE UNIT by Ninni Holmqvist

Named one of the Best Novels of the Year by the *Wall Street Journal*, a gripping story about a society in the throes of a cynical, utilitarian way of thinking disguised as care

"Echoing work by Marge Piercy and Margaret Atwood, *The Unit* is as thought-provoking as it is compulsively readable." —Jessa Crispin, NPR.org

KATHERINE CARLYLE by Rupert Thomson

Unmoored by her mother's death, Katherine Carlyle abandons the set course of her life and sets out on a mysterious journey to the ends of the world.

"The strongest and most original novel I have read in a very long time... It's a masterpiece."
—Philip Pullman, author of the best-selling His Dark Materials trilogy

ALL DAYS ARE NIGHT by Peter Stamm

A novel about survival, self-reliance, and art, by Peter Stamm, finalist for the 2013 Man Booker International Prize

"A postmodern riff on *The Magic Mountain*... a page-turner." —*The Atlantic*

"*All Days Are Night* air[s] the psychological implications of our beauty obsession and the insidious ways in which it can obscure selfhood." —*New Republic*

Also recommended:

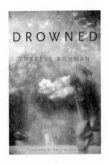

DROWNED by Therese Bohman

This spellbinding novel of psychological suspense combines hothouse sensuality with ice-cold fear.

"Therese Bohman could be lumped in with the other Scandinavian authors who have taken over the mystery world since *The Girl with the Dragon Tattoo*, but her story is more quiet and nuanced, her writing lush enough to create a landscape painting with every scene." —*O, The Oprah Magazine*

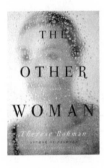

THE OTHER WOMAN by Therese Bohman

A psychological novel where questions of class, status, and ambition loom over a young woman's passionate love affair

"[Bohman's] characters are curiously, alarmingly awake, and a story we should all know well is transformed into something wondrous and strange. A disturbing, unforgettable book." —Rufi Thorpe, author of *The Girls from Corona del Mar*

WILLFUL DISREGARD by Lena Andersson

"Gripped me like an airport read ... perfect." —Lena Dunham

Winner of the August Prize, a novel about a perfectly reasonable woman's descent into the delusions of unrequited love

"[A] story of the heart written with bracing intellectual rigor. It is a stunner, pure and simple." —Alice Sebold, best-selling author of *The Lovely Bones* and *Lucky*